To Joy.
Thank you for making married life such a thrilling adventure.
You make the magic possible.
Shane

To my best friend and wife Renee.
Thank you for believing in whatever lies
beyond the realm of possibility.
Darryl

CONTENTS

Across the Fourwinds

SHANE TRUSZ
— AND —
DARRYL FRAYNE

ACROSS THE FOURWINDS

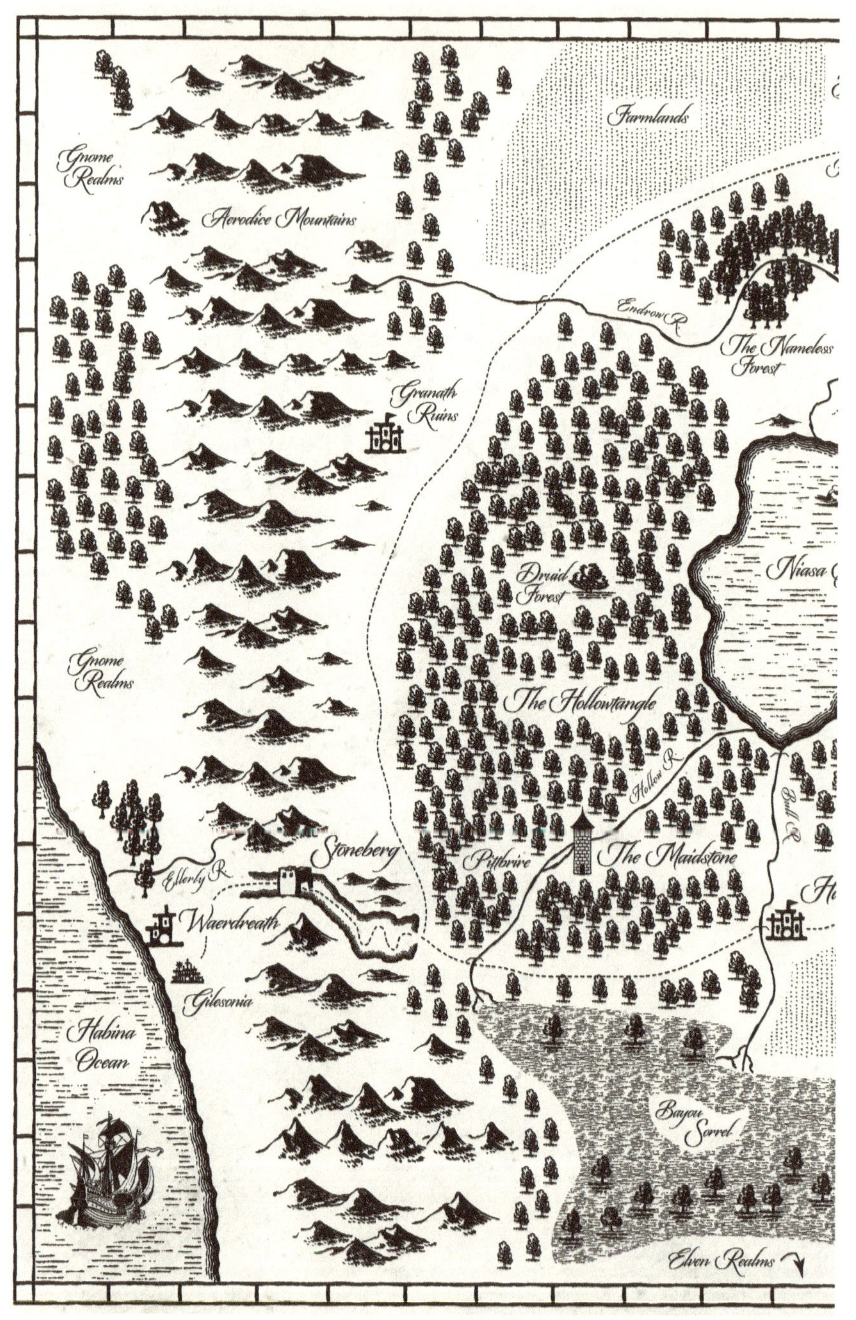

THE FOURWINDS
MAIDSTONE CHRONICLES MAP

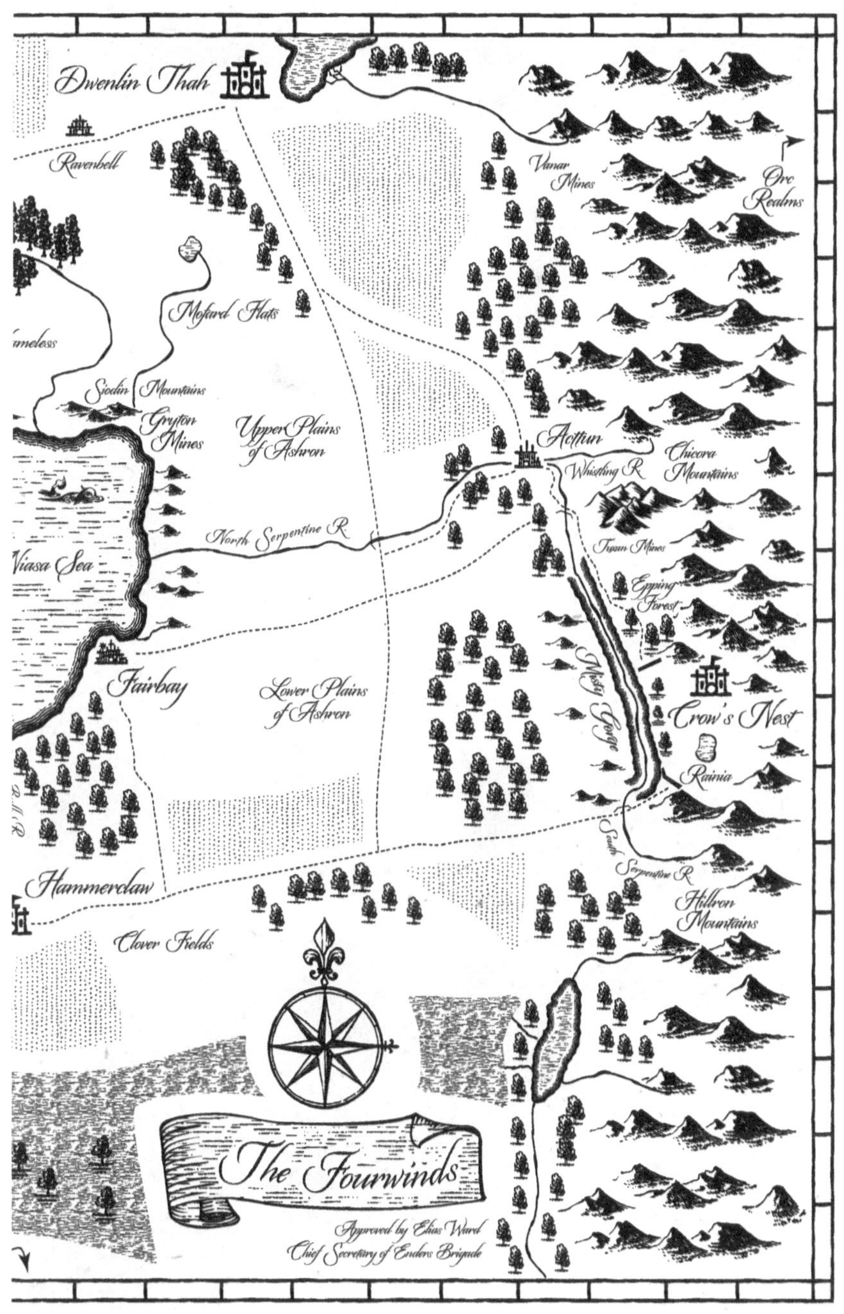

FULL DOWNLOADABLE VERSION AT:
WWW.MAIDSTONECHRONICLES.COM/MAPS

CHAPTER 1

DARK DAYS

Morgan stepped back as her blade whistled through a circular parry, deflecting the advancing foil with a loud *snap*. Against anyone else, Coach's powerful attack would have certainly taken the point. He outmatched the young fencing virtuoso in both size and experience, but Morgan remained poised, tendons tight as piano wires.

Without hesitation, she lunged. As Coach parried, she shifted her feint, moving with savage grace. Before he had time to counterattack, Morgan lunged again, this time below his guard. She extended her foil and jabbed his bright-white jacket low in the chest.

"Match!" she shouted, whipping off her mask and bib. Strands of sweat-soaked auburn hair clung to her tanned face as she raised her gloved hand, foil pointing up in salute. Her black-flecked hazel eyes flashed with the energy and maturity of someone about to graduate from university instead of high school.

Coach returned the salute. "Impressive, Miss Finley."

He pulled a small towel from his back pocket and dabbed a line of sweat rolling from his high forehead. "A well-executed passata sotto," he said between heavy breaths. "Bold move."

Morgan's full lips parted into a brilliant smile. Her lean form drew appreciative glances from a few boys warming up along the periphery. Five other fencing matches in the school gym continued around them, their footwork echoing off the walls. From the rafters, two World Fencing Championship banners with Morgan's name on them swayed beneath the air ducts.

Coach wiped the towel over his thinning gray hair. "Thought I had you there."

"Oh please," Morgan said, placing a hand on her hip. "I was watching the clock."

Coach smirked and drank deeply from his water bottle. "Well, I'm not foolish enough to stick my hand in the same fire twice; let's call it a morning."

"Want me to stay and help?" Morgan asked as they approached the main doors.

"No, I'll be fine. Off to class with you, Finley. Fencing earned you that nice Yale scholarship, but you'll need to keep your grades up to maintain it."

Morgan paused at the gym door, observing her favorite teacher in action. Of all the people in this hick town, she would miss him most after she moved away to attend university.

Coach's commanding voice jolted students into fearful acquiescence. "Hops! Now!" he shouted.

Morgan walked down the hall to the girls' locker room as the pounding and squeaking of running shoes filled the gym. She smiled, knowing Coach would not blow his whistle until the students' legs burned, or until one senior boy vomited across the floor.

As the soothing warmth of the shower cascaded over her body,

Morgan's adrenaline subsided. Thoughts of the odd little town flooded her unsettled mind. Only during practice could she truly be herself, uninhibited and confident. Even there, she was finding it difficult to be genuine. She missed the simple authenticity of childhood friendships.

Opening the hot water tap as far as it would go, she tried to relax as steam filled the locker room.

Morgan's family had moved four times in her life, making it challenging to form deep friendships. Her mother always found stable part-time work as a nurse, but her father struggled to find a church that would keep him as a long-term pastor. Three years ago, her father had uprooted the family from Cleveland, Ohio. He had told Morgan she would have more opportunity to stand out as a young fencer if they lived in Canada. She had hoped that meant returning to her birthplace in Niagara Falls, Ontario; instead, they moved to a small northern town where she couldn't help but stand out.

On the surface, Cochrane appeared a quiet hamlet. But Morgan was sensitive to what most townsfolk accepted as commonplace: rumors, innuendos, and the secrets revolving around the Arden Forest that bordered the eastern edge of town. At first, she had thought the gossip rather comical, like childish ghost stories told by old-timers in wallpapered kitchens. Now, her father was being pulled into something she did not understand.

As she stood motionless in the unveiled solitude a shower provides, Morgan considered how her family had drifted apart since coming to Cochrane. Until a few years ago, her parents had openly displayed their affection for one another. But recently, tension and angry words filled their home.

The latest argument between her parents burned in Morgan's

memory. Her father routinely raised his voice, but that day, he'd also spoken with his hands. The kitchen wall bore the brunt of his outbursts before he'd left the house, slamming the door behind him. Morgan had recoiled in the shadows of the dining room as her mother cringed in silence as if expecting the blows to shift in her direction. Fear of her father was subverting childhood adoration.

Since her first class was a spare, Morgan decided to run home and check on her mom before second block. The combination of the chilly tile floor and dark thoughts of her father strengthened her resolve as she dried off before slipping on socks, a T-shirt, and baggy track pants. She grabbed her favorite oversized hoodie she often wore to hide her form from prying eyes while she ran. It rarely worked.

With every step, anxious thoughts cooled the calmness she had sought in the warmth of the shower. Her father's simmering anger over the past few months threatened to boil over into open hostility. The thought of angry words turning to a physical attack on her mother was not as outlandish as it had once been. She turned down her street and noticed her father's car was still gone. She breathed a grateful sigh.

The house was silent. Her mother had worked the night shift, so Morgan hoped she was asleep. She entered and tiptoed upstairs. Halfway up, she stopped. In the upstairs hall, the spring-loaded ladder hung down from the ceiling. She had never seen the attic open since the day they moved in.

A soft glow emanated from beyond the small rectangular opening. Morgan listened. There was no sound, but she sensed someone was up there. Her pulse quickened. A knot tightened in her throat, stifling a breath as a brief image of her mother's beaten body flashed in her mind.

Morgan clutched the creaking ladder and climbed. Cool, dusty air floated down through the opening, and the hairs on the nape of her neck bristled. She shivered and strained her ears. Adrenaline surged through her veins like nervous fish in shallow water. With shorter breaths, she reached up before she lost her nerve.

The dark rooflines of the short attic formed sharp angles that prevented most adults from standing upright. A light bulb dangled from a single wire several feet away. Morgan shifted her view, avoiding the cobwebbed corners. At first, the room appeared empty, but at the other end of the attic, her mother kneeled in the shadows.

Still wearing her work scrubs, Julie Finley stared at the floor before her. Morgan exhaled as her mother turned her head, but her familiar features were unreadable.

"What…are…you…doing up here, Mom? You okay?" Morgan pulled herself through the trapdoor.

Julie blinked. The usual subtle creases around her limpid eyes now resembled miniature chasms. Her skin had an ashen tint to it.

Morgan approached one slow step at a time. She knelt beside her mother and gasped.

A long, wide floor plank was missing, revealing a shiny object.

"Don't get close," Julie warned, her voice raspy.

Morgan was transfixed. "I don't understand."

"I tried to pick it up, but…" Julie raised her reddened palm.

In the space beneath the missing floorboard was a sword unlike any Morgan had ever seen. Its blade was slender and graceful, with an ethereal green glow visible deep within the unblemished alloy. The grip, wrapped with tightly woven strands of black leather, could easily accommodate two hands. A simple round cross guard separated the area between the grip and the blade. The weapon was lying on a crimson fabric that added a regal aura to the humble surroundings, like a prince come to live with a pauper. It was magnificent.

"I've seen this before," Morgan breathed.

"What do you mean, you've seen this before?" Julie's eyes were wild and bloodshot.

Morgan squinted in the harsh light cast by the single bulb. She gripped the hilt before her mother could stop her and pulled the sword from its hiding place.

Julie was dumbfounded. "How… Why isn't *your* hand burning?"

"I don't know why it burned you, Mom, but I know I've seen this before." She raised the sword into the light, never flinching as she studied the weapon. The size and weight were a perfect match for Morgan as though the sword had been forged specifically for her.

Julie stared. "Where did you see this before, Morgan?"

"Not sure. I was young." She paused. "Dad was there."

"Put it back," Julie snapped.

Morgan gazed at the sword. It felt so alive, so majestic in her hand, that returning it to the humble hiding place would be a dishonor. Coach had once allowed her to hold an expensive saber at the World Championships, but that one paled by comparison. After a moment, she responded to her mother's command, placing the sword gently on the soft fabric. The difficulty with which she released her grip, however, was not lost on her.

"How'd you find this?" Morgan asked.

Julie ignored the question as she slid the wooden plank back into place. "Don't say anything to your father."

"Do you think *he* put it here?"

"I don't understand any of this," Julie said as Morgan helped her stand on shaky legs. A labored stretch suggested that Julie had been up here for hours.

She raised a stern finger and held Morgan's gaze. "Not a word to anyone, Morgan."

"I won't say anything, Mom."

Julie spoke quickly now as she ushered Morgan away from the sword's hiding place and back to the attic opening. "He should be home tomorrow afternoon, and I know you'll want to ask him about it. Lord knows I certainly do, but something isn't right here. I don't know why, but we need to keep this from him."

"Okay… Sure." Morgan had grown accustomed to secrets—even in her own family—but this was frightening. Without another word, she helped her mother down through the narrow opening. As she followed, an unfamiliar sensation washed over her. Morgan gazed into the attic as if the sword were drawing her back. Despite the strange seductive summons, she managed to ignore it.

At the foot of the ladder, Julie gave Morgan a tight hug. "Good. In the meantime, I need to get some sleep, and you need to get to school, kiddo."

Her mother spoke as if everything were normal but held Morgan longer than usual. When they broke from the embrace, Julie turned and walked into her room. The door closed softly, leaving Morgan unsettled.

She considered her options. She could wait until her mother was asleep and return to the attic, but respect for her mother trumped the impulse. With a sigh, she headed downstairs to the kitchen. But walking away from the sword took a concentrated effort.

Morgan was eager to leave the house, but she could not ignore her growling stomach. She poured herself a bowl of Shreddies and ate while pacing the kitchen. The attic captivated her thoughts. She was certain she had seen the sword before and could not forget how its smooth leather pressed against her palm. After starting to leave the house twice, she conceded and tiptoed upstairs.

Without checking to see if her mom had fallen asleep, she climbed the rickety attic rungs as quietly as possible. She trembled with excitement and inhaled sharply as she removed the floorboard. She wrapped both hands around the grip, lifting the gleaming blade in front of herself.

Her breathing slowed to a steady rhythm. A sudden burst of self-confidence mingled with profound peace, lifting the burdens of adolescence she had carried for three years. She felt like a child again. All was right in her world. She admired the intricate details of the sword in the same way she had on the first day her father introduced her to fencing.

As soon as Morgan's thoughts turned to her father, the sword became lighter as if intentionally drawing her away from the hiding place in the floor. Instinctively, she knew she had to move the weapon to a safer location in the house.

Moments later, Morgan stepped outside and welcomed the sun's warmth against her skin. She flexed her fingers into fists as though the sword remained in her hands. At least now the mysterious blade was safe. She was not so confident about her mother, who had shown genuine fear at the mention of her father. The thought of him using such a weapon on his own family provoked a shiver from Morgan, despite the comforting sun.

Morgan walked down the front steps and stretched in preparation for her return run to school. There was no one on the sidewalk, and not a single vehicle on her street.

The empty driveway reminded her of her most recent conversation with her father before he had left for his conference. It was not *what* he had said that unnerved her but *how* he had said it.

From the pulpit, his speech was always fluid and practiced, but that day, he spoke one awkward word at a time. Something was wrong. He had been withdrawing from the family and spending more time in his musty church office. Even as he spoke to her in the driveway, she had sensed a new aggression in his tone. She felt it more than heard it, like a shift in the wind before a storm.

"I won't be able to come with you to Germany," he had said without a hint of regret.

"But, Dad…this is the World Championships. My last tournament before I go to Yale. I thought…" Morgan fumbled for words. She had been so focused on defending her title in women's saber that she had little time to think about what had happened to her biggest fan. A former successful college athlete himself, her father had always encouraged a strict training regime. He had never missed a tournament, came to countless practices, and had supported her every chance he could. That had all changed since their sudden move to Cochrane.

He stepped forward, raising a warning finger. "Don't question me again, Morgan!"

Morgan could not believe what she was hearing. She had stared at him as if he were a stranger, as if someone were trying to impersonate him without knowing who he truly was. Before she could respond, he had backed out of the driveway and pulled away without another look.

Determined to shake the bitterness that now fused with her growing fear of her father, Morgan started a fast pace down the driveway. Her first few strides felt sluggish, so she opted to take the long way to school, along Nineteenth Avenue. She needed time to consider the possible connection between her mysterious affinity with the sword and the expanding alienation from her father.

Nineteenth Avenue was as close as anyone went to the Arden Forest these days, but Morgan was tired of secrets.

⊰ 10 ⊱

CHAPTER 2

DREAMS AND REALITY

With almost every light on in the house at 25 Nineteenth Avenue, Will Owens studied the shadowy border of the Arden Forest across the field from what had once been his parents' home. He stood alone in the kitchen, waiting.

Two small forms darted from the trees and scurried into the grassy field. Once in the open, they rushed to Will's house. In the front yard, they stopped in their tracks and glared at Will standing behind the kitchen window.

Will drew his father's old Springfield 1911 handgun from the back of his cargo pants and raised it threateningly. The creatures narrowed spiteful yellow eyes as their shadowy forms cowered. One flashed a small claw and spat at Will before they both turned and fled down the street.

Will released the breath he had been holding and carefully placed the .45 caliber handgun on the counter. The presence of the hideous creatures frightened him, but not as much as the increasing frequency of their emergence from the forest over the past month. They were also becoming bolder. A week ago, Will had chased one from his house. In his panic, he had fired a shot at the creature, but the bullet passed harmlessly through its lanky body and into the hallway wall outside his bedroom. He was amazed the police never came by. Neighbors had grown accustomed to Will's oddities since his parents died three years ago. Now people only offered sideways glances and whispers that fueled the town's busy rumor mill.

Will had first noticed the dark creatures shortly after his mother's tragic accident. He had searched the internet in a vain attempt to identify the small humanoid beasts. For lack of a better name, he referred to them as Lessers, perhaps because he expected a more significant creature to follow. He had quickly figured out that, while he could see the Lessers, other people could not. Each attempt to point them out or describe them to others further alienated him, so he stopped saying anything about them. Like a miry swamp, a deep loneliness gradually pulled Will into its bottomless pit.

The flat metal finish of the handgun absorbed the light in the small kitchen like an anglerfish in the darkness, luring him closer. Will blinked and turned away. Too many times, he had thought about using the 1911 to end his crippling loneliness as his father had done three years ago. Threads of hope slipped through the fingers of his soul, but he gritted his teeth and resolved that today would not be his last. With clenched fists, he rubbed his eyes as if trying to erase the vision of a dream that persistently interrupted his life.

He inches across a frozen river, and the ice collapses. In the frigid darkness, he tries to cry out, but he is alone. When he opens his eyes, he is standing on a high ridge staring down into seven waterfalls spilling into a yawning canyon. With every recurrence of the dream, the roar of the waterfalls grows with alarming clarity. He turns his left shoulder to see a massive dark tower. Ancient blackened mortar holds rough stone blocks, their lines barely visible behind centuries-old moss and vine. A cone roof covered with weathered shakes protects the structure from the rain that falls relentlessly from dark-gray clouds, nourishing the seven royal waterfalls like obedient cupbearers. The tower's design whispers of an age Will could not begin to fathom. There are no window openings. A solitary solid wooden door at the base of the tower, set back in the stone behind a shroud of mist, offers the only access into this enigmatic fortress.

Over his right shoulder, within his peripheral vision, Will sees the snout of a large horse whose hide mirrors the darkness of this place. Despite his attempts to turn and examine the creature, something prevents him. Then, like the water's crash at the base of the seven waterfalls, the horse releases a sudden, impatient huff. With each huff, Will awakens with a start in a cold sweat.

When the dreams had first begun, Will spent hours at his computer trying to find a place in the world with seven waterfalls cascading into a single canyon. He could find nothing close to his vision, but each time, his search ended with an image of the Arden Forest spread across Google Earth. Like the mystery of the Lessers, the dream baffled him. And with each futile attempt to share his unique visions with someone, the deep loneliness tightened its grip.

He poured himself another cup of coffee and stepped out the front door to breathe more clearly. Like the ivy of the dark tower in his dream, a deep-rooted conviction spread over him. The creatures and the forest were inextricably linked to the images in his dreams.

The two small creatures had gone, so Will sat on the front steps. He stretched his legs, stiff but strong and lean from the endless miles he walked each night while the town slept. He rubbed his hands on his faded jeans, then hugged his chest and shivered. His favorite red T-shirt with a Coca-Cola logo was wearing thin, but he couldn't decide if the chill was from the temperature or his nerves.

With a dry mouth, Will pursed his lips and swallowed hard, trying to shrug off the inexorable heaviness settling on his shoulders. The morning sun glinted off the basketball hoop above the garage door, reminding him of simpler days a few years ago when he had a smooth jump shot and friends at every turn. He raked his fingers through thick hair, reminiscing. Even the forest was different then. Now he watched it with apprehension.

A few lower branches shifted, and something broke from the trees.

Will stiffened. He rubbed his eyes to be certain of what he was seeing. To anyone else, a tall brown-haired middle-aged man had stepped out of the forest for an early-morning walk. Dressed in pleated khakis, black dress shoes, and a crisp blue oxford shirt, the man was vaguely familiar. Beyond the simple shell, Will saw someone—no, something—terrifying. The Lessers were little more than dried leaves in this impending hurricane of evil.

A flash of movement where Iroquois Road curved into Nineteenth Avenue caught Will's eye: a young female jogger wearing an oversized hoodie ran alone down the street. Will turned his attention back to the forest and saw the pseudo-man now halfway across the field, walking the land like a king. Will's mind raced. He realized the jogger would not make the distance to the next street without a confrontation.

By the time the creature passed behind the tranquil houses on the far side of the avenue, the jogger had come to a halt. Will sprang to his feet. The girl stood in the pathway between two houses for a second, then strode up a driveway.

"Don't!" Will shouted, shattering the morning silence.

The girl disappeared behind a white van in the driveway.

A pang of fear struck Will so hard, it nearly threw him off the porch. *That thing could kill her!* Instinctively, he wanted to turn and run into the house, but a flicker of inner strength held him steadfast. He balled his hands into fists. His natural urge to dissociate himself from the affairs of the town faded, and he opted to intervene.

As if struck in the heart with a syringe of adrenaline, Will leapt off the concrete porch and sprinted across the lawn. He widened his stride and leaned forward to keep his legs beneath him. The houses blurred as he charged past them.

The girl jumped back as Will skidded to an awkward stop a few feet from her. He had expected to confront the creature, but the girl stood alone next to a small dog tangled up in its chain.

"Wh-what the…?" the girl said.

"I…saw…thought I saw…big dog follow…neighbor has a vicious…" Will stammered while she regained her composure.

"You scared me." She picked up the dog's chain. "I was just gonna give this little guy a hand."

Aware of the evil lurking close by, Will cleared his throat but could think of nothing to say.

"Are you new to Cochrane?" she asked.

Her calm, tolerant tone surprised Will. In the moment he took to find his voice, he was startled by her gentle eyes.

"Kind of," he replied, wiping a line of sweat from his face with the back of his hand. "I grew up here, but…I was away for a while."

He shifted his weight evenly between both feet, bracing himself for the inevitable jeering and judgment that most people extended him. She must have something to say about his stilted speech or his pasty skin and weary eyes that betrayed too many nights without decent sleep.

Instead, the girl bent down and quickly untangled the dog's chain that was caught in a small bicycle.

"That about does it." She stepped back from the excited puppy intent on climbing her legs. "Guess that other dog must be inside."

Will waited for her to say more. Most people in town avoided him. A few openly mocked him as a lunatic, especially after he spent six months in the North Bay psychiatric ward. But this girl's simple acceptance of his peculiar presence and the unpretentious way she spoke astounded him.

The puppy shifted its interest to him, chewing on his leather moccasin. The girl smiled as they both noticed the other moccasin was missing entirely. Embarrassed, Will tried to think of some explanation for his odd behavior, but nothing came.

"I'd better get going. I'm already late for class," the girl said with a wave of her hand.

Will lifted his arm to return the gesture as the girl continued her run down Nineteenth Avenue. She turned left on Seventh Street and was gone.

Left alone, Will backed away, glancing from house to house, expecting the creature to materialize at any moment. What he failed to realize was that it was already inside a house, harvesting.

CHAPTER 3
SOME DAYS

Morgan walked through the open door of Coach's small office cluttered with sports equipment, stacks of textbooks, and an undersized desk. She rarely skipped class, and math was important to her, but the odd encounters with her mother in the attic and with the boy on Nineteenth Avenue consumed her thoughts. Moreover, her fascination with the strange sword refused to be ignored. The only person she could trust to help declutter her thoughts worked in this messy office.

While Coach finished one last report, Morgan had a chance to catch her breath. She plopped down on the old couch across from his desk, squeezing between a cardboard box of small trophies and a mesh sack of baseball helmets. She breathed in the comforting smell of coffee already dripping from an aging four-cup maker.

"Not interested in class this morning, Miss Finley?"

"Don't worry, Coach; my A is all but in the books. I decided to run home for a second breakfast, and I took the long way back," she said before considering her words.

Coach stopped writing. Morgan had grown accustomed to

him peering over the thin silver frame of his glasses with a disapproving gaze.

"I know, I know." She sighed, mimicking his familiar phrase before he could remind her. "*It's a dangerous part of town.* But I didn't go anywhere near Arden Road."

"Nineteenth Avenue?"

She nodded.

Coach tossed her a water bottle filled with orange Powerade and sat back thoughtfully.

"I can offer you advice, Morgan. But it's up to you what you do with it."

Morgan wrenched off the wide lid and took a drink, spilling some down the front of her hoodie. "Do you know how crazy it sounds, the way you all talk about the Arden Forest? I mean, to someone who hasn't grown up here?"

"I suppose."

"I did have a good scare, though. I went to untangle a little dog from its chain, and some guy came running over. Scared the bejeebies outta me."

The disapproving expression on Coach's face led her to believe she had said too much.

"Who was it?" he asked, setting down his pen.

"Just some guy—about my age, I think. I haven't seen him in school, though. He said something about a dangerous dog in the area."

"Did he tell you his name?" Coach pressed.

"The dog?" Morgan tried to break the uncomfortable seriousness of the early-morning lecture.

"The boy. Did he have a name?"

"Probably." Frustration crept into Morgan's voice. She made a mental note to consider her words more wisely next time.

Coach walked over to a small bookshelf between two trays of basketballs and pulled out a few yearbooks. He brought one back to his desk and flipped through the pages.

"Is this him?" he asked.

Morgan leaned forward to scan the page. Coach tapped his index finger next to the photo of a boy.

"How on earth did you know that?" Morgan narrowed her eyes.

Coach pulled the yearbook back and, after another brief look at the photo, closed it. Somehow, his brow furrowed even deeper than it had before. "Since you're blowing off math class, let's head up to the gym and I'll tell you on the way."

He pushed aside the messy heap of papers on his desk, found a Toronto Maple Leafs cup, and filled it with fresh coffee. With his free hand, he grabbed a bulging file folder and motioned with his head for Morgan to follow.

As soon as they entered the hallway, Coach began. "His name is Will Owens. He used to hang around with my son when we lived on Eighteenth. He had some…well…emotional issues. Soon after that yearbook picture was taken, he had a small breakdown. He was sent to a psychiatric facility in North Bay for help, and shortly thereafter, his mom drowned in the Frederick House River. Her snowmobile had crashed through the ice."

"That's horrible," Morgan whispered.

"Worse, they were unable to recover her body from the river. His father had been driving the sled and, overcome with guilt and grief, took his own life a month later. The last I heard, Will was back in his parents' house."

Morgan stared in stunned disbelief as she slowed. At the top of the stairs, Morgan found her voice, but it sounded faint and quavering in her ears. "How could anyone *not* have emotional issues after that?"

Coach remained silent as she processed the story.

"That explains after the accident," she said. "But what kind of issues did he have before? I mean, what teenager doesn't have issues?"

"This was different." Coach faltered as if deciding either how to continue the story or if he even wanted to say anything at all.

Without knowing why, Morgan pushed the subject. Maybe she was tired of the secrets surrounding the Arden Forest. Or maybe it was her family's secrets, hidden behind church office doors and beneath attic floorboards. Whatever the cause, she realized she was in too deep now.

"Does all this have anything to do with the forest?" she asked.

Coach's expression hardened so much she reconsidered her question.

"Why would you ask that?" he asked, brushing a few wisps of hair from his forehead.

"Does it?" she pressed.

"Listen, Morgan." Coach paused to reposition the file folder under his arm. "Some things are best left alone."

Morgan sighed as she opened the gymnasium door. "I hate this town! Spinning stories is all it is, one rolling into the next."

She paused in the doorway as Coach gulped some coffee.

"I'll tell you this, Morgan, only because I trust you." He lowered his voice. "This has to remain between the two of us."

"You know me, Coach."

"I do, but Will has endured a lot, and I don't want to add to his… Well, he's had a hard go."

"I can appreciate that."

"I'm not sure you can," he said as they walked across the polished hardwood.

"What do you mean?"

"He started having severe mood swings about three years ago," Coach explained in a hushed voice. "You could be having a normal conversation one minute, then the next, he would act strangely, frantically glancing this way and that, often staring into the shadows of a room. His swings kept getting worse, and after several months, he finally confided in a friend, and word got out. The teasing was relentless. We tried to help, but you know how kids can be."

"What did he tell his friend?" Morgan raised her voice. "Coach. What did he tell him?"

Coach was fiddling with the keys to the equipment room. His hand trembled as he turned the lock and pushed the door open with his foot. He turned to her.

"That he could see strange creatures lurking…everywhere."

CHAPTER 4

First Found

The quiet streets of Cochrane filled with residents driving to work, parents taking kids to school, and business owners opening shops. At the always busy Tim Hortons, one of two squad cars on duty pulled up to the drive-thru window. An urgent dispatch interrupted the officers' coffee break.

"All units, we have a 10-35—possible 901—at number Thirty-Three Eighth Avenue."

Constable Tom Bondy accepted his usual coffee—the popular Double Double—and gaped at the radio as if seeing it for the first time. He handed the coffee to his rookie partner, Andy Barnet, before reaching for the mic. Inside the cruiser, the temperature rose several degrees despite the crisp morning air passing through the opened window. He eased the car forward to avoid being overheard.

"Car four, 10-9."

The dispatcher repeated the message.

"10-4. Car four responding. ETA two minutes."

"10-64, car four."

Tom did a quick shoulder check and, careful not to screech the tires, maneuvered the cruiser out of the parking lot without the sirens. If the dispatcher was right, the last thing he wanted was to draw attention to his arrival.

"Isn't that old man Lafleur's place?" Andy asked.

Tom nodded. He slowed through the stop sign at Third Avenue and continued along Fifth Street. At Eighth Avenue, he turned left.

A small crowd was gathered in front of the Lafleur house.

Experience from almost twenty years of service quickly organized in Tom's mind, allowing him to act on instinct. He pulled to an abrupt stop in front of the driveway.

"Get those people back to the sidewalk and wait with them until backup arrives," Tom said as he stepped out of the squad car.

"Don't you think—?"

"Lord, have mercy! 10-35 means Major Crime Alert, and 10-64?" Tom glared at his partner. "Proceed with caution!" He closed his door and placed his sizeable hands on the window frame. Leaning forward, he met Andy's eyes and offered a short nod that set Andy in motion.

"The sidewalk. Gotcha."

Tom surveyed the burgeoning crowd. A woman was crying on the front lawn with several people trying to console her. She was so hysterical that no one had yet ventured into the house to investigate what she had seen. As Tom walked past them and up the steps to the house, he felt their frightened eyes following him.

At the door, he sensed something was terribly wrong. He tried to collect his wits, but the feeling worsened. With a sweaty palm nestled around his service Glock, he opened the screen door and peeked through the partially opened inside door. The inner darkness prevented a clear view.

Tom forced himself to ignore the wailing behind him and focus on the stillness of the front room, listening for clues. The soft click of his flashlight broke the eerie silence within. He slipped his Glock from its holster and nudged the door open. An overwhelming impression washed over him, a warning that he was about to see something he would try to forget the rest of his days.

He stepped into the living room and used his foot to stop the aluminum-framed screen door from slamming shut behind him. The moment it closed, Tom forgot about the commotion outside. Trained to observe the details, he waited as his eyes adjusted to the shadows inside. With both flashlight and gun held up at eye level, he scanned the room. All the blinds were drawn. An old clock ticked softly on the mantle lined with numerous framed pictures of the Lafleur family. Tom recognized everyone. His pulse fell into pace with the clock. The scant furnishings appeared undisturbed, the lamps unmoved on their small end tables. Yesterday's *Cochrane Times* lay folded on the coffee table opposite the sofa. Next to the newspaper was a half-empty teacup and a saucer. Tom could not detect a single sign of forced entry or struggle.

Two purposeful steps forward provided a view of the hallway; nothing had been disturbed.

Everything slowed as he moved farther into the house. He started toward the bedrooms, but his instincts redirected him to the shadowy kitchen.

Before he could move his feet, he attempted another calming breath. He took a small step into the kitchen around an overturned chair. His finger slid over the trigger. Two more chairs were pulled away from the kitchen table. His next step revealed the table itself—and what was on it.

Tom shone the flashlight on the center of the table and gasped. The room shifted beneath his feet as he fought the urge to vomit.

He stumbled backward against a wall, almost dropping both flashlight and gun, sending a potted devil's ivy crashing to the floor. Before his weakened knees gave way, the front screen door opened. Tom snapped back to reality.

Andy's face reflected Tom's horror. The young rookie stopped in the hallway.

"What is it, Tom?"

"Don't come any closer." Tom forced a dry swallow. "Set up a perimeter around the property. No one comes in."

"What's going on?"

"There's a body on the kitchen table."

"A—a person?" Andy's voice trembled.

"I want a man posted at the back door, and one at the front. No one—and I mean no one—goes inside. I need to get CIB here right away."

Within an hour of his call, two special investigators from the Criminal Investigation Branch in Toronto were on their way to Cochrane. What took eight hours by car was only a one-hour flight. With a jet capable of landing at Cochrane's single-runway airport, the investigators would be arriving shortly.

It was not yet noon when Tom drove out to the airport, anxiously awaiting the two promised CIB agents. He sat in his car, reeling from the ghastly murder scene. He needed experienced investigators and hoped the short notice of his request would not mean they sent rookies.

Moments later, a small plane came in on final approach. After a short taxi, it pulled in front of the small hangar. A door opened the moment the wheels stopped rolling.

"So, people *do* live this far north," the first investigator said.

Tom feigned a smile as the man with boyish facial features

and a bowl haircut stepped down onto the tarmac. Before Tom despaired that he had, in fact, been sent two rookies, another man emerged from the plane.

"Easy there, Morley," the other investigator said, stepping out behind him. "You're talking about my land here."

The large man appeared to be in his midfifties, with weathered skin and shoulder-length jet-black hair. He had a rugged face, but his dark eyes revealed a mix of warmth and wisdom rarely seen in Tom's line of work.

"Constable Tom Bondy?" the first investigator said, appearing younger with every step.

"Yes, sir," Tom said, extending his hand. "Call me Tom."

"Special Investigator Josh Morley, but everyone calls me Morley. And this is Special Investigator Joe Cheechoo."

"Please call me Joe. Pleasure meeting you, Tom." Joe's voice was slow and resonant, and his broad smile deepened the creases in his face. Tom reassessed his initial estimate of the man's age.

"I appreciate you boys getting here so fast. I'm sure you'd rather be a hundred other places."

"I can sympathize with such sentiment, Tom," Joe said. "I grew up in a small town where everyone knows everyone. It's always difficult when you know the families involved."

Their eyes met briefly, and Tom sensed that this guy was the genuine article. These investigators might actually be able to help.

"It always helps in these circumstances for outsiders to come alongside," Joe added.

"We have a few minutes until our gear's unloaded," Morley said. "Mind telling us why our CO had us on the first available plane to the North Pole?"

Tom turned and led the way across the warm tarmac to the car waiting beyond the fence. "I'm not sure where to begin."

"Were you the first officer on the scene?" Joe asked.

"I was."

"Just tell us what you saw, Tom. You'll be surprised at how much it'll help," Joe said.

Tom was silent a few moments as they walked. He wished he could purge his mind of the scene, but he knew the key to solving any crime was in the details. They sat down at a picnic table near the car. Morley pulled out his BlackBerry and selected the recorder app as Tom began.

"There was a small crowd outside the house when my partner and I arrived this morning. It was strange. A woman was having a meltdown. Some people were consoling her, but most were staring at the house. I walked in through the front door. It was dark inside, and a heavy, pungent smell hung in the air, like the scent of a recently lit match. I was about to head toward the bedrooms but turned instead to the kitchen. There I saw old man Lafleur's body—what was left of it—stretched naked across the kitchen table."

Morley glanced at Joe while Tom continued, picking up the pace, unable to stop for fear of not being able to finish.

"He was lying there peacefully like he was under sedation. At first, it didn't even resemble a murder scene. I've seen open heart surgeries on TV, and that's the first thing I could think of." Tom cleared his throat. "His chest was opened neatly, except…only he…his insides were gone. I didn't need to see any more; I knew who it was, and I knew he was dead."

Tom finished abruptly, wiping sweat from his forehead.

"Did you approach the body?" Morley asked.

Tom shook his head.

"That's good. The kitchen must have been a mess."

"That's the weirdest part," Tom said. "Aside from an overturned chair, everything was in its place." His voice quivered. "There was no blood anywhere, not even on the table. Hell, I can still picture the place mats."

Tom waited for a reply from either investigator, hoping that last clue might trigger a positive lead.

"Interesting," Joe mumbled, shifting his gaze from Tom to the forest bordering the small airport. "We'll need to examine the crime scene, but I also want to get familiar with the area and speak with some residents. We need suspects, of course, but answers to difficult questions often arise from unexpected sources."

CHAPTER 5

DAWN'S NEW DAY

Tiny beads of sweat clung to Will's forehead despite the coolness of his home office. He paced between his desk and the window a few times, then stopped at the window. Through a thin crack in the curtain, he peered outside. In the distance, pale harbingers of light clawed the night sky, but in the neighborhood, all was still.

Will eyed the desk. The antique oak workstation filled the space like an imposing employer. He rubbed his hands together and stole another glimpse outside. Visions of the latest creature from the Arden Forest, news of three mysterious murders, and a perplexing recurring dream converged on him. But the desk didn't care. The demands of daily work refused to be ignored.

Will returned to his desk and switched on the TV mounted above his computer monitors. A repeat of last night's broadcast of the eleven o'clock news held his attention but was not surprising.

Yellow police tape surrounded a third murder victim's home. Reporters from towns as distant as North Bay huddled as close as they could to the crime scene. Three officers with puffed-up chests and outstretched arms struggled to keep the crowd at bay.

It seemed like a losing battle. The local newscast reported that police were still without a suspect. Major network news vans would soon arrive, forcing the detachment to call in officers from neighboring South Porcupine and Kapuskasing. The town had previously only experienced one murder in the past twenty-five years, and the local OPP had caught the assailant within hours of the crime. Now, in less than a week, there were three deaths, and no suspects. Inexperienced reporters stuttered unfamiliar terms like *serial killer* and *grisly murders*. The lowly town of Cochrane would soon be headline news across Canada.

Will shut off the TV and sat down at the desk. He hunched forward and rubbed his hands against his thighs. A few deep breaths offered little relief for his general state of exhaustion.

The recurring dream had visited him again, but it had changed slightly last night. He recalled standing on the ridge surveying the seven waterfalls and feeling as though he and the horse were at the end of a difficult journey together. A featureless woman stood before him. He could not discern whether she was good or bad, but he knew he must confront her. The outcome of this meeting would affect many people. *Right*, Will thought. *Like that would ever happen.* Despite his self-doubt, he could not deny the premonition. His actions would determine the difference between living in the depths of unimaginable sorrow or rising to find lasting freedom. None of it made sense. In fact, the dream now obscured more than it revealed.

Will stood again and stretched his arms in front of himself. He shook his head a few times as if doing so might somehow reorder and settle the turbulence inside. Brushing the hair from his eyes, he sipped some water and sat down again to focus on the day's work.

A series of numbers on a graph flashed across the large monitor to his right, measuring the buying and selling pressures of six currency combinations. The monitor before him displayed his active trading account. He was seeing some large currency swings that indicated, in his opinion, a dramatically oversold Euro against the US Dollar. He expected a bounce soon. Investors would realize the end was actually not as imminent as expected.

Before passing, Will's parents had always assumed he squandered his nights playing video games over the internet with people far away, people who knew nothing of his *problems*. They had been right about the internet but mistaken about what he had been doing there. Ostracized by everyone, including childhood friends, Will had become a recluse.

In his travels throughout the internet, he had discovered some articles about currency trading. He studied day and night. For whatever reason, he could decipher the charts and developed a discerning eye for key global indicators like retail sales and CPI numbers.

After his parents died, Will buried himself in currency trading. He sometimes wondered if this was simply a defense mechanism to evade the trauma, grief, and depression that threatened to consume him. Spurred by his desperate need to leave Cochrane and never return, he had amassed a trading account that was $37,500 short of $3 million.

Will stood and walked around his office that doubled as an exercise room. He offered a few feeble blows to a punching bag hanging in one corner before wandering over to a large open closet that held his scuba gear. *No,* he thought, *not today.* Turning back to his desk, he paused before a floor-to-ceiling bookcase that filled the space between two blacked-out windows.

Books had been an important part of Will's childhood. He'd

rarely made time to read them over the past few years, but their presence offered him a small source of comfort. He ran his fingers along the spines of some of his favorites. His mother used to read aloud every night, and together they enjoyed countless adventures. She had been an amazing storyteller. Until a few days ago, Will had considered picking up one of the old books, but the thought of venturing to an imaginary realm without his mother had prevented him. More importantly, the realities of the past few days kept him grounded in this world.

It was time for his morning walk, but Will decided to check the TV news one more time. He laced up his running shoes as the reporter wrapped up her story. Behind her, a large dark-haired man with the letters *C-I-B* on his jacket emerged from the barricaded house. He conferred with several officers and then reentered the house.

Curious, Will switched one of his monitors back on, leaned over to his keyboard, and searched the web for *CIB OPP*. The top result led him to the Ontario Provincial Police's website that described the Criminal Investigation Branch's duty to provide specialists to investigate homicides and other serious crimes.

With a heavy sigh, Will shut off the TV and slouched in his chair with three simultaneous thoughts: *That new creature is responsible for the murders. Why? Who's next?*

Will licked his lips and swallowed hard. He spun around in his chair to face the closed office door, holding his breath. Someone—or something—was behind it.

Was that breathing? Will stared at the tarnished brass doorknob. *Don't start turning. Please don't open.*

He strained to listen, but the thrumming pulse in his ears muffled everything else. In one swift motion, he grabbed the

Springfield 1911 from the desk and stood, gun aimed at the door. He shook his shoulders to release a shiver tickling his spine as he crept across the room. Before he could think of possible consequences, he wrenched the door open and jumped back with gun raised, shouting something incoherent. Somehow, he refrained from pulling the trigger.

In the empty hallway, Will noticed the bullet hole left behind from the last time he was certain something had been lurking there.

Silence filled the house. Will could see nothing, but something had been there a moment ago. He could feel it. Or could he smell it? *Is that sulfur in the air?* Reality and fantasy flickered under the soft glow of the solitary hall light.

"Is anyone there?" His cracking voice broke the insufferable silence. He ventured a few steps down the hallway to the kitchen but saw nothing. Still, he was sure something had been there.

He inched along the kitchen counter until he reached the door to the basement. His throat tightened when he saw the darkness below; he remembered changing those light bulbs last week! Something shifted in the shadows below.

"No!" Will shuffled away from the basement doorway, scrambling for the front door. His pounding heart almost stopped when the locked door resisted his efforts. He slammed the dead bolt to the side, flung the door open, and leapt outside.

On the short concrete porch, a small, crooked form sprang from the top step. The Lesser landed two steps down and lost its footing, tumbling backward. With a startled look, it disappeared into the shadows.

Will jumped backward, then stopped, fearing something worse inside the house. He pointed the 1911 at the shadows, but a remnant of sanity reminded him that the bullets would pass harmlessly through the creature. *Idiot,* he thought. *A gunshot will alert the entire neighborhood, and you'll be shipped back to North Bay.* Will tucked the gun into the back of his pants and grabbed the garden rake leaning against the porch wall.

He charged down the concrete steps and swung the rake in a wide arc as the little hate-filled form melted into the heavy shadows against the house. Will spun around. Several more shadowy figures darted around the yard. Until recently, only a few Lessers had dared to come this close to his house. Now, almost a dozen boldly taunted him.

"Ya! Ya!" Will cried out in a shrill voice, chasing the creatures across his front lawn. Tiny sets of yellow eyes blinked out of sight as the Lessers dodged his attacks. Will's chest heaved, pumping adrenaline through his veins. He spun around, expecting to see the new large creature at any moment.

Then he saw it. On the sidewalk across the street, an outlined form stood motionless. Will squared to face it and lifted the rake above his shoulders like a batter ready for a curveball. He clenched his jaw. If he had the gun in his hand, he would have emptied the clip, regardless of the consequences.

The morning light had chased away most of the darkness. Will blinked in utter shock as he focused on the form before him. It wasn't the creature. Instead, Will found himself staring at the jogger he had encountered the other day. Confusion spread across her face. Will assumed she couldn't see the Lessers, and he imagined she was probably wondering why he was flailing the rake around his yard like a madman.

He longed to say something logical to explain his actions. Although he moved his mouth, he couldn't form the words. He thought briefly of the reactions of past friends and neighbors.

Their mocking voices rose again to belittle him. Each time he had tried to describe the creatures visible only to him, Will had slowly pushed people farther from his life. Everyone had given him the same silent disregard—everyone except this girl.

For a few seconds, neither of them moved. Will's mind whirled like a fleeting wind. He squeezed his eyes shut, wanting to cry out, but nothing came. The rake slipped from his fingers. Fear, exhaustion, embarrassment, and confusion attacked him through the strong whispers of the Lessers hiding in the nearby shadows. He wheeled around and ran between his house and the neighbor's.

The girl called out to him, but he raced past Eighteenth Avenue, Seventeenth Avenue, and all the way to Lake Commando, running like a man possessed.

CHAPTER 6

INVESTIGATIONS

Will stopped running at the footbridge that spanned the narrows between both halves of Lake Commando. Heaving breaths provided little relief. Tears came without warning, but Will didn't care. He had thought he was on the road to recovery after months of treatment. His success at currency trading had boosted his self-confidence and given him an inkling of hope for a brighter future. He had even hoped that his ability to see the Lessers might keep him alive or help him save others in town and redeem himself. That fragile hope was snuffed out like a dying ember in the showers of loneliness that now overwhelmed him.

The town slowly came alive as the sounds of light traffic rose from the streets. The faint laughter of children, probably on their way to school, drifted across the lake. Out at the narrows, Will was far enough away to find sanctuary.

As he wept alone in silence, the sun nudged shadows from the footbridge and warmed his face. He realized that his tears came not from fear of the Lessers—or even the mysterious new creature—but from the growing gulf they created in his life. Each encounter with them deepened the chasm between him and those he cared for: friends, teachers, and…yes, especially his father. *Dad never tried to understand. I was one more tragedy he couldn't deal with.* He wiped both eyes with his sleeve and stared across the lake, wondering if that jogger might appear and prove him wrong.

"Do you ever get the feeling things are not always as they seem?" The unanticipated voice beside him should have startled Will, but the soothing tone calmed his fear.

A large man with dark hair and rugged features stood watching him. Slightly over six feet tall, the man had a solid frame that could only be built from years of hard toil. He wore a navy-blue windbreaker and faded, loose-fitting jeans.

The man stepped closer. "Like with you, for instance."

Will met his penetrating eyes, and a hint of recognition reflected back at him. The man composed himself so quickly that it would have been easy to miss his surprised expression, but Will caught it.

The man raised his eyebrows, deepening the weathered creases in his forehead. "People see you and they make assumptions."

Will's eyes burned again, threatening another bitter deluge. "No one cares if I live or die."

"I see. So, you also make assumptions about yourself?"

"Wh-what?"

"How are you called?"

It was a strange way of asking a person's name, but Will played along. "Will. Will Owens."

The man's eyes narrowed, and his high cheekbones sharpened. "Did your parents always call you Will?"

Half memories swirled around in Will's head. "Mom used to call me something when I was young…" He remembered how good it had made him feel. *What was that name?*

The man remained silent for a moment as Will worked through some of his earliest memories, then continued. As he spoke, the man leaned casually against the railing, viewing the crystal waters of the lake.

"One's heritage can sometimes reveal much about an individual. Bloodlines, lineage, and lore all play into who we are, and *why* we are. People today have largely forgotten their heritage, and thus their purpose for being. I suspect you know little of your heritage because, if you did, you might not be sitting here feeling sorry for yourself."

Will stared at him, nodding in silent agreement. There was so much about his family he didn't know.

"Who *are* you?" Will asked.

The man hesitated. He turned and gazed at Will the way one looks at an old friend, content to be together. After a moment, he spoke.

"My name is Joe of the Mushkegowuk. But that does not answer your question. There is more to both of us than our names suggest—more than anyone's assumptions about us. And there is more going on around us than our eyes can see."

A chirping cell phone broke their conversation. Joe reached into his pocket and retrieved an old flip phone.

"Go," Joe said, answering the phone. He nodded several times. "One moment," he told the caller, lowering the phone behind his back.

"I must go now, *masitaw*," Joe said with confident recognition in his eyes. "We will meet again soon."

Will stared back at him, but Joe simply turned and walked away with the phone against his ear.

That's it! That's what Mom used to call me all those years ago! Ma-

sitaw. Will wondered if this stranger could help him make sense of recent events in town, of his broken family, and of his disturbing visions. It was wishful thinking, but for the first time in the past few years, he'd met two people who hadn't shunned him: a girl he barely knew and a man who knew more than he revealed.

Later that afternoon, after two hours with the forensic team from the CIB, Joe exited a house amid a flurry of camera flashes and frantic questions. In a town where everyone knew each other, he thought it was odd the way the townsfolk hungered for details as much as the foreign reporters. Something wasn't tracking, and Joe was running out of time.

The unfortunate individuals who had found the victims' bodies were flown to Toronto via air ambulance for *observation*. They were haunted by the images of what they had seen and needed trauma counseling. But the main reason Joe sent them so far away was to limit the spreading panic. He had heard the diversity of rumors floating around, and as bad as some were, none came close to what he suspected to be the truth.

"Hey, Joe!" The familiar voice stopped him as he was about to get into his car.

Joe turned and recognized Constable Tom Bondy as he drove up in his squad car.

"Time for a coffee?" Tom asked.

With a nod, Joe slid into the squad car before the media cornered him. He glanced over his shoulder as he fastened his seat belt. The back seat was packed with three open filing boxes. Large yellow notepads were tucked between the boxes.

"Sorry for the mess," Tom said. "Most of our cars are like this these days. I think we've interviewed everyone in Cochrane. Some people have been interviewed two or three times by different officers. Unfortunately, our investigation is turning up a whole lot of nothing. How goes it at your end?"

"Seven crime scenes, and not a single print or DNA signature," Joe said. He thought briefly of his encounter with the boy at Lake Commando but wasn't ready to call that a solid lead.

Tom sighed. "People are getting pretty riled up. Some have even left town. Even heard the sawmill might close early for maintenance."

"You're doing a good job at keeping the peace, Tom. Large-scale panic would simply allow our perpetrator easier access around town."

"That's just it. A lot of people are more curious than afraid. I sent my wife to North Bay for an impromptu visit with our daughter. And if my other kids hadn't already left the nest, I would've made them leave until we catch this perp. Hell, I'm scared to death. Last night, I slept with my shotgun across my chest."

Joe laughed, a deep, vibrant laugh that caused Tom to smile despite the stressful time.

"It's a good thing your wife didn't decide to surprise you," Joe said, generating more laughter from both men. "Tom in his skivvies with a loaded shotgun across his chest!"

The shared laughter quickly subsided. "Boy, that sure felt good," Tom said, turning up the Sixth Avenue hill.

"You should consider taking an evening off work," Joe said. "We need you to be strong for your community."

Tom turned onto the highway toward Tim Hortons. "Thanks, Joe, but I'm good. A coffee break is all I need for now."

"How's your partner holding up?"

"I sent Andy home early. He's seen some horrible things over the past few days. It's a lot to take for a rookie."

Joe nodded. "This is a lot for anyone to take, but it's especially frightening for young people." His thoughts turned again to the distraught boy he'd met by the lake. Had Will Owens seen some horrible things that might shed light on the investigations?

Tom parked the car in the Tim Hortons parking lot and sighed. He must have noticed that Joe was deep in thought. "What is it?" Tom asked.

Joe rubbed at a tingling sensation on the back of his neck. His suspicion was growing stronger, but he still wasn't ready to discuss it with Tom. "Oh, it's nothing. Just thinking about someone I met today who reminded me of a girl I once knew."

The following morning, Will sat on the top step of his porch, stunned by the commotion taking place seven doors down at Constable Andy Barnet's house. Flashing lights, chirping radios, the hum of satellite dishes on network vans, and the familiar *wop-wop-wop* of a helicopter were difficult to ignore. A few reporters had gathered, but police kept them well back from the house, near the street that had been closed to local traffic only. The police, ambulance, and media vehicles had displaced three cars from neighboring homes. Those families had thrown suitcases into the trunks of their cars and made a hasty departure.

Amid the swirling activity, several Lessers lurked in the shadows of the crime scene. Not since his encounter yesterday morning on his front lawn with the small, repugnant creatures had Will seen so many in one place. He estimated there to be at least a dozen skulking about the neighborhood.

Will turned his attention to the Arden Forest. Until recently, the dark-green spruce trees had appeared lush and healthy, but today, part of the forest was sick and dying. The needle colors were changing into shades of orange, and some trees were showing signs of loss. Even the branches drooped as disease overtook the forest. Will realized that the death of the forest paralleled the death of the town, and he wondered if it were mere coincidence. Knowing what had emerged from the forest, however, he suspected that answers to the brutal murders would be found there.

Shouts from reporters down the street redirected his attention to the crime scene. A man emerged from the house, and Will recognized him as Joe, the stranger he had met on the trail by the lake.

As Joe worked his way toward a car, the crowd of Lessers scurried away. Joe slipped into the car and chirped his siren several times, parting the crowds. A single Lesser appeared from behind a low shrub, and then another from beneath a news van. They watched with hard stares as Joe's unmarked squad car pulled away. Will had never seen them act this way, as if they were actually afraid of Joe. Then, as quickly as they'd appeared, the creatures were gone again, slipping into the shadows.

As Joe's car turn off Nineteenth, Will remembered the name Joe had called him. Before falling asleep last night, Will had done a quick internet search. He discovered that *mâsihtâw* was a Cree word meaning something like *he fights with, or undertakes, a difficult task*. He had laughed cynically at the meaning, but the sound of the word echoed in his mind.

Footsteps crunched the gravel in his driveway, and Will froze, seeing the girl who had been jogging by his house quite regularly recently. He braced himself for a barrage of questions about the other morning.

"Hi, Will." The girl took short breaths as she slowed from her run. She brushed back some stray hairs from her face. Sweat glistened off her smooth skin. She was taller than he remembered, with athletic legs and muscle-toned arms. But her eyes were red and puffy. Something had changed.

"Hey," he answered. He couldn't remember getting the girl's name, but it didn't surprise him that she knew his—people in town liked to talk.

She stopped at the foot of the steps and gaped at the media circus down the street. Will put on a stoic face as he struggled to stifle his embarrassment and shame.

"They, uh, showed up a few hours ago," he mumbled.

"Another one?" her voice cracked. "I saw the news yesterday but assumed that would be the last one."

"Yeah. That's Andy's house."

"Did you know him?"

"He was fairly new in town, but he was one of the nice ones."

Her eyes softened as she pursed her lips and swallowed. "I'm so sorry."

Will could think of nothing to say as they observed the scene unfolding at Andy's house.

"Do you have any water?" she asked.

"Yeah, sure. Be right back."

A moment later, Will returned with two glasses. The girl was sitting on the concrete steps.

"Here you go." As he handed her a glass, a light breeze ruffled her hair, and Will smelled apple-scented shampoo that reminded him of his mother. He sat down one step higher, waiting for her inevitable questions about his odd behavior.

"Thanks." She drained most of the water in a few seconds.

She didn't seem interested in talking about the other morning, so Will decided to avoid the subject. "So, are you training for a marathon or something?"

"I sure feel like it sometimes, Will."

"How'd you know my name?"

"I…noticed you in a yearbook from a few years ago. Your hair was shorter."

"Happened to have an old yearbook lying around?"

"As a matter of fact, I did," she said, meeting his gaze.

Will pretended not to notice her slight smile. "So…I didn't get *your* name."

"Sorry. It's Morgan. Morgan Finley."

"How long have you lived up here in the deep north?"

"Going on three years. My…" She sucked in an awkward breath. "My dad's the pastor of the Baptist church." Her words were strained.

A helicopter flew above the house, drawing their attention back down the street.

"Do you think they'll catch the killer soon?" she asked.

Will reflected on the stranger he had seen emerge from the woods and decided it was unlikely anyone could ever stop him. But he dared not say anything to Morgan about that.

"With the number of resources they're bringing in to this hick town, you'd think so."

"Mind if I stay here awhile to watch?" Morgan asked.

"Sure. I mean, no problem."

The silence soon became comfortable. But Will could see as plain as the flashing lights down the street that Morgan was struggling with something besides the murder of Andy Barnet.

"I don't…" she started. "Will, this might sound strange, but I'll say it anyway because I think I can trust you." She took a shaky breath. "I need a friend right now."

He stared at her as a small tear rolled down her cheek.

"I need someone I can be real with, someone I can talk to, someone who will see beyond my accomplishments and my family…" She turned away, staring idly at the front lawn. "My family's coming apart, and whatever I say or do only makes things worse, you know? I pray sometimes Dad would leave us, but there's no hope of that. It's almost like there's a reason he doesn't go and that the reason has little to do with us. Sorry for babbling. It's just… Well, I feel so lost."

Will remained quiet, staring at the family next to Andy's house as they loaded a few suitcases into a minivan. Seconds later, they pulled away. "I know about families coming apart. And about needing a friend."

Morgan fidgeted with the empty glass in her hands. "Before I was born, my parents were missionaries in Nigeria. Dad once told me that, soon after they arrived, a local man who the missionaries referred to as *the witch doctor* sent a demon to terrorize them so they would leave. But when the demon arrived at our house, it found the entire place surrounded by a wall of fire. It walked all the way around the yard but couldn't get close, let alone enter the house. When it returned to the witch doctor, he sent it back two more times with the same results. One day, there was a knock at our door. It was the witch doctor, coming to ask my dad who his god was."

Will was speechless.

"My mom has a similar story." Morgan sighed. "She told me that about a month after we moved here, she woke in the middle of the night and came into my room. She found something standing at the foot of my bed, apparently watching me sleep. It was small and dark, with yellow eyes."

Will raised his eyebrows. "What did your mom do?"

"She quoted Bible verses at it until it jumped out a window. Mom said she spent the rest of the night sitting on the edge of my bed praying."

Will could not have been more stunned by the conversation than if a giant Stay Puft Marshmallow Man had come walking over the houses of Nineteenth Avenue. Why would the Lessers be interested in Morgan's family?

"I've heard and read about stories of angels and demons that we can't begin to comprehend, Will. I tell you my parents' stories to give you the freedom to talk to me. I *will* listen, though I might not understand. We barely know each other, but I have a feeling you'll listen to me as well. I think we have more in common than meets the eye."

Will stared at her, afraid to risk another friendship but more afraid to continue sinking into his deep loneliness.

⁂

News of Constable Andy Barnet's death spread quickly. By the following day, the spirit of the town changed dramatically. Despite official notices that withdrawing from normal routines like going to work or school was unnecessary, the streets were almost void of traffic. Many families left to visit out-of-town relatives. Cochrane's largest employer, Tembec, advanced its summer maintenance shutdown by almost three weeks, providing an excuse for more residents to leave early for holidays. In the old downtown core, most store owners closed their businesses indefinitely. Even the Empire Theatre, with the carpet shop in the lobby, closed until further notice.

It was, however, the perfect time for Will to be out walking. Since the regular gawkers had lost interest in him, he savored the solitude. With each step, he breathed deeply. The newness of the midmorning air filled his lungs like a gentle breeze through the newly opened windows of a boarded-up house.

Will stopped and gazed across the stillness of Lake Commando. Despite the tranquil scene, he remained guarded. After his recent encounter with the Lessers at his house, he kept his eyes open, wary of every shadow.

As he rounded the lake for the third time, he crossed Eleventh Avenue to the sidewalk, and a car pulled up beside him. He continued walking with his head down, bracing himself for either hurtful words or for something to be thrown at him from the car.

The driver pulled ahead of him, and the passenger window rolled down.

"*Masitaw*," a familiar voice called.

Will peered through the window at Joe sitting behind the wheel of his unmarked police car.

"Can I offer you a ride home?"

Will stopped and squinted. "Why do you call me *masitaw*?"

"You have Cree blood flowing deep within your veins. I can see that as plainly as the lake behind you. I suspect your father was white, and that the Cree side comes from your mother."

"That explains the name, but why *masitaw*?"

"It means—"

"*Fighter*," Will interrupted. "Or something like that. I Googled it. You talk like you know more about my past than I do. And *masitaw*. I think that's what my mother used to call me when I was a toddler. How do you know so much about me?"

Joe smiled. "Come, and I will try to answer your questions. It is a difficult task worth fighting for."

Will studied Joe's eyes the way he often examined the lake's surface, trying to determine how deep or how cold the water was before taking the plunge. After a moment, he pulled the car door open and slid into the passenger seat.

Before Joe had even pulled away from the curb, Will began the questioning. "So, you're a cop?"

"I am Inspector Joe Cheechoo of the OPP Criminal Investigation Branch, Yorktown Division."

"Yes, but who *are* you?" Will repeated, shifting in his seat.

"I am Joe of the Mushkegowuk."

"You mentioned that the other day. Did you know my mother?"

"If she was who I think she was, then yes, I knew her a long time ago. I see her in your eyes."

Will stared at him with his mouth open and his mind brimming with questions. He had not expected that answer, nor had he understood it. He considered his next question.

"Who was she?" he asked.

"She was a Callum Sage."

"I beg your pardon?" Will managed. "What's a Callum Sage?"

Joe kept his eyes on the road, but the lines in his forehead deepened.

"Entire books have been written on the subject, books that have been lost for so many generations, most people do not even believe they ever existed."

Will forced his questions aside. As the car approached Nineteenth Avenue, he straightened in his seat.

"Are you a…a Callum Sage?"

"I am," Joe said, pulling to a stop in Will's driveway. He turned to Will with a somber expression. "You may ask me one final question, then it is I who will ask a question of you."

Before he could think of a better question, Will blurted out, "Am I a Callum Sage?"

Joe drew in a breath and answered with a simple nod.

Will relaxed his shoulders and slumped into his seat as Joe's reply lifted a weight from his shoulders. He almost smiled but then stiffened again as the weight was replaced by another.

"Now for my question, Will. What do you know about these murders?"

"I know enough."

"I need details now, before something terrible happens."

"You mean worse than what has already happened? My parents used to be friends with the people who've been killed. And Constable Barnet…he at least acknowledged me on the street, well… sometimes. This town's not safe anymore."

"The events that have taken place will not even be remembered if we fail to stop what is coming."

Will gripped the door handle to stop his shaking hand. He pushed the door open and breathed in the fresh air. "Follow me. There's something you should see."

Will climbed the concrete steps to his house and sat at the top. Joe sat beside him.

"Something tells me you'll believe me," Will said, "So, I'm gonna tell you everything. This won't be easy."

Joe furrowed his dark eyebrows, his eyes fixed on Will's face.

Will pointed beyond the three vacant lots across the street. "See the road across the back of that field?"

Joe nodded.

"That's the Arden Road. It's an old road that leads north to what was once a town called Arden. It's pretty much a ghost town now. Over there…" Will pointed down the avenue to their left. "That's

Seventh Street. Follow it to where it intersects with Arden Road, then look directly across the road. You'll see a faint outline of a trail that cuts straight back through the Arden Forest."

Joe squinted. "I see it. To the right of the trail, the forest basically ends at those power lines."

"That's the Polar Bear Riders' snowmobile trail. To the left of the trail is the forest I'm gonna tell you about. The trail is narrow, ending at a massive lot with logging trucks and storage bays. It stretches way back, dividing into several large farming fields and toward a couple of lakes. The forest is an island of thick, dense spruce trees."

Will became more animated as he spoke. Having someone take him seriously was intoxicating.

"Ask people about that forest. No one will talk about it; everyone avoids it. People are terrified of that forest, and the funny thing is, they don't even know why. Well, I can tell you why."

Will hesitated but knew he was in too deep now. "I've seen them. Hundreds of small, terrifying creatures walk out of that forest and straight into town. I call them Lessers. I've never seen any go back into the forest.

"One day, I followed a Lesser into town, right through the front door of Canadian Tire. It kept running from me, so I chased it around the aisles. Unfortunately, in my struggle to keep up with it, I knocked over a display and crashed into a woman's shopping cart. People gathered around me as I lay on the floor, murmuring to each other and staring at me like I was from another planet—even though the Lesser was standing right beside me! I made the mistake of asking the store manager why he couldn't see it, and he promptly kicked me out."

Joe smiled. "You cannot tell me you blame him?"

"Before the killings started last week, I saw something far worse walk out of the forest. It was some kind of nightmarish creature that walked like a human. I saw past its disguise, more demon than human. It walked out in the early morning and disappeared behind that house there." Will pointed to the house surrounded by yellow police tape.

"Constable Barnet's house," Joe observed.

"I haven't seen it since, Joe, but I believe in my heart it's responsible for the killings."

Joe cleared his throat. "I believe what you saw was a creature called a harvester."

Will cocked his head to one side, then launched into a series of questions. "How—how could you know that? What's a harvester? Does—"

"I need to share more with you, but our time is short."

"Does this have to do with you being a sage? And how—"

"That is certainly part of it."

"How do you know me?"

"When I first saw you on the bridge, I was surprised by the resemblance to my granddaughter. I have not seen her in many years, but I always believed she would come for me. As the years turned into decades, I confess that my faith faltered…until a few days ago."

Will opened his mouth but couldn't speak.

"Your mother and I share an ability to manipulate the element of ice, but she also possessed the ability to see what you can see. And more." Joe paused. "She was a powerful Callum Sage, Will, and a warrior in every sense of the word."

Will swallowed hard. He shivered once, struggling to grasp the outlandish yet undeniable implications. "So, what are you saying?"

"I need some time before I can speak to the possibilities."

Will stood and threw up his arms. "Pardon me, but you basically told me we're related, that we're Callum Sages—whatever that means—and now you tell me you need *more time*?"

"These are delicate matters, Will, and must be treated as such until the time is right."

Will struggled to comprehend the ramifications of this otherworldly information. "Does your control of ice give you the ability to operate in the cold without needing heat?" he asked.

"We have few equals in environments of extreme cold."

"I've been told my mother died when our snowmobile broke through the ice. The only time Dad spoke of the matter was to tell me that, after the crash, he woke up fifty feet away from where the snowmobile dropped through the ice. Mom's body was never found."

Joe sighed so deeply that it almost sounded like a groan.

Will sat down again on the step. "Could she still be alive?"

Joe stared at him. "There's a lot at work here."

"So, what, then? How do we unpack all this?"

"Suffice it to say we need to find the harvester. I will need your help to make that happen because I can see only its human form."

"What do we do when we find it? Can you kill it?" Will asked.

"That is unclear for the moment."

Will leaned back with a deep sigh. "This is unbelievable."

"Whatever you believe to be within the realm of possibility will change over the next few days, Will. For the moment, however, I need to do some research before I can offer much more—" Joe cut his words short as a jogger strolled up the driveway.

"It's okay, that's Morgan," Will said. "She's…uh…she's a friend, Joe. I told her everything."

"Morgan *Finley?*" Joe's eyebrows raised, and a smile replaced his concerned expression as he introduced himself. "Joe Cheechoo."

"Nice to meet you," Morgan said, breathing heavily.

"You know her?" Will asked.

Joe released Morgan's hand and stepped back. "Morgan Finley," he repeated.

"That's me," she replied, shrugging her shoulders.

"How do you know her?" Will repeated as he turned and led them into the house.

"The world knows her, Will. Morgan Finley."

Will gaped at Morgan, then at Joe, then back again at Morgan.

Joe smiled at his obvious confusion. "Two-time world fencing champion. But I became a fan before that."

Will noticed Morgan regarding him carefully as they walked into the kitchen.

"Fencing? Like—like sword fighting?" Will asked. "With the white storm trooper outfits?"

Joe frowned. "Calling it sword fighting would be like comparing checkers to chess."

"I've never heard that analogy before," Morgan said. "I like it."

"It is a good one, I believe," Joe replied. "I have become quite a fan of the sport. I love the strategy required at breakneck speed. Every step, every lunge, every thrust, every riposte—all part of a larger plan. It is poetry in motion."

"What were you saying about being a fan before the World Championships?" Will asked as he opened the fridge and produced a bottle of water and a can of Coke. As expected, Morgan accepted the water, and Joe took the Coke and opened it right away.

"A few years ago," Joe said, "I was doing some paperwork late one night at the office in Toronto. As usual, the TV was on. TSN featured a live broadcast of the Junior Nationals in Moscow. All eyes focused on an eighteen-year-old Russian girl named Larionoff. Apparently, she had never lost a match since the ripe old age of eight. In her final match as a junior, she faced an unknown from Canada. The broadcasters predicted the match would be a mere footnote in Larionoff's career. The Canadian had been to the Junior Nationals the year before where she placed eleventh. So, there I was, mesmerized by the drama as the jewel of Russia entered to thunderous applause."

Will grew impatient as Joe sipped his drink. "And…?"

Joe set the can down on the counter. "Larionoff was tall and built like a Russian tank. I imagined she was taking steroids because nothing about her was right." He shot a proud look at Morgan. "And then I saw Morgan Finley step out to face the giant. She was much smaller than Larionoff. But what she lacked in stature, she made up for with emotion. I'll never forget the fire in her eyes before she put her mask on. She was there to win, and nothing less!" Joe clapped his hands together.

"You beat her!" Will exclaimed.

Morgan shook her head. "She beat me in overtime."

"What?"

Joe held up a hand and waved off Will's disappointment. "Oh, but, Will, you should've seen Morgan. When Larionoff made the winning point, Morgan bent her own saber over her knee and threw it as far as she could. Her mask flew in the opposite direction as she cried out in anger."

Will curled his brow as he turned to Morgan, who said nothing.

"Morgan was all fire—and apparently all memory as well. Two years later, Morgan met Larionoff at the World Championship—for the title Larionoff was defending—and Morgan took her down without giving her a single point. It was a perfect shutout, the first of its kind during a World Championship match."

"Wow." Will grinned. "And I thought you liked to run for the fun of it."

"Well, that was a fun trip down memory lane," Morgan said. "I have to be heading home. My dad's getting back from another conference, and with the way my parents have been shouting at each other lately, I want to be around."

"I am sorry to hear that," Joe said. "Marriage can be a difficult journey. Where was the conference?"

"He's been leading a series of Promise Keepers conferences at the First Baptist Church in Timmins."

"Is that the big church on the south side of town?" Joe asked.

"No, it's the one on Algonquin on the right as you head into the city."

"Can I come with you?" Will asked.

"Thanks, but no. I want to hang out with Mom."

"All right, then." Will wished he could keep the conversation going. It had been so long since he had enjoyed something so wonderful.

Joe offered Morgan a wave as she started jogging down Nineteenth Avenue. When she was gone, he pulled out an iPhone and did a quick search before placing a call.

"I use this one for personal calls," Joe said, tapping the screen. "I'll put it on speaker; you should hear this, Will."

A woman answered. "First Baptist Church, Timmins, how may I direct your call?"

"Is this the First Baptist Church on Algonquin, near the highway?"

"Yes, it is."

"Then I have found the right place. Who could I speak to about the Promise Keepers conferences?"

"I'm sorry, sir, but I'm not aware of any Promise Keepers conferences."

"Oh. Perhaps I've missed them."

"No, I don't believe so, but let me transfer your call to our senior pastor to confirm."

"I would appreciate that, thank you," Joe said.

"Good afternoon, Mike speaking."

"Hi, Mike, I understand you had some Promise Keepers meetings going on."

"No, sir. We had a citywide Promise Keepers convention over a year ago that most churches were involved with, but, unfortunately, there are no churches holding any meetings at the moment."

"Well, that's too bad. I had heard that a Pastor Grant was putting them on. Maybe he was doing them at another church."

"No, sir. I know Pastor Grant, and he's not involved with any church in Timmins."

"Are you sure?"

"Yes, sir, we're a pretty tight group of churches here. We do have several other courses taking place, though, that you may find interesting."

"Is the info on your website?"

"Yes, and if you have any questions about any of them, feel free to give me a call."

"Sure thing. Thanks for your help, Mike."

Joe tapped the screen to end the call.

"What's that all about?" Will asked.

Joe leaned on the kitchen counter and gazed out the window

toward the Arden Forest. "I need to find Morgan's father. There may be more to him than meets the eye."

CHAPTER 8

TRACKS

During her run home from Will's house, Morgan maintained a rigorous pace but struggled for every stride as if she were running up a rocky hill. The moment she turned down her street and noticed her father's car in the driveway, she slowed. Her breathing quickened as she approached the house on legs that felt like they belonged to someone else.

She opened the front door and pressed her hand against the doorjamb to steady herself. Her eyes darted around the room. Pieces of furniture lay overturned with contents of drawers and closets scattered between them. A bloodied handprint smeared the far wall.

"*Mom!* Mom, are you here?" Morgan called as she stepped inside, careful to leave the door open.

Silence responded.

Morgan cried out again, desperate for the sound of her mother's voice. Several more streaks of blood marred the kitchen walls. Morgan ran from room to room. The house seemed abandoned. Frightened tears flowed between her shouts as she ran up the stairs. She stopped when she saw the attic ladder lowered into the hallway; she had closed it before she'd left the house this morning.

"Mom?"

All was quiet, so she stepped around the ladder to go to her room. Despite her mother's stern warnings about the sword they had found in the attic, Morgan had hidden it in the fresh air return beneath her bed. Now she was terrified she may have cost her mother her life. She could only imagine that her father had found the sword missing from the attic and had taken out his anger on her mom. Morgan prayed she was still alive.

She entered her bedroom and inhaled sharply. Her dresser was overturned, its contents scattered about the room. Her twin-size mattress had been removed from the bed frame and was leaning awkwardly against the back wall. Morgan squeezed between the mattress and the wall, pulled the grate from the fresh air return, and reached inside. Her tense muscles eased slightly as she drew the sword from its hiding place.

Downstairs, the front door slammed. "Hullo?"

Morgan recognized her father's voice, but it sounded gruff, like he had a deep chest cold.

She jumped to her feet. Eyes darting around the room, she ducked behind her mattress. The smell of blood and sweat choked her, forcing sharp, staggered breaths. Heavy footfalls pounded up the stairs. Morgan clasped a hand over her mouth. She fought to control her breathing. Her other hand cramped, and she realized she was gripping the sword. The blade sparked in response to her touch like a dog's hair bristling in warning.

A strange tingling sensation, seductive and unrestrained, charged up her arm. Her body trembled with energy. The sword vibrated as if responding to impending peril. An ethereal green glow radiated from within the polished adamantine blade. Morgan blinked several times as faint traces of vivid green lines marked her vision. Now she couldn't release her grip even if she tried, as if the sword were holding her instead of the other way around. The sword was surreal, alive, dreamlike yet nightmarish. It was like—she tried to push the word from her mind, but it remained—*magic*.

The footfalls stopped at her bedroom door. Morgan recognized her father's breathing, but it sounded raspy. Each second tumbled into the next. She squeezed her eyes shut. Her overwrought muscles twitched as the silent stimulating energy from the sword intensified. The hoarse breathing stopped, and a floorboard in the hallway creaked. After a moment, the attic ladder rattled.

Morgan tried to clear her thoughts. The sword's energy, like a magical force, roused her to her feet as her father's steps scraped the attic floor. The plank that had previously hidden the sword clattered. Morgan crept out from behind the mattress and slunk into the hallway. She held her breath, trembling like a sprinter poised to dash from the starting block.

She peered up to the attic opening, raising the sword in front of her face. Swirling shades of green previously hidden within the sword now became clearly visible, forming distinct patterns. Drawn to the unseen power, she wasn't frightened. In fact, she was suddenly struck by the notion that she did not have to flee. She could kill him. Yes, she could… *No!* She shook her head against the grim proposition, fighting to suppress the weapon's allure.

Instantaneously, her father bounded across the attic floor toward the opening. The vibration in the sword increased. Without thinking, Morgan ran down the stairs as fast as her shaking legs would carry her. By the time she reached the bottom, the attic ladder was creaking wildly.

Swept up in a single surging wave of energy, Morgan ran toward the front door. In a fluid instant, she grabbed her father's keys from the wall rack, burst through the front door, leapt off the front steps, and slid into the old Honda Civic. She placed the sword on the floor of the back seat and fixed her eyes on the front door as she jammed the key into the ignition.

The engine roared. Morgan jerked the shifter into reverse, and the tires squealed all the way down the driveway. She pulled the shifter into drive and stomped the accelerator to the floor, inciting another screech from the tires. With a single glimpse in the rearview mirror, Morgan saw movement inside the doorway, but no one emerged from the house. She never looked back.

Ten minutes after Morgan had left Will's house to check on her parents, Joe drove away, saying he needed to meet with someone before looking for Morgan's dad. Will sat on his front steps and ran a hand through his hair, trying to piece together his conversations with Joe and Morgan. Will wanted to help in some way but knew he couldn't get involved in police business. Besides, he didn't know where Morgan lived. But he also had no desire to sit around and wait for more creatures to appear from the forest, so he decided to walk to Lake Commando.

As he strolled along the quiet streets, he turned his face to the sun, lost in thought. The honking of a car horn behind him shattered his reverie. He turned midstride, tripped, and then struck the sidewalk hard with the palms of his hands, tumbling to the ground. He blinked in astonishment as Morgan swerved to a stop and jumped out of a white Honda Civic. Her hair was messy, and her eyes were wild, red, and puffy. She dropped to her knees beside him.

"Will! I'm so sorry!"

"Wha-what's going on?" he asked as Morgan examined his hands. Blood oozed from deep scrapes on both palms. His right knee was bleeding freely through a hole in his cargo pants. He scanned the street behind Morgan, expecting to see someone chasing her, but the way was clear.

Morgan helped him to his feet and launched into a volley of fragmented sentences. "My house… The blood… Dad came back… Mom's missing."

Without waiting for a response, she pulled him to the car, threw the passenger door open, and tried to push him in.

Will considered offering to drive, but she ran around the car and jumped into the driver's seat. The car lurched onto the empty street.

"Where—where are we going?" Will asked, trying to break through to her.

"I need you to see something, Will. Tell me what you see!"

"I will, Morgan, but I want you to tell me what happened."

"It's my dad," she said, jerking the car onto Sixth Avenue. Partway down the street, she signaled to turn into the First Baptist Church parking lot. "I think he did something to Mom—"

"No!" Will exclaimed, seeing the church building covered with Lessers. Before she could turn, Will grabbed the wheel.

"Don't stop here!" he shouted, pointing down the street. *"Go! Drive!"*

Morgan drove her foot down, hit the far sidewalk, and barely managed to keep the car on the street. She sped past the vacant parking lot and turned down Seventh Street. Will shifted in his seat to see through the rear window, expecting to see Lessers chasing them. Fortunately, none had left the church.

Will had seen countless Lessers over the past three years, but never had he seen so many in one place. For some reason, they were gaining momentum. But why? Things had definitely changed since that creature that Joe called a harvester arrived. Could the Lessers be rallying around it? And with all the activity at the church, was Morgan's father in danger?

Suddenly, Will recalled Joe's words: Whatever you believe to be within the realm of possibility will change over the next few days.

"Get us to my house, Morgan!" Will shouted as he pulled out his phone.

Joe answered after one ring. "Go."

"It's Will. Something's happened, Joe!"

"Calm down, Will! Where are you?"

"Heading to my house."

"Is Morgan with you?"

"Yes!"

"Go inside, lock the doors, and hide. When I get there, I'll knock twice, then twice again, then twice again. Don't answer it otherwise. I'll be there in fifteen minutes."

"Hurry, Joe!"

Joe responded in a slow, deep voice. "What do I need you to do when you get home?"

"What?"

"What do I need you to do when you get home?" Joe repeated, his voice calm.

"Lock the doors and hide," Will answered, his mind swirling.

"Very good. I'm on my way."

Morgan turned the car sharply into the driveway.

"Let's get the car inside the garage," Will said.

He threw his door open and jumped out, stumbling toward the garage door. He heaved the old door open and waved Morgan in. Somehow, she parked between the wall and the vintage Land Cruiser without hitting anything. Will slammed the garage door down, and they scrambled up the front steps. He pressed his ear to the door and listened, his lungs heaving. Hearing nothing, he eased the door open and entered, one careful step at a time.

Will locked the door behind Morgan and hurried to his bedroom. From the top dresser drawer, he grabbed his 1911. He crept from room to room, searching for any sign of an intruder. Finding nothing unusual, he tucked the gun into his belt as he walked to the office. Blood dripped from his hands onto the floor.

"Stop!" Morgan shouted, slowing his reeling thoughts.

She grasped his arm and led him to the bathroom. Will placed his hands over the sink, and she fumbled with the faucet. As the temperature adjusted to lukewarm, she examined the gravel embedded in each palm.

"This is gonna sting," she said, easing his hands beneath the water. He winced and tried to pull away, but she held him fast.

"What did you see at the church?"

"What does that place mean to you?" Will asked, staring at the thin red water in the sink.

"My dad's the pastor there. I don't know what's going on, but…" She closed her mouth, and her tight lips quivered. "I don't know what's happened to Mom…"

"I couldn't even see the walls, Morgan."

She straightened her back as Will continued his description of the church.

"They were everywhere, clambering over one another. All up

the walls… There were hundreds…maybe thousands. It looked like—like a membrane surrounding the entire building. The roof was covered with them…the windows…the doorway. They were fighting wildly at the front entrance as if they were trying to get inside a place that was full."

He ignored her confused look and continued before he lost his nerve altogether.

"Lessers. I've never seen so many in one place before. It was like an ant farm. The building was covered with them…"

"What's a Lesser?"

Will let out a deep breath. "Three years ago, I started seeing strange small creatures emerge from the Arden Forest. It started one day while playing basketball in my driveway with my friend Todd. Something caught my attention. It limped through the field, across Nineteenth Avenue, and right past my house. I tried to get Todd to see it, but he couldn't—even though it was hobbling a few feet away. At first, Todd thought I was joking around. By the time I realized he couldn't see what was so obvious to me, it was too late."

Morgan adjusted the faucet, and water dribbled over his hands. "Can you describe the creature?"

"Like something from a horror movie. Its arms and legs were all different lengths, with claws and talons you wouldn't believe. Its skin was sickly gray. Several small horns protruded from a skull that was too big for its body. I kept pointing at it, shocked, terrified, and when Todd realized I was being serious…well, I'll never forget the look in his eyes."

Morgan listened in silence as she picked gravel from his hands as if strange forest demons were as common as bloodied hands.

"I have vivid memories from that first in a series of terrible days," he continued. "The clearest memory is the way my friend gawked at me when the shouting stopped. It's the way everyone's treated me since." He raised his eyes. "Everyone except you. And Joe, who seems to know more about me than I do for all the sense that makes. Heck, he pretty much said he's my great-grandfather."

"What? How could you be related?"

Will shrugged. "I have no idea, but that isn't even the strangest part. He said he was a sage, and that my mother was a sage, and that I'm a sage too. Something about bloodlines."

"What's a sage?"

"I don't know. But it probably has something to do with what I can see that others can't."

"Like…magic?" Morgan had an odd look on her face.

"Maybe. Not really. I dunno. It all sounds crazy." Will's cheeks warmed.

"You don't need to be embarrassed, Will. Does it truly sound crazy to you?"

He held her gaze and then swallowed hard. "You think I might be a sage?"

"I have no idea. There's definitely *something* different about you. Who's to say your ability to see those creatures isn't, well… something *real*? It's different from the stories my parents told. Maybe you *are* a sage. And maybe Joe's a sage too. Can *he* see the creatures?"

"No, but apparently my mother could."

"Well, maybe he's a different type of sage, with different…magic."

"Never thought of that. I've always had a hard time believing any of it was real. And I've certainly never called it *magic*."

"It's hard to believe something when no one else believes, or when someone else has different beliefs they hold so strongly, they're deaf to other ideas."

Will lowered his head. "I told Joe about the creatures and about the Arden Forest."

"Did he believe you?"

Will smiled slightly. "He did."

As Morgan wrapped his hands with cloths, two sharp knocks at the front door startled Will like a dog kicked awake.

"That's Joe," he said.

By the time Morgan was finished with his hands, the last two knocks sounded. Will rushed from the bathroom, peered around the corner, and saw Joe standing outside. As soon as he released the dead bolt, Joe burst in and surveyed the room.

"Morgan's here," Will said as they walked into the kitchen.

She materialized from the hallway and, with a heavy sigh, started toward the door to the garage.

"Where are you going?" Will asked.

"I need to get something from the car."

"Morgan, you need to stay—" Will began, but she was already gone.

Joe leaned toward Will and whispered, "I just left her house. Someone ransacked the entire place."

Will stared. "Her mom?"

"I saw blood on the walls, but no body…" The door reopened, and Morgan stepped inside. Will gaped at the sword in her hand.

"My goodness," Joe breathed.

Morgan placed the sword on the kitchen table, holding the hilt of the weapon as if some unseen force refused to release her. Joe cleared his throat, and she pulled her hand away.

Morgan recounted the story of how she had found her mother

staring at the sword in the attic and how she needed to hide it. She described the way the sword had burned her mother's hand but melded seductively to her own grip.

"And when I got home earlier today…" Morgan's voice trembled as she told them what had happened at her house only moments before she had startled Will as she fled in her father's car.

Will stood in silence, hoping Joe could offer some kind of explanation.

Joe pulled out his phone and turned speakerphone on. "I need to call Constable Bondy so we can send some investigators to your house."

The dial tone sounded twice before a man answered. "What's up, Joe?"

"Tom, do you know the Finleys?"

"I beg your pardon?" Tom answered.

"Grant is a pastor at—"

"I'm watching Grant right now," Tom interrupted.

"Come again?"

"He was walking with a weird gait, sorta limping, and he had a wild expression on his face. I waved to him as I drove past, but he acted like he didn't recognize me."

"Where are you now?"

"I'm on the edge of the Arden Forest east of town. I think… Yeah, he's heading into the forest now. Something isn't right."

"I'm with his daughter, Morgan, who just left their house. She said it's been ransacked, and she couldn't find her mother."

Tom cursed. "I'll pick up Grant now before he steps into that blasted forest."

"No, come get me first."

"Where are you? We could lose him in that forest!"

"I'm at Will Owens's home on Nineteenth Avenue. My car's in the driveway."

"Be there in two."

Joe ended the call, and Morgan gaped at him. "Why is he going into the forest?" she asked. "Do you think he has my mom somewhere in there?"

Joe grimaced. "We do not know yet. And there is something I need to explain to you, Morgan. As you might have guessed, this is no ordinary sword. I recognized it right away. The fact that you can wield it can only mean one thing. This will be difficult and confusing to hear, but times being what they are…" He paused. "Without the proper bloodline, this weapon would harm you as it did your mother. But it doesn't hurt you, meaning your father was a Callum Sage…and so are you."

Morgan shared a shocked expression with Will, then turned back to Joe as he continued.

"Was it your father who led you into fencing?"

"He was so excited when I first started."

"He wanted you ready to wield this weapon should the need arise."

"But he's been against my fencing for…for three years now, since moving us here. He's been a different person this entire time."

"A harvester," Joe breathed.

"What's a harvester?" Morgan asked.

"Do you have a picture of your father?"

She pulled out her iPhone and, after a few swipes, slid it across the table toward Joe. He looked briefly at the picture and passed the phone to Will.

"No!" Will exclaimed softly, recognizing Morgan's father as the disguised creature he had seen emerging from the Arden Forest the day he met Morgan in the neighbor's driveway.

The doorbell rang, jolting everyone to attention.

"What—wait!" Morgan shouted. "What's going on?"

"We need to go after your father in the forest," Joe said, standing by the front door. "Does he know you have the sword?"

"I think so."

Joe groaned and pulled the door open, and Tom stepped inside, dressed in full uniform.

"Mind telling me why I let Grant walk away?" Tom said, folding his arms.

"Will knows where he is," Joe said.

Will stared, hoping Joe knew what he was talking about.

"All right, then," Tom said. "I have officers en route to the Finleys' house, so let's go find Grant and figure out what going on here! For heaven's sake, I can't imagine why anyone would want to go in that blasted forest! We'll pick you kids up on the way back."

"I'm coming with you!" Morgan blurted out.

"Pardon me?" Tom shot back.

"I need to be there in case we find my mom."

Joe glanced at her sword. "As long as you keep out of the way."

"Grant could be armed," Tom said.

"Just the same, we may need her there if her mother is being held."

Tom huffed. "We don't need any more—"

Joe cut him off. "Let's go. Morgan, bring that machete in case we have to cut our way through any tag alders."

Tom gawked at the sword. "Machete?"

Joe placed his hands on Tom's shoulders and marched him toward the door. "We're good, Constable. No more questions."

Will ran to his bedroom. He threw off his ripped pants and strapped a holster around his thigh over his boxers. In the closet, he found his baggy green cargo pants with an opening in the pocket that would allow him easy access to the 1911. With the pants buttoned, he slid the gun into the holster and changed into a clean black undershirt.

He returned to the kitchen to discover the others were already outside, ready to venture to the Arden Forest.

CHAPTER 9

THE FOREST

During the five-minute ride in Joe's unmarked police car from Will's house to the forest, no one spoke. From the front passenger seat, Tom fired irritated looks at Joe, then over his shoulder at Will and Morgan, his jaw set, brow furrowed. Not angry, Will thought, but clearly at odds with Joe's decision to bring the two young civilians. Joe's eyes remained fixed on the road, both hands clutching the wheel. As they approached the edge of the Arden Forest, he parked a few feet from the tree line.

An unnatural silence from the forest replaced the car engine's drone. As foreboding as the forest was from Nineteenth Avenue, it now stood before them like an impenetrable wall.

As the four stepped from the car, the stench of rotting vegetation rose from the ground like an invisible warden. Creaking branches and groaning trees added their warning as the intruders scanned the area. Here at the outskirts of the forest, a remnant of brittle rust-colored spruce needles testified to the decay that had stripped the woodland of its former beauty. A low mist weaved its way slowly between the tree trunks. No one moved.

A loud crack in the forest broke the silence. Morgan inhaled sharply and rolled her shoulders. Will did the same but found it did little to release the tension.

Joe opened the trunk and pulled out a short-barreled tactical shotgun and handed it to Tom. He reached in further and pulled out a dark-red garment. Without a word, he unfolded it and swung the cloak over his shoulders. The tightly woven fabric had a medieval style, but the smooth, tight weave and absence of wear alluded to something much newer. A single brooch that resembled a solid black orb polished from a rare stone connected the garment at Joe's neck. The cloak covered his body except for a narrow opening along the front.

"What the—?" Tom exclaimed, gawking at Joe in a strange cloak and Morgan holding a sword.

Will stared at Joe. An unseen power radiated from the man and electrified the air around them. Since their first meeting, Will had been comfortable around Joe. Now, he felt like a kid in the principal's office, small and exposed. He shifted his weight from side to side and rubbed his hands on his hips a few times before shoving them into his pockets.

"What *is* that?" Morgan whispered.

"It's called a Trannalun cloak, a symbol of our order."

"Callum Sages," Will mumbled.

"It's—it's magnificent," Morgan said, reaching a hand toward it.

"And dangerous." Joe stepped back, eyes narrowing as he faced Morgan before he addressed everyone. "Great power has been woven into the fabric of this garment."

Tom rolled his eyes and let out a quiet whistle as he ventured closer to the forest.

"All right, Will," Joe said. "Which way?"

The question surprised Will. He had been expecting Joe to lead. Self-doubt threatened to smother him. He looked at Joe's expectant face and ventured a few awkward breaths. Morgan offered him a slight but encouraging smile. Wearing blue track pants and a baggy sweatshirt, she looked oddly underdressed next to Joe. But her hazel eyes radiated confidence. Will turned to Joe to see the sage's eyes had softened. A quick nod of affirmation from him was enough to suppress Will's rising fear.

"I—I think we should find the place where they all emerged," Will suggested. "If they left some kind of trail, we could follow it back to…to who knows what."

"*They?*" Tom snapped, eyes flicking about. "Who—"

Joe moved quickly now and stood behind Will. "Single file. I'll follow Will. Morgan will follow me, and Tom will bring up the rear."

Will inched forward, surveying the edge of the forest to find a suitable point of entry. A light breeze stirred the mist now climbing the trunks of the dying spruce trees, and the lower branches responded to the slight shift in the air. Slowly—so slowly, in fact, that Will almost missed it—gnarled limbs reached out as if attempting to interlock with the branches of other trees. He inhaled a deep breath, then another. His heart pounded as nature itself stood against them. This was no place for the living.

"I believe in you, Will," Morgan whispered.

He walked toward a spindly spruce that swayed in response to his movement. After a few steps, he stopped abruptly. To the right of the spruce, he noticed a narrow path. Feeble branches stretched across the trailhead to form a barrier but fell short. Will's smile at their plight quickly faded upon seeing the blackened forest floor. Through shadows cast by the trees, he could see the ground had been scorched. Small tag alders—shriveled and sickly gray yet somehow alive—marked the sides of the trail. It was a pathway of death.

Like wraiths, the group moved forward, crouching low to avoid the branches. Will turned often to check on the others behind him. Joe continued to scan the forest ahead while Tom and Morgan cast quick glances in every direction. Will focused on one step at a time. Gradually, everything familiar became distant: the usual forest scents faded, the burnt-orange needles dwindled, and the pallid trees ahead swayed like ghastly gray ghosts.

After a half hour of steady progress, Will passed the last tree showing any sign of life, and stopped. Sparse tag alders stood rigid and brittle. The dense undergrowth they had come through dissipated. The blackened ground became moist, covered ankle deep in a mist so thick it obscured the feet of the four trespassers. They slowed their pace. A pungent, unidentifiable odor drifted up from the unseen earth beneath them and blended with a hint of sulfur.

They trudged through this new landscape for another hour. Without warning, Will stopped and lowered his head, straining to see something through the mist and deathly trees. A few more steps revealed the outline of an old cabin about fifty yards from where they stood. Will turned to the others, and their frozen expressions verified what he was seeing. The image burned into his memory: this was no ordinary cabin.

A dark, coarse, hairy material covered the roof. Small veins in the bare logs pulsed as if the decaying structure were somehow a living thing. Thin, translucent membranes covered two window openings, fluttering in and out despite the stillness of the forest air. An old wooden door hung tenaciously from a single rusted hinge. Large cauldrons awash with glowing runes hung from the four corners of the cabin, connected to the logs with thick umbilical-like cords. From the outside, Will saw no sign of Morgan's father.

A sudden movement at the cabin door revealed what might be a person, but as the mist shifted, Will reconsidered. A large humanoid creature covered with plate armor blended with the darkness of the doorway. Its head was huge, with two horns curved back above its forehead. In one hand, it held a short piece of wood topped with a length of heavy chain that fell to its feet before disappearing in the mist. The other hand gripped a broad, jagged sword with chipped and dented teeth along the length of a dark metallic blade.

Joe leaned close and whispered into Will's ear. "Death knight."

Had it not been for Joe's firm grip on his shoulders, Will might have lost his footing. He turned and drew upon the strength clearly reflected in the older man's face. Morgan and Tom stood motionless next to them.

Loud crackling from within the cabin shattered the silence. A brilliant-white light flashed in the windows, and a gust of wind carried the acrid smell of sulfur out from the cabin. A rush of battle cries and the high-pitched sounds of metal clashing against metal rose and fell so quickly Will wondered if he had heard correctly. The death knight took one step away from the door but otherwise remained stationary.

Joe grimaced. "How unfortunate for us."

Dropping into low crouches, they huddled behind a large stump, waiting. Will peeked at the cabin. A huge form materialized behind one of the membrane-covered windows. Deep, guttural groans and growls reverberated from within as something thrashed about the small space that confined it. Then, as unexpectedly as the terrifying noises had begun, the forest was silent again.

"Keep it together, keep it together." Will folded his arms and rocked slightly.

Joe leaned back and whispered to Tom, "Those cauldrons are a power source. We need to empty them before we can destroy the cabin…" He trailed off.

Tom was staring, mesmerized by the death knight. Without warning, he stood and pointed his shotgun at the cabin.

"Get out of here!" Joe hissed at Will before setting off after Tom, who was now running toward the cabin. Will swallowed hard and struggled to regain some semblance of control as events accelerated to breakneck speed.

Tom had run about twenty yards when a monstrous form stumbled from the cabin. The creature hit the ground so hard, the sound of snapping bones filled the air. With its face in the dirt, it writhed and thrashed wildly. Bulky deformed muscle shifted and twisted as the unrecognizable creature raised its massive head.

Tom stopped in his tracks, half mad and fully stunned by the abrupt appearance of the terrible beast.

"Shoot it!" Joe shouted.

Tom remained motionless.

Slowly, the creature rose to reveal dark-gray scales covering its massive skull and narrow muzzle that frothed with black fluid oozing from rows of sharp teeth. One high-set ear was severed and dripping thick dark blood, while the other was missing altogether. Scales covered the heavy muscle mass hunched low to the ground, giving the creature the appearance of an unwieldy gator with the head of a monstrous bear. Its narrow yellow eyes were open and alert despite the gaping wounds. A serpentine tail lined with tiny horns shifted about dangerously. With a gravelly huff, it spat black vomit before turning back to the cabin as if checking to see if it had been followed.

"Harvester!" Joe shouted again. "Shoot it, Tom!"

Crouched low and somehow advancing once again, Tom shuffled closer to the beast, shotgun held high. He was about fifteen yards from the cabin when the harvester shifted its immense body and faced him. It remained low, balanced on all fours as it roared and snapped at the air. Tom stopped as if he had come to the edge of a cliff with nowhere left to run.

With an incomprehensible battle cry, Tom fired four rounds in rapid succession. The first slug flew over the creature's head before tearing a jagged hole in its back. Dark blood sprayed behind it while the remaining three slugs missed entirely, each smashing through cabin logs. A similar black fluid oozed from the damaged logs.

Tom continued to pull the trigger until the *click click click* warned him to reload. He drove a hand into his pocket for more shells, eyeing the hideous creature snapping and growling as it closed the gap between them.

The death knight loomed from the shadows of the surrounding trees near Tom.

"Tom!" Joe shouted. "Three o'clock!"

As Tom turned his head, a spiked iron ball from the end of the death knight's chain whistled and raked his jaw. His head snapped to the side as a mouthful of his teeth and blood flew in a wide arc into the surrounding forest.

Recognizing the death knight's weapon as a crude mace and chain, Will was amazed to see Tom standing. The dazed constable turned to face the death knight as the harvester sprang nearly a dozen feet in a high arc.

Following his warning cry to Tom, Joe charged at the harvester.

While it was in midflight, Joe flew into the fracas, driving a shoulder into the creature's sizable girth.

Tom ducked as the death knight swung its mace and chain again, and the spiked iron ball flew over his head.

The moment Joe and the harvester crashed to the ground, the creature grabbed him like a rag doll in the jaws of a vicious dog and tossed him through the air. The harvester was all talons and teeth as it attacked again, pouncing on the red-cloaked sage and slashing wildly. A brilliant flash burst from the Trannalun cloak, which absorbed the blows that would have otherwise torn Joe to pieces.

From beneath the cloak, Joe raised his forearm as a target for the creature's jowls. He spoke two unintelligible words, and a thick layer of solid ice instantly covered his arm. The harvester's teeth shattered against the icy forearm as its jagged claws grated harmlessly down the front of the Trannalun cloak. Sparks flew as Joe pummeled the creature's head with powerful punches from his other hand. The harvester collapsed, flattening the forest undergrowth. Rolling once, Joe rose to his feet.

Will remained where Tom and Joe had left him, huddled next to Morgan as if frozen to the ground. Seeing the harvester motionless, Will knew he had to act before something else emerged from the cabin. The runes on the cauldrons glowed brighter, and he remembered Joe's words to Tom: *Those cauldrons are a power source. We need to empty them before we can destroy the cabin.* Without considering the implications, Will was moving toward the cabin.

Morgan rose to her feet as the unbelievable scene unfolded before her.

Despite his shattered jaw, Tom squeezed off two more rounds but failed to hit anything. The death knight struck the end of the shotgun barrel with its mace and chain, following immediately with the sword. In shock but still able to move, Tom deflected the blade with his gun, losing his left-hand grip in the process. Then, in one fluid motion—astonishing for such a large creature clad in plate armor—the death knight kicked across Tom's vulnerable midsection so quickly that it might have missed. Unfortunately for Tom, a hooked blade protruding from the creature's armored boot had opened his abdomen. Tom's arms dropped feebly to his sides, and his eyes glazed over. As Tom's innards spilled onto the ground, the death knight's blade fell across his neck.

Morgan's stomach lurched as Tom's body fell, his head rolling several feet away. She averted her eyes from the horrific sight, then noticed the death knight spinning around to attack Joe. In that moment, she found her voice.

"Joe!" she screamed, running in his direction. "Behind you!"

Joe wheeled around as the death knight's mace and chain flew at his head. The spiked iron ball slapped across his back, knocking him off-balance.

Morgan stifled another shout as Joe's cloak took the brunt of the attack.

The harvester stirred and lunged at Joe, but the sage rolled onto his back, using the creature's momentum to carry it over his body. It flailed and crashed into a cluster of alders.

Joe rose to his knees as the death knight moved closer to Morgan. He stepped toward her, but a clanging sound near the cabin stopped everyone as Will grunted and shoved one of the cauldrons over. Blood and gore splashed to the ground. The harvester turned and let out a terrifying roar. It sprang toward the cabin.

Will froze as the nightmarish beast bounded toward him. There was no time to run.

When the harvester was only a few strides from Will, Joe thrust out one hand after the other as he spoke two arcane words, sharp and rhythmic. Shards of ice shot from his hands and pierced the creature's hindquarters, slamming it flat against the ground. Before it could recover from the crushing attack, Joe sprinted and leapt at the harvester, landing across its back. Again, they rolled amid snarls and battle cries.

The creature struggled to break free of the icy spell. It jerked so violently that Joe lost his grip, allowing the harvester to swing its massive head around.

Joe waved a hand in front of its eyes. The result was instant, freezing both eyes shut, but the harvester had already clamped its teeth around Joe's exposed wrist. He bellowed in pain.

The harvester now had most of its hulking mass on the sage's cloak, pinning him to the ground. It released its hold on his wrist, seeking his throat instead. With his good hand, Joe twisted the brooch to release himself from the cloak. He dodged the first snap of teeth and rolled as the creature pounced for him.

Morgan watched Joe and Will, wishing she could help, but the death knight resumed its slow approach, blocking her way. She had no choice but to stand and fight it.

A warm, tingling sensation ran through her body and into her right arm. She glanced at the sword in her hand. Multiple shades of green flickered within the blade. As it had done when she was hiding from her father in her house, the weapon responded again to imminent danger. The sword's power was exhilarating yet somewhat reckless. Morgan trembled as the blade rose up before her outstretched arms. When the sword was fully extended before her, the fear that had paralyzed her moments ago melted away, replaced with raw courage. With feet firmly planted and knees bent, Morgan shifted to the en garde position and glared at her opponent.

The death knight raised its sword, strode forward, and drove the huge blade down. Morgan parried, bracing herself for the impact of a much larger sword in the hands of a behemoth. The clash of metal rang out, startling a murder of crows into flight from the treetops high above. Morgan gasped as electrifying currents of pure energy coursed through her body. She knew the beast's powerful blow should have knocked her off her feet, but somehow, she stood firm.

The death knight drew back. As if adjusting its strategy, it dropped the mace and chain, gripping its sword with both hands. This offered Morgan a brief opportunity to study her horrifying adversary. Two fiery-red eyes narrowed behind an iron mask that was all jagged angles. Where the mask ended below its nose, a skeletal jaw froze in a deathly grimace. Large metal plates covered its shoulders with a row of spikes running down to its elbows. The decomposed flesh on its forearms revealed ancient gray bones. Thick gauntlets gripped the hilt with the skill of a master swordsman. Battle-worn iron plates covered most of its chest, but a few chinks in the armor revealed a gruesome mess of flesh and bone beneath.

The death knight let out a strange guttural purr as it raised its sword in challenge. "In life, I have slain hundreds; in death, thousands."

Taking a short step backward, Morgan heard Coach's voice as clearly as if he had been standing beside her at the World Championships.

Keep it simple. Footwork first. Back straight. Patience, patience, patience. Let your opponent come. Give nothing and take everything.

Morgan was only vaguely aware of the marked change in her posture. She eased her body back a step as the death knight's sword sliced through her sweatshirt, narrowly missing her midriff. Again, it attacked, unnaturally quick. Morgan shouted as she parried, intercepting the blade. She was acting on instinct, but her sword's…*magic*—the only word she knew to describe the powerful weapon—kept a tight rein on her fear. She prepared her riposte, realizing now that her sword could withstand the death knight's attack.

As magical sparks lanced from her blade, Morgan lunged as she had done countless times during years of practice and competition. She advanced so quickly, the death knight was forced back a step, barely deflecting her small but significant weapon. The creature lunged forward, wielding its sword in a smooth arc. Morgan recognized the movement as an unpolished moulinet, which she parried before returning to the en garde position.

She planted her rear foot against the ground. As the creature attacked again, she lunged forward in a perfect passata sotto, ducking low beneath her opponent's blade and driving her own past its guard. Magical green sparks erupted as the blade cut cleanly between armor plates covering the creature's thigh. The death knight grunted and tried to backhand her with a spiked gauntlet, but she retreated so fast that it missed entirely, exposing its midsection.

Morgan drove her back foot into the ground yet again and lunged with lightning speed before the creature could recover. With a shout, she thrust her sword through the chest armor, sinking deeply into rotting flesh. With a final effort, she shoved the blade through the creature's backplate. The sword sparked and crackled.

The force of the thrust brought Morgan face-to-face with a nightmare.

For a fraction of a second, neither of them moved. The creature's flesh sizzled. The death knight slowly lowered its enormous head and glowered at Morgan through the eyelets of the iron mask. She drew in a short, desperate breath, expecting another attempted blow from its gauntlet. Instead, the magic flowed first through her body and then through the sword. Glowing red eyes narrowed and flared. The death knight's body jolted as magic lanced from the blade, lighting up its entire chest in a spectacular green blaze. One red eye turned sparkling emerald as the creature gasped, and its huge body shook. Morgan held fast.

The death knight dropped its sword and grasped the small exposed portion of the magic blade. With a sinister hiss, it tried to pull Morgan's sword from its body. A flurry of dazzling green sparks lit the surrounding forest. For a second, Morgan considered withdrawing. She couldn't believe the creature could survive such an attack and feared its next move.

Instead, the death knight dropped first to one knee, then to the other. Stepping forward, Morgan forced the weakened creature onto its back. She held the sword fast until the creature's other eye turned green before closing one last time.

⚜

At the first resounding clash of sword blades, Will stood in awe as he gaped at Morgan battling the huge armored monster. But he was unable to watch for more than a few seconds as Joe wrestled with the harvester a dozen feet from where he stood.

The harvester pounced again, catching Joe off guard. Vulnerable now without his cloak, Joe grunted as a claw ripped through his side. He stumbled backward and rolled to his knees. The creature leapt again.

From his boot, Joe drew a long knife. The harvester dropped onto him in a mass of thrashing claws and snapping jaws. Joe's blade plunged into scale-covered hide three times before another set of claws raked his body. He slashed furiously at the beast's muzzle as it sought his neck. Now visibly weakened, Joe raised both hands in defense of the final blow. Instead, the creature reared to attack Will.

"Get under the cloak!" Joe shouted.

The Trannalun cloak lay only a few feet from Will. He dove on it and rolled the fabric around him a split second before the harvester landed on him. Claws scraped harmlessly across the cloak. The enraged creature reared up and dropped down harder in an unsuccessful attempt to tear through the garment.

Will peeked out to see Morgan running toward him. Her sword glowed. Before she could reach him, Joe dove across her path, tackling the harvester away from Will. Morgan dropped to Will's side and helped him roll over, untangling him from the crimson fabric. He gulped air into his winded lungs. Morgan gaped as if shocked to see him alive.

"Run!" Joe bellowed as the harvester wrestled from his weakening grip.

Morgan pulled Will to his feet as Joe grabbed the creature's hind leg, slowing its attack. Will stood feebly, the Trannalun cloak draped over his shoulders. A pang of guilt stabbed his heart as he met the older man's eyes, but Joe nodded once as though relinquishing the cloak to its new owner.

The creature slashed the air at Will and Morgan.

Joe's deep voice boomed over the harvester's roar, and a layer of ice spread over the entire area.

Morgan held out her sword with one hand as she pushed Will behind her with the other. Together, they jumped backward toward the cabin door, away from the harvester's gaping maw, and tripped over the slick threshold.

As the two of them stumbled into the cabin, Morgan reached for the doorframe, but her hand slipped off the smooth, cold surface. She lost her balance and slammed into Will. As they fell, Will grasped for a handhold but found only chilling air before crashing through a thin layer of ice.

Instead of remaining in a heap on the cabin floor as expected, Will and Morgan continued to fall at a terrifying pace, down into the cold, unknown darkness.

CHAPTER 10

WORLDS APART

Morgan plummeted through the dark, empty space, wondering why she hadn't hit the ground. Or maybe she had and was now unconscious and dreaming. But her tense muscles and the sudden assault on her senses were far too real. Streaks of lightning flashed around her, the light penetrating her tightly closed eyes. Then came the first squall of sounds: unidentifiable snarls, howls, and hissing mixed with distant battles cries. With limbs flailing, she screamed. A blast of dry heat from beneath her, followed immediately by a gust of humidity, covered her in a sheen of sweat. Down she went, fighting for every breath.

The falling sensation soon changed to one of floating, but she continued to descend. Unseen things brushed against her. With both hands on her sword in a viselike grip, she slashed in every direction. The blade flashed, warding her against the unthinkable evil around her. Terrifying grunts and bone-chilling shrieks filled her ears.

Her grip on the hilt slowly weakened until her frenzied battle ended suddenly. She careened into something hard, and silence enveloped her.

The stop was so abrupt that she vomited between gasps. She convulsed several times, then released the sword and curled her sweat-soaked body into a fetal position. The last of her breakfast spilled onto the wooden floor, and she rolled over.

Before she could open her eyes, something grabbed her by the hair. Physically and emotionally shattered, Morgan cried out. Unable to fight her way free, she yielded to the hand that pulled her to her feet in a single powerful motion. Her exhausted legs failed to support her, and she slipped down until an arm caught her around her neck.

<hr>

Wrapped in the protective power of the Trannalun cloak, Will rolled awkwardly after slamming onto the same wooden floor. He forced his eyes open against a rush of dizziness and lifted his head to orient himself.

Five men were staring at him. Each one was panting, sweating profusely, and holding a medieval-style weapon.

As Will's depth perception returned in waves, he noticed two of the men were not men at all. They stood as men but were much larger with uniquely shaped heads, almost apelike. Their bristling, coarse hair was cropped short, exposing large gray-skinned foreheads sloping into broad noses. Tightly braided beards covered wide jaws that were barely able to contain their sizable chipped teeth. Solid leather breastplates and metal-studded shoulder guards protected their enormous frames. Their boots, laced tightly to the knees, were made from the same type of leather, with sheaths for long knives. One creature carried a giant battle-ax with a varnished wooden handle topped with a jagged spearhead between the two ax blades. Dark blood dripped from the tip. The other creature carried a broadsword with a blade as wide as his head. Colorful strips of material flowed from the hilt of each weapon. Will blinked in bewilderment, struggling to pry his eyes from the creatures.

He was immediately aware of distinct smells: the familiarity of Morgan's apple-scented shampoo; wafts of dust and leather; and the pungent odors of blood, sweat, and filth. Overpowering all these was the distinct stench of sulfur.

Will traced the nauseating odor to an enormous creature sprawled on the floor. Black sludge oozed from several gaping wounds in its coarse dark-gray hide. The ichor flowed freely from its protruding jowls teeming with jagged teeth. One eye was missing where a large section of its gruesome skull had been hacked. Its other eye was closed, and black fluid trickled down its face. Will gasped and covered his nose. Without a doubt, it was what Joe had called a harvester, and somehow these people had found a way to kill it.

A soft whimper broke the quiet, and Will turned his head.

Less than ten feet away stood a disheveled man, his sunken eyes shifting back and forth. He was holding Morgan up with his left arm around her neck. With his right hand, he pressed a rusty knife below her jawline. Blood flowed from his swollen lips that parted to expose broken yellow teeth. A swath of freshly bloodied leather hung beneath his chest guard. Although clearly wounded, he appeared strong enough to threaten Morgan's life.

Will tensed as Morgan's eyelids fluttered. He wanted to cry out, to beg for her release, but the words caught in his parched throat. Questions about where he was and who these strangers were clamored in his mind as he pushed himself to his feet. His muscles resisted. He ignored his pain and confusion and took stock of the strange group around him.

Near the apelike creatures were three men: two carried swords, and one stood farther back with an arrow notched in a longbow. Will was startled to see the archer was actually a harvester disguised in human form.

A young soldier instantly separated himself from the others by his red cloak and the sound of his voice cutting through the electrified air. "Let her go, Alkin. It's over."

The soldier's green shirt and dark-brown leather pants were splattered with blood and black ichor. His sun-browned face was awash in sweat. Fierce blue eyes glared beneath dark brows, firm and unassailable. The man had the look of someone determined to finish what he started.

Morgan's captor tightened his grip. "Get out, Rowe!" he shouted. "Out now, or I drive dis dagger deep!"

Morgan winced, managing a hard swallow as the man pressed the blade against her neck. Her eyes flickered as she slumped closer to the floor.

"I said it's over, Alkin," Rowe replied, pointing with his black-stained blade to the dead harvester. "That thing's dead, and we both know you're not going through the Gateway. Let the woman go."

Will's mind whirled as he tried to assemble the pieces of the puzzle before him. The young soldier named Rowe seemed concerned about Morgan, but Will was unsure about the others. The one holding Morgan was human and clearly a bad guy. The apelike creatures stood near the dead harvester, their weapons dripping with ichor, making them good guys. The second harvester—definitely bad—stood back with a bow at the ready while the other swordsman stood within an arm's length of Rowe. Will needed to determine which side that swordsman was on before he exposed the second harvester, and before Morgan ended up dead.

"Her days fer mine, Sage," Alkin snapped, drawing another drop of blood from Morgan's neck. This time, she did not respond.

"All right, Alkin." Rowe sheathed his sword and raised his hands. "What do you have in mind?"

Alkin scowled at Will, who suddenly remembered he was wearing Joe's Trannalun cloak. It looked remarkably similar to the red cloak that Rowe wore. Will then remembered that on his hip, hidden beneath the cloak, was the Springfield 1911.

"You! Wit' de odders!" Alkin snapped with an awkward nod at Will. The man held the knife tight against Morgan's neck but was struggling as she grew limp.

Will considered the archer's position again and realized Alkin must be trying to help the harvester. He was unclear, however, as to what Rowe meant by "the Gateway."

"Take me instead," Will offered, his voice hoarse.

All eyes turned to him.

With a shaky hand, Will quietly slid the .45 caliber handgun from its holster and surveyed his surroundings. The walls were all made of large stone blocks, the kind one would expect to see in an ancient castle. At one end of the room, two horizontal beams barricaded a solitary wooden door reinforced with metal slats. Other than the narrow embrasures high up in the stone walls and one wider embrasure across the room, the only way of escape was a yawning gap in the wall near Morgan that appeared to lead to complete darkness. This, Will assumed, must be the Gateway.

"I know," Will said in a raspy voice.

"You know *what*!" Alkin snarled.

"I know…" Will coughed as he tried to square his shoulders.

He glanced at Rowe, who was studying him. Despite the man's display of strength and confidence, it occurred to Will that Rowe did not seem much older than him.

The other men moved toward Alkin.

"Please, order them back." Will's voice cracked.

Rowe raised a hand that stopped everyone.

"Enough!" Alkin shouted. "Or I'll spill her blood!"

Rowe turned his attention back to the ruffian. "Why not take me, Alkin? I can have the main gates left open."

Alkin spat a thick wad of bloody phlegm that hit the floor hard. "I decide here!"

"Who do you want?" Rowe asked.

"Danton!"

Without looking, Will knew Danton had to be the archer, and the final puzzle piece fell into place. The other swordsman must be on Rowe's side if Alkin didn't want to take him.

"Only if you take me too," Will said.

Rowe studied him.

Will tried to sound calm. "I'll lead Danton to you by the red scarf around his neck, and you give me the woman in exchange."

Rowe turned slightly, and his eyes flicked down to the ragged red cloth around the archer's neck. He raised an appraising eyebrow at Will.

"You can let her drop now," Rowe said.

As Alkin loosened his grip, Morgan slipped to her knees, but he clutched her hair to keep her from completely falling.

Will slid the 1911 from beneath the folds of the cloak and carefully raised it. His hand trembled and twitched under the weighty prospect of shooting someone, making the familiar weapon almost too heavy to lift.

"What's that!" Alkin yelled, gaping at the gun pointed at his face.

Will inhaled deeply, held his aim, and shut out everything but Alkin, Morgan, and the incessant pounding of his pulse in his ears.

"Down! Put it *down*!" Alkin shouted, struggling to lift Morgan back to her feet.

Will lifted the gun to eye level. He steadied his grip with both hands and exhaled. "Please forgive me," he whispered and gently squeezed the trigger.

The report was instant. Everyone jumped in shock—everyone except for Alkin, whose body was driven back in a heap against the shelves, and Morgan, who slumped to her hands and knees for a second before lying down and passing out.

With his ears still ringing, Will spun around and fired again at point-blank range. The bullet struck Danton square in the chest, forcing the archer back a step. He stumbled but did not fall. New skin rapidly covered the wound as the creature shed its human guise. Before anyone recovered from the shock of the blasts, the harvester drove a clawed fist into the chest of the swordsman standing a few steps from Rowe and made a powerful lunge for the Gateway.

Rowe's sword flashed, driving deep into the harvester's side as it flew past. With a grunt, Rowe twisted his arm, causing the creature to spin awkwardly. The large soldier with the battle-ax struck the harvester's back. Slammed to the floor, the wounded beast roared and thrashed. Rowe's sword erupted in a crackling, ethereal blue flame that burned through its helpless body. The battle-ax came up and around a second time, striking the creature so hard, its body bounced off the floor. Blue flames erupted from every orifice in its body. Only a few feet away from its goal of reaching the Gateway, the harvester burned.

Will cringed against the sound of Rowe's blade sliding free from flesh and bone.

"Dench," Rowe snapped. "Take Dossan's body to the infirmary, then fetch Ellywick—and be tight-lipped about it."

The large apelike soldier with the broadsword sheathed his weapon. He lifted the body of the swordsman the harvester had clawed, unlocked the large wooden door, and ran from the room.

Rowe rushed to Morgan's limp form on the floor and raised her in one quick motion. He carried her to a plush leather settee, laid her down, and examined her face. A bruise was forming beneath her right eye, and a trickle of blood trailed down her neck. Rowe swept the dark hair from her ashen face and placed a hand on her forehead. She shivered beneath his touch. For a brief moment, her eyes opened before she fainted.

"Grab that coverlet, Ruint," Rowe said with his eyes fixed on Morgan.

The soldier leaned his battle-ax against the settee and pulled a dark-green blanket from the back of a massive leather chair. Together, they tucked it around Morgan. Rowe rushed over to a small shelf and folded another blanket into a tight bundle. Ruint lifted her legs, allowing Rowe to place the bundle beneath them, and then slipped a giant finger against her neck with surprising gentleness.

"How is it?" Rowe asked.

"Slow," Ruint replied in a deep, guttural voice. "But still."

"Is she…?" Will lowered himself against the bookshelf.

A gentle tap at the door interrupted his anxious thoughts. A small creature walked in, followed by Dench.

Will gasped. Standing about four feet tall with bulbous eyes and small round ears beneath a shock of ponytailed white hair, the creature tested the air with large round nostrils. His milky-green eyes narrowed at the lingering smell of burnt gunpowder.

"Ellywick," Rowe said, bowing his head slightly.

"Came from here the great sounds did." Ellywick's deep, raspy voice sounded like someone nearing the end of his days.

He brought one hand up and smoothed his white beard that was braided neatly down to a green belt that held his flowing light-brown robe in place. He did not seem pleased. His eyes scanned the dead harvesters before falling upon Will with the Trannalun cloak wrapped around him.

Will held his breath as Ellywick stared. The creature's gray cheeks paled as his eyes flickered toward the dark opening in the wall, then back at Will. A thin, crooked finger silenced Rowe, who had opened his mouth to speak. Ellywick turned from Will to the settee where Morgan was lying; his eyes widened.

"The less you know, the better, Ellywick," Rowe said. "How did you know the explosions came from here?"

"Came from here many suspect." With a pronounced limp, Ellywick approached Morgan. "Search they will but not here, not soon."

Rowe and Ruint stepped away from Morgan as Ellywick carefully lifted one of her eyelids, then the other. He took both her wrists into his spindly fingers and closed his eyes momentarily. The room grew silent. After a moment, he reached into the folds of his robes and withdrew a tiny glass vial. He popped the cork and tipped the vial upside down against a fingertip, shook it twice, then dabbed the clear liquid on his finger under her nose.

Will recognized the scent of basil, but there were other smells unfamiliar to him.

"Injuries she suffered?" Ellywick studied her face. The rasp of his voice prevented Will from following the conversation.

Rowe looked at Will as if expecting him to respond to the question.

"U-uh…" Will stammered. "Pardon me?"

Rowe turned to Ellywick. "She was conscious when she arrived through the Gateway."

"Strange secrets you keep, Sage." Ellywick adjusted the coverlet under Morgan's head, and her labored breathing eased.

"Haven't had the chance to keep it a secret, Ellywick; they arrived moments ago."

"Keep this from the duke, will you?" Ellywick's voice grew quiet. "In chains you will be, if misstep you make."

"That one was wearing the cloak, and she was carrying that sword." Rowe pointed to the weapon lying close to the Gateway. "And he can see the harvesters while they're in human form."

Ellywick stared at the sword but seemed unsurprised. "Difficult journey for these two. Great care will I need to aid their transition to our world."

He pulled a small wooden bowl from his robes and placed it on the floor as he knelt. From an outer pocket, he retrieved five small vials and examined each. He chose the one containing green powder and slipped the others back into his pocket. Reaching into another pocket, he carefully withdrew two small dried leaves. His fingers hovered over the bowl as he crushed the leaves, and tiny flecks floated down. From the vial, he poured several grains over the leaves. With a pointy fingernail, he stirred the contents, and intoxicating fragrances filled the room.

Will breathed deeply and relaxed immediately. His eyes grew heavy as he looked around the room. Sunlight streaming through the high embrasures bathed the room in a warm light, revealing rows of wooden shelves. Despite the immensity of the timbers, each shelf sagged under the weight of large leather-bound volumes. Confused and disoriented, Will realized this room was too immense to be the inside of the cabin. He remembered crashing through a layer of ice, and suddenly wondered if he was in the tower from his recurring dream. Or maybe he was dreaming now. The surroundings, the men, and the creatures were unbelievable, yet the images, sounds, and smells were undeniably real.

Ellywick placed the bowl of herbs and spices on the floor next to Morgan. He rose slowly to his feet and motioned for Rowe to follow him to a nook with three large, heavily padded chairs.

"Time I have precious little of, Rowe of the Nest. Listen well. Many battles, much betrayal. More of both your future holds. Needed a second Callum Sage and eyes to see friend from foe. Both it seems you now have." He glanced at Will. "Mindful of your footsteps you must be, Rowe. Return I will after my summons." Ellywick paused, studying Morgan as she slept. "Rest she must; calm must her breathing become. The bowl, keep close." He stood. "The duke hears much, knows much."

Rowe followed Ellywick to the door. "Thank you, old friend."

"Time to leave the Crow's Nest, for you it may be." Ellywick turned and left, and Rowe closed the door behind him and secured the locks.

Will studied the three remaining strangers. Rowe was surveying the room. Three chairs were overturned, a table was smashed, and another lay on its side next to a few scattered volumes. Rowe brushed some stray hairs from a weary face that was all hard angles. He stared at the Gateway.

Dench and Ruint stood like stone statues.

After a moment, Rowe turned to them. "We need to dispose of the bodies and clean up the mess before one of the duke's men appears at a most inopportune time."

Dench and Ruint scanned the room and then faced one another.

"Throw them out that embrasure," Rowe said. "We can gather them up and burn them later."

Ruint furrowed his bushy eyebrows and grabbed a dead harvester's lanky arm.

"Can you do it without cutting them in half this time?" Rowe sized up the embrasure that was more than three feet wide but nearly five feet from the floor.

Ruint nodded as Dench walked over to help.

"Someone might see. Big drop." Dench's accent was so thick, Will could only understand every second word.

Rowe had his hands on his hips. "If you two have a better idea, speak up or get to work."

"Now"—Rowe pointed at Will—"you and I must talk."

Will climbed to his feet, stretched, and followed Rowe to the nook where he and Ellywick had spoken together.

"Where are we?" Will asked, trying to glimpse the outside world through the embrasure.

"Crow's Nest. The oldest castle in the Fourwinds. This tower is the Records of Time where we safeguard the Histories. Wars have been fought in attempts to gain control of the Gateway, but the Crow's Nest has always proven sound—save for two occasions in nearly a thousand years. Both times, a single harvester breached the Gateway, and for reasons I do not understand, the power of their kind here in the Fourwinds dramatically increased."

Will struggled to keep up. None of these names or places were familiar.

"During the first breach," Rowe continued, "almost two hundred years ago, two Callum Sages followed a harvester through the Gateway. Then, fifty years later, another Callum Sage followed another harvester through. None were ever heard from again, and nothing has ever come through the Gateway from the other side…until today."

Will shook his head, bewildered by Rowe's stories. He studied the room around them, slowly raising his gaze high above the bookshelves to the cone-shaped ceiling. His mother had read many mythical tales to him as a child, but he always assumed they were imaginary. Still, he could not shake how this place reminded him of her stories and also of his dream.

"Are there waterfalls beyond this tower?" Will asked.

Rowe sat in the chair opposite Will and cocked his head slightly. "It's about two days' walk to the nearest waterfall."

Will slumped. "What…who are…*they?*" He gestured with his head in the direction of the soldiers as they heaved the first harvester body out the embrasure.

"Dench and Ruint. My personal guards."

"But—but *what* are they?" Will stammered, trying not to sound offensive.

"Half orc, half human."

"Half *what?*"

"There are tribes of orcs and human barbarians living deep in the highlands beyond the Hillron Mountains. Over the centuries, the close relationship has resulted in mixed-race children born into an unwelcoming world. The Callum Sages have always had an affinity with the half-orcs. According to the Histories, they have been the backbone of our defense since the beginning. In keeping with this tradition, these two make up my personal guard. A small guard compared to others who have commanded the Callum Sages in the past, but times being what they are…" He trailed off.

"Half-orcs…Callum Sages…" Will rubbed his eyes, fighting waves of fatigue and stress.

"Do we need to worry about others following you through the Gateway?"

"What?" Will blinked and followed Rowe's gaze to the dark doorway. "You mean we came through there?"

Rowe nodded. "Were you followed?"

"No, I don't think so."

"Are you certain of this?" Rowe waved at Dench to join them.

"There were only four of us in the forest," Will said. "And I'm pretty sure only Morgan and I survived. Most of the people in Cochrane are leaving in droves."

Rowe and Dench picked up the settee with Morgan sleeping on it. With the utmost care, they walked it over to the far seating area, facing away from the door. After moving a sturdy, low-backed leather reading chair beside the settee, Rowe motioned for Will to join them.

Will sat heavily and let out an uneasy sigh as Dench brought over Ellywick's scented bowl, then went back to help Ruint.

Rowe set the bowl between Will and Morgan. He then slipped a footstool beneath Will's feet and covered him with the Trannalun cloak.

"Keep covered at all times in case someone comes. It is unlikely, but if that happens, pretend to be asleep," Rowe said.

"That, I think I can do," Will muttered as he inhaled the soothing aroma.

"Now, how are you called?"

"I'm Will Owens. And that's Morgan Finley."

"You are both sages?" Rowe asked.

"What?"

"Callum Sages. You must be one of those who passed through the Gateway long ago."

"I, um…" Will recalled Joe's words to him about being a sage, and then he noticed Rowe's eyes lower to the crimson cloak. "No, no. It's not mine; it was Joe's."

Rowe leaned forward. "Yet you wear it, and the magic responds to your need."

"I'm not sure how I ended up with this cloak. A harvester and something dressed in armor were trying to kill us."

"The death knight."

Will shuddered. "It sure looked like death."

"It passed through over a hundred years ago."

Will raised his eyebrows. "Morgan killed it with that sword, but I'm not sure what happened to the harvester. I remember seeing it half covered in ice but still fighting. I can't see how Joe could have survived."

Rowe was clearly surprised. "Ice? Did this *Joe* have anything to do with the ice?"

Will hesitated. "I can't imagine where else it came from."

"That must have been Johanissan of the River Country. The Histories say he was the first to pass through the Gateway. That happened almost two hundred years ago." Rowe scratched at a few days' growth beneath his strong jawline.

"Here." Will untied the cloak. "You take it."

"No," Rowe said, holding up his hands. "It has been passed to you."

"It wasn't *passed* to me, I-I'm not sure what happened."

"You do not simply pick up such a garment. The magic only responds to someone with the correct lineage."

Will remained silent.

"To a man without the bloodline, the cloak is nothing more than fabric," Rowe explained.

"But how is that possible?"

"The bloodline is essential."

Will closed his eyes for a few seconds before opening them again. "Did Joe—Johanissan—have a relative go through the Gateway after him?"

"Yes, his granddaughter Alyssa, some fifty years after him."

Will stiffened.

Rowe raised his eyebrows. "You know that name?"

Will nodded and swallowed hard. "My mother."

Rowe leaned back. "Yes…the bloodline. Is she…?"

"She died after her snowmobile crashed through the ice on the Frederick House River."

Rowe stared. "Was her body found?"

"No."

"Was she alone when it happened?"

"My dad was with her, but he ended up sprawled across the ice fifty yards from the hole. What are you getting at?"

Rowe folded his hands. "Alyssa had a powerful command of the element of ice, greater even than Johanissan. Ice water to her would feel like warm water to us, and she would have complete control of it."

"What can you do with control of ice water?" Will asked, rubbing his clammy hands on his thighs.

Rowe shrugged. "Form a block of ice and have it lift you from a river, for example. One legend says Alyssa's control was such that if the air was below freezing, she could form the cold crystals into invisible steps and walk in midair."

"So, what are you saying? Is she…could she be alive?"

"When did the accident happen?"

"This winter, it will be three years."

Rowe turned his eyes toward the ceiling and scrunched his face slightly as if sorting through a surge of memories. "She certainly was not killed in any accident," he said slowly.

"How can you say that?" Will asked, desperately hopeful.

"You knew nothing of her as a Callum Sage?"

Will was so confused, he could barely shake his head.

Rowe brushed a hand through his thick shoulder-length hair. "There is much that I know of her, though it is not my place to discuss such things with you. Not yet."

"You can't expect me—"

"Such sentiment is justified, Will, but if you will give me time, I promise I will have more to say on the matter."

Will leaned his head back against the cushioned chair. He sighed and closed his eyes. "This is too much." He tried to ask another question, but the words faltered on his lips as he yielded to exhaustion.

※

Rowe listened to the steady breathing of his two strange guests. He contemplated Will's story for several moments, then stood up and examined Morgan, who turned onto her side under the coverlet. Strands of dark hair fell across the small cushion under her head. Rowe hoped her eyes would open, but they did not. The spark of life he had glimpsed earlier hinted at an ardent fire within her that captivated his curiosity, lighting a colorless place in his heart.

He noticed Ruint standing beside him.

"Not a day goes by when me don't wonder about what's on the odder side of de Gateway," Ruint said. "Now dat we have two people here who know, dey bote sleep."

Rowe smiled and knelt beside Morgan. After some silence, Ruint continued.

"Remember de ambush at Chilton Pass?"

"Of course." Rowe examined the foreign fabric of Morgan's small boots. He untied the laces, studying the strange material.

"When me saw dat rock troll swing his ax, me tought for certain it would go right trew your back. De power dat creature had… and its size! De biggest one me ever saw—and fast."

"Your point?" Rowe gently pulled off Morgan's boot.

"De ax blade struck you, and your cloak flashed bright red. Dat nearly made me blind, it was so bright."

"Hurt for days," Rowe recalled.

"Such a small area flashed with magic. Did you see Will's cloak as he came trew de Gateway?"

Rowe paused. "I had to turn away; it was so bright."

"De entire cloak was awash in magic. Me had to look away too."

Rowe gazed at Morgan. "She didn't have a cloak to protect her."

"Dat's what draw you to her."

Rowe said nothing as he pulled off her other boot.

Ruint's brow furrowed into a familiar half-orc smile. "She a fighter."

"She is," Rowe agreed, covering her feet and tucking the boots beneath the settee. "They will both need to be fighters to make the transition after their journey through the Gateway. But Ellywick's healing magic will also do its work as they rest, helping them adapt to a new way of life."

A gentle knock at the door shattered the quiet moment.

"Dench back wit' de water, so we can clean de ichor," Ruint said, moving to the door.

Rowe placed his hand on Morgan's forehead. He removed one coverlet and was about to leave to get some wet cloths when Dench walked in carrying two mops and buckets.

"Duke would like to see you," Dench said.

Rowe's face slackened. "Did he speak to you?"

"No. Me bumped into a herald on de way here. Me told him dat me pass de message to you. No worry, he no follow me; no one like dose stairs."

"Best not keep the duke waiting." Rowe stood. "When I leave, secure the locks and do not let anyone enter. By my order: *no one*."

"What if—?"

"Kill them," Rowe interrupted. "No one enters until my return. And keep an eye on the Gateway. If anything else comes through, be ready. I will return as soon as I can."

Ruint threw the locks behind Rowe and immediately joined Dench with the mops.

"Ichor," Ruint said with disgust.

"Stinks, and sticks to everyting," Dench agreed with a low huff. After some scrubbing, he noticed Ruint watching Morgan with interest.

"You tink she will see anodder sunrise?"

Dench sniffed the air. "Ellywick's magic will see to it dat she does."

Ruint pointed at Will, who was fast asleep. "What do you tink der land look like?"

Dench shrugged.

"Let's wake him and ask," Ruint said.

Dench glowered but then saw his companion's familiar smile. He returned to scrubbing the floor. "Why Rowe trust you, me never know."

CHAPTER 11
THE FOURWINDS

With the door to the Records of Time safely locked behind him, Rowe began the dismal descent down the winding stone stairwell. Although he had taken this passage many times over the years, he proceeded with caution. The ancient, worn steps could barely accommodate the length of his boot. Two narrow embrasures provided minimal light, so he continued around and around with his hand on the railing. His left hand gripped the hilt of his sword; these were uncertain days.

He emerged from the tower and almost collided with a servant carrying folded light-brown linens. Instinctively, Rowe sprung back, ready to draw his sword, but then eased the blade into its sheath and sighed.

The servant cried out but somehow kept the linens in hand. "Begging your pardon, my lord," he muttered as he bowed and shuffled away.

Rowe turned and walked down the expansive hallway beneath the arched ceiling. Curious about where the servant was headed, he glanced over his shoulder but saw only the intricate tapestries lining both walls. He descended another flight of steps and opened a small wooden door that took him out of the Upper West Hall. Breathing the fresh air, he crossed the skywalk that spanned the gap to the main keep, three stories above the courtyard.

Once through the labyrinth of the superstructure, Rowe turned down a short hallway leading to a massive pair of doors. He inhaled and slowed his pace.

Two soldiers stood like sculpted pillars on either side of the doors, guarding the entrance to the great hall. Their blend of plate and banded armor with floor-length red capes identified them as members of the duke's private guard. Both men held menacing glaives: the shafts, nearly twice as tall as the guards, were topped with flat curved blades that were clearly more than ceremonial decoration.

As Rowe approached, the guards opened the doors, and Elly-wick walked out. Rowe started to speak to him, but the warning in his old friend's eyes commanded silence. Ellywick's eyes flicked upward, motioning for Rowe to look above the doorway.

"Know well your history, Sage."

At first, Rowe didn't notice anything unusual about the door-way, but as he drew closer, he could see something etched into the wood. The symbol resembled three fishing hooks tightly linked together. His jaw slackened as he recognized the sign he had only read about: *the Mark*. The Histories described how the appearance of the Mark on the crown of a doorway would signify that the resident's heart had aligned with the will of the mythical creature Natas. Rowe was amazed at how easily some people succumbed to dangerous deception.

As he pulled his gaze from the Mark, he wondered if he, too, had been deceived. An alarming question struck him as he recalled the servant that he'd bumped into moments ago: *Who would require linens in the Upper West Hall?*

He slowed, overwhelmed by a sense of urgency to turn back. But it was too late. Ruint and Dench could be trusted to guard the tower and protect Will and Morgan until his return. And if he left the Great Hall now, without a plausible explanation, the guards would be on him in a second. He braced himself for his meeting with the duke.

Ellywick slowly made his way through the Upper West Hall, groaning under his breath as he approached the narrow stairwell leading up to the Records of Time.

Kill me in the end, these stairs will, he thought.

Four of the main lanterns were out. Ellywick squinted. The lack of light added to his negative sentiment about the climb before him.

Something moved in the shadows ahead.

Ellywick stopped. "Who's there?"

A calm voice eased his concern. "I didn't mean to frighten you, my lord. This blasted darkness… I tripped and dropped some linens."

"*Frighten?*" Ellywick snapped. "Failing my gnome vision is, but not hearing."

Ellywick could not yet see the servant hidden in the shadows. "Show yourself!"

"There," the calm voice replied. "All nice and folded."

The servant materialized from the shadows carrying tightly folded light-brown linens. Two hellish yellow eyes glared at Ellywick. He widened his own bulbous eyes as he realized the linen was, in fact, a robe identical to his own. Knowing that harvesters had to replace their victims' bloodied clothes before they shifted into their form, Ellywick stepped back. Only a bold harvester would attempt to take on the form of a gnome, especially one so prominent.

The creature shuffled forward with stunning speed.

Ellywick stumbled back, driving a steady hand into his pocket. He had spent years pulling useful items from his pockets, but now he grasped a tiny gray pill he had never needed until this moment. In a single, fluid motion, he popped it into his mouth half a second before a set of six-inch claws slashed his wrist. The harvester reached for his throat but was too late. Ellywick had swallowed the pill that stopped his heart before the harvester could strike again. The dying gnome barely sensed the wretched stench of the creature's breath on his face as it hissed a seething curse. Ellywick convulsed once before his lifeless body fell to the floor.

✦

Every time Rowe entered the Great Hall, his mind drifted back to the history of the place that, until recently, had been the King's Court. The courtroom was long and narrow, with twenty-one rows of benches on either side of a wide center aisle. He placed a hand on a thousand-year-old bench, drawing strength from the Catalina ironwood. The rows of benches ended ten feet from three sweeping steps leading up to the dais. Behind a giant wooden desk sat an ornately carved throne. Six heavily padded, high-backed leather chairs surrounded the majestic centerpiece—three to the right, and three to the left. Rowe smiled slightly as he recalled the legend that the fabled dwarf craftsman Maxhan Barak, had fashioned the throne from a single block of Catalina ironwood using nothing more than his carving knives.

On the throne sat the duke of the Nest, Renaldi, nephew of King Malaqui, conversing quietly with six councilors.

The flickering firelight of the lanterns bathed the room in a myriad of shadows that ebbed and flowed in the stale air. Rowe masked his disdain for the duke as he quietly pondered the same perplexing question that he'd asked himself whenever he saw the man. Rowe was one of the few living who knew that Renaldi had won the privilege of becoming duke of the Nest during a game of chance the king himself had been playing. Rowe also knew the hand had been won on a bluff, but what had always baffled him was the wager itself. How could Renaldi, who had not yet reached the age of marriage and had little in the way of wealth, offer anything as a counter to something as utterly priceless as the Crow's Nest? With the king dead, Rowe knew he might never have his question answered.

"The remains of another body have been found in the loft above the front stables," the duke said in a cold, flat voice. He leaned forward slightly, and Rowe observed that Renaldi's boyish features had grown somber, with creases around his eyes. That was new.

"We can ill afford to condone the old-fashioned ideals of the Callum Sages," Councilman Tranas said, folding his thick arms neatly against a barrel of a chest. "Either we open the Records of Time and allow those abominations passage through the Gateway or we close the main gates."

"That would not be wise," Rowe said. "But wisdom has been in short supply in these parts as of late."

A threatening curved blade materialized beside Rowe's right ear as a guard admonished him. "Your lack of respect has no place here."

The duke leaned back.

Rowe fixed his eyes on Renaldi as he quietly responded to the impudent guard. "And yours is about to have you struck down with that glaive you carry."

The duke was quick to defuse the sudden tension, but his voice quavered. "Stand down, gentlemen. This is a place for conversation, not battle."

The glaive disappeared from Rowe's field of vision.

"Tell us, Rowe," the duke asked. "What choice do we have?"

"My lord, we are all aware of what happens to their kind when even a single harvester passes through the Gateway. Our realms are interwoven."

"Do we know this as a fact?" Tranas asked.

Rowe glanced at Tranas, then at each of the others. He sensed something had already been decided. "What are you suggesting?"

The duke raised a hand and tapped the air with a bony finger as if lecturing a child. "We close the main gates."

Rowe glared at the duke.

"We are at war, after all," the duke continued. "Perhaps we should start behaving as such. We have neither time nor resources for those who are too weak or too young to fight. They shall simply have to fend for themselves."

"The weak and the young are our responsibility," Rowe said, raising his voice slightly. "Sheltering widows and orphans is what men do in times of war."

The duke's eyes narrowed. "If only we all had cups that overflowed."

"If memory serves, the vaults were full until recently," Rowe said.

Tranas opened his mouth, but the duke interrupted him, tapping the air again. "Perhaps… No, you are correct. We *have* become accustomed to strong drink and pleasurable women." The men surrounding him smiled. "But I digress."

The duke smirked at Rowe. "I've considered ordering the Records of Time forsaken, but I know you and your half-breeds would die fighting me on that. My guards would not be happy about confronting a Callum Sage, but if pressed, they would, and they would eventually kill you and your two guards. I want you to understand that I hold that option. Something else I have considered is taxing your food shipments—let's say one hundred percent, seeing as your wealth seems to have no bounds."

Rowe clenched his jaw.

"As a side note," the duke continued, "what of the rest of the Callum Sages? If the Gateway is so important, why are they not here protecting it?"

"What makes you so certain they are not?" Rowe asked.

"A mysterious explosion—two, in fact—that cannot be explained." The duke paused as if trying to judge Rowe's reaction. "There are few events within these walls I am not aware of. Not many, but there are some. You have secrets, and I have secrets. Since no love is lost between us, we could simply purge the castle of all the refugees…unless you introduce us to your mountain of treasure." The duke snickered. "Just a thought."

"It is your choice to make," Rowe said.

"Yes, I suppose it is." The duke sighed. "There *is* another option. This one I do not think you would care for, but it certainly is something I have discussed with my council."

"Does it involve strong drink and pleasurable women?"

The duke sniffed at Rowe's sarcasm. "I was recently approached by an emissary representing Queen Sidara. It would appear that if I give her emissaries access to the Histories, she would bypass the Crow's Nest and head to Dwenlin Thah. She even offered to exterminate anyone less than enthusiastic about allowing her emissaries this access." The duke paused. "I can only imagine she was referring to you."

Rowe sighed. "The Mark appears on the crown of your doorway, and now you negotiate with Sidara? My lord, your foolishness has no bounds."

"Nor does my desire to rule the Nest," the duke said, laying both hands on his lap. He continued quietly. "Besides, have you not considered that the Mark appeared as a sign that Natas means to *bless* us in our hour of need?"

"Indeed, no bounds." Rowe shook his head in wonder. "Please inform your private guard that their first step into my stairwell will be their last."

"And no warning for the garrison?" the duke asked.

"They have sense not to take that step."

"Would you indeed dare touch a private guard of the crown?" Tranas sneered.

"Without a doubt, my lord. It will become increasingly difficult to command soldiers you can ill afford to pay."

"I think I may have that situation worked out, Rowe." The duke winked. "Is there anything else before we discuss your fate?"

"Be careful who you invite into your bed. The fall from duke to slave could be a short one."

The duke flashed a mocking smile. "In my experience, Sage, authority is something difficult to attain but quite easy to maintain."

"With your leave, then," Rowe said with a short bow.

CHAPTER 12

CLOSER THAN
A WORLD APART

Candlelight flickered in the Records of Time, chasing shadows between the rows of bookcases like mischievous children in a school library. In contrast to the shouts and clashing of steel the previous day, only the soft flutter of flames disturbed the dark of night. Morgan lay motionless, suppressing a rush of nausea. Her eyes darted from side to side.

One thing at a time, Morgan, she thought as she considered her situation.

A soft pillow supported her slightly aching head. She was warm, wrapped tightly in a thick blanket. Elevated, her legs rested comfortably on rolled-up blankets. Her left side was snug against what felt like a soft couch. She was dressed.

Inhaling slowly, she detected the aroma of basil first, then something so sweet, her palate moistened immediately. Another breath brought the scent of dust that reminded her of her grandma's attic, followed by the distinct fragrance of cedar.

She slowly opened her eyes, wanting to be sure the spinning

116

had ceased. Next to her, Will lay in a chair with his feet up on a stool. Joe's brilliant-red cloak enveloped him. He shifted once before settling back to sleep.

Beside Will, a young man sat in an old, worn reading chair with a massive book opened in his lap. Three short candles flickered softly on a small stand beside him. She blinked, trying to focus. The stranger's tousled sandy-brown hair fell to his dark eyebrows. His eyes—a blue so clear they might be considered cloudless—were sharp, discerning, and confident. His strong jawline was covered with a few days' growth. The dim candlelight revealed a light scar on the right side of his neck that disappeared beneath a dark-green wool shirt. The top two hooks were undone, revealing tanned skin.

He shifted his attention from his book and met her gaze with an ease that calmed her mounting fear. She drew in a slow breath.

"Lady Morgan," the man whispered, bowing his head slightly. "How are you feeling?"

She cleared her throat quietly, wondering if her voice would even work.

"Would you like something to drink, my lady?"

Thoroughly confused by the way he spoke but certain of her thirst, she nodded, licking her dry lips.

The man closed the leather-bound book and slid his feet off the stool. He rested the book on the floor and stood. About six feet tall, he had a well-defined body like a young construction worker, but he moved with the grace of an athlete. He walked over to a table heavily laden with enormous books, poured something into a beautiful ceramic goblet, and returned, kneeling in front of Morgan. She stole a glimpse at his toned arm as he reached a hand down to her back and gently helped her into a sitting position.

Nothing around her looked familiar, but she was too disoriented and thirsty to care. She lifted the goblet, but her hand trembled, her muscles utterly spent and uncooperative.

"Take your time, my lady; you've been through much." His voice was soothing yet resonated with unmistakable authority.

With his help, she held the goblet with both hands and raised it to her lips. A cool eruption of flavor spilled into her mouth, and she momentarily forgot her pain.

She quickly drained the contents. "What *was* that?"

"Water." He smiled and took the goblet from her shaking hands, refilled it, then knelt again as he handed it to her. This time, her hands were more cooperative.

"My name is Rowe of the Nest."

Morgan peered over the rim of the goblet.

"Does that name sound strange to you?"

"What does 'of the Nest' mean?" she asked, her cheeks warming.

"It is the order in which I serve."

"What kind of order is a *Nest*?" Morgan asked. In addition to her curiosity getting the best of her, it was good to talk.

"It refers to the Crow's Nest, the name of this castle. This library is located in a tower called the Records of Time. I, like you and Will, am a Callum Sage, my lady."

Her heart beat faster as recent memories returned to her in sudden bursts. "Castle?"

"Lady Morgan—" Rowe began.

"Please, call me Morgan," she whispered, distracted by images of the Arden Forest flashing in her mind.

"Are you hungry, Morgan?"

Her stomach grumbled, but she wasn't sure if it was hunger or nausea.

"I'm not sure what I feel." She took another drink. "I need…I need to get a grip."

"I think I can help." Rowe went to the table and returned with a pitcher filled with a transparent light-green liquid. She raised her goblet, and he filled it. The aroma of the drink reminded her of autumn harvests when her parents would bring in fresh produce from their garden.

"And what is this?" Morgan asked, sniffing at the unfamiliar drink.

Rowe shrugged. "Something to calm your nerves, my lady."

"Please, Rowe, I need you to call me Morgan."

"Very well." Rowe placed the pitcher on the table and returned to his chair.

Morgan took a generous sip with less shaky hands and opened her eyes wide. The taste of the water had enlivened her palate, but this—whatever *this* was—was inexpressibly delightful. She savored the first sip, then closed her eyes and swallowed. When she opened them, Rowe was smiling at her, clearly amused.

"You remind me of the first time I tasted elven mead many years ago."

"Mead? So, *elves* made this?" Morgan laughed softly, but Rowe wore a serious expression on his face. She stiffened and frowned slightly as she took a larger mouthful.

"It is said men have come back from the dead for a taste of this mead." Rowe raised his goblet and drank.

After a few more swallows, Morgan relaxed, feeling almost human again. "I saw you," she said. "I thought I was dreaming."

"I beg your pardon?"

"I remember seeing you with several others, and Will," she said with a thoughtful pause. "And I remember you leaning over me, taking my shoes off."

"It will all come back to you with time."

"I'm not sure I want it to," she whispered, followed by a sudden hiccup that surprised her. She stretched her back and rested her head against the thick cushion, enjoying the tingle trickling through her body. "But if this is a dream, I'm starting to like it."

"You are a strong woman. And from what I understand, you have few equals with this." Rowe reached beside his chair and lifted the sword. The firelight flickered across the polished steel as he laid it across his lap. He traced a finger along its fuller. "I was reading about the history of this sword as you slept."

She smiled slightly, feeling the effects of the mead. "Not much to read about, I'm sure. Just a typical magic sword—probably made by the elves."

Another brief scene from the Arden Forest flashed across her memory, and she tensed her muscles.

Rowe was watching her with a furrowed brow. "You should get some rest, Morgan."

"That would be good," she muttered, still wondering if she were dreaming. "Whenever I can't sleep because I'm worried about something, my mother challenges me to think of one thing I'm grateful for. Whenever I do that, I always sleep well and the next day is better."

"She sounds like a wise woman."

Morgan paused. "Tell me something you're grateful for, Rowe. What's the last fun thing you remember doing?"

Rowe rubbed his eyes with the palms of his hands. He sighed heavily and squinted at her. Morgan was unsure if he was thinking of an incident or deciding if he trusted her.

"Last week—or maybe it was the week before," he began, "I was riding in the Misty Gorge and came across a young boy named Soveigh. Eleven years old. He was clambering up an old goat trail. Shale rock was falling away beneath his feet, down to the river below. One wrong step might have cost his life. He was old enough to know the danger, but he climbed at a frantic pace, nonetheless. At first, I could not see below him, but after watching for several minutes, I saw his five pursuers: slave runners."

"Sounds like they were really motivated," Morgan said as Rowe sipped his mead.

"They are paid by the Dark Queen, Sidara, to collect children she can twist into heinous creatures."

"You consider that *fun*?"

Rowe held up a hand and continued the story. "This boy—I'll remember until the end of my days—he worked so hard to reach the crest of the canyon. And even from a distance, I could see his body heaving as he struggled for breath. I assumed he would pause to rest before disappearing into the safety of the forest, but he didn't. Instead, this boy—who had been chased up a canyon wall—started picking up rocks. He even had the wherewithal to wait until the men were within range before throwing the rocks at them."

"Did he knock them into the canyon?" Morgan asked before finishing her mead.

"A few rocks, even well-placed ones, would never slow a slave runner. There's far too much at stake for them."

"What do you mean?"

"If they return with children, they receive sizable fortunes and, more importantly, the favor of their queen. If they do not…well, some have been crucified for less. Suffice it to say that once they have a child in sight, they do not require extra motivation. So…" Rowe continued, cutting off Morgan before she had a chance to ask another question, "the rocks bounced harmlessly away, but Soveigh had decided he was not going to run anymore. He continued throwing rocks until the slave runners made their final rush up the goat trail."

Morgan placed her goblet into Rowe's outstretched hand. "What happened? Did he make a run for it?"

"No."

"But—but…what did you do?"

"I rode up behind Soveigh to see if he would eventually run, but he didn't, not even when the first slave runner grabbed at him. Instead, he swung his fists—which did nothing, of course."

"Did you have anyone with you? Could you stop them?" Morgan asked impatiently.

Rowe leaned forward. "Slave runners prey upon the weak. They do not fare well against those who recognize their shortcomings."

"So, what happened to Soveigh?"

"I brought him to live with us here in the Crow's Nest."

Morgan huffed. "How was that fun? I—I don't understand. He could have been killed. *You* could have been killed."

"Morgan, most people will go a lifetime without seeing such a display of courage. He risked his life, not because he had a chance to save himself but because he believed in life, in freedom, in goodness. Sure, he may be too young to have thought through all that, but the spark was there inside him. That day forever changed me, Morgan. And I am very grateful for that boy."

An unexpected warmth filled Morgan as she looked deeper into his eyes.

"And you, Morgan?"

"What?"

"A good memory that makes you grateful tonight?"

"Hmmm. I don't know why this came to mind, but a few weeks ago, I was slicing mushrooms while Mom worked the pizza dough. No one makes homemade pizza like Mom, and I can't remember why, but we laughed and laughed the entire time, singing along with a John Mellencamp song—Mom's favorite. It seems like years ago…" She trailed off, her eyelids beginning to droop.

"That sounds nice."

Morgan sensed he was merely being polite. "It was," she said quietly. "It was the last time I remember Mom laughing."

"Think upon such things tonight, Morgan."

"Are you staying?"

"I am." He put his feet up and pulled the book into his lap.

Morgan peered into the impenetrable shadows of the ceiling. She wondered again if she were dreaming but felt strangely calm and safe. She closed her eyes. Moments later, the sound of Rowe's book slipping startled her, and she noticed him sleeping. A minute later, Morgan's breathing settled into a restful rhythm.

DAY TWO

Early the next morning, Will lay in the silence as he watched Morgan sleep. He had hoped to awaken in his own bed and realize yesterday's events were all part of a crazy dream. But the strange room was very real. The smell of basil and other herbs reminded him of the threat on Morgan's life, and the odd creature who had come to care for her.

A shuffle of paper broke the silence. Will lifted his head to see Rowe strolling around the great library, reading from a book.

Will sat up and stretched. "So, yesterday *did* happen," he whispered.

Rowe motioned for him to move away from Morgan. Will removed the Trannalun cloak and joined Rowe at the table.

"How do you feel?" Rowe asked, handing him a cup of water.

Will took a few gulps. "All right, considering."

"May I ask you a few questions before Morgan stirs?"

"Sure."

"Have you come to help us?"

"What do you mean?"

"Why have you come?"

Will collected his thoughts, staring at the dark doorway on the wall. "We had no idea this—whatever this is—even existed."

Rowe sighed. "What exactly happened to Johanissan before you came through the Gateway?"

"Well, that's hard to say." Will took another drink. "The fighting was terrifying, and this harvester was…well, like a cross between a bear from hell and a hungry alligator. I think I remember Joe grabbing its leg when it tried to attack Morgan and me. We were close to a cabin, and when we jumped back, we tumbled into it. The last thing I saw before falling was the harvester rearing around to attack Joe as ice was forming around both of them."

"The creature you describe is the harvester called Eurynome." Rowe hesitated before continuing. "Do you believe it is possible Johanissan survived?"

Will winced. "There was a lot of blood."

"There are many accounts written in the Histories of Johanissan's life that should have described his end, but he's a fair hand at avoiding defeat. Besides, his magic has been able to keep him alive for over two hundred years. Those stories give me hope."

Will shook his head. "What d'you mean by two hundred—?"

"Are you certain there will not be others coming through?"

"If you could have seen the cabin, you wouldn't wonder another second."

Rowe released a small sigh. "The harvesters here in the Fourwinds are somehow drawing strength from what is happening beyond the Gateway. Shades! They now have the ability to keep their identities hidden even from me. In all of history, they have never been able to do such a thing."

"It doesn't sound like things are any better here," Will said.

"Recent years have not been kind. Until now…when *you* arrived."

Will tilted his head to one side, and Rowe pointed to his eyes.

"I don't know how or why," Will said, "but I can see them, clear as day."

Rowe tapped his book. "I have done some reading about the third Callum Sage that passed through the Gateway a hundred and twenty years ago. His name was Tannis of the Nest. He had no equals with the sword that Lady Morgan arrived with. If she can wield it, she must be a direct relation."

"But I saw her father; he was a harvester."

Rowe slouched against the table. "Most unfortunate."

"I—I don't understand."

"As far as we know, a harvester can only be killed by a Callum Sage. They've gone to great lengths to hunt us. I suspect Tannis fell prey to a harvester, and knowing he had a daughter, the harvester then assumed Tannis's form."

"Why would it matter that he had a daughter? Why didn't it kill her too?"

"Something prevented it from doing so." Rowe shrugged. "Does Lady Morgan know about her father's fate?"

"I'm not sure." Will watched Morgan sympathetically as she slept. He wondered how she would accept the news, remembering vividly the day he learned of his father's death.

"You asked me about a waterfall yesterday," Rowe said. "Why is that important to you?"

Will told Rowe about the dream. "It's getting more intense with every sleep—except for last night. It was the first time in months I haven't woken up in a cold sweat. But here's the crazy part: the dream always starts with me falling back and crashing through a layer of ice, like when I fell through the cabin! It makes me wonder if maybe I'm getting closer to where I need to be."

Will squinted at Rowe, expecting the usual blank stare that often followed his strange stories. Rowe simply raised an eyebrow and waited quietly for him to continue.

"I can't explain it, Rowe. It's more than a dream, and I'm terrified of what will happen if I don't find that black horse and the tower. It has to be here somewhere—*has* to be."

"What you described is a tower called the Maidstone that overlooks seven waterfalls. I am uncertain about the horse."

Will's mouth opened slightly. "Wha… Maidstone? Have you been to the Maidstone?"

"I've passed through the area twice but have never ventured up near the tower."

"I'm scared to ask why."

"The constant torrents of water there have unearthed remnants of the old world. Rumors passed down through generations whisper of secrets to be found in the Maidstone, secrets that apparently reveal much about the breaking of the old world."

"Not sure what you mean by all that, but wouldn't a student of history be interested in confirming those rumors?"

"I have spent much time pondering the Maidstone. Many have gone in search of its secrets, but none have returned. None. Whatever is protecting those secrets is efficient."

"Could you take me there? I am a Callum Sage, after all."

Morgan yawned suddenly, slowly shifting her weight to one elbow. "What's a Callum Sage?"

"Please, Morgan, give yourself a moment before getting up." Rowe walked over and placed a hand on her shoulder, and she rested her head back down.

"We are seekers of truth," he said. "Disseminators of knowledge. Those who forget their history are bound to repeat it. And a great deal of history must never be repeated." Rowe paused. "I could say more about the Callum Sages, but for now please allow me to indulge in a short lesson from the Histories."

Will and Rowe helped Morgan to sit up slowly.

"Half a century ago," Rowe began, "the Fourwinds was a land dominated by five powerful kingdoms, the Crow's Nest being one of them. War broke out between four of the kingdoms, a war many sages believe was kindled by Natas—"

"Natas?" Morgan echoed, shuddering as she spoke the word.

"A creature of chaos that many people consider as nothing more than a spinster's tale. Some believe in an actual creature, but others think such a being merely represents a spirit of destruction. Personally, I find it difficult to deny that the influence of Natas is responsible for our present time of upheaval.

"As I was saying, the war between the kingdoms continued for years while the king of the Crow's Nest, with the help of the Callum Sages, worked tirelessly to broker an end to the fighting. Eventually, they were successful but not before each kingdom was decimated. Those who survived were now vulnerable to timeworn enemies previously held at bay by powerful alliances. Less than a fortnight after the war ended, trolls, gnomes, grizzons, and other creatures sent raiding parties into the kingdoms. These throngs grew into legions.

"After years of fighting on all sides, it became clear that the only way the kingdoms could defend their lands was to centralize power under a single banner. Peace had been easier to broker than unity. The kingdoms lost ground with the passing seasons, so a final effort was made to secure what was left of the kingdoms of man.

"After months of negotiating and voting, an aristocrat by the name of Malaqui of the House of Aldor was crowned the first king of the Fourwinds. Under his leadership, a new army was formed. When his second son, Raric, was old enough, he enlisted in the army and quickly rose through the ranks. He eventually became a general. He had a tactical mind that few strategists could equal. His victories became bedtime stories that inspired many young men to enlist, adding greater strength and unity to the army. In a few short years, Raric's leadership had ushered in a new era of peace."

"We're not going to get a silver lining here, are we?" Will said.

"Throughout those turbulent years, we lost track of Sidara, the Dark Queen who ruled enormous tracks of land beyond the Aerodice Mountains. By the time we sent our spies back over the mountains, it was too late. Her armies had assembled, and her surreptitious dealings were complete. She even united the gnome lords, winning over their warriors and teaching them all to speak the common tongue."

"Why was she forming an army?" Morgan asked.

"Many of us believe she has been but a human face for Natas. He has been extremely influential, slowly gaining adherents in the shadows."

Rowe paused to take a drink. "King Malaqui's firstborn son, Harroc, was a politician living in the palace in the capital city of Dwenlin Thah. As heir to the throne, he feared his brother's control over the army. Raric had no interest in court politics and no regal aspirations; nevertheless, fear eventually drove Harroc to murder his father and crown himself king."

"But if Raric controlled the army, why not remove his brother from the throne?" Will asked.

"He would have, but Harroc had struck a deal with the Dark

Queen. He promised to give her the location of his brother's secret camp in exchange for a treaty that would bring about an end to the war. She would be allowed to keep the western lands she had conquered, and he would become the hero king who brought an end to the war.

"What Harroc failed to realize was that his sister, Alarra, had a lust for power greater than his. She discovered what Harroc had done and sent out her own emissary with a proposition to Sidara to deliver *both* Harroc and Raric. Alarra's terms were accepted. Sidara sent in Uluk the Shadowfallen, who commanded half her forces, and he attacked with terrifying efficiency—"

"What's a *Shadowfallen*?" Morgan asked.

"It's extremely rare; in fact, Uluk is the only one alive that I am aware of. His father was an angel who bedded a human. Uluk grew up with the might of an angel—wings and all—but without the necessary tutelage from his celestial kin, he fell under the control of an evil power." Rowe paused. "Even so, Raric nearly escaped. In the end, Uluk's skullduggery and brute force served him well: Harroc was killed in the ambush, and Raric was captured. Uluk carried him to the Dark Queen. I can only assume she wielded her considerable power to learn everything Raric knew about the army, which remained strong even after it had lost its warrior general."

"That sounds awful," Morgan whispered.

"Is Raric still alive?" Will asked.

"I believe he is."

"Do you know where he is?"

"The Waerdreath, the Dark Queen's iron fortress, far to the west."

"You intend to go after him, don't you?" Morgan said.

"I have considered this option, and I believe time is not our companion in the matter."

"Do you think the queen is planning to do something with the knowledge she gained from the general?" Will asked.

"Sidara's roots run deep in the study of alchemy, and she has ample resources to further such knowledge. She has always savagely protected her efforts, but sometimes light shines in dark places, giving us a degree of insight. Recently, one of our spies returned from the Waerdreath, and we learned that Sidara's alchemists have finished creating an elixir. They are now in the final stages of developing a delivery system."

"That doesn't sound good," Will said.

Rowe's voice became somber. "The elixir is called Phyriad. And, just as it sounds, it is something to be feared. The information we have is somewhat fragmented. Apparently, if a person becomes infected with it, they change into something that is no longer human. The most disconcerting rumors imply that once a person changes, the transformation cannot be undone. Some say that those infected can then spread Phyriad without physical contact. But all we have now are rumors."

"Spreading fear," Morgan said with a tone of disbelief. "Mom was a nurse and worked with some rare diseases in Africa. I've heard her talking about pandemics and how difficult they are to stop once they hit the general population."

"What do people change into?" Will asked.

Rowe's brow furrowed. "No telling for certain. If the fragments of information we have carry any truth, victims become more like animals than people. Their humanity is lost, and even their bone structure is altered. They become irrational and aggressive, and no longer have any recollection of what they once were."

"Pandemics spread quickly," Morgan said. "They're impossible to stop without a vaccine or an antidote."

Will took a nervous drink. "So, what did you mean by *the final stages*, Rowe?"

"It is my understanding that Sidara requires a way to transport and unleash Phyriad into a broad population to ensure it spreads like a tidal wave."

"Transport it to where?" Will asked.

Rowe was silent for a moment.

Will raised his eyebrows in realization. He answered his own question with two words that caused Morgan's face to pale. "The Gateway."

Rowe pursed his lips and nodded. "We have reason to believe Sidara plans on unleashing Phyriad beyond the Gateway. But our capital city of Dwenlin Thah seems to be her first target."

"This can't be happening," Morgan breathed.

"Are you guys trying to stop her from finishing this little science project?" Will's voice grew a little louder than he intended.

"Every able-bodied soldier in the kingdom has been called to arms, Will, but the winds of war have not been at our backs since the loss of the general. Uluk has been commanding an army of over fifteen thousand strong to attack the city of Hammerclaw. If we lose that battle, we expect them to march north to Dwenlin Thah. Eventually, Sidara's poison will come to the Crow's Nest… and the Gateway."

"So, she could destroy *both* our worlds!"

A knock at the door gave both Morgan and Will a start. Rowe walked over, threw the locks, and opened the door enough to accept a large basket.

"Let us take time to eat before continuing with our spirited banter." He carried the basket to a small round table and unpacked a large salver with pheasant covered in a light peppercorn sauce.

Bright vegetables—from red potatoes to green peas—surrounded the tray of meat. A glass pitcher filled with fresh berry juice completed the virtual rainbow of color. Will was certain Morgan's stomach grumbled in unison with his.

"Please sit and enjoy," Rowe said, handing them each a long, narrow fork.

With his own fork, Rowe stabbed a bite-size piece of meat. Will pushed his fork in and withdrew a small potato. He dipped it in the sauce, placed it into his mouth, and groaned with delight. Morgan echoed the sound, slowly chewing some meat.

"The one constant here in the Crow's Nest is the food," Rowe said. "It matters not if we are enjoying a warm spring day or in the throes of a siege, the food is always the same. Well-fed soldiers are effective soldiers—or so the maidens say."

The food provided a brief respite from their conversation. Will savored a drink, allowing it to linger in his mouth. Admiring his goblet, he enjoyed another mouthful and leaned back.

"You mentioned you considered going after the general," Morgan said.

Rowe set his fork down and wiped his mouth with a cloth napkin. "Sidara's armies have not been able to overtake the stronghold city of Hammerclaw—the last major obstacle in her path to the Crow's Nest. I have recently discovered that she plans to leave the Waerdreath and personally lead the army through Hammerclaw. Her magic is formidable, but it is my hope that the journey to Hammerclaw will leave her in a weakened state upon her return to the Waerdreath."

"And you mean to be waiting for her in her castle?" Morgan asked.

"I have been trying to gather a small assemblage to journey into the Waerdreath, but none have heeded my summons."

"Would you go alone?" Morgan asked.

"I believe there is a Callum Sage in the city of Acttun who may join me. Another has remained silent. In truth, I have come to accept the possibility of journeying west alone."

"To save the general or to kill Sidara?" Will asked.

"I would seek out the general, and if an opportunity presented itself, I would not hesitate to bring about an end to the Dark Queen."

"But what if you run into more harvesters?" Morgan asked. "What if they attack before you recognize them?"

Rowe started to respond, but Will spoke first. "Would you take me to the Maidstone if I helped you get to the Waerdreath?"

Rowe stared at him as though he had not considered such an option.

"And I have that magic sword," Morgan added.

Rowe faced Morgan as she lifted her goblet to her mouth. It was a full minute before he spoke.

"Prudence." Rowe was slowly shaking his head. "You have both endured much, and careful contemplation is warranted."

Will glanced at Morgan. "The alternative would be walking back through the Gateway," he said, "back into a nightmare we can do nothing about, and then what? Can we simply hope Sidara and her army never show up in Cochrane?"

Rowe met his gaze but said nothing.

Will raked his fingers through his hair. "I don't know, Rowe. Back home, I've lost everything because of what I can see. But here, it's a pretty big deal. I think I have a chance to find out what it all means."

Each of them took another piece of food and ate in silence.

"How far is it to the Waerdreath?" Morgan asked.

"Better than ten days of hard travel."

"If we helped you here, would you come back to Cochrane and help us kill those harvesters?" Morgan asked. "After taking Will to the Maidstone?"

Rowe placed his fork on the table. "If we were to bring about an end to the war, thousands of lives would be spared. If we could stop Sidara, humankind in our world and in yours could be saved. Such are the stakes. If you two stepped into our plight, there would be no way we could ever repay such a debt."

"So, you *would* travel back to Cochrane with us?" Will pressed.

"Without hesitation," Rowe replied. "In truth, I *must* go there with you. As long as those two harvesters live in your world, the strength of Natas grows. I'm afraid stopping Sidara is merely the first step."

"I can't go back until I find out what my dream means," Will said.

Morgan stared at the Gateway, biting her lower lip.

"How dangerous would it be?" Will asked. "I mean, I can't imagine we simply arrive at the Waerdreath and ring the doorbell."

Rowe's face darkened. "The journey would take us through war-torn lands inhabited by powerful enemies. But I believe a small assemblage could pass through these lands undetected. I have studied the Histories carefully; there is a secret way into the Waerdreath and a series of passages I believe even Sidara is unaware of."

"What would happen if she found us?" Morgan asked.

"I cannot say for certain, but a chance for a merciful death is doubtful." Rowe sipped his drink. "The only certainty is that the journey would be fraught with peril soon after leaving the Crow's Nest.

"It is a heavy yoke set before you. If you choose instead to return to your world, I will provide you both with warding magic to protect you through the Gateway. But I cannot protect you once you are through. If you choose to journey with me, I can promise nothing. In fact, it would be wise to consider the likelihood that not all of us would survive."

Again, silence filled the room as they considered Rowe's warning.

"I'll be honest, Rowe," Will said. "Back in Cochrane, I've been hospitalized, medicated, and counseled to death—all against my will—in an effort to fix me. Now, I find myself in a place where my ability might help. In a crazy way, I feel more normal *here* than I did back in Cochrane. I think I'm staying."

"That was fast," Morgan said.

"Not sure I have a choice in the matter."

Will waited for Morgan's response as she stared at her plate.

She turned to Rowe. "So…why did I find a magic sword in my attic?"

"I do not believe there is an easy way to hear what I am about to say," Rowe said, taking another bite.

"Say it."

"A Callum Sage named Tannis of the Nest carried that very sword with him through the Gateway years ago. He was hunting a harvester called Abaddon and was never heard from again. Because the magic responds to you, I assume Tannis was your father."

"But I don't understand. Why not—"

"Please allow me to finish," Rowe interrupted. "Will shared with me that his mother, Alyssa—who was also a Callum Sage and the granddaughter of the man you knew as Joe—had apparently died in an accident three years ago. Will also said your family moved to the same village as him, about three years ago."

"Yes, that's right," she answered, wringing her hands.

"Three years ago," Rowe echoed before taking a drink.

She stiffened. "That was when Dad changed…and when we moved to Cochrane! But if he was a Callum Sage, what would he have to do with Will's mom's accident?"

Rowe hesitated. "I am sorry, Morgan. I believe your father was killed by the harvester Abaddon, who took on his form."

Morgan stared at the embrasures high above them, her eyes brimming with tears. No one spoke or ate for a few moments.

"That explains why he's been dead to me since then," Morgan said after several moments. "I guess I've been mourning his loss for the past three years."

Rowe set down his fork. "I am truly sorry, Morgan."

After another moment, he continued. "Three years ago, Natas, in the form of the Iron Dragon, returned to the Fourwinds."

Morgan sat up straighter and raised her eyebrows. "Dragon?"

"Three years ago…" Will muttered.

"Magic works in ways we do not understand," Rowe said. "It drew the three of us together. And I believe it drew your mother to a cause greater than herself, Will."

"Then I started seeing all those creatures materialize from the forest, and my life fell apart."

"Perhaps your mother returned to the Fourwinds to stand against Natas," Rowe suggested.

Will's mind ran wild. "But why wouldn't she connect with you and other Callum Sages?"

"Your mother's power was unique, as mysterious as an ocean. But there are times when power can endanger the lives of loved ones."

Will stared at Rowe, wondering if he was talking about the same woman who used to make delicious lasagna and drive him to basketball games.

Rowe stood suddenly. "There are matters I must attend to before you leave this room. May I ask that you remain here? I shall return soon."

Morgan continued to stare at the ceiling, probably still thinking of her father, but Will nodded as Rowe left them in silence.

Will reclined in his chair, pondering the mystifying story he found himself in.

CHAPTER 14
PURGE

Morgan noticed a dramatic change in Rowe's appearance when he returned to the Records of Time. His Trannalun cloak flowed behind his shoulders like a cape, revealing the shallow hilt of the sword on his right hip. Beneath a leather vest was a dark-blue chemise tucked into a wide belt that held up loose-fitting leather pants. Armguards that looked like tree bark covered his forearms, and similar shin guards were strapped above soft leather boots.

Ruint and Dench followed Rowe across the room carrying several fragments of armor and a bundle of tightly folded clothing.

"Morgan, this is Dench and Ruint of the tribe of Harkarsh," Rowe said. "They are my personal guards. Will met them last night. They are committed to protecting you when we leave the Records of Time."

Dench and Ruint both stood over seven feet tall with imposing frames like carved granite. They offered Morgan smiles that revealed enormous bone-crushing teeth.

"Uh…hello," Morgan said, trying not to stare.

Rowe handed Will some armor. "These should fit you."

"Looks like birch bark," Will said.

"Using a mold, we add dozens of thin layers of bark, brushing a root extract between each layer. While it remains wet, it can be form-fitted to an individual, then slowly dried for two weeks in the kilns. A final extract is brushed on, making it this clean shade of green. The intricate process takes three months, but when finished, the armor is nearly as strong as steel at a fraction of the weight."

Will held one of the shin guards. "Amazing."

"I have a breastplate that buckles to a backplate, armguards, and shin guards for you, Will." Rowe handed him a stack of tightly folded clothes and gave Morgan another. "I also have some clothes you both can change into. Yours will attract too much attention here."

"No armor for me?" Morgan asked.

Rowe stared at her a moment. "You wear armor where you are from?"

"No one wears armor back in Cochrane," Morgan said.

"You would be the first woman to grace the halls of the Crow's Nest with armor, and we can ill afford the attention," Rowe said. "Besides, you would stand out like a gnome in Harkarsh if you are seen with your sword."

Dench and Ruint gave a short, guttural laugh, nodding in agreement. Morgan failed to see the humor in any of it.

"Morgan, you may change over there," Rowe said, pointing to a tall bookcase that jutted out from the wall in a semicircle.

Morgan obliged and carried her bundle behind the bookcase. She unfolded the green fabric, and it flowed to the floor. After examining it for several moments, she removed her clothing and slipped the frock over her head. The material slid smoothly over her shoulders and hips; she was surprised by how well it fit. It covered her shoulders and formed a shallow V above her breasts with a wide black neckline stitched with light-green thread. A similar black border ran from her wrists to her forearms, stitched with the same light-green thread. The frock was form-fitted to her hips, where it widened considerably and flowed to her ankles.

In stark contrast to the deep-green fabric, she buckled a wide brown leather belt around her waist. Attached to the belt was an empty scabbard. She unfolded a brilliant-red shawl bordered with yellow stitching and slid it over her shoulders, noticing how it concealed the scabbard. She pulled her hair back and stepped out from behind the bookshelf.

"If you ever get tired of this place, Rowe, I bet I could get you a job selling wedding gowns back home," Morgan said. "Fits perfect."

Rowe stared with his mouth slightly open as she drew near.

"I'm not much for dresses," she said, "but I've never felt such soft material." Morgan brushed past Rowe. "You look great, Will," she said, examining him from head to toe.

Will had changed into a dark-gray tunic that covered the gun and holster strapped to his right thigh. He wore a brown leather belt with a short sword hanging from his left hip. The tan-colored canvas pants fit well, as did the short leather boots that resembled the pair Rowe was wearing. He buckled the shin guards and chest plate into place but had trouble getting the armguards buckled.

Dench offered some help, working the buckles with ease. "Master Will. Speak wit' me?" he said in a deep voice.

"All right." Will followed Dench's massive strides across the room, keeping his distance.

As Will and Dench walked to the center of the library, Rowe stepped close to Morgan. "My offer still stands. If either of you wishes to return to your home, I will make the trip back with you to make certain the way beyond is clear. I will not be able to remain for long, but I will make certain it is nothing like the experience you had coming here."

Morgan caught a glimpse of genuine concern in his eyes. "Thank you, Rowe. That means a lot."

"Are you certain you are ready to leave the Records of Time?"

"As soon as I can get my legs to stop shaking."

Dench spun around. Before Morgan could blink, the tip of the half-orc's sword was touching Will's chest plate. "We have some minutes, so me share tinking wit' Master Will."

Will managed a shaky nod.

"Good," Dench said, sheathing his sword in a single fluid motion. "Harvesters be strong, but not as much while human in form. You can see dem but must be careful. Once dey know we know, dey will start fighting. Dat is bad. We must fight when good for us, so dey must not know you know. Dis sound good, Master Will?"

Will scratched his head. "I think so."

"Good. We need to fight when it is good, and tings never good wit' harvesters. Dey old and knowing. When fighting starts, dey move fast. You need to have sword out. You have no sword fighting skills, but dey cannot know. Dey will kill easy prey to make room to fight us. No look like easy prey. Learn to draw blade. It is short like toy; you need to draw in wide arc. Follow angle of sheath. Dis to set pace for fight."

His broadsword barely rang as it left the sheath in a wide arc. Almost as quickly, Dench slid it back in place. His beady eyes probed Will, then a smile crossed the broad expanse of his mouth.

"Is your sword, um…magic?" Will asked.

Dench shook his head. "It can no kill harvester. Slow it, yes, but no kill. Strong magic needed to kill harvester."

"What about *this* sword?" Will placed a hand on the sword at his hip.

"No magic," Dench said. "Cloak strong magic. Keep cloak on. Keep sword up."

Will drew his sword awkwardly and tested its weight, swinging it around several times. Morgan winced as he fumbled to slide it back into the sheath. He repeated the process several times with some encouragement from Dench. After Dench seemed satisfied, Will walked over to the reading chair and held his Trannalun cloak in his hands. He pulled the crimson material over his shoulders and attached the brooch.

Rowe approached Ruint, who was adjusting his ax. "Did you find Ellywick?"

"Messenger told me dat he in his chambers feeling old today. He will join us here dis evening for eats but no happy about so many stairs."

"I had hoped to talk with him, but it can wait till this evening."

Morgan stood with Will as he adjusted his holster and fiddled with the hood of his cloak. "You did fine, Will. Confidence with a sword takes time, believe me."

He drank a full goblet of water and, with shaking hands, quickly refilled it.

Rowe stepped close to him. "Thank you for being patient, Will. Rest assured, we will speak of Alyssa as time allows. I know of three texts that speak of her in the Histories."

"I guess I know why she didn't have any pictures of her parents," Will said with an unconvincing smile.

Rowe scrunched his cheeks and glanced at Morgan. She smiled at his confusion. "Very well," he said, leading the way through the main door. "Follow me."

A thin iron handrail helped guide them down the winding steps of the tower. Morgan traced the dark-gray stones with her fingers, trying to estimate the age of the castle. She noticed Will casting nervous glances at every turn. The look on his face reminded her of the day he had claimed to see Lessers at her father's church building. He was probably expecting a similar encounter, so she tried to calm him.

"Hey, Will, I toured the Tower of London when I went to England for a competition. As old as that castle was, this feels much older. How old do you think this place is?"

Will maintained his grip on the handrail. "No idea. I've never seen anything like it, but I think we're in for more than a nice guided tour."

After a few minutes, they emerged from the narrow confines of the tower and stepped into a wide hallway with a great arched ceiling. Enormous timbers spanned the gap high above, and two bright-red tapestries covered the wall, floor to ceiling, on either side of the tower entrance. Bright sunlight streamed through seven large embrasures centered perfectly on the far wall. Morgan rushed across the empty hallway to the nearest embrasure, eager to see if the outside world looked as foreign as the inside. Would the sky be blue? Would the sun rise in the east and set in the west? Were there clouds? Were there trees?

The embrasure had a flat bottom sill made from giant stones fixed together with mortar; the opening arched several feet upward. The wall was nearly three feet thick. Morgan placed her hands on the rough, cold stone sill and leaned forward on tiptoes into the opening. The vista took her breath away.

Will joined her, peering over her shoulder. "Wow! Those trees are bigger than the Douglas firs on Vancouver Island."

A majestic forest covered the hillside, rolling gently to a valley below. Morgan stared at the lofty trees for several moments before looking down their length. She gasped, realizing they were several stories above a great expanse of sprawling walls with countless pitched rooftops that formed a spectacularly large keep. A solid curtain wall surrounded the courtyard and the myriad of smaller buildings around the keep. The stone wall was made of battlements, parapets, and smaller towers. The enormity of the Crow's Nest left her feeling small.

She leaned forward and surveyed the courtyard approximately sixty feet straight down. She nudged Will with her elbow, pointing to a large crowd of people. Will let out a despondent groan.

"The faces of war," Rowe said.

Morgan was surprised to hear such a compassionate voice from a seasoned soldier.

"We are losing ground every day while the Fourwinds is ravaged by war," Rowe explained. "The Crow's Nest has always been a place of hope for the hopeless…until the harvesters arrived."

Morgan watched the crowd amble through the courtyard. "But there's hundreds of them…so many children."

"Every man capable of lifting a sword has been commissioned. The children have been left in the hands of people that, in many cases, are too old to care for themselves. The towns in this valley are overwhelmed by the steady influx of refugees. Space here is filling by the hour."

"Why are they not being allowed inside the keep?" Morgan asked.

"Any one of them could be a harvester," Will suggested.

Rowe nodded. "The refugees will remain within the curtain wall until the duke decides what to do with them."

"What if we can kill the harvesters?" Morgan asked. "Would people be allowed in?"

"Those unable to care for themselves would, but the others would be sent out into the valley. Regardless, we would have to convince the duke we have purged the castle without revealing you." Rowe shrugged. "Difficult, but not impossible."

"I guess the pleasantries are nearly over," Will said.

Rowe's face was stoic as he turned and ushered them onward.

The end of the hallway offered two options: straight down the long flight of stairs or left down a narrower hallway. Even at midday, the narrow hall was a shroud of shadows. Rowe turned left around the corner and almost collided with two men wearing studded armor. He started to address them, but Will interrupted with a shout.

"Holy crap!"

Will's face went pale. Morgan stepped back as Rowe drew his sword with a flourish. The steel blade radiated brilliant blue. Before anyone could react, Rowe drove it deep into the soldier closest to him. Will leapt back into Morgan, and they both tumbled to the floor as Ruint's battle-ax came down. The curved blade caught the second man's shoulder and would have cut him in half had he truly been human. A grumble reverberated from deep within the creature as Ruint withdrew his ax. Three tentacles slithered around from the harvester's back as it dropped to a knee from the force of Ruint's blow. The first tentacle wrapped itself around Ruint's neck, the second around a leg, and the third around the ax handle.

An unnatural blue flame, crackling wildly, lanced from Rowe's blade, electrifying the air as he held it fast in the first harvester. Dench stepped in, cutting the tentacle around Ruint's neck as his own leg was pulled out from beneath him. Another tentacle knocked the ax from Ruint's hand, narrowly missing Dench. Ruint drove a boot into the creature before it could regain its feet. He pulled a long knife from the boot and hacked at the tentacle encircling his feet.

"Me ax, Will!" Ruint bellowed as another tentacle came at his throat. He grabbed at the tentacle with his hand, trying to cut it, but it pulled free from his grip and immediately aimed for his throat again.

Will rolled onto his back and scrambled away from the onslaught. Seeing the terrified expression on his face, Morgan sprang to her feet and seized Ruint's ax that had bounced off the far wall.

Tentacles emerged from the second harvester with stunning speed as Dench stood over the creature, cutting one, two, then three, of them before one broke through and gripped Dench's ankle. It jerked his leg out from beneath him. Dench fell down hard but not before driving his sword through the demon's chest until the tip struck the stone floor.

Rowe kicked out the feet of the first harvester, and it landed in a heap. He yanked the blue blade from its carcass and brought it down in a high arc, cleanly severing the second harvester's head.

The dim hallway was silent.

"Spectacles," Rowe gasped with a heaving chest. "We need spectacles."

Ruint sat up. "What?"

"Dench, run up to the Records of Time and fetch the spectacles on Brin's old reading table—and be quick about it!"

Without a word, Dench sheathed his sword and was off.

"Will, I will tell the duke you have a set of spectacles that allows the wearer to see harvesters," Rowe explained. "That will allow me to negotiate the opening of the main gates for those in need. We will have to move quickly to kill them all before the duke has a chance to test the spectacles." He turned to Ruint. "How's your leg?"

Ruint rubbed his knee. "Me can walk but no want to run."

"You thought of spectacles during all that?" Will asked.

A sudden grin formed across Rowe's lips. "*Holy crap?*"

Will released a nervous burst of laughter. "Sorry, Rowe, but that was crazy. I panicked. I mean…they were right there, and I panicked."

Rowe crouched beside Will. "Clearly you have had no experience with combat. And clearly, it terrifies you. Despite this, you chose to use your gift to help instead of using it to save yourself." He extended a hand, lifting Will to his shaky legs. "Imagine what could have happened if they had been able to strike on their terms."

Morgan silently observed Rowe interacting with each one. He brushed the sweat from his brow as he checked the harvesters' bodies, then looked at Morgan. She held his gaze until Ruint stepped between them.

"What we do wit' de bodies?" he asked.

"Drag them back to the storage room around the corner," Rowe replied.

"Why harvesters always so heavy?" Ruint grumbled.

⚜

The keep was an immense five-story structure housing a vast assortment of rooms. Morgan quickly became disoriented in the endless series of halls and wings. Dench caught up with them and slipped Rowe the eyeglasses. As they continued, they passed several soldiers; some offered polite greetings, while others regarded Rowe and his two guards with disdain. Few showed any interest in Will, but several stole sidelong glances at Morgan.

After several hours touring the keep, they slipped through a narrow back entrance to the main stables. Morgan followed Will inside behind Rowe and stared down the alleyway. Two horses were being led from their stalls not far from where they stood. As Will entered, the horses stopped and turned to face him. One mare huffed, and one by one, heads appeared from the stalls. Each horse turned its full attention to Will.

"Shades!" said the stableman leading the mares. "What manner of man are you?"

Rowe cleared his throat and escorted Will onward. "His cloak has always drawn such reaction from horses."

Will resisted as he stared at the horses, but Dench pushed him forward. Both mares standing in the alleyway stepped aside and dipped their heads. Dench had to push Will again to keep his feet moving as Rowe led them quickly from the stable through the giant front gates. It was a few moments before anyone spoke.

"Me never seen anyting like dat before," Dench said as they climbed a set of steps.

"I've never even read of such a thing," Rowe said.

Will held up his hands. "Don't look at *me*."

"Did you see the black horse from your dream in there?" Morgan asked.

"No."

"So, what was that all about?"

Will thought of his brief history with horses. "Not a clue, Morgan. I've been around horses a few times, but nothing like that ever happened. Man, my heart is still racing. That was weird."

"Let us finish here, and I will give the matter some thought," Rowe said.

They walked along the wall near a section of the courtyard

packed with refugees. The entire leading edge of the wall was lined with battlements made from single blocks of stone. Metal railing anchored to the inside of the wall walk contained bundles of tightly wrapped arrows and tall spears. Sentries stood alert every dozen paces as if expecting an attack at any moment.

They came to a bench, and Morgan was quick to take a seat. She rubbed her feet through her slippers. Ruint joined her, massaging his knee. Will stood against the guardrail, studying the crowd below. Rowe and Dench disappeared into the gatehouse. After several minutes, they returned with frowns on their faces. Rowe handed Morgan a skin of water.

"Thanks, Rowe. Did everything go all right in there?"

"The duke will be closing the main gates shortly."

"Is there anything you can do about it?"

"There are no easy answers, Morgan. If we keep the gates open, more harvesters will enter, and more people will die—both here and perhaps in your homeland."

"Lot of faces," Ruint said, passing Will the skin.

"I don't see any harvesters," Will said. "I think we're good down there. Hopefully, now we can get the people inside." He drank some water and wiped his mouth. "My word, look at them. Some are so young, but others are older than dirt."

"Rowe will see to it dey are safe," Ruint said.

Morgan sighed as the weight of the refugees' plight settled on her shoulders like a stone block. "Someone has to let them in. They'd never survive the elements."

"Let us go down to be certain we have no more unexpected guests," Rowe announced.

They stepped into the courtyard among hundreds of refugees

carrying what was likely all their earthly possessions. Each person, smooth or wrinkled, wore the same despondent look.

Rowe turned to Morgan. "Servants of the Crow's Nest have been providing food and water, but shelter from the cold is something these people no longer hope for."

Morgan and Will followed Rowe and the half-orcs slowly through the crowd. Dressed in ragged clothing, several refugees wore blank stares as they walked past.

As the crowd grew, Will bumped into an old woman hunched low and covered in a dirty, tattered shawl. He apologized, but the woman ignored him, keeping her head low. Morgan regarded her for a moment, but someone else caught her eye.

She crouched on the hard ground, removed her shawl, and draped it over a young girl who sat scratching at the dirt with a small stick. The girl flinched, and a glint of fear sparked in her eyes.

"This will keep you warm, little one," Morgan said.

The girl relaxed her shoulders as Morgan wrapped the shawl around her. Morgan shivered as the sun disappeared behind the forty-foot curtain wall. The darkening sky was brewing an ugly evening.

"What's your name, sweetie?" Morgan asked.

"Lillie, my lady."

"That's a pretty name, Lillie. My name is Morgan."

Lillie curled her nose slightly.

Morgan smiled. "Strange name, isn't it?"

The girl nodded.

"Are you drawing a picture, Lillie?"

"Yes, my lady. It's my horse, Blackie."

"That's a very nice—"

"*Morgan!*" Will shouted, startling everyone in the courtyard.

Morgan leapt to her feet in time to see the old woman Will had bumped into skittering in her direction. Morgan was momentarily confused as the old woman straightened to a height of nearly six feet. From beneath the old shawl, giant, crooked claws produced a jagged-edged sword. The harvester quickened its pace.

As the creature rushed past several people cowering in fear, a sudden calmness washed over Morgan. She was instantly face-to-face with everything that was wrong in both this world and her own. The pain and anguish her mother had gone through the past three years, along with the murder of her father, now had a face. It was a face void of humanity, and it was gaining ground. She barely heard Ruint shout as he, Dench, and Rowe ran to intercept the harvester.

Morgan knew no one would make it in time to save her. But that suited her need. No one could save the approaching creature either. Without hesitation or fear, she reached across her waist and drew the sword from its sheath. Instantly, the magical tingling returned, at once electrifying and tantalizing.

The creature closed the gap with a final powerful stride. Its eyes flashed with abhorrence. The crude sword came up and then descended in a quick motion.

Morgan kept her back straight as she retreated beyond the harvester's sweeping blade. The sword struck the ground with a clang. Morgan counterattacked as she had done countless times throughout her fencing career. But this time, she was holding a sword pulsing with magic, and this time, her attack was meant to kill. She executed her powerful lunge so quickly, the harvester was unable to offer any defense. Morgan grunted as she drove the narrow blade through its chest to the hilt. Green sparks of magic danced wildly around Morgan's body, arousing an unfamiliar passion within her to obliterate the creature.

The harvester reached for Morgan's face with its terrifying claws. Morgan retreated from the danger, pulling her sword free in the process. The harvester shielded its eyes from the green flames arcing from the blade and made a final desperate lunge. Morgan parried and shuffled back two quick steps before attacking with an explosive riposte. She drove her sword deep into the creature's chest and this time the eruption of magic almost pushed her back. She screamed. The sword's grip vibrated and bucked hard as the magic flashed through what remained of the harvester's human disguise. Morgan held fast. Stunning green light burst from the harvester's eyes, nose, and ears as if they were expelling the darkness within.

By the time Rowe and the half-orcs arrived, the creature was dead.

"Me no understand." Ruint lowered his ax. "She not normal."

Rowe gaped at the smoldering corpse and then at Morgan.

"Two-time…world champion," she managed between breaths.

"She surprises," Dench said.

Rowe sheathed his sword. "Morgan, I'm—"

She placed her hand on his shoulder and drew strength from his compassionate eyes. "It's all right, Rowe. I'm fine."

The threatening clouds were breaking up. Panic within the courtyard subsided. Morgan sheathed her sword and stepped closer to Rowe. "Can we bring them into the keep now?"

"Morgan?" Lillie spoke in a small, trembling voice.

Morgan reached down, lifted the little girl into her arms, and scanned other faces in the courtyard. "There are at least two hundred refugees, Rowe. They're frightened, but I see hope in them when they look at you."

"They're not just looking at me," Rowe said. "Would you like to help, Morgan?"

"More than you could imagine."

"Very well. Let's get started."

A thundering voice caused another ripple of fear throughout the courtyard. *"Make way!"*

"Duke Renaldi," Rowe huffed under his breath. "Impeccable timing."

Twelve armored soldiers carrying large glaives forced the refugees back to form a perimeter as a man in royal robes strode into the courtyard, eyes fixed on Rowe.

"Head over with Dench and Ruint," Rowe told Morgan as the young aristocrat closed the gap with a broad-chested man at his heels.

The tension that had begun to dissipate from the courtyard became palpable again. Morgan joined the half-orcs, who were scowling at the duke's pompous entrance. She cringed at the sound of their grinding teeth.

"Am I to understand that another harvester has been found within my walls?" the duke shouted.

"Found and killed, my lord," Rowe said.

"Were any of my men hurt?"

"Not one, my lord."

"Good. When did *he* arrive?" the duke snapped as he glared at Will, who was wearing the telltale red cloak. "I had assumed you were the last, Rowe."

"Not so, my lord. This is—"

"I care not who he is."

"Perhaps you should, my lord. He brought us these spectacles that allow the wearer to see a harvester while clothed in the form of a human. We have completed a sweep of the castle and have found and killed three harvesters."

The duke's eyes narrowed slightly and shifted to Will. "Is that so? Who *are* you?"

"I'm afraid he is three years into a seven-year vow of silence, my lord."

The broad-chested man scoffed. "If only you would do the same."

"I would consider it, Tranas," Rowe said. "But then the duke would lose the only council he does not pay for."

Tranas's face reddened, but the duke kept his focus on Will for a lingering moment. A sheen of sweat appeared on Will's forehead.

"There is no reason for these people to remain in the courtyard, my lord," Rowe said. "As per your conditions for allowing them entry, I suggest we begin the process."

"I will decide the *ifs* and *whens*," the duke snapped.

"You already have, my lord, when you agreed to let them in as soon as you had assurances that there are no harvesters among them."

"How dare you speak to the duke in such a manner!" Tranas spat as he strode forward with the duke's private guard one step behind him.

The refugees moved backward, creating ample space in the courtyard for a small battle.

"You would be wise to stand down," Rowe said.

"You would allow your words to place your life at risk?" the duke asked.

"My words will always be my own and carry with them simple truth. I have received *your* word as to the conditions required to allow these people entry, and *that* is what is going to happen. The question remaining is not *if* or *when*, but *how*."

The duke's soldiers shifted slightly, raising the handles of their glaives off the ground. Dench and Ruint shuffled their feet and flexed their thick arms. Rowe's feet remained bolted to the ground.

"I will confer with my council when next we convene to decide whether to allow them entry," the duke said.

Rowe stepped forward and planted his hands on his hips. "The time to confer was before you spoke of conditions, my lord. Now is the time to act upon your word."

"The duke decides, not you *or* your kind!" Tranas hissed through gritted teeth.

"Let's get on with it," Rowe said, flourishing his arms in a wide, welcoming gesture.

"Shades!" Tranas shouted. "Twelve seasoned soldiers against you, a deaf-mute, and two half-breeds? Ha! That is obtuse even by *your* standards."

"What about you and the duke?" Rowe asked. "Have you forgotten to count yourselves as part of this? Or is twelve as high as you count?"

"Enough!" the duke said, raising his arm. "Are you willing to die to have these beggars allowed into the keep?"

"I am willing to die to make certain you keep your word to these people," Rowe said. "In any event, the chance of myself or Dench or Ruint or the deaf-mute dying this evening is unlikely."

The duke stared at Rowe as if calculating the odds before placing a bet.

After a moment, he lowered his voice. "Very well, Rowe. I did say that if you could guarantee that no harvesters were among them, I would allow entry. But this will be the last group. The main gate will be closed shortly, and the castle locked down. All others will be forced to fend for themselves in the valley."

With that, the duke spun around and started back to the keep with his entourage.

As soon as they were gone, a collective sigh rustled through the courtyard. Morgan examined the faces of the refugees and saw a lingering fear as though they were afraid to hope.

An older woman pushed through the crowd toward Rowe.

"Gloriana!" Rowe called out.

The woman, dressed moderately better than most refugees, met his eyes. She squinted, brushing some straggly gray hairs from her face. Her eyes brightened in recognition of the Callum Sage.

"We can bring them in now!" Rowe shouted.

The woman's wrinkled, weary face softened as she limped toward him. Rowe waved at Morgan to join them.

"Gloriana, I would like you to meet Morgan. I think you will find her a welcome ally in your work."

The old woman beamed and immediately gave Morgan a warm embrace.

"So good to have your help, child," Gloriana said. She led Morgan into the crowd with Lillie holding tight to her hand. "We have several rooms with bunks where we will keep the wee ones this night, but we must be quick as the sun has forsaken us."

"What about the elderly?" Morgan asked.

Gloriana turned to face the courtyard. "I have others to tend to their needs. You and I will do our part."

Before Morgan could ask her next question, Gloriana was well ahead of her.

Will worked alongside Rowe as they assisted the refugee workers with the elderly. Questions flooded his mind, so he took the opportunity to speak with Rowe.

"You mentioned someone who had yet to answer your summons, Rowe—someone who could help us."

Rowe leaned close and whispered, "His name is Bremer."

"Is he a Callum Sage?"

"There was a time he was part of our order, but the mere mention of his name here is grounds for imprisonment," Rowe said.

"What happened?"

"The duke arrived—a politician among politicians. Bremer, on the other hand, was an idealist among idealists. With him, your word had better be your bond or there would be trouble—and trouble there was. He almost killed the duke twice, and after the second time, he removed himself from the order, and from the Crow's Nest. I have not seen him in five years."

"Can he fight like you?"

"Bremer was born to fight. He's thirty-three years old, but one would think he has done a hundred and thirty-three years of living. Since his departure, there have been rumors he has been training with Yonaan Silvanas."

"Who's that?"

"A master rogue."

"Should we be worried?" Will asked.

Rowe smirked. "Suffice it to say that Bremer *was* a good man."

"Why doesn't that make me feel any better?"

"Wasn't meant to," Rowe said as he helped an elderly man to his feet. "But I'm hoping I can still trust him."

Will ran his fingers through his hair. "I'm out of my element here, Rowe. This place is so different. And I have nothing to offer these people."

Rowe placed both hands on Will's shoulders and captured his attention. "Much needs to be done here, and there's more for us to discuss. But we have so little time to talk, and their need is great."

"I can't even fight when the need arises, Rowe. I feel immobilized…useless."

"Do not be discouraged or afraid. Your lineage is without equal. Johanissan was a leader of many and has killed more harvesters than the queen's army. At a young age, his granddaughter Alyssa, your mother, commanded the ice elemental like a seasoned sage, and so she entered her grandfather's ranks. Peace followed wherever they went."

"But she was my mom… She used to drive me to basketball practice and badger me about homework like every other mom."

"I cannot explain her reasons for settling in your town. I assume she had not been able to find Johanissan and eventually started a family of her own. Love has a way of changing a person."

Will stared at the ground, recalling childhood memories. "You know, now that I think about it, before the accident, Mom started traveling a lot—or at least said she was. She would be gone for days at a time, and even when she was at home, she was distant. Something was happening; maybe she was out searching for Joe."

"I believe that quest has now passed to you, Will. When we have finished our work here in the Fourwinds, one day you must find Johanissan."

Will considered these words as Rowe wrapped a blanket around an elderly woman. "You know, Rowe, in some ways, you remind me of Joe. And I like the way you said *when* we're finished."

Rowe smiled. "Come. Let's get some rest. Tomorrow will hold new challenges for us all."

CHAPTER 15

NO LONGER SAFE

An hour before sunrise the next morning, Morgan sat on the floor of her assigned bedroom wearing a dark-gray robe. She was wide awake. Her hair was damp and combed straight, and her spirits were lighter after a hot bath. Sleep beckoned, but she couldn't resist the innocent sound of a child's laughter. In contrast to the sadness and tears of many refugee children that she and Gloriana had cared for last night, the little girl she had met in the courtyard was a spark of joy.

Morgan raised her eyes at the sound of a knock on her partly opened door, and her pulse quickened.

Rowe peeked inside and flashed an infectious smile. His hair was combed and his face clean-shaven. The thin, short-sleeved shirt he wore revealed the smooth curves of his shoulders and chest.

Morgan smiled. "Hi, Rowe. I thought everyone was asleep. Are we too loud?"

"It doesn't look like you've been to sleep yet."

"This little girl," Morgan said, reaching out to give Lillie a tickle, "has been keeping me awake!"

Rowe sighed and smiled as if the sound of giggling was long-forgotten music and the notes lingered in his ears. Morgan studied his kind eyes as he met her gaze. After a moment, he blinked and turned to Lillie.

"And who might this be?" he asked.

"This little rascal is Lillie."

"Are you certain?" Rowe crouched to Lillie's level. "I recall her being covered in dirt yesterday."

"I got a baff," Lillie told Rowe, adding another giggle. "I splashed Morgan."

"You did, did you? Well, she probably deserved it."

Morgan feigned an offended expression but smiled at him. She found it difficult to turn away from his captivating eyes. They had a magical way of disarming her.

"So, Lillie," Rowe continued, "are you two planning on getting any sleep at all tonight—or should I say, this morning?"

Morgan stood and peered through a crack in the shutters. "I suppose we don't need this lamp anymore. Okay, Lillie, I think we *should* catch a few winks."

Lillie scrunched her nose.

"Sleeps," Morgan explained. "Get some sleeps."

"I can sleeps with you in the big bed?"

"I wouldn't have it any other way."

Lillie let out an excited squeal, sprang to her feet, and ran over to the bed. The thick mattress was too high for her, so Morgan helped her up.

"Now, I'm going to step outside the door a minute to speak with Rowe," Morgan said, tucking the blankets around Lillie. "I'll be back so soon, you won't even notice I'm gone."

"Hurry, the bed is freeeezing," Lillie said, rubbing her feet together beneath the thick down-filled blanket.

"I will," Morgan said with a chuckle as she followed Rowe outside the room.

"I think you have made a true friend," Rowe said.

Morgan's voice quivered. "Her father's been off to war for so long, she barely remembers him, and her mom was taken in a raid. No one knows what happened to her younger brother. She has no one, Rowe, *no one.*"

"That is not true, Morgan."

"How can you say that? They're all gone. Who does she have?"

Rowe stared at her. "You, Morgan. She had *you* this night. In times like these, we must cling to such moments. That will give her the courage she needs."

Morgan moved closer to him. "Is that the wisdom of Callum Sages?"

"I suppose it is."

"The Fourwinds is so foreign to me, Rowe. But in *this* moment, I feel at home. That's something *I* can cling to." She shivered and wrapped her robe tighter.

He closed the gap between them, and his fingertips brushed her hand. "The castle hallways are cold at night."

She held her breath, wondering if he might take her in his arms, but a door opened across the hall, and Dench stepped out.

Rowe stepped away from Morgan and patted the half-orc's massive shoulder. "Thank you for standing watch, old friend."

Morgan moved to her doorway. "I'm coming with you and Will to the Waerdreath."

Rowe's warm smile returned. "You should get some sleep, then. Gloriana will need you later this morning."

Morgan awoke too late to help Gloriana with serving lunch to the refugee children, but there was no shortage of tasks. Ruint stayed close to Morgan, guiding her around the castle and carrying the heavier loads. As the two of them were leaving the main hall with some linens, Morgan spotted Rowe scurrying down a crowded hallway, keeping his eyes down as if trying to avoid attention.

"Rowe!" Morgan called.

He spun around and waited for several soldiers to march past before crossing the hallway. A light sheen of sweat covered his forehead, and both sleeves were rolled up past his elbows.

Morgan pushed back her tousled hair, which was now tied back in a loose ponytail.

"Gloriana has obviously been keeping you busy this morning," he said. "And I expected to see Lillie at your side."

"There's a few of us checking on her. I think she'll be sleeping right through the day."

Rowe nodded. "That will do her good."

"Where are you off to?"

"I still have not heard from Ellywick, and I need to talk with him before we leave."

"Is he all right?"

"His years are numerous. But I do not suppose he is quite ready to step into the next."

Morgan paused, still unattuned to some of Rowe's unique terms. "Can I come with you?"

"Most kind, but Gloriana would have me in stocks if she lost her best worker."

Morgan brushed a few stray hairs from her face. "Where are you meeting him?"

"He insisted we meet in the Records of Time, but it's odd because he hates the climb." Rowe rubbed his chin. "Something's not right."

"Maybe he simply wants to be somewhere with you where he knows you won't be interrupted."

"Perhaps."

Morgan squeezed his hand and was away before he could react. "Let me know if you change your mind."

"I will."

Turning midstride, she was surprised to see him standing in the same spot, watching her. "Have you seen Will this morning?" she asked.

"Yes. He's never been on a horse before, and after the incident at the stables, he's terrified of them, so Dench has him out riding before we leave." Rowe tilted his head slightly. "I cannot imagine those carriages you described moving without horses. What did Will call them?"

"Trucks." Morgan chuckled. "You'll see."

"I suspect I might," Rowe mumbled.

<hr>

Will stood outside the stables fidgeting with the brooch that fastened his Trannalun cloak. He watched in silence as Dench readied the saddles for two horses. One was much larger than the other, and Will assumed the larger horse was for Dench; it would take a strong mount to bear the weight of the half-orc. As all the horses had done the day before, these two bowed their heads and remained calm around Will, patiently waiting for the morning ride. Neither horse resembled the black stallion of his recurring vision.

Will had dreamed again during the night, but this time, the images included scenes from Cochrane. First, Constable Tom Bondy's final terrible moments in the Arden Forest. Then, an image of Joe covered in blood with a frozen, enigmatic stare followed. His final vision was a stable full of black horses with bowed heads. Over his left shoulder, the familiar snout of the great black horse huffed, and Will awoke.

He shook the images from his mind and adjusted his sword until it rested comfortably at his side. He hoped he would never be called upon to use it. But then a funny thought occurred to him.

"If Luke Skywalker can learn to use a lightsaber, I can learn to use this," he mumbled.

Dench must have overheard him. "You will learn to use de sword, but me have better plans for you today."

The riding lesson taught Will more than how to handle himself in a saddle. He also got his first real look at the surrounding landscape. Like the waterfalls in his dream, this place was unlike anything he'd seen before. But this was no dream.

As they rode, Dench explained some of the key points of reference. The Crow's Nest was strategically established high on a cleft in the Hillron Mountains at the northern end of the sprawling Rainia Valley. At the western border of the valley, the towering Epping Forest formed a lush, protective wall that stretched all the way back to the Misty Gorge. The thousand-foot rock bluffs of the Hillron Mountains walled the eastern border of the valley for twenty miles. Alpine streams nourished a patchwork of crops before meandering into the deep saltwater Rainia Lake. The inhabitants of the town of Rainia tended the crops to help feed the countless refugees streaming in daily.

Will did his best to keep his horse tight against the rocky wall and away from the steep drop on the other side of the road. He scanned the hodgepodge of homes around the original town, built along the northern shores of the lake. Dense thatched roofs and timber-framed buildings formed the core of the town, reminding him of a quaint Swiss village he had seen in travel guides. Judging by the narrow roads that snaked from the town center, there had clearly been little planning for the town's rapid expansion.

After about two hours, they returned to the looming castle wall, and Dench rode ahead. Will shifted in his saddle to enjoy a final sweeping view of the valley. A sharp bend in the road led him between two massive walls for nearly three hundred feet, ending at the main gates of the Crow's Nest. He rode awkwardly through the passage, which Dench had referred to as *the Gauntlet*, aware of soldiers watching him from the battlements.

Dench dismounted and waited beside his horse at the gates. A number of other horses and riders came in and out, each one paying special attention to Will. The horses would stop, wait for him to pass, and then continue. Their behavior unnerved him, but so did the gawking of confused and angry riders.

Despite the odd behavior of horses and most people, the riding lesson had been a success. Will had loosened his death grip on the reins about halfway through the ride, and he actually thought he could go another hour.

"Dench, I never figured you for a riding instructor."

"Keep riding," Dench said, casting a nervous glance at some nearby soldiers.

Will didn't respond, but sat stiffly, staring at the crowd of people.

"Holy crap!" he said.

Will had used those same words with the same tone when they'd encountered the harvesters inside the castle, so he didn't need to explain himself to Dench now.

"Down," Dench whispered.

Will slid from the saddle.

"Where it be?" Dench asked.

"That gnome—the one who helped Morgan." Will's mouth was dry enough to spit cotton.

"Ellywick? What about Ellywick?" Dench's voice became gruff.

"It's not Ellywick anymore."

"You certain? Me tink harvesters only take form of humans."

"Absolutely certain."

***

Morgan and Ruint finished Gloriana's task list, then joined her in a large room where dozens of refugees waited for fresh clothing. The elderly and the young were all helping one another. In addition to clean clothes, many were enjoying their first warm meal in weeks.

Morgan pulled a child's dress from one of the sacks Ruint had carried in and handed it to Gloriana. "Do you know Ellywick?" she asked the older woman.

Gloriana unfolded the dress and held it up to a little girl. "He's been a healer here since before I arrived and the only gnome ever to be welcomed in this part of the Fourwinds, to be certain. He's like a father to Rowe." She lowered the dress and furrowed her brow. "Why do you ask?"

"Rowe is going to meet him up in the Records of Time."

Gloriana let out a light huff. "Why there? Ellywick's always said the climb would be the death of him."

"I don't know, and Rowe doesn't know either."

"What's bothering you, child?"

"I—I don't know, Gloriana, but Rowe sounded uneasy about his meeting with Ellywick."

"Ruint!" Gloriana said sharply, surprising everyone in the room.

The half-orc spun around with a hand at his ax.

"Where's Dench?"

"He be here soon."

"Where is he *now*?" Gloriana snapped.

"Ridin' wit' Will."

"The stables are on the way," Gloriana said as she limped quickly to the far door with Ruint on her heels.

Morgan ran after them. "What's going on?"

"Something has alarmed you, and I mean to find out what."

"It's probably nothing, Gloriana," Morgan insisted. "I think I'm overtired."

"No harm in finding out for certain."

"Do you think he's in danger?"

Gloriana lowered her voice. "He's been in danger since the duke arrived. You would never know it by the way he carries himself. Was he wearing his cloak?"

"He was. Why?"

"Well, that's something." Gloriana pushed through a large set of double doors, out into the courtyard, leading them to the main stables.

Morgan lowered her head to avoid undue attention. "The duke wouldn't do anything to Ellywick, would he?"

"That would be the last thing Renaldi did. Rowe would tear the castle down to the footings to find anyone who brought harm to Ellywick, and the duke knows this."

At the stables, they found Will and Dench returning their horses. "Where's Rowe?" Will asked. "We've got some bad news."

"He's supposed to be meeting Ellywick in the Records of Ti—"

"No!" Will said. "We've got to stop him!"

Without waiting for an explanation, Ruint turned and ran back into the castle. "Come, Morgan! Someting no right!"

Morgan chased Ruint toward the Upper West Hall, assuming the others would follow but not bothering to look back. She always considered herself a fast runner, but Ruint led the way, incredibly quick for his size. They rounded a curve in the hallway and came to a sudden stop when they saw Rowe near the stairwell entry to the Records of Time. Four soldiers were about to enter.

"I beg your pardon, Tomas," Rowe said.

The soldiers turned in surprise.

"Rowe," Tomas said, his eyes wild like those of a skittish horse. "You surprised me. We were on our way up to find you."

Rowe slowed his approach. "Seems I saved you the trip."

"Apparently, you have a pair of spectacles the duke wants."

"What spectacles?"

Tomas wiped his brow. "He said you would know."

"Does he want me to bring them to him?"

"No. He would like *us* to bring them to him."

"Interesting," Rowe said, stopping a few paces away.

Tomas shifted his weight and broadened his stance.

Rowe reached into his Trannalun cloak and pulled out the spectacles, keeping his eyes on the soldiers.

Tomas glanced at Morgan and Ruint as they approached. "We don't want any trouble, Rowe." He reached out a trembling hand and moved closer to Rowe. "The duke is waiting. I need them now."

Rowe stepped back. "Do not make that next step the last thing you do in this life."

"Please, Rowe. I beg you."

Rowe raised the spectacles, and each soldier gasped. But before he could put the glasses on his face, footsteps scuffled in the tower stairwell behind the soldiers. Rowe stopped short.

Ellywick stepped out of the stairwell, and Rowe lowered his hand as he watched his old friend. In the brief distraction, one of the soldiers snatched the spectacles from Rowe's hand and passed them to Tomas, who slipped them into his pocket.

"Done here are we?" Ellywick asked.

Morgan wasn't clear what he meant by that or whom he was speaking to, but Rowe answered, "Yes."

The soldiers eyed Ellywick, then Rowe. No one moved.

"Tell the duke I would like the spectacles returned when he is done with them," Rowe said.

Tomas opened his mouth to reply, but a sudden commotion from down the hallway interrupted him. Steel flashed as the soldiers drew swords in unison.

Rowe unsheathed his sword and stepped back. "Run, Ellywick!"

The sound of footfalls grew closer. Ruint raised his ax, but Morgan stood with her hands at her sides, confused as to why Ellywick hadn't moved.

Dench and Will rounded the corner in a full sprint, weapons in hand.

"Cape!" Will shouted as Dench and Ruint closed the gap between them and the soldiers. They immediately turned on the only soldier wearing a cape.

As Rowe clashed swords with the caped soldier, Morgan shouted, "Rowe! Behind you!"

Rowe leapt away from the soldier and turned around.

Ellywick stood a few yards away, but his face was rapidly transforming. Large eyes void of life glared at Rowe, and jagged fangs protruded from a widening, unnatural grin. Two massive hands with deadly, crooked claws reached out. In the center of each palm was a gaping maw lined with snapping teeth.

Rowe glanced beyond the creature as if looking for Ellywick. But the hallway was empty.

Morgan gaped at the approaching harvester. The realization that Rowe's friend had suffered the same fate as her father sucked the breath from her lungs.

Dench and Ruint roared fierce battle cries, but instead of rising up to fight, Rowe hesitated. He stumbled and dropped to a knee as the action swirled around him.

Will appeared at his side, gun pointed at the gnome harvester.

Ruint swung his battle-ax in a high arc that struck the soldier wearing the cape so hard he crumpled to the floor. Instantly, the caped soldier began transforming into a terrifying beast. Ruint hacked like he was chopping wood. The creature thrashed wildly, unable to transform fully from soldier to harvester.

Dench rushed past the other soldiers toward Rowe. The gnome harvester raised its deadly claws, preparing to slash Rowe's head. Dench cried out, and Will pointed his gun. Two explosions echoed throughout the massive hallway, and the gnome harvester's chest burst open. The creature staggered backward but quickly recovered from the punishing blows.

Dench launched his sword. The blade made one full rotation before sinking into the gnome harvester's chest, exactly where the gunshot holes were closing. The enraged beast roared as the force of Dench's sword knocked it against the wall, but somehow the creature kept its footing.

The gnome harvester started to pull Dench's sword free from its chest, but Morgan charged in along the wall, driving her blade deep into its side. Green flames erupted from the sword, enveloping the creature within a tornado of emerald fire. Morgan leapt back with a shout, shielding her face. Fire continued to arc from the blade, burning the gnome harvester to ash.

Dench's sword lay on the ground beneath the green firestorm, out of reach. He drew two long knives from his boots and turned to help Ruint, who continued chopping at the caped harvester. Before Dench could lift the knives, his arms dropped to his side as a soldier's blade emerged from Ruint's chest. The blackened battle-ax clanged on the floor.

As Ruint collapsed, Will shifted his handgun and fired another round. The bullet struck the soldier who had stabbed Ruint, sending a spray of blood across Ruint's body. Will shot another soldier, blowing a large hole in his chest as the final soldier fled.

Morgan stood in shock; the two dying soldiers were not transforming into harvesters as she'd expected. Instead, they remained in human form.

She drove her blade, awash in green fire, into the weakened but transforming caped harvester. Searing flames burned first through both eye sockets and ear canals before exploding out of a mouth opened wide in a silent scream. The harvester fell to the floor as green fire burned it to ash along with Ruint's lifeless body.

"Have mercy!" Gloriana breathed, limping slowly around the corner. She had taken longer to catch up, and Morgan was thankful she was not there to see the fight.

Dench was on his knees in front of the scorched floor and pile of ash, holding his face in his giant hands. Rowe sat against the wall, his mouth agape.

"They knew," he gasped.

"Knew what?" Gloriana asked.

"The soldiers knew one was a harvester. They were on the same team," Will said. "Did the duke arrange this?"

"I saw a soldier run past me in the hall," Gloriana said.

Will holstered his gun. "I—I don't know why I didn't shoot him." His face was pale and drawn.

"He must be heading straight for the duke," Gloriana said.

"What do we do now?" Morgan asked.

"The duke will have no choice but to come for you all," Gloriana said, placing a hand on Dench's shoulder. She whispered something in his ear, and he climbed slowly to his feet.

Rowe was sitting on the floor with his head between his knees. Morgan sheathed her sword and knelt at his side. She draped her arm around his shoulders.

"I'm so sorry, Rowe."

A moment later, Tranas ran around the corner. Recognizing him from the courtyard encounter with the duke, Morgan shot to her feet and raised her sword.

The councilman raised his empty hands and slowed as he scanned the area. "Oh my…"

At the sound of his voice, Rowe raised his head. "It's all right, Morgan."

Tranas rushed to his side. "Are you hurt?"

"I don't think so. You were right, Tranas."

"Is the duke aware that you know?"

Morgan exchanged a confused look with Will as the two men spoke as friends.

"It's all right," Rowe repeated. He turned to Tranas. "He *must* know."

Tranas sighed as he surveyed the area again.

"Ruint is dead." Rowe fought back tears as he pointed to the ash pile. "And *that*…that was Ellywick."

Tranas was silent for a moment before he spoke. "You do realize Ellywick didn't suffer?"

"How can you say such a thing?" Rowe snapped.

Tranas spoke quickly. "Rowe, you knew Ellywick. Do you think he would have allowed himself to die on *their* terms?" He paused, but Rowe did not reply. "No, he had something in one of his many pockets that would allow him to step into the next on *his* terms."

Rowe sighed. "I need to believe that."

"Believe it, because you know it to be true—and wipe your blubbery cow eyes."

Rowe sniffed and rose to his feet.

"You need to leave," Tranas said as he stood with Rowe. "Are you two going with him?"

Morgan nodded numbly.

"Are you certain of this?" Tranas pressed.

"Yes," Morgan and Will replied in unison.

"Very well. No time to waste! I need to return to the duke to buy you some time." Tranas placed a hand on Rowe's shoulder. "Help Dench. Do not allow him to consider retribution at this time. And, Rowe, return the general to us—and be quick about it."

Rowe rubbed his eyes.

"There will be time for reprisals upon your return, so do not kill the duke before you leave," Tranas added. "That shell of a man has undoubtedly surrounded himself with a hundred soldiers."

"We are in agreement," Rowe said as he clasped Tranas's forearm.

Dench joined them and embraced Rowe. "Me wish to come wit' you."

"I wish it too, but we need you to rally your people for our return," Rowe said. "When we hang the duke from the gatehouse, we may need to defend the castle from the Dark Queen's forces. For that, we will require an army."

"Me know. Me try."

"His death will be avenged, Dench, but not today," Tranas offered.

Dench groaned. "It happened so fast, Rowe. Too soon. No say goodbye."

"No goodbye was needed, Dench."

"Me know. Me sad."

"I know how you feel, my friend," Rowe said.

"Don't you get killed, Rowe." Dench placed his enormous hands on Rowe's shoulders.

"Unite your people and it will be *us* doing the killing, Dench—starting with the duke."

Dench hung his head. "Me tink dat good, Rowe. Me will."

Rowe walked to the foot of the stairwell. "The Records of Time is no longer safe. It's time to seal it off. Each of you knows what to do. Will and Morgan, wait here until I return."

CHAPTER 16

KINGS AND GENERALS

Shortly after Rowe went up to the Records of Time, Dench, Gloriana, and Tranas left Will and Morgan alone in the Upper West Hall. The clamor of the brief but violent skirmish with the harvesters and soldiers rang in Will's ears.

Rowe returned from the tower and handed small backpacks to Will and Morgan. "I only had time to collect some basic supplies and a little food and water."

He opened his hand to display a small, polished dark-colored sphere he had retrieved from the library. It was an unassuming object, but he handled it with great care.

"What is it?" Will asked.

"The only thing the duke could offer Sidara is access to the Records of Time," Rowe explained. "This is the crag orb. It will ensure Sidara never gains access to the Histories or the Gateway."

"How does it work?" Morgan asked.

"The ancient magic protecting the Records of Time will transfer the Histories and the Gateway into the orb. The tower will be completely hidden and inaccessible. Only a Callum Sage can

176

wield its power, and only a Callum Sage can retrieve the Records of Time from the orb." He faced them. "Should I not return from the Waerdreath, you will have to do it."

"And if none of us make it back?" Morgan asked.

"This journey will be fraught with danger, Morgan. There is still time to reconsider…"

"I'm coming," Morgan insisted.

"Have you ever used that thing, Rowe?" Will asked.

"This has never been done."

Will exchanged a skeptical look with Morgan.

Rowe stared at the crag orb. "When the magic is released, we will have to move quickly." He stepped toward the stairwell opening, extending his arm until the orb crossed an unseen threshold. A sudden deep boom louder than Will's 1911 thundered throughout the Crow's Nest and across the Rainia Valley. All three of them jumped and clasped hands over their ears. Seconds later, the hallway was silent again, and they lowered their hands.

Will gazed at Rowe, tugging his ear. "Sonic boom much?"

"That was certainly loud," Rowe said. "This is no ordinary thing we've done, to be sure." He tapped the solid block wall where the entrance to the stairwell had been moments before. "Best get into the mines before the duke realizes what we have done."

Will stood in awe. "I can't imagine Sidara will be happy the duke allowed this to happen."

"I wish I could see his face when he discovers this," Rowe said.

Will flinched as Rowe slapped a hand against a block before turning to lead them away. Although the wall had not been there a moment ago, it looked as though someone had built it centuries ago.

Halfway down the hall, Rowe stopped at a partially opened door in the stone wall. All three stepped inside, and Rowe closed and locked the door behind them. After a moment, a soft glow cut through the impenetrable darkness, illuminating Rowe's face. He lifted his cupped hand, revealing a small glowing stone, then knelt on the floor.

Rowe motioned for them to come closer. "I am going to leave the orb in this wall," he explained, pulling a small piece of stone from a block with the tip of his long knife. Behind the stone was an indentation the exact size of the crag orb. He nestled the orb in place and returned the cover. The only sign of the hiding place was a small circle etched in the stone.

"If I do not return, one of you will have to use the orb to restore the Records of Time. Do not forget what you have seen here."

They both nodded as they adjusted their backpacks.

"Follow me, and stay close," Rowe said. "We have an uncertain journey ahead of us tonight."

After walking about fifty feet through the tight passage, they came to a junction. Smooth stone walls lined the passages to the right and left. A narrow passage straight across the junction seemed as if it had been crudely carved into the granite over a thousand years ago.

Rowe walked straight ahead to the crude opening and paused. "This is one of two passages leading to the mines deep in the Hillron Mountains."

Will soon became completely disoriented as Rowe led the way through the narrow passage through the mountain. Minutes drifted into hours; the only thing Will knew for certain was that they were gradually climbing. They passed three more junctions, but Rowe did not hesitate or speak, leading confidently.

Will followed the shadows cast by Rowe and Morgan. He

traced his fingers along the granite walls to steady himself until he wore his skin raw.

In the silence, Rowe handed Morgan a waterskin. She took a small drink and passed it back to Will, who was surprised by how thirsty he had become. He stopped to wipe his brow. As he drank, Will noticed for the first time that the crude ceiling was only a few inches above his head. His stomach tensed at the sudden sense that the walls were closing in on him.

"Will!" Rowe snapped. "We're almost there. Let's keep moving."

Their pace increased slightly, and Will grew light-headed. His mind drifted between images of soldiers and orphans, of kings and generals, of friends and sages. He had seen so many unexplainable things in the Fourwinds, things that were easier to label as *magic*. He thought of his strange new friends and how they were beginning to feel like family. He thought of his mother and could not help but embrace the hope growing inside him that he might see her again.

A sudden rush of fresh air caressed his face, snapping Will from his reverie. Ahead of him, Morgan and Rowe disappeared around another bend in the endless procession of twists and turns.

"Watch your step," Rowe said as they came to a crude set of stairs in a section so narrow they had to turn and walk sideways. Each step was a different height and depth, making the climb even more challenging.

Morgan quietly numbered the steps as she followed the flickering glow of Rowe's sunstone. She stopped around three hundred. Abruptly, the steps ended at another junction. Rowe held Morgan's hand, helping her onto the final tall step. A cool breeze flowed from right to left, and they continued up another section of wider steps.

"That other way leads into the mines," Rowe said.

At the top of the stairs, the wind shifted, cooling Will's clammy skin.

"Will, what time do you think it is?" Morgan turned around briefly and bumped into Rowe, who had stopped abruptly in front of her.

Will rubbed his eyes. Ahead of them was a small clearing bathed in the pale light of a cloudless blanket of stars. They had passed through the mountain passage. Will breathed deeply, awestruck by the countless shimmering lights in the velvet sky.

"Middle of the night?" Will answered, exchanging a relieved smile with Morgan.

Rowe led them toward the silhouette of a cabin. "We will stay here the night and set out in the morn," he announced. "Would you like to eat something before we get some sleep?"

Will stepped onto the front porch. "I'm too tired to chew."

"Morgan?"

She was staring at the stars. "I'm okay. Are you eating, Rowe?"

"I do not eat before I retire to bed, but that is not to say you may not."

Will and Morgan followed him through the doorway. Rowe lit a lantern hanging by the door, instantly casting a warm glow. The sunstone went dark.

The cabin was sparse but comfortable. A small table with four wooden chairs and a narrow counter for preparing food furnished the front area. Three sets of bunk beds, anchored to the back wall, were neatly made. In fact, the entire cabin was like a well-maintained guest lodge.

Rowe opened the shutters, and a cool breeze freshened the cabin. Will strode across the room, slipped off his cloak, and tossed it at the foot of his chosen bunk. He sat on the edge of a bed, pulled off both boots, and before another word was spoken, was fast asleep with one hand on his 1911.

⚜

Overnight, the wind shifted and grew colder as dawn approached. Back in the Crow's Nest castle, Duke Renaldi rose from his bed and pulled a fur-lined robe over his shoulders to ward off the morning chill.

Five courtesans lay motionless on his bedroom floor, surrounded by large, plush pillows. After a sleepless night with the duke, they were finally able to rest. Renaldi grinned and rubbed his hands together as he recalled what the girls had allowed him to do until the wee hours. Of course, they had no choice in the matter, but that meant nothing to him. His days were laden with troubles, so why shouldn't his nights offer a dash of pleasure? Unfortunately, a new day dawned, ushering in a tide of problems that would require the utmost care.

He opened the door to find thirty of his private guards bleary-eyed but watchful. The duke's fear of known enemies and traitors had driven him to insist on such a large number. But the price of his neurosis was a sizable audience for the nightly rumpus in his bedchambers.

The guards stiffened to attention and cleared a path as Tranas strolled down the hallway. The councilman's eyes were dark, and his hair unkempt. He suppressed a yawn as he approached Renaldi.

"We searched all night, my lord, but there is no trace of the opening."

"It must be an illusion of some sort," the duke said, rubbing his head.

"We pounded on the walls with hammers. No way any type

of illusion could withstand that." Tranas threw up his hands and huffed. "It's like the passage to the Records of Time never existed."

"I need to see this with my own eyes," the duke said. "Has there been any sign of Rowe or the remaining half-breed? Or his mute friend?"

"None, my lord. The night watch claims no one has left the castle."

"So, they are somewhere in the castle?"

"I cannot say yet. I have dispatched men into the depths of the dungeons while others are sweeping the keep room by room. If they are within the castle walls, we will find them."

"Have two fresh troops meet us in the King's Court. I want thirty men with me inside, and thirty beyond the door, until we locate this brood of vipers."

"Do you still wish to come to the Upper West Hall, my lord?"

The duke shook his head sternly. "Best to keep to the King's Court for the moment."

"We are expecting an emissary in as little as three days, my lord—"

"You don't think I'm aware of that? Whose body stands to get stretched across two timbers?" A stream of spittle showered Tranas's cheek. "Certainly not yours!" The duke lowered his voice. "Find Rowe and bring him to me alive. If you fail to do so before that emissary arrives, I'll crucify you myself!"

Tranas bowed slightly. "What if Rowe has fled the castle?"

"That would be most unfortunate for both of us."

"Should we send men out to search the valley?"

The duke grinned. "If Rowe has left the castle, he's probably dead by now."

"How so, my lord?" Tranas's voice quavered.

Renaldi rubbed the sleep from his eyes. "I was understandably nervous about the alliance with the Dark Queen, so I withdrew the patrols in the Epping Forest beyond both the North and South Crow Gates."

The color drained from Tranas's face. "When did you do that, my lord?"

"Last week. I imagine the holgs have ventured down from the trees by now." The duke shivered slightly and smirked. "And if we're lucky, those beasts will also kill the emissary before it arrives, giving Sidara a reason *not* to kill us."

CHAPTER 17

JOURNEY'S FIRST STEP

Morgan stepped from the cabin with a woolen blanket draped over her shoulders. She closed the door behind her and yawned. A puff of mist dissipated around her face in the crisp morning air. Will was fast asleep, and Rowe was nowhere to be seen. She wondered if he ever slept. When she turned around, her breath caught in her throat.

The cabin stood on a ridge hundreds of feet above the northern reaches of the Rainia Valley. An ancient forest spread west to the edge of a deep gorge that was thinly veiled by the old-growth canopy. The valley to the south was partially obstructed by mountain ridges, but Morgan could almost see the edge of a large lake fed by multiple streams. Behind her, majestic snow-covered peaks promised to keep the cabin in the cool shade until midday.

You sure are a long way from home, Miss Finley, she mused as she recalled her simple life in the small town of Cochrane.

"Huh," she muttered under her breath. It had only been a few days, but it seemed like weeks since she had given a second thought to the sport that had all but consumed her back home.

But here—wherever *here* was—fencing aspirations didn't seem the least bit important.

A tinge of guilt colored her memory as she realized how important her personal goals had become in light of how good it had been to help Lillie and the refugees. Attending university was important, but if Sidara's plot succeeded, all would be for naught. She sighed. Funny how perspective could change in such a short period. But change it had, and she wondered if life would ever be the same again.

She stretched her arms wide in a silent embrace, holding the trees, the mountains, the clean air, the simple song of joyful birds. As strange and dangerous and different as this world was, Morgan breathed deeply, trusting she was in the right place—for this moment, at least.

A soft scraping sound behind the cabin drew her around the wide porch. A low mist lingered, saturating the lush grass around a small clearing where Rowe tended three horses. He was murmuring something to a chestnut mare. Morgan could not make out his words, but he appeared so content.

He raised his head, and an easy smile crossed his weathered lips. "Morgan Finley. Did you find any sleep without Lillie's elbows and knees in your back?"

She folded her hands in front of her and stretched her arms. "It was enough."

"She will be excited to see you upon our return."

As she approached, Morgan noticed Rowe's bloodshot eyes. But there was something more. Despite his weary appearance, he was studying her face as if reading a favorite line from one of his treasured books. Her heart beat a little faster, and she hoped he wouldn't turn the page.

Morgan stepped closer. "Did you get any sleep at all?"

"There will be plenty of time for sleep—" Rowe began but stopped as Morgan placed a hand over his.

A light breeze blew through her hair, and a few strands caressed Rowe's cheek. "I'm so sorry about Ellywick and Ruint," she said. "Gloriana told me Ellywick was like a father to you. And I think Ruint was like a brother."

"My parents died when I was young," he said. "Ellywick became my closest friend and mentor. I suppose he was like the father I never knew."

Morgan moved closer. Feeling him tense, she wrapped her arms around him. Seconds later, he exhaled as his body melted into her embrace. She rested her head on his chest as his arms slowly reached around her. "I'm sorry, Rowe."

She breathed in and out. It was good being held so tight. It awakened feelings of safety and admiration she had tucked away since her father…

Morgan loosened her arms suddenly and stepped away. The pain of loss stabbed at her heart, but she wasn't ready to welcome grief right now.

Rowe stood motionless as she moved across the grass to the stable looking for a diversion. She grabbed one of the brushes hanging on the wall and returned. Rowe had not moved.

She patted the mare Rowe had been brushing. "And who is this?"

"Her name is Riverwind. She may be the elder mare, but she is the truest."

Morgan brushed Riverwind's powerful shoulder. "She's beautiful."

Rowe and Morgan worked together in silence for a few minutes, then flinched as the cabin door creaked open.

Will stepped out and squinted, dark circles beneath his eyes.

His wild hair caused Morgan and Rowe to laugh softly. Beneath his opened red cloak, his clothes looked as if he had slept in them for a week.

"Doesn't anyone sleep around here?" he mumbled.

Rowe threw a saddle over a mare that had shifted its attention to Will. "When did you begin your days at home?"

"I traded currencies on the spot forex market. Most days, I would just be getting to bed at this time because I was chasing the action half a world away."

Rowe bit his lip and narrowed his eyes as if struggling to interpret a foreign language.

Will turned in a slow circle, scanning the majestic scene around them. "If this place came with internet access, I'd say it was perfect."

Morgan laughed as Rowe quietly worked the saddle straps.

"Imagine trying to explain the internet to someone from here, Morgan."

"I suppose it would be as difficult as trying to describe the view from up here to a blind man," Morgan said.

"What is this place anyway, Rowe?" Will asked.

"It's an outpost camp. The caretaker is an old man who has maintained the cabin for nearly fifty years."

"Where's he now?"

"Retracing our steps to ensure our passage is hidden."

"Speaking of our steps," Will asked, "what's on today's agenda?"

"We will ride into the valley and head north. If Bremer decided to heed my call, he would be coming from that direction."

"When I asked Dench about Bremer, he didn't seem to like him very much," Will said.

"I did not like him much either," Rowe said, adjusting a saddle.

Morgan contemplated Rowe's reaction. "Sounds like there's some history there. When was the last time you saw him?"

"Five years ago."

"A lot can happen in five years," Will said.

Rowe finished tightening the final saddle. "A lot *has* happened. I only hope none of the rumors are true."

Morgan sensed the tension in Rowe's voice and changed the subject. "Were those clothes on the table inside for me?"

"Riding garments, compliments of Gloriana."

"I'd best go change."

"Please do, because she would have my head if you were forced to ride in a dress."

After Morgan had gone inside the cabin, Will joined Rowe, greeting each horse as they lowered their heads. It seemed normal to Will even though he knew nothing of horses.

"Riverwind seems especially fond of you," Rowe said, "but Morgan will be riding her. This one is yours."

"Guess we have a lot of riding ahead of us."

"We do," Rowe said. "How was your lesson with Dench?"

"Good. He's a great teacher. I wish he were here. And Ruint."

"As do I."

"I'm sorry about Ellywick too, Rowe. I wish I knew what to say."

"He will be missed, but his wisdom lives with us."

The cabin door creaked again. Morgan stepped from the porch wearing a pair of black riding breeches made from a tightly woven fabric. They looked soft and warm, with a slight stretch to them. A thin, long-sleeved white undergarment was visible beneath a forest-green tunic. Tall brown leather boots with a low heel were buckled at the sides below her knees.

A gentle breeze swept her hair to the side and exposed her neck. She shivered and wrapped a leather riding cloak across her chest.

"Looks…uh, looks like we're ready." Rowe's voice nearly cracked. "I suggest we set off now and stop to eat when we get off the mountain."

The trio rode in silence in the shadows of towering rock bluffs, following an old wagon trail down through tight switchbacks carved through rolling fields. Colorful wildflowers sprinkled the alpine meadows. Like a trail guide, Rowe named them: red paintbrushes, golden flame's eye, and purple wolfsbane. Morgan appeared to soak it all in, but Will shifted constantly in his saddle, wishing he had his morning coffee.

"The Crow's Nest is on the other side of that ridge," Rowe said as they neared the giant fir trees. "We're heading in the opposite direction. With luck, the duke will not bother to send soldiers after us. All the same, we'll keep to the trees just in case."

Very little direct sunlight reached this part of the valley, and a dense layer of moss covered the ground like an old shag carpet. Will thought it would be a perfect place to sleep for a bit longer. His body relaxed as his mind drifted, trusting his horse to follow Morgan's.

Rowe seemed wide awake. He routinely scanned the surrounding forest and the canopy above. He was uneasy, but Will was too tired to worry about it. He ventured several glances upward but saw only the underbelly of branches that were thicker than most tree trunks back in Cochrane.

The sound of a gently flowing stream turned his attention downward as they crossed an arched stone bridge. The clear water teemed with rainbow trout meandering downstream.

By midmorning, they'd reached a thirty-foot-high rock wall

spanning the gap between a thousand-foot cliff face and a vast gorge. A wide set of stairs led up to a well-maintained wall walk protected by battlements.

Rowe slowed as they emerged from the forest into an outcropping of weathered structures. Although the wall was worn and mossy, the enormous wooden gates appeared new.

"What is this place?" Morgan asked.

"The North Crow Gate," Rowe said, "marking the northern border of the kingdom. It is the only passage in this part of the Rainia Valley between the Hillron Mountains and the Misty Gorge."

"Where is everyone?" Will asked.

"A sound question." Rowe led his mare to the wall and scowled. "This place should be manned by a regiment."

Morgan rode her mare to a clearing high above the yawning gorge that stretched into a clear, majestic vista. A river raged hundreds of feet below. Sharp ledges, breathtaking cliffs, and multi-shaded rock formations rose from the narrow gorge.

Will's horse stopped beside Rowe's with no guidance needed from Will. "What are you thinking, Rowe?"

"Things are not as they should be." Rowe urged his horse closer to the yawning gates. "We should proceed with caution as we pass through the Epping Forest."

By noon, they were pushing a steady pace through the heart of the forest. With the last of the rocky outcroppings now far behind them, they reached a prominent junction. The intersecting road was twice as wide as the one they traveled and was covered with heavily worn cobblestone. Cracked and heaved, the patchwork of stones had been overtaken by clumps of moss filling every available gap. Large sections of stone were missing altogether, while other sections were completely covered by thick grass and roots.

A six-foot, narrow block of finely chiseled stone marked the end of the trail they had been on. Without slowing, Will and Morgan followed Rowe as he led his mare past the headstone, keeping a pace that burned up the miles.

As they ventured farther from the North Crow Gate, they saw no one. Because everything was new to Will, he thought it only mildly odd. But Rowe brooded in silence as if this were highly unusual.

"I would think such a well-used road would have more traffic," Morgan said.

"Or *any* traffic," Will offered from behind.

Rowe paused. "The regular patrols have been withdrawn. I understand why the duke did such a thing, but shades, the man already has one foot soundly in his own grave. Why rush to get both feet in?"

"Do you think we'll meet up with your friend…Bremer?" Will asked.

"One cannot say. Bremer follows his own path." Rowe pulled a short piece of dried meat from a small sack in his saddlebag.

Will pointed to the nearest tree. "How high do you think that one is, Morgan?" The dark-brown trunk rose perfectly straight with not a single branch for two hundred feet.

"No idea," Morgan said. "But they're getting bigger as we go."

"I bet there's a couple hundred grand worth of lumber in there," Will mused, turning away to stop the rush of dizziness. He decided to keep his eyes on the trail.

Rowe continued to peer into the canopy. The uppermost branches formed an impenetrable layer of green, but Will saw nothing to be alarmed about.

"What are you searching for up there?" he asked.

Rowe stretched in his saddle. "We best keep moving."

"What's going on?" Morgan arched a dark eyebrow.

"Without the patrols," Rowe said in a grim tone, "the holgs will be moving soon."

"What's a holg?" Morgan asked.

"Just keep moving forward."

"So…should we go back?" Will asked.

"No turning back now, Will. Keep your hood up."

Will slipped the cowl over his head and sat high in his saddle. He was wide awake now.

"We need to break from the forest before they make it down," Rowe said. "We're three miles from the edge of the forest. We'll be safe there."

Will's knees ached as they continued at a hard pace. He tried to find a comfortable position in the saddle but could not. Unable to see clearly around him, he threw his hood back. Having fallen several lengths behind the others, he was about to call out when a sudden eruption of bone-chilling shrieks cut him off.

The horses reared. Will crashed awkwardly to the ground, grunting as his head struck a moss-covered rock. An explosion of tiny stars filled his vision, instantly followed by a painful ringing in his ears. He lay motionless, squeezing his eyes shut to help slow the spinning sensation.

As he refocused, a gray beast landed at the base of a tree not ten yards away. It resembled a giant gorilla, crouched low from the fall. Its muscular chest shook from the impact with the ground. Without hesitation, it sprang forward on powerful legs.

The creature clutched an ax with a crude stone blade in one hand and a small dented shield in the other. It bounded toward Will, piercing the air with a set of rapid, terrifying shrieks. The clanking of fragmented bits of armor filled the gaps between howling. A protruding jaw opened unnaturally wide, revealing puffy pink gums and large, sharp teeth oozing with saliva.

Will froze.

The holg was about to land on him, but his horse kicked furiously with both hind legs. One hoof struck the holg in the chest, shattering ribs, while the other hoof struck its neck. The beast hit the ground a dozen feet away, broken and lifeless.

Through bleary eyes, Will saw Morgan barely able to stay in her saddle. She shouted at the mare, but Riverwind reared again.

Rowe charged past. Several yards from Will, he drew his sword as a second holg appeared around a tree. But Rowe was too far away.

Morgan screamed as the holg's ax came down onto Will. Fortunately, in the fall from his horse, Will had become entangled in his cloak, a bungle that saved his life. The Trannalun cloak flashed a brilliant red as the protective magic woke to his need. The ax deflected off Will as if striking a rock.

With his horse at a gallop, Rowe leapt from the saddle and drove his sword into the holg's side, knocking it to the ground. He rolled once and gained his feet, then slammed a boot down on the creature's neck to pull his sword free. He jumped back, narrowly avoiding a studded club from a third holg. The crude weapon bounced off the ground with a dull thud. Before the holg could recover, Rowe kicked the weapon from its hairy hands. In the same motion, he brought his sword up, slicing through its neck in a vicious onslaught. The sudden silence that followed was nearly as shocking as the first eruption of shrieks.

Morgan regained control of Riverwind and joined Rowe, who dropped to the ground and gently lifted Will's head. Blood trickled down to Rowe's wrist as he spoke quietly. "You're all right, Will. Let's get you back in your saddle where you can rest."

Will's mare knelt, making it easier for Rowe to help Will into his saddle. Morgan reached over to take his reins as Rowe guided Will's hand to the saddle horn and one foot into the stirrup. With a heave, Rowe pushed Will's other leg over the saddle.

Morgan guided Riverwind to be tight against Will's mare. She reached down to stop him from collapsing over the other side as his horse stood.

"Lean forward and don't let go of the horn," Rowe said.

Will slumped and vomited over the side of his mare. Rowe jumped back and came around to face Morgan.

"You need to keep heading up the path and get clear of the forest."

"But what are—"

"Listen to me, Morgan. I need you to keep Will moving. It's a little more than a mile. We're so close—keep moving." He placed a hand on her leg. "You can do this, Morgan."

She clutched Will's reins, spun her horse around, and adjusted herself in the saddle to maintain a tight grip on both sets of reins. Will remained hunched over the front of his saddle as they started forward.

Morgan had to jerk the reins several times to stop Riverwind from circling around to follow Rowe's mare. By the time she had both horses back on the path, another eruption of shrieks filled the air.

"*Ya! Ya!*" Morgan shouted between staggered breaths. She kicked Riverwind's flanks, struggling to control the reins.

After a few agonizing minutes, Rowe came riding up the path behind them. Fresh blood spattered his cheeks. He slowed his horse beside Will's and reached over to pull the hood over his head. Will turned and wiped vomit from the corner of his mouth. He blinked several times, but everything looked foggy.

"Well done, Will," Rowe said. "Just keep hanging on."

"Yeah," Will managed, his tone tinny in his ears.

They slowed their pace, and Rowe stayed near Will for several strides before pulling alongside Morgan.

"We need at least a trot, Morgan. We must get him to safety. He's growing weaker."

Will made a strange burping sound, convulsed, and vomited again.

"I don't know if I can keep this pace," Morgan said, breathing heavily.

"We have no choice, Morgan."

About a hundred yards away, a holg charged forward, its fur-covered muscles shaking. Rowe reached over and placed a finger beneath Morgan's chin and gently pulled her to face him.

"There's only one, Morgan, and that's nothing to get excited about. Just keep the horses under control and follow the path."

The pounding footfalls grew louder.

Rowe spun his horse around. "I'll catch up."

Will threw up again right before Morgan kicked Riverwind's flanks. She had to fight with the reins to coax the mare in the opposite direction of Rowe's horse.

The crude path led around several trees and down a gradual slope. Will quickly lost sight of Rowe.

High-pitched sounds of metal striking metal followed a sudden eruption of shrieking. Rowe was obviously fighting more than one holg.

Morgan pressed on. The horses slowed around another bend in

the path, and Morgan had to reach out to steady Will. If he fell, it would be over for both of them.

The path led into a gully with a wide creek. They followed the water's edge to a moss-covered stone bridge. The horses' hooves clacked loudly across as they increased their pace. On the other side, the path climbed a gentle hillside.

About halfway up the embankment, the horses froze as six holgs appeared at the top of the ridge. Both horses stamped and snorted, flicking their manes as Morgan tried to maintain control. She pulled Will's mare closer to Riverwind.

"Do you think Van Halen will ever get back together?" Will's voice sounded like it belonged to someone else.

"What?"

Will stared off into the trees. "Have you heard the new live album?"

"Will, stay with me!"

"Sammy Hagar…he needs to come home. Hey, where's my phone?"

"Look at me, Will!" Morgan snapped.

Will blinked. "Give me my reins," he groaned.

He lowered his head, closed his eyes, and reached for the reins.

Morgan hesitated. "You could have a concussion. Try to stay awake."

"I have ten shots in my gun and six in the extra clip, but I can't get my eyes to focus."

"Will it kill them?" Morgan asked, heaving staggered breaths.

"I dunno, but Dave can't sing anymore."

"God, help us," Morgan whispered.

It sounded trite, but that little prayer seemed to help her relax enough to pass the reins to Will.

The holgs waited atop the ridge, flailing arms and snapping jaws. Ravenous, bulbous eyes opened wide as if the creatures were craving an impending kill. Matted gray hair stuck out from beneath fragments of dented, banded armor as they brandished various weapons. But for all the aggressive show, they were not attacking.

"Is there room between the trees?" Will mumbled as he wiped his mouth.

Morgan pushed several strands of sweaty hair from her face. "Lots. Think you can handle a gallop?"

Will nodded but wasn't confident.

"I can see a break in the trees beyond the ridgeline. We're so close."

"Can we ride along the creek and climb out of the gully ahead?"

"Yes," Morgan answered. "I think we could."

All at once, one holg was jerked back from sight. The remaining five turned and shrieked.

"What's happening?" Will asked as, one by one, the holgs fell silent.

"No idea."

"Is Rowe up there?"

All of a sudden, Rowe approached from behind them.

"No, there's Rowe!" Morgan gasped.

"Then who's up there?"

Before Rowe reached the bridge, two more holgs dropped from the trees and sprang onto the bridge.

"No idea, but we have to move!" Morgan cried.

"Draw them out to the creek so Rowe can kill them. I'll head up the path. Say a prayer for me, Morgan!"

"I will!" She slapped Riverwind on the rump, and they bolted from the path. Both holgs chased her.

Will slumped over his saddle and whispered to his mare, "Let's go."

The horse spun slightly and broke into a slow gallop.

Barely able to keep in the stirrups, and with shooting pain in his head, Will realized they were not heading up the gully as he had planned. He blinked hard several times, trying to maintain his equilibrium. To keep from falling, he pressed his knees inward but eventually slipped from the saddle.

He slammed to the ground, then lifted his face from the dirt as the sound of footfalls grew louder.

One holg must have turned from Morgan to pursue him. He knew there was little chance he would survive the next few moments.

From deep within, a gentle but commanding voice called for him to press on. Filled with a desperate need to live, Will reached back and pulled up his hood. He gripped his 1911 and braced himself.

The holg drove its club into Will's red cloak with full force, then raised its powerful arms to strike again. As it did, Will pulled the trigger.

The report brought everything in the forest to an instant standstill. The bullet struck the holg beneath its protruding snout and ricocheted off its forehead without penetrating the thick skull. At that range, the bullet would have killed a human, but the force only knocked the holg backward a few feet.

The wounded creature rose to its feet and lurched toward Will, its face a mess of blood.

Will tried to raise the gun again but was too weak to focus on his target. As his vision faded, he saw Rowe slide from his saddle and end the holg's misery with his sword.

CHAPTER 18

HAPPENCHANCE

Morgan slowed her mount and turned back to see Rowe kill one of the holgs pursuing her. She could not see Will. As Rowe chased the second holg in another direction, Morgan turned Riverwind back up the bank, hoping to find Will and whomever had killed the other holgs on the ridge. She crested the hillside and stood in her stirrups, searching the path ahead. Riverwind was sweating.

As they rounded a gigantic maple tree, Morgan pulled the reins, and Riverwind stopped.

A small, lanky-armed creature blocked their way. Less than three feet tall, it had a flat face, large flared nostrils, and a grim mouth with two small fangs on permanent display. Fragments of ratty leather covered patches of its coarse dark hair. Despite its disturbing appearance, Morgan first noticed its eyes: narrow, set close, and dark purple. They flicked to the sword at her side and narrowed further.

The creature pivoted, raised a wooden handle topped with a

spiked iron ball, and drove it into the forehead of a dying holg it was standing on.

Morgan pried her eyes from the creature. A short distance behind it stood a man dressed in black with a brace of knives buckled across his chest. Leather guards protected his bare arms, and shin guards were tightly buckled over his loose-fitting linen pants.

The small creature made a short whistling sound, drawing the man's attention, and pointed at Morgan. The man turned to face her.

Morgan couldn't flee if she wanted to. Dead holgs lay scattered across the forest floor, and their killer stood among them. Slightly shorter than Rowe, his piercing eyes burned into hers. His finely toned chest heaved, and his bald head and face dripped with sweat and blood. He quickly perused the forest with hawkish features before sheathing his slender sword and moving toward her. His face was unreadable.

Morgan sat motionless, unable to kick the horse's flanks as she desperately wanted to. The man was utterly calm despite his recent fight with so many holgs. If not for his bloodied, sweaty face, he might have been out for a leisurely afternoon stroll.

"Has your day become better, or worse?" He clutched Riverwind's bridle and stroked the mare's face.

Morgan swallowed hard, uncertain whether he was speaking to her or the horse.

He turned, and sunlight glinted off the brace of knives. "Is it so difficult a question?"

His eyes, so dark they were almost black, fell upon the hilt of her sword. His intentions were difficult to discern. Morgan was grateful he had killed the holgs, but his tone was hostile. If he wanted to steal her sword, she would rather hand it to him and flee, but she was paralyzed.

He patted the horse's cheek. "How about you, Riverwind? Has your day become better, or worse?"

Morgan exhaled a small breath. The man knew Riverwind by name, which meant he knew Rowe. But as a friend or foe?

He gave the forest a long hard scowl before returning his attention to Morgan.

"Better?" she managed with a dry mouth.

He shrugged. "Perhaps. How are you called?"

"Morgan Finley," she answered, daring to move only her lips.

"I am not familiar with that name. And that person down there with Rowe, how is he called?"

"Will Owens."

The man turned Riverwind around and led them back along the path. Morgan shivered as they passed the dead holgs, imagining what she would have ridden into if this stranger had not arrived.

"Would have been a shame to die with that sword resting comfortably in its sheath," he said.

They left the path to where Rowe was kneeling beside Will, who sat with his back against a tree, eyes closed.

"Your timing is sound, Bremer."

"And your choice of company is a curious thing, Rowe."

"How is he?" Morgan asked.

"Not good," Rowe answered. "We have to get him out of here."

"That will be difficult," Bremer said. "Been quite some time since holgs have graced the dirt. They're thirsty for blood."

"Let's get you up," Rowe said as he helped Will to his feet.

"Looks like a dog that's been beat too much," Bremer said.

Will's skin was turning pale and clammy, his eyes drawn and unfocused.

"Can we make it out to the gorge?" Rowe asked.

Bremer made a grumbling noise in his throat as he surveyed the forest. "If we scatter the horses to give the holgs something else to chase. But we'd better get to the downhill side of this—and soon!"

"There's no way Will can run," Morgan said.

"Can you walk?" Rowe asked.

Will nodded.

"Where were you headed, Rowe?" Bremer asked.

"Acttun."

Bremer's eyes widened. His short, purple-eyed companion appeared over the ridge. "Seems our time is short."

"What *is* that creature?" Morgan asked.

Bremer glared at her as if she had asked him the color of the sky.

"Not *what*, but *who*," Rowe answered. "Urk is a goblin. Not friendly, but a friend…of sorts."

The goblin pointed two fingers to his eyes, then down beyond the gully. Two fingers raised, then all four.

"They're coming down everywhere now," Bremer said.

Urk twirled a finger in the air, then disappeared over the ridge.

"Get us to the gorge, Bremer, and I'll take you into the Waerdreath," Rowe said.

Bremer offered him a sideways glance. "You have a way in?"

"Yes."

"And Raric?"

"Still there," Rowe said.

"Time to stretch these pretty legs," Bremer said as he sent the horses off with a slap.

Shrill howling and the thumping of holgs dropping throughout the forest quickly overpowered the sound of heavy galloping.

The goblin appeared in the distance, pointed, and disappeared like a wisp of smoke in a summer squall. Bremer led them down into the gully beside the shallow creek. They maintained a slow jog. With one arm around Rowe's shoulder and the other around Morgan's, Will stumbled along.

"My head's pounding, Dad," Will mumbled.

The goblin appeared at intervals, guiding Bremer's path. It moved with surprising speed, darting in and out of the trees.

The fleeing horses provided a distraction, but not for long. The holgs noticed their human riders missing and returned, seeking their favorite soft meat.

After a few hundred yards, Will convulsed. Bremer pointed to a massive hollowed-out cedar that would provide enough space for a quick break. Morgan and Rowe lowered Will so they could catch their breath. Will vomited, then crawled in next to Morgan.

"You must keep Will alive," Rowe whispered to Bremer. "He can see harvesters."

Bremer raised his bushy eyebrows, studying Will.

Morgan stepped close. "What are you gonna do?" she asked in a harsh whisper.

"Will is an important part of helping us rescue General Raric," Rowe replied.

Morgan grasped Rowe's shirt with both hands. "You can't get yourself killed!" she demanded, careful to keep her voice down. "If you think you'll run off and—"

"Stay calm, Morgan." Both Rowe and Bremer gaped at her, but Rowe's voice was steady, his piercing-blue eyes confident. "I will lead the holgs away and let you three slip over that ridge and make a break for the tree line."

"What happens if they catch you?"

"I think Rowe can run faster scared than they can hungry," Bremer said.

"We need to focus on getting Will to the gorge, Morgan. That is what's important right now. I'm going around to the other side of this tree. If need be, I'll draw them away and meet up with you as soon as I can."

He spun on his heels and disappeared around the immense tree trunk.

"My eyes," Will mumbled.

"Can you see the ground?" Morgan asked.

"Everything's blurry."

She winced. "Don't worry about it, Will. I'll lead you."

Bremer pointed ahead at Urk, who was up on the ridge waving wildly for them to follow. A group of holgs followed.

"There's too many! I have to help Rowe!" Morgan drew her sword and rushed around the tree, thinking she would only need a minute to warn Rowe and then return to help Will.

On the opposite side, she crashed into Rowe.

"Stay with Will!" Rowe snapped.

A holg dropped from a tree behind Morgan. She screamed and slashed at the creature as shrieks rose from all around.

Rowe plunged his sword into the creature's chest. "Run, Morgan!"

Morgan spun around to return to Will and Bremer, but they were already racing up the hillside, pursued by more holgs. She sprinted in the opposite direction.

"Don't let up or look back until the only sound you hear is your own breathing," Rowe called. "I'll be right behind you!"

CHAPTER 19

INTO THE MISTY GORGE

The air exploded with shrieking as the holgs advanced with stunning speed. Will convulsed again as Bremer pulled his arm over his shoulder and scrambled up the hillside after Urk. Will kept his head down, frantically trying to move his feet.

The holgs split into two groups. Some raced to cut off Bremer and Will, and the others targeted the hollowed-out cedar. Within seconds, they had cut off Morgan's path to Bremer and Will.

Bremer dropped Will and planted his feet to confront the advancing holgs. "Get to the top of the ridge and don't stop!"

Will crawled half blind up the hillside. He turned to see Bremer's blurred form drawing a sword.

The first holg to appear around the nearest tree was cut down with a blade across the throat. Without slowing, Bremer rushed past it and stabbed the one following. Urk threw a knife into the chest of the third and leapt off a stump. He drove his morning star into the back of another holg's head as it closed in on Will. Three holgs bounded in from the side, cutting off Will's escape route.

Will drew his 1911. He located the approximate direction of

the shrieks and squeezed off two quick rounds. He shoved the gun back in the holster and continued uphill without a clear picture of what was happening. The sound of growling and grunting behind him fueled his adrenaline as he scrambled forward.

While Urk continued to ward off several holgs, Bremer grabbed Will's wrist and, in a single motion, pulled him onto his shoulder and continued at a fevered pace. Bremer wheezed as pursuers gained ground with every stride. He broke from the trees and raced across a well-traveled road bordering the edge of the forest. The holgs reached the road before he had even crossed it, but Bremer surged forward despite Will's weight on his shoulders.

Scarcely aware they had broken from the trees, Will cringed as he bounced on Bremer's shoulder. They crossed the road and the dozen feet beyond at a full sprint.

"*Here we go!*" Bremer shouted.

Before Will could comprehend what Bremer was doing, his eyes flew open as gravity separated him from Bremer. Will flailed wildly as he fell over the cliff and down into the Misty Gorge.

⁂

Despite falling two hundred feet, Bremer somehow hit the water feetfirst. The impact echoed across the imposing cliffs as he plunged into the frigid waters of the Serpentine River. The icy shock was cut short by a jarring impact with the stony river bottom a dozen feet below the surface. His body crumpled, and his chin slammed into his knees. With little breath remaining, he pushed himself off the bottom and rose to the surface.

He coughed several times and spat blood, then thrust his head beneath the surface in search of Will. The boy was nowhere to be seen. Bremer floated with the current closer to shore until his feet touched the riverbed. He submerged his head again and this time caught sight of Will's bright-red cloak drifting gently along the river bottom. He kicked his feet and swam toward it.

Where he found Will, the water was not even waist deep. Bremer despaired, realizing that at this depth if the impact with the water had not killed him, smashing against the riverbed certainly would have. The garment was glowing slightly. Bremer reached down and dragged Will's motionless body over the shoals and onto the rocky shore.

Bremer dropped to his knees and pulled at the cloak, trying to untangle Will. His teeth chattered, and his shivering hands were making the simple task very difficult. The cloak was becoming warm, but Bremer untwisted the hood to see Will's face and turn him on his side. He slapped his back three times. Will coughed mouthfuls of water but failed to regain consciousness. Bremer leaned close to listen for breathing. It was steady, albeit shallow and labored.

"You look like an old cracked dish, kid," Bremer muttered.

He pulled at Will's cloak until he had it unraveled enough to wrap him properly. The cloak was now too hot to touch, which Bremer knew to be a sign that its healing magic was at work. That either of them survived the fall left Bremer feeling as if he had stepped into the kind of story that would be told for millennia.

Bremer stood slowly, massaged his aching knees, and surveyed the area. They were on a rocky shore less than twenty feet wide between the lofty cliffs and the frigid river. Only trace amounts of direct sunlight reached this area each day, and today's light had passed several hours earlier. Bremer rubbed his arms and stomped his feet.

High above the jagged shale cliffs, the holgs shook their weapons and howled in rage. As angry as they seemed, none had the courage to leave the safety of the trees and follow the humans over the edge. Instead, they shrieked in vain as Bremer lay back on the rough shore, his adrenaline slowly subsiding.

He had not been in the Misty Gorge for many years, so he gazed in wonder at the sheer rock formations walling in the Serpentine River. There were signs of slides along the shore, and the one straight across from where he sat was the reason they had survived. The narrowing of the gorge deepened the river at this precise point, adding to the eeriness: if they had splashed down a little farther in either direction, the water would have been so shallow that their shattered remains would have been fish food.

As the holgs disappeared one by one, Bremer considered his next move. Part of him wanted to leave Will, who could, in all likelihood, die before nightfall. But his instinct whispered to him that Will's journey was far from over.

A gust of southerly wind brought a pungent smell of fish, offering Bremer his answer. He had heard stories of nomads who spent two months every spring catching huge quantities of freshwater salmon from the Serpentine. They would cure the fish in crude smokers on the shore before transporting them farther downriver by boat to the city of Acttun. If Bremer could procure one of their boats, they could be on their way to Acttun in short order. He checked Will's breathing once more and left without a second thought.

Piles of deadwood were scattered around the stone smokers. Several barrel-chested men with arms thick from days of toil cut the wood into small, thin pieces. Dozens of women wearing dirty, threadbare dresses cleaned fish behind three makeshift tables. Iron shackles on their ankles limited their movement. Bremer grimaced at the stench of dead fish, but the sight of the enslaved women affirmed his decision.

He scanned the river's edge. Amid piles of fish guts were two canoes and a small rowboat. The rowboat would serve him well.

As soon as the men noticed the stranger, shouts rang out. The women cowered as nine men turned to face Bremer, raising their machetes. Without slowing or making any move for a weapon, Bremer closed in on the men.

⁂

Will stirred. The smell of rotting fish, combined with a gentle rocking motion, made his stomach churn. His pounding headache caused everything to go dark again but not before he opened one eye. His vision was blurry, but he glimpsed the edge of a small boat, the gentle ripples of a river, and, before he passed out, bloodied bodies littering the shoreline.

INTO THE TUXAN MINES

Morgan scrambled alone through the forest, longing to turn around to see Rowe and the others but knowing if she slowed down, the holgs would be on her in seconds. A minute later, Rowe caught up and passed her. He took the lead, guiding them carefully through the trees.

"Holgs are quick for short distances," Rowe explained between breaths. "But they lack endurance."

They ran up one side of the gully and back down the other before settling along the edge of the creek for several miles. The sound of the holgs grew sporadic, but Rowe maintained their fast pace.

Running had always come naturally to Morgan, and here the air was so clean her energy seemed inexhaustible. Every breath invigorated her. Neither the sword on her hip nor the unfamiliar clothing slowed her.

As one minute tumbled into the next, she prayed for Will but wondered how he and Bremer could have survived.

They broke through the trees and Rowe reduced his pace. The

shrieking continued behind them, but it was distant and scattered, so they eased into a fast walk.

They came upon the ruins of some ancient stone dwellings. The roofs of the stark structures had decayed into nothingness, and thick green moss covered the crumbling walls. Larger structures materialized around them like frozen ghosts. At their feet, a low mist weaved slowly over the centuries-old cobblestone between them and the stone walls. It reminded Morgan of the hike into the Arden Forest.

Faint, indiscernible sounds whispered in the mist for a fleeting moment. Morgan looked at Rowe, but he either ignored them or didn't notice. After a moment, the sounds returned: children playing, wagons rustling, people working. It was none of them and all of them at the same time.

"Rowe, did you hear—"

Rowe held up a hand to silence her. He stood motionless under the remains of a giant archway at the entrance to a small coliseum. Most of the arch had collapsed centuries ago, but the massive pillars remained.

"See these marks, Morgan?" Rowe pointed to an image of what looked like three linked fishing hooks etched into a pillar. "It is the Mark of Natas. His influence is spreading."

Rowe entered the coliseum ruins, leading the way down a set of broken steps between a stone seating area. At the bottom, they crossed a large open field. Again, Morgan heard the whispers on the wind, but this time, they were mixed with the sounds of battle. At the far end of the field, Rowe led them through a tall tunnel and out onto another cobblestone street. In the distance, the holgs' howling intensified.

They jogged down a narrow street surrounded by two-story stone structures and turned down a smaller lane that led to a village square. At one time, it was probably a prominent marketplace, but now fallen walls and statues lay crumbled on the uneven cobblestone.

At the center of the square was a large rectangular platform rising several feet above a dilapidated ornamental fountain. The statue that once graced the fountain now lay in pieces.

Rowe stopped in front of the platform. Without hesitation, he pushed on one section while reaching over and pressing his fingers into a narrow crack. He applied steady pressure and held his breath. There was a loud click, and the platform shifted to reveal a hidden staircase. A rush of stale air rose from the darkness. Morgan stepped back and covered her nose. Beyond the first few steps and a myriad of spiderwebs, the narrow passage disappeared far below the surface.

Morgan pressed against Rowe to settle her jittery nerves. The whispers in the old village had subsided, but the holgs sounded like they were gaining on them. "Where does this lead?"

"Down into a series of caverns," Rowe said. "We need to get away from the forest and stay off the main roads for a while. The caverns lead north to Acttun where we will meet up with Will and Bremer."

"So, you believe they're still alive?"

Rowe stared at her. "This entire time you thought them dead?"

"I could only imagine…"

"I'm sorry, Morgan, I had no idea." He placed a hand on her shoulder. "I have no doubt we will find them in Acttun waiting impatiently for us."

Morgan loosened her grip on Rowe's shirt and exhaled, but her relief was short-lived. The holgs shrieked again, and her muscles tensed. "Will those things follow us down?"

Rowe withdrew the sunstone from his pocket. "They will never find this passage. Holgs avoid human dwellings—even abandoned villages where spirits may linger."

"I don't blame them for staying clear of this place."

Rowe drew his sword and cut away the shroud of spiderwebs from the tunnel entrance. He took her hand, and they descended the stone stairs. The final step sank into the floor, triggering a mechanism that closed the opening above.

In the silence, Rowe led the way through the pungent, crudely cut passage that barely accommodated one person.

"I still can't imagine how they could've made it," Morgan said, trying to settle the feeling that everything was closing in on her.

"I suspect Will is sipping from a mug of dwarven ale if he has any taste at all." Rowe turned to offer a heartening smile. "Before this journey is over, we will see and do things we will ponder the rest of our days."

After a few hours, they emerged from the first narrow passage into a massive cavern. They followed a series of switchbacks down, then crossed a small stream over a narrow stone bridge. A gap in the rock led them into another cavern.

They rested here for a drink from Rowe's waterskin and a light snack from Morgan's backpack.

"Did you see the way Will's horse came to his aid in the forest?" Morgan asked.

"I've never seen anything like it, nor am I certain of its significance."

"Do you think it has to do with the horse in his dream?"

"It is possible, Morgan. I suspect we will have our answer soon enough."

They crossed the second cavern and came to a series of tall, rocky outcroppings where the path ascended again. Rowe stopped in front of a jagged wall. He traced his hands across the uneven surface. When he found a prominent crack, he followed it down to where it opened large enough to get a hand inside.

"There's an iron handle inside this crack." He twisted his wrist, then gave a hard pull. Something clicked loudly, and a narrow section of the wall opened wide enough for one person to pass through. "We are beneath the Chicora Mountains. This is a secondary entrance into the Tuxan Mines. Once inside, we need to keep quiet and travel quickly."

"Why do we need to be quiet? Does someone live down here?"

"The dwarf nation of Tuxan once inhabited these mountains. Over the centuries, their mining quest pushed them deeper into the mountains. No one has seen the dwarves for about eighty years."

"Where'd they go?"

"Deeper, is the accepted theory, although no one has ever found any evidence."

"How many were there?"

"Between thirty-five and forty thousand."

Morgan gaped as Rowe explained.

"When their massive subterranean city became vacant, various races moved in. Some came hoping to find vast piles of gold mined by the dwarves, while others came in search of a secluded place to hide from the reach of man. Few survived in such barrenness. I have passed through the mines on two occasions."

He placed a hand on her shoulder. "This section is narrow, but if we move quickly and quietly, we will be through in short order."

Morgan stared at the ground, searching within herself for the courage to continue. She failed to find an ample supply and realized she had to trust Rowe. "All right, Rowe," she whispered.

He stepped through the crack, and she followed. A dank, bone-chilling wind greeted them. Together, they pushed the secret door closed, and the latch clicked.

They were in a narrow, low tunnel, forced to walk hunched over, which quickly strained their backs and necks. After several minutes, they reached a junction with two options. The passages were identical, with smooth floors and rough walls and ceilings. Rowe didn't pause at this junction or at the fifteen similar ones that followed as they crept deeper into the mountains.

When Morgan thought she could go no farther, Rowe stopped. She was relieved to see a smile on his face.

"Let's take a moment to rest," he suggested. "How is your back?"

"Good," she lied.

"They were not accommodating to those of taller stature." Rowe sat and stretched his back. "They did this in case the mines were breached. Most of their enemies were taller, so by the time the fighting started, they would be half crippled. Each of those tunnels we passed branches off into a labyrinth designed to render trespassers fatally lost. One could walk for days, but there's only one correct way through."

"And this is where you tell me we're right on course?"

Rowe nodded. "Not far ahead, the tunnel opens into what was once the heart of the Tuxan kingdom. Unfortunately, we need to pass through it without the light; current residents do not take kindly to visitors."

Morgan's heart beat faster. "Have you done it in the dark before?"

"That is the only way I have done it. Once we pass through the city, we can use the sunstone again."

Morgan shook her head. "How do you know all this?"

"Some say I read too much." Rowe smiled. "I have committed

the map to memory. A steady pace will have us through the area in two hours."

He wrapped the sunstone, and darkness covered them like a heavy blanket. Morgan gasped. Rowe held one of her hands as she clutched his cloak with the other. Since her eyes were useless in the darkness, she closed them tightly. With each step, she trusted Rowe to lead them through the unknown, to see what she could not.

The air grew colder and more humid. "We have just crossed the threshold into the ancient city."

Immediately, a strange humming vibration started. "There's the familiar droning," Rowe said. "The first time I heard it, I didn't understand what it was. Only after days of careful contemplation did I realize it is the sound of production. Someone, somewhere deep, is working."

Before Rowe's next step hit the smooth stone floor, the air exploded with bright flashes. He stumbled back into Morgan, shielding his eyes.

Morgan cried out and tripped. Rowe pulled her to her feet before she had any idea what had happened and put his lips against her ear.

"We've just triggered a trap that gave away our location," he whispered.

Within seconds, dancing rays revealed glimpses of statues, archways, parapets, and intricate scenes carved into the smooth rock. There was no visible light source.

Beautiful stone bridges stretching over the street flickered in and out of view, each one joining rows of large buildings several stories high. Morgan gaped at the sheer enormity of the city.

"It's more than I had imagined," Rowe breathed. "But we cannot stop and study now." He took Morgan's hand and ran between a set of pillars larger than the trees of the Epping Forest.

The smooth stone buildings reflected the light, creating the illusion of movement all around. As they passed between the pillars, something darted between the shadows to their right. Rowe gripped Morgan's hand and sprinted down the street. Seconds later, something struck him from the side, sending him sprawling through an arch and down a flight of stone steps. He rolled to a stop and turned to point at Morgan. "Behind you!"

Morgan ducked to avoid the swing of a dark, furry arm.

A large humanoid beast stepped into the dancing glow of light. It stood over seven feet tall on massive legs and cloven hooves. Two curved horns stretched to either side of its giant bull's head. Its hulking torso heaved in and out. Enormous teeth and savage red-glowing eyes flashed as the creature examined Morgan briefly before taking the steps, three at a time, down toward Rowe. For something so large, it moved with ease.

"*Morgan!*" Rowe shouted. "The tunnel's straight ahead! *Go!*"

She stared, gape-mouthed.

"Morgan!"

She tried to run but couldn't move. "M-minotaur?"

Rowe drew his sword, which seemed inadequate to fight the creature bearing down on him with ruthless abandon.

Another minotaur emerged from the deep shadows, blocking Morgan's escape. She drew her sword.

The first beast slowed, eyeing Rowe's blade.

Rowe's head whipped back and forth between the two creatures as if trying to decide which one to fight first. The second minotaur hesitated, stamping the stony ground as it watched Rowe. Apparently, Morgan was less of a threat. But the first minotaur lowered its head and charged forward with a surprising burst of speed.

"All right!" Rowe snapped. "You first!"

He waited until the last moment before sidestepping the charging beast. Blood squirted from a deep cut across the side of its neck. But as the creature passed, its whiplike tail slashed Rowe's face, snapping his head back. Somehow, he kept his footing. The minotaur dropped to one knee, then collapsed as its life bled onto the floor. Rowe touched his face, but the tail had not broken skin.

The second minotaur was in motion, and two curved horns charged toward Rowe.

Morgan shouted his name as Rowe rushed forward to meet the second attack. The impact would have crushed every bone in his body, but Rowe shouted a strange battle cry and jerked the edge of his cloak to cover himself.

The creature roared its own battle cry before contacting the Trannalun cloak. Brilliant-red streamers exploded from the garment. The minotaur let out a bone-jarring grunt, slamming into the cloak as if hitting the side of a mountain. One horn shattered, and a deep gash opened across its brow. It stumbled backward and its legs buckled. Rowe brought his sword up in a broad sweeping motion, opening the creature's chest.

A third minotaur chased Morgan around a giant pillar, gaining ground with every stride. After seeing the attacks on Rowe, she dared not attempt a duel.

"Run, Morgan!" Rowe raced up the steps, and when he reached the top, the creature chasing Morgan turned on him. Another appeared from the shadows.

The first charged, cutting off Rowe. The other attacked from the side. Pounding hooves and deeps grunts filled the air. Rowe would not have time to fight both. The creatures lowered their great sloping heads. Rowe cursed. He dropped to his knees and drove the hilt of his sword down onto the stone street.

A single spark erupted from the hilt and flew up the length of the blade before arcing from the tip into two bolts of pure energy. Rowe's body flew several yards backward as lightning surged from the blade, striking the two minotaurs before their glowing eyes closed. Deep wounds covered their smoking carcasses.

With a weary groan, Rowe gained his knees, then his feet. He fell back twice before cursing.

"Mor-*Morgan*!" Rowe shouted, but before he could move toward her, a hulking mass of wet fur dropped between them with a hideous squishing sound.

Morgan jumped back and raised her sword, but the blood-soaked and bone-pierced mound didn't move. Before she could identify the mangled body, two more minotaurs emerged from the shadows. They were identical to the ones Rowe had slain, but these stood motionless, eyeing their dead companion.

A strange breeze blew Morgan's hair back, and her breath caught in her throat. A flash of movement drew her attention upward, and an immense form dropped from the darkness.

Morgan and Rowe stumbled back as a radiant silvery-white dragon landed on a minotaur, crushing it like an ant.

The remaining minotaur turned and ran, hoofbeats clacking across the stone floor.

The dragon reared. It tracked the fleeing creature with its ice-blue eyes, then drew in a raspy breath and shot its gigantic neck forward. Morgan expected a blast of fire, but nothing exited the dragon's mouth. Even so, the fleeing minotaur let out a terrible grunt as its body crashed against a wall.

Morgan stayed seated on the ground, gaping at the magnificent fairy-tale creature. The scale-covered body was a monochromatic mosaic in countless shades of white. The great beast lowered its large catlike legs to the ground as if ready to pounce. Powerful talons etched the stone floor with a terrible grating sound. Enormous wings were now folded tightly at its sides. The dragon lowered its head toward Rowe, revealing a giant tooth-riddled mouth topped with rows of small horns stretching over its narrow head and down the length of its neck. Two gaping nostrils flared as its eyes narrowed.

"Sage," came a powerful female voice resonating with an authority that would cause the most valiant king to quake. Her eyes narrowed further as her nostrils sniffed twice.

"Ah, so you recognize me?" the dragon said, moving so close that her protruding teeth must have filled Rowe's vision. He shifted his feet, but his legs failed him, and he fell to his knees. The dragon raised her head, allowing him space to breathe.

"A-Alyssa?" Rowe said.

The dragon nodded.

"Y-you—you have…" Rowe stuttered.

"Returned to the Fourwinds," she said with a gentle nod.

"To keep Natas on the periphery?"

"There is understanding in you, Rowe of the Nest."

"You know my name?"

"I have sat for countless hours in the Records of Time. Sometimes to read, sometimes to observe."

"But…how is that possible?"

"Many things are possible, things that you will never understand. Like what you see before you."

The dragon lifted her head further and flashed her intimidating teeth. Her voice was kind, but Morgan was having trouble separating images of fire-breathing monsters in books and movies from the creature standing before her.

Rowe must have noticed Morgan trembling. "Morgan!" he blurted. "Are you all right?"

"Fear not," Alyssa said. "She is under my care."

Rowe sighed, but Morgan could only stare in silence.

"This is the Ice Dragon, Morgan. Don't be afraid."

The dragon's head bobbed. "You travel with intriguing company, Rowe of the Nest. Had you known Morgan in her world, you would think so all the more." The dragon's eyes sparkled. "And my son whom I love…" She trailed off.

"I knew he was your kin," Rowe said.

"The pain he has endured…" Her voice softened. "How I longed to stay with him."

"But had you not returned, Natas would have destroyed us all."

"Even so, I ache every day for my son."

"He is becoming a mighty force."

Alyssa drew in a long breath. "Yet the journey ahead will be difficult for him—for all of you."

Morgan's mind reeled as she struggled to follow the conversation and understand who they were talking about. She watched and listened in still and silent wonder.

"Will you not go to him now?" Rowe asked.

"Natas has grown too strong. Standing in the gap is more onerous than ever for me."

"Are you *unable* to go to him?"

"He is not yet ready to see me in this form, and I must remain as you see me now until we can turn the tide."

"I understand," Rowe said. "And I will fight to keep him safe with everything I am."

Her eyelids drooped, and her head sagged. "We are in the throes of foreboding changes for humankind. Here, the implements of war are steel and brute force. In Will and Morgan's time, the implements of war are subtle yet sinister and crippling. There, many people live in quiet desperation. They have lost their way and have become broken, empty vessels. It is not unlike the brilliant but evil subversion we have experienced here in the Fourwinds. We share a common enemy. Remember this, Sage: I am not the only one who can travel between our time and theirs."

"Was there nothing you could have done to prevent this evil?" Rowe winced as if regretting the question as soon as he finished asking it.

"How could I, Rowe of the Nest? They prefer their blissful life and are blind to what is coming."

"I'm so sorry. I should never have assumed—"

"It is in your nature to make such assumptions, and it is fair to speak freely with me in this place. But beyond these mountains, assumptions are dangerous." She leaned forward. "Now tell me, what would a Callum Sage be doing traveling through this place with someone from another realm?"

Morgan had the distinct impression she did not require an answer. The dragon's eyes bore into his as if reading his mind.

"The general," Alyssa said. "You plan to rescue General Raric. And your heart desires the destruction of Sidara. Perhaps to make certain she cannot complete her life's work?"

"Yes."

"It is a terrible thing that happened to Sidara all those years ago, and more terrible what she has become."

"She is an enemy of all that is good!"

Alyssa huffed. "That may be. Fortunately for you, there is one in your company who can perceive friend from foe. Trust Will's eyes. But even if you are successful in your quest, do you think the general would be of any use after the vile things that have been done to him?”

“I dearly hope so.” Rowe hung his head. “Otherwise, all may be lost.”

“You risk much on an undertaking that in all likelihood will fail. You journey to rescue what could be but a vague remnant of past glory. You attempt to destroy what may be indestructible.”

“Has Sidara completed the elixir?”

“In time, she will.”

“She must be stopped!”

“Is that what you believe?” The dragon exposed another row of teeth. “Do you believe Sidara is our real enemy?”

Rowe stared.

“I see understanding in you, Rowe of the Nest, an understanding of the dangers ahead. Yet you march on despite your insecurities and fears. I have not seen such faith in a human for many years.”

“I cannot stand to see the faces of war one more day, Alyssa. They haunt my dreams, and I feel their pain with every waking moment. I fear I have not seen the last of war.” Rowe cleared his throat. “Is our quest for the general warranted?”

“Your yoke is heavy, and your path is unclear. Yet you travel with someone who has settled in your heart, someone to share your burden. A wonderful but dangerous thing.”

“I do not understand,” Rowe said.

“The future, and sometimes the past, are not for you to understand. What would you ask of me, Rowe of the Nest?”

Rowe was quiet as if weighing his words before responding. “Could General Raric turn the tide in the war?”

“Your hope is not misguided.”

“Do you know if Will is safe?” Rowe asked.

Morgan held her breath.

"He has suffered much but is nearing Acttun even as we speak."

Rowe's sigh blended with Morgan's and echoed off the surrounding walls.

"Hear this, Sage: there is much required of me as I keep Natas at bay. It is my heart's desire to care for my son, but I cannot go to him lest all become lost. You must journey to the Waerdreath without my protection."

Rowe nodded.

"However, the iron ladder is sound if you were to approach the Waerdreath from the north."

Rowe's eyes brightened. "That is good news."

"Indeed."

"Thank you, Alyssa."

With that, two enormous wings, larger than the sails of a tall ship, spread out to form wintery-white tapestries. Despite deadly razor talons at the edges of the wings, it was one of the most beautiful sights Morgan had ever seen.

Alyssa leapt into the air, and with one great flap of her wings, then another, the dragon was soaring high above.

Brilliant flashes of light reflected off the creature, bright enough to illuminate two giant towers that Alyssa flew between. She gained speed and altitude, her wings displacing tremendous volumes of air with each flapping motion. In a matter of seconds, the Ice Dragon rounded a bend in the cavern and disappeared from sight.

CHAPTER 21

ACTTUN

Morgan shielded her eyes from the morning sun as she followed Rowe through a small opening in the rock. The brightness contrasted with the gloom of the Tuxan Mines, but she welcomed the sun with a grateful smile. She breathed the fresh air as though she'd been underwater too long.

"Where are we?" she asked.

"The foothills of the Chicora Mountains," Rowe replied. "We will need to push hard all day if we hope to reach Acttun before nightfall.

A small creek nearby provided the opportunity to wash and refresh. A half hour later, Morgan spread her cloak across the sand and sat next to Rowe to fasten her boot buckles.

"I don't understand what the Ice Dragon meant about her son. Who is he? And how will you keep him safe?"

Rowe held her gaze a moment before responding. "It is probably better that we discuss this later. But I think you have an idea."

In truth, Morgan did not. There was already so much about this place she didn't understand.

"I wish we had another hour of sleep." Morgan reclined on her cloak. "But I'm thankful to leave the mines behind. The constant darkness was one thing, but deadly minotaurs and a friendly dragon…it's a bit much for me. Unbelievable, in fact."

Rowe stretched. "Here in the Fourwinds, most people believe only in things they can see. But I have to believe there is more to life than what I see. I've experienced so many things I cannot explain in the same way I speak of things I see with my eyes."

Morgan nodded slowly. "There's so much here that doesn't line up with what I grew up believing. I'm not sure what to think about it all now."

"Do not be afraid of doubt, Morgan. It can be a strong force to strengthen who you really are, and what you truly believe."

Morgan smiled and placed a hand over his. "Thanks, Rowe. One thing I *do* see: *nothing* is as clear as it seems."

Rowe laughed softly. "And nowhere will you see that more clearly than Acttun."

After walking for hours, the trail grew warm. Morgan brushed beads of perspiration from her forehead. Rowe maintained an unrelenting pace in the heat of the midday sun.

"Are you all right, Morgan?" he asked. "You have not spoken a word for some time."

"I was thinking about Lillie…and Acttun."

They crossed a footbridge spanning a narrow stretch of the Serpentine River. "Acttun?" Rowe said. "What are you wondering?"

"I can't imagine what a city in this place will be like. We've already been through so much…" She trailed off. "Here I go doubting again, but do you really think Bremer and Will are there?"

"Sitting at a pub, hoping we take our time." He stopped. "I won't lie to you, Morgan. The city of Acttun is unique to the Fourwinds.

People there prefer to believe in the *unseen* rather than what they see. And it has a foul history that speaks to the unbridled nature of people's arcane lusts and depraved pursuits of power."

The footpath they were on crested a hill and intersected with a narrow road. Rowe removed his cloak, rolled it up, and tucked it under his arm.

"We are coming to some outlying homesteads soon. It is best not to talk about Callum Sages and the Tuxan Mines. Eyes and ears abound even beyond the city's borders."

Morgan laughed nervously. "How about talking dragons or flying monkeys? Can we talk about those?"

A smile touched the edge of Rowe's lips. "Probably not a good idea either."

They approached a community Rowe called the Head Stone. Within minutes, they came to the first homestead. It was a simple shanty set back from the road and partially hidden behind a cluster of evergreens.

Several faces stared back at Morgan. Disturbed by the intensity of their gaze, she had to look twice before discerning five small children and one adult. Morgan could not distinguish male from female. They were all clean and fairly well groomed; each one wore similar loose-fitting clothing and short-cropped hair.

"Staring back will only draw attention," Rowe said as they passed a narrow path leading to the homestead.

"Are they…?" Morgan faltered, searching for the right words.

"Human?" Rowe asked. "Yes. Most of the people living in and around the city are human."

"Most?"

"Best to see it with your own eyes. But do not stare, and trust little of what you see. It is a…well, you will see," he said with a smirk.

She poked a stiff finger into his shoulder. "Not funny."

"I disagree."

They continued down the road in relative silence, passing a few more homesteads. Through the trees, they glimpsed the river but saw very few people. In the two hours spent on the main road to Acttun, only one wagon and three riders passed. Although they had the winding road mostly to themselves, Morgan sensed eyes watching them every step of the way.

"Do you think your friend will be in Acttun?" Morgan asked. "What was his name?"

"Gunthru," Rowe said. "If he is in Acttun, he will be easy to find."

They climbed about a hundred feet above the banks of the river, and Morgan's breath caught at the sight of the city sprawled out in the valley below.

A waterfall spilled into the valley's eastern side, and the Serpentine River snaked through the city where it joined the Whistling River. Together, the winding rivers carved the city into five islands. A hodgepodge of walkways and unique bridges connected each island. Some spans were made from giant timbers, some from stone, and others from a combination of materials. Some were painted, most were covered in art, and some even had colorful banners and tapestries hanging from them.

"Welcome to Acttun," Rowe announced.

"It's so…it's…"

"It can be overwhelming," Rowe said, raising an eyebrow. "I reacted the same way the first time my eyes took it all in."

"It's amazing. But why is that part so different?" Morgan pointed to a section of the city.

An island at the far side of the city resembled a war zone that had been bombed for days. Few walls stood taller than three feet high. It was a mess of rubble. The only part intact was a massive stone building that had an institutional feel to it. An imposing iron fence surrounded the structure. Between the fence and the building was a courtyard of waist-high grass and shrubs, some of which were well on their way to becoming trees.

"That's the asylum." Rowe put a hand on her shoulder and gently pulled her away. "I will tell you more about it later."

Apart from the desolate island, most buildings were at least two stories tall. Murals abounded, tapestries flowed, and flags flew. Despite the color and creativity, everything was incongruous as if multiple architects had competed for the city's most unique design award. Morgan wondered if there had been a citywide paint explosion.

"The more you stare, the harder it becomes to look away," Rowe said.

They walked several paces before Morgan pried her eyes from the city. The road jogged to the left away from the valley and then down sharply. With every step, the sounds of the city came alive, but like the architecture, the sounds also lacked harmony.

"Remember, Morgan: it is a city of magic. There will be fortune-tellers, seers, wielders, warlocks, magicians, sorcerers, wizards, and many others—all in close quarters. Some work on the streets, but others will try to draw you in. They will use different approaches, but they all want to know your secrets." Rowe stopped. "You must be wary. Keep your eyes lowered and do not respond to anything or anyone. If you can keep your curiosity in check, we will go about our business as we would in any other city."

Morgan stole another peek at the city.

"Oddly enough, once you learn to ignore their eyes, most people are friendly."

Morgan studied him. "So, this city isn't part of the kingdom?"

"It is the only human city that is not. Kings have tried to draw them in but to no avail. The other option would be military action, but forcing a city without a garrison to bow to a king is never a good idea. Especially if the city produces nothing—no taxes, no exports, no industry, and no leadership or hierarchy."

"What do the people do for work?" Morgan asked.

"You will see."

Only one way down into the valley existed, a narrow road carved into the bank of the hillside. Had Morgan not witnessed a wagon's descent into Acttun, she would have never have believed the feat possible. The wagoner guided two powerful horses around a series of tight turns and forced Morgan and Rowe against the bank. The wagon's wheels came to the edge of the steep drop on the other side. Despite the treacherous descent, the wagoner had the wherewithal to eye them both suspiciously. Morgan self-consciously pulled her cloak a little tighter and gazed at her feet. With her sword tucked beneath the folds of her cloak, she waited for the wagon to make the next turn before raising her head.

Morgan pulled her cloak around her neck. "Why do I feel… violated?"

"They cannot take what you do not offer," Rowe said.

"Are you sure about that?"

He smiled. "Absolutely."

He walked to the edge of the road and wiped his sweaty forehead with his sleeve. Morgan followed his gaze down into the valley.

The road made one final switchback before reaching the Whistling River. A large bridge topped with a massive timber sign held up by two giant pillars marked the entrance to the city. The last time Rowe had traveled beneath the timber, the word *Acttun* was burned into it. Now, the Mark of Natas obscured the letters.

Morgan gasped. On either side of the sign hung a dead body. One was decomposed and most of the flesh had been picked away. What remained of the person's hair was falling in clumps. It was covered in filth and dried blood, but the Trannalun cloak was unmistakable.

Rowe stared at the body, but Morgan had to look away. "Gunthru," he sighed.

Morgan held her stomach.

"How many have succumbed to the same fate?" Rowe spoke quietly. "This explains why no one answered my summons."

The second body was less than two days dead. A few crows fought for morsels of flesh hanging from the fattened figure.

Rowe wondered aloud as they approached the bridge: "What would a bard be doing in Acttun?"

"How do you know he was a bard?" Morgan asked.

"I can tell by his clothing. Golden hooks hang from the front of a many-pocketed vest designed to carry various objects such as notepads, small instruments, and exotic tobaccos. And there's a faint imprint of a shoulder strap that once carried a mandolin—a bard's favorite instrument."

He turned to Morgan and lowered his voice. "These people do not like foreigners, and bards are drifters by nature, always following their next song. They are outsiders no matter where they travel, but they are usually welcomed—and even sought after—for the wonderful tales they weave into their melodious songs. But in Acttun, those qualities can get a person killed."

"Apparently." Morgan's voice cracked, and she swallowed hard. She followed Rowe past the bodies, resisting the urge to vomit.

At the far end of the bridge sat a small, thick-spectacled man behind a table. A woman stood in front of the table and nodded when the man waved her forward. Morgan expected Rowe to walk up to the table, so she drifted toward it until his hand slid over hers.

"Names and citizenship?" the aged man snapped impatiently as if he had been interviewing refugees all day. Rowe led Morgan past the table without a word.

"Be you deaf?" croaked the man with an undeniable air of authority. "Names and citizenship!"

Morgan tightened her grip, but Rowe rubbed his thumb across the back of her hand. Without acknowledging the man, they walked past the table and entered the city.

The road led them between two giant stables alive with activity. Men were leading horses in or out while others carried saddles to and from the stalls. A small group of older men were oiling and repairing saddles on the racks lining the wall beneath a low over-hanging roof. Four men with pitchforks unloaded the hay wagon that had passed Rowe and Morgan on the road in. Everyone knew their place and was working with sleeves rolled up. Some men whistled a tune, and a few sang along quietly. Others chatted as they worked, but everyone was clearly enjoying the warm evening. Those who noticed the two strangers bowed slightly at Rowe and cast appraising looks at Morgan.

"Do you remember when I told you that everyone in this town wants to know your secrets?" Rowe asked under his breath.

Morgan leaned in.

"That is what the man on the bridge was trying to do. They will try many ploys to start a conversation. Once you engage them, many will use dark magic to help learn what they can without you even realizing what is happening. Since we ignored him, the man assumed we either live in the city or we come here often enough to know better. This is how we will deal with most people who speak to us."

Morgan released his hand and locked her arm around his. He tensed but eased into step with her. It was some time before her breathing slowed and she could swallow again.

Beyond the stables, the dirt road gave way to cobblestone and soon they reached a Y in the road. Two bridges stretched across the river to diverse sections of town. Rowe followed the stone bridge to the right. A massive arch with strange symbols burned into it spanned the width of the far end of the bridge. Morgan could not read the script, nor could she see any pillars holding up the arch, as if it were floating fifteen feet above the bridge deck.

"This section of the city is predominantly inhabited by spell casters," Rowe explained. "The magic resonates close to the surface here, so be careful."

"About what?" Morgan pulled her hood over her head.

"You will see," Rowe answered.

Morgan rolled her eyes, pressing closer as they crossed midspan.

"Do not touch the hilt of your sword until we pass through this part of the city," Rowe said as they approached the arch.

Morgan raised an eyebrow. "Let me guess: I'll see?"

As they passed beneath the arch, a jolt of electricity shot through Morgan, giving her body a start. Her sword vibrated, absorbing the brunt of the force. She looked around but could not locate the source of the energy. The air was charged, calling the hairs on her arms to attention.

"It's all right, Morgan. It will not harm you."

Tiny sparks arced from her sword's hilt, reminding her to listen to Rowe's warning against touching it. Morgan heard—and felt—a strange humming sound throbbing in her ears. Rowe led her onward.

"What *is* this place?" she breathed.

"Another unique part of Acttun. We will be through it soon."

A myriad of tiny shocks, strange and sensual, raced through Morgan's body with every step. She wanted more than anything to leave this place, but the city was spellbinding.

After about four blocks, the street narrowed. Two-story stone buildings lined both sides, joined so closely, it was hard to see where one ended and another began. Faces peered out of wood-shuttered windows, curious and captivating, but Morgan averted her eyes. An intersecting street opened to a market crowded with people clothed in colorful flowing robes, wide bright sashes, and accenting belts. Everyone, young and old, had waist-length hair tied back with vividly colored braids, ribbons, and kerchiefs.

The architecture was vaguely familiar to Morgan. Interlocking blocks and small roofs above the windows reminded her of something she had seen somewhere else. But she had trouble focusing. The air sparked around her, distorting her senses. It was electrifying and exhilarating yet somehow wrong.

"The mines," she muttered.

"What about them?" Rowe asked.

"The buildings here are similar to the ones we saw in the mines," she said, focusing on each word as she spoke.

Rowe smiled. "You heed the details—something few people

know how to do these days. These buildings were designed by the same dwarves who built the ones we saw in the mines."

"Will we be seeing any dwarves here?"

"Not likely. The ones who did much of the stonework in this city were slaves."

"Slaves?"

Rowe waited until they passed a small crowd walking in the opposite direction. "It happened three hundred years ago during a terrible civil war that almost caused the demise of the dwarves. It was a dark period in their history, and in ours."

They passed a dozen large-wheeled carts buckling under the weight of an assortment of trinkets. Morgan paused at one or two carts, but Rowe kept her moving.

They turned down a narrow path between two tall buildings and crossed a footbridge. The moment they stepped off the bridge, everything changed. The sparks, the crackling energy, and the drowning hum all ended as quickly as they had begun. Morgan stopped midstride in the intensity of the stillness.

"It all just… Did you feel that?" She was relieved but disappointed.

Before Rowe could answer, she inhaled rich fragrances, making her stomach grumble. "That smells wonderful!"

Rowe breathed in the aromas. "We have entered the part of the city known as Nullac, home of the alchemists. One nice thing about alchemists is their ability to cook."

Morgan breathed in hints of spices, herbs, and ingredients she could not even begin to process. The buildings here were unique too; they were all timber framed and smaller than the stone buildings designed by the dwarves. But they were similar in that the Mark of Natas remained above many of the doors.

The people in Nullac were unique. Instead of brightly colored clothing, the local fashion favored modest, hooded robes in various shades of brown. They all went about their business with little regard for others. Morgan and Rowe must have appeared so peculiar to these people. Fortunately, everyone ignored them.

"Ready for a hot meal?" Rowe asked as they turned down an intersecting street.

"Is there anything I need to know before we eat?"

"Not this time, Morgan. The Cauldron's Stew is a simple inn. I have eaten there many times, never disappointed."

"Good, because I don't think I've ever been this hungry."

"We are almost there. We'll follow the river and then pass a few more streets."

They rounded another corner, and the street widened into a round open-air market. Carts were stationed like permanent fixtures against the buildings while robed patrons walked quietly from one to another. In the buildings behind the carts, shops with narrow doorways and no windows supplied vendors with an endless supply of goods. This market was less crowded than the others, and much quieter. Some vendor carts displayed fruits and vegetables, but most carried jars of every conceivable shape and size. Some jars were smoking, and others bubbled and churned. The colors and smells were as foreign to Morgan as everything else in this city.

The market stretched down to the riverside. Across the dark waters stood a group of people with shaved heads, various body piercings, and tattoos of detailed runes. Ink covered their exposed skin. Most of the people were barefoot and bare chested, wearing baggy canvas pants cut raggedly below the knees.

"Don't take me there, Rowe," Morgan said under her breath.

"Not to worry."

"What are they?"

"Sorcerers. Outsiders are not welcomed there."

Farther along the river, between the two shores, was an island surrounded by a soft green glow. The land was barely large enough to accommodate its only building: a single structure made of stone and wood with no visible doors or windows.

"What is that?" she asked.

Rowe was silent. She wondered whether he had heard her question until she noticed the warning in his eyes.

"That is the home of Marlay Bonicle."

CHAPTER 22

THE CAULDRON'S STEW

Morgan and Rowe walked in silence along the river past a few more narrow side streets. Morgan wanted to ask Rowe about the home of Marlay Bonicle, but she knew he would say more in his own good time. She was experiencing information overload anyway, and her growling stomach made it difficult to think about anything beyond the promise of a hot meal.

Minutes later, the waiting ended, and Rowe stopped at a large building with a sign that read *The Cauldron's Stew*. The letters were burned into a thick tree branch growing through the wall above the large entryway.

"That's strange," Rowe mumbled.

Morgan followed his gaze, noticing this doorway did not have the Mark across the top. But Rowe was reading a bulletin hanging on the wall that read: *The Bard's Yarn is canceled tonight and tomorrow night. Refunds at the bar!*

"What's a Bard's Yarn?" she asked.

"Bards sing their tales in hostelries like this one all over the Fourwinds," Rowe explained. "The problem is that bards pen from experience. Since Acttun is a city that protects its secrets, I never thought I would see the day one was hired to perform in *this* city."

Morgan followed Rowe through the narrow doorway and was surprised by the size of the room. From outside, the building appeared small and insignificant. Inside, however, it opened into a massive dining area with over thirty well-ordered tables and a large, elevated stage in the far corner. A long bar spanned the entire length of the far wall, its countertop carved from a single tree. Several tiny branches sprouted from the bar, and Morgan realized it was alive. Nutshells crunched beneath their feet as they crossed the wide-planked floor.

A barrel-chested brute of a man burst through the kitchen door. He dropped a splintered keg onto the bar and slid it down the well-buffed surface. Three barmaids busied themselves with wiping everything down, careful not to get in the man's way. Another man emerged, bald with bushy eyebrows and tiny nests of hair in each ear. Almost seven feet tall, his arms were the size of most men's legs. He dropped two racks of mugs onto the bar and returned through the swinging door. A barmaid unloaded the racks.

A second swinging door slammed open several feet away, and another barmaid entered carrying a giant round tray covered with four plates piled high with steaming food. She glided across the nutshell-covered floor and set the tray on an empty table. Four people were chatting together at the table next to it, and she began serving the dishes to them. Three more groups occupied other tables, but not one person acknowledged Rowe and Morgan as they entered.

Morgan followed Rowe to a table off to the side. Old weapons hung on the walls like relics from another time. She wanted to examine them, but Rowe quickly sat down with his back to the room. Morgan thought it strange he would not want a full view of the room but realized he had positioned himself next to a large metal shield on the wall that provided a clear reflection of the room behind him.

Morgan sat next to him as the barmaid with the round tray headed straight for Rowe.

"Rowe, lad? That really you?" the barmaid asked in a raspy voice. Her wrinkles deepened, and her eyes sparkled.

"How is it you look younger every time I come in here?" Rowe said.

She croaked something so fast that Morgan missed it, but Rowe laughed.

"This is Morgan. Morgan, this is my dear friend Meagan."

Both women smiled politely as Rowe continued. "How's the big man?"

Meagan let out a huff. "In a foul mood."

"Anything to do with the bard?"

Meagan huffed again and sat down so heavily that Morgan expected the chair to collapse. "That fool of a man brought a bard in by the name of Silvin Tao. I warned him, Rowe, but filling this place is a never-ending burden, so he made a contract for two nights. Silvin was supposed to arrive this morning, but instead he showed up two days ago. I had gone over the contract with him in Bealwitch. I had made it clear what needed to happen in order for this venture to be successful. But the moment he arrived… well, you know the way people gather around bards. Conversations started, and one thing led to another."

"How could you expect a bard to not speak with the locals?" Rowe asked. "That would be like asking your man not to eat meat."

"You know how stubborn that innkeeper can be, Rowe. He

insisted we try, so I did my best." Meagan sighed, wiping her forehead with a dishcloth. "For a while, I caught myself thinking it might work. We sold out both nights and were considering extending the contract an extra night."

"Should I ask what happened?"

"When Silvan arrived early, I knew I had made a mistake. I offered to relieve him of his obligations and sneak him out of the city. But he would have none of that. I turned my back for two minutes, and he was gone. At first, I thought he'd gone up to his room, but he had left the inn. He decided he needed to write a song about Acttun." Meagan's eyes reflected genuine pity. "He couldn't help himself."

"What happened?" Morgan blurted. "Did someone kill him?"

"His body is hanging at the entrance," Rowe answered.

Morgan gasped, but the old woman merely sighed again. "I'll have one of the boys go cut him down after dark."

"They killed him?" Morgan said.

"Well…" Meagan answered, tilting her head toward the inn-keeper as he reemerged with another keg. "*He* did."

Rowe nodded as Meagan continued. "He had no choice, but still… He's many things, but the big man is no killer. They would never have let the bard leave the city with his song. Since we held the contract, it was our responsibility. If he hadn't killed him, someone else would have, and this place would have been burned to the ground, and we…" She trailed off, shuddering.

"But—" Morgan managed before Rowe cut her off.

"Better that the big man did it instead of an angry mob."

Meagan leaned forward, looking into Rowe's eyes. "It's good to see you, Rowe." She stood abruptly and tapped the table twice with her knuckles. "Now, then, what can I get you two?"

The evening meal did not disappoint: mutton, roast potatoes, and greens—all covered in a rich blend of unforgettable apricot-and-rapeseed sauce. After finishing a tall goblet of delectable mushroom wine, Morgan relaxed enough to begin taking it all in.

Lanterns were lit throughout the Cauldron's Stew as the evening sky grew dark. The workday had ended, and a steady flow of patrons were entering the pub. More than half the tables were now occupied. Intoxicating smells from the generous platters being served permeated the room. There was not a vacant spot at the bar where four barmaids cracked kegs and filled mugs as fast as they could serve them up.

Morgan tried not to stare at each person who entered, but the diversity was captivating. Not all the patrons were wearing the local heavy brown robes. Some were spell casters, and even a few sorcerers had donned attire suitable for an evening among the masses. There were others Morgan had not seen on the streets on their way through the city. One group wore tight-fitting red suits that looked like a blend of fine leather and tightly woven wool. These were the most boisterous, and even this early in the evening, it was clear they were heavy drinkers.

Rowe enjoyed a long pull of his favorite golden gnomish ale and followed her gaze. "Those are cosmic decriers."

"You mind explaining that?" Morgan let out a slight giggle followed by an unexpected burp that led to another giggle.

Rowe laughed. "They derive their power from alternate planes of existence. They say some can even tap into multiple universes."

"Well, that about clears things right up." Morgan gave him a wry smile and leaned back.

With all the noise and people moving about, Morgan and Rowe were free to keep to themselves without much worry of a confrontation. Meagan reappeared to replace Rowe's mug of ale and provide another goblet for Morgan, but this one was filled with water. She whispered something in Rowe's ear and tapped the table three more times before leaving.

"What was that about?" Morgan asked.

"Will arrived the day before yesterday. He's in a room upstairs."

Morgan sat up straight. "What! When can we see him?"

"Whenever you are ready."

She gulped down her water and slid the goblet into the center of the table. "I'm ready."

Rowe stood and stretched. "Follow me."

As they crossed the room, Morgan noticed Rowe making eye contact with Meagan as they climbed the stairs. He leaned close. "She'll be watching to see who might follow us."

At the top of the stairs, they followed the hallway to the end and turned right down a dimly lit corridor of closed doors. When they reached the end, Rowe turned and peered back down the corridor.

"When this door opens," he whispered, "you need to go straight in before saying anything."

She nodded as he knelt and slid something under the door. A moment later, the door flew open, and Will stood before them.

"Will—" Morgan said before Rowe clasped a hand over her mouth and pushed her inside.

The door closed, and Will stepped forward for a brief but warm embrace. "Man, it's good to see you, Morgan!" He grinned and laughed as he held her at arm's length. "Bremer told me you two would make it through the forest, but I couldn't see how!"

Will turned and hugged Rowe. "I thought I was stuck here alone with Bremer!"

"But how did you…?" Morgan began. "The last time I saw

you, the holgs were everywhere! And you were blabbing something about Sammy Hagar and Van Halen."

"Hmmm…I don't remember that part. But apparently Bremer threw us both over the cliff into the Misty Gorge. I vaguely remember tumbling and a few other fragmented bits and pieces before I woke up here last night."

"Are you well?" Rowe asked.

"Pretty much. Bremer has had a steady flow of people in here making me eat this and drink that. I've had a full-body massage with oil that left my skin tingling something ferocious. I've had people rubbing stuff beneath my nose and even spent the night with some kind of gel covering my eyes. I have a bit of a headache, but my vision returned to normal this morning and the dizzy spells are pretty much gone."

"That's incredible!" Morgan said. "I expected you to be laid up for days if not weeks."

"Bremer sure seems to know the right doctors—or *healers*, as he calls them."

"Do you have your cloak?" Rowe asked.

"It's under the bed." Will pointed to one of the two bunk beds.

Rowe was staring at Will. "Went over into the gorge, did you? What about that weapon of yours?"

Will rubbed his hands together. "It's wrapped in my cloak."

"You must have dropped almost two hundred feet," Rowe said.

"Crazy, eh?"

"How has Bremer been?" Rowe stood by the window and opened a heavy curtain slightly. He peered out, then closed the curtain tight.

"That's a strange dude," Will replied as he and Morgan sat at a small table. "He came in this morning and asked me to keep watch at that window until I spotted a harvester. He sat there staring at me. The streets were so crowded, but after about two hours, I saw one. The moment I pointed it out, Bremer left."

"Did he say anything to you?" Rowe asked.

"No."

"Have you eaten?" Morgan asked.

"A few hours ago, a woman named Meagan brought me some of the best soup I've ever had." Will scratched his head. "Boy, it's good to see you two."

A hint of a smile crossed Rowe's lips, but he was less enthusiastic than Will and Morgan. "Can I trust you both to remain until I return?"

"No way I'm going anywhere," Will said. "I've seen quite enough from that window."

"Where are you going, Rowe?" Morgan asked.

"To talk to Bremer." He paused before opening the door. "I'll be back shortly. Lock the door, but feel free to open the curtains if you would like to see more of the city."

"Not on your life," Will said. "Bremer told me if he caught me looking out the window, he'd return my eyes to me once we left Acttun—and I believe him!"

Rowe grinned as he left and closed the door behind him.

Morgan rose to lock the door. "Have you seen the sorcerers, Will?"

Will nodded. "I've seen two or three walk past. Bremer explained a few things to me, at least."

"There's an entire section of the city where they live."

Will raised an eyebrow. "I don't think I'll ever get used to this place."

"Oh, you haven't seen the half of it." Morgan sat on the bottom bunk across from the one Will had slept on and unlaced her riding boots. She tugged them off, then climbed to the upper bunk.

"It feels so good to talk," Will said. "Bremer doesn't say much."

Morgan leaned over the side of the bed. "Well, I've got some stories for you. We traveled through caverns deep beneath some mountains, and Rowe had a conversation with a dragon that saved us from a group of creatures that looked like minotaurs. Short of that, this place isn't all that different from Cochrane."

Will gaped at her.

"I'm not kidding, Will."

Rowe returned to the pub and found the same small table Meagan had kept vacant despite the growing crowd. Taking a seat, he leaned back and quietly studied the room.

Meagan appeared with a fresh mug of gnomish ale. "I suspect he'll be here soon," she said.

It was not until Rowe approached the bottom of his second mug that Bremer stepped through the doorway. A hush fell over the crowd as the rogue scanned the room. Rowe knew his old friend was setting out the order in which he would eliminate threats should the need arise.

To Bremer's right stood a stunning young woman wearing a brilliant-white semitransparent gown. Her skin appeared to have been rarely kissed by the sun, and her hair was a fiery red. To his left stood another woman with short raven-black hair. A collage of tattoos covered her neck. She wore a dark-blue cloak that opened in a large V at the front, giving those brave enough to stare a vista they would carry to the grave.

Rowe caught Bremer's eye, and the rogue whispered something

to both girls. He gave them each a gentle pat, and they climbed the stairs. Almost every set of eyes in the pub followed them as Bremer slipped out the front door.

Rowe finished his mug, slipped two coins onto the table, and waited for a few people to stumble out before he left the building. Outside, he turned sharply left and then left again. He found Bremer sitting alone in the shadows of an eatery that had closed for the night.

"You were not dealing me false iron," Bremer said. "But I do not understand. I have enlisted the aid of formidable wielders to no avail. Yet here is a lad with no magic or training who can see what others cannot."

Rowe sat on the cobblestone next to him. "Perhaps it is not for us to understand."

Bremer gently scratched fresh stitches on the back of his neck. Rowe recognized the wounds immediately; harvesters were all claws and talons.

"What does this change?" Bremer asked.

"I would argue it changes everything. We can travel freely now."

"I've always traveled freely."

"Not like this."

Bremer glared, and Rowe was thankful their history ran deep.

Rowe stood. "I am going to the Waerdreath, Bremer, to rescue the general and put an end to Sidara's destructive ways. You would be a welcome addition."

Without another word, Rowe returned to the Cauldron's Stew.

<hr>

The room was dark. All was quiet except for the heavy breathing of Will and Morgan as they slept. Rowe sat up and rubbed his eyes after only a few hours of sleep. He pushed the warm covers aside and pulled on his pants. The bed creaked as Morgan turned in the upper bunk, but she continued her steady breathing. Rowe grabbed his shirt from a chair and left the room in his bare feet.

The smell of ale lingered in the unlit hostelry. Bremer sat in the shadows at a corner table. Rowe quietly crossed the room, stepping between swept-up piles of nutshells.

"Morning." Rowe sat across from Bremer, who was finishing a plate of eggs.

Bremer spoke with his mouth half full. "I have news: the western gate has fallen. They will not hold the bridge for long."

"The Bull River." Rowe rubbed his temple with his fingertips. "It will be a devastating loss to the Iron Lord. How will he defend Hammerclaw now?"

Bremer kept his head down and shoveled another scoop of eggs into his mouth.

"I have learned that Sidara is on her way to personally oversee the final assault against Hammerclaw," Rowe continued. "Rumor has it she has a weapon that will make short work of the stronghold."

"So, that's why you want to kill her and rescue our good general?"

"War is a persistent plague, Bremer. But a weapon capable of annihilating an entire race must be destroyed."

"How long before Sidara reaches the bridge?"

"A few days."

Bremer lowered his fork. "Forsaken the Crow's Nest, have you? If they succeed at Hammerclaw, they will continue to the Rainia Valley."

"The Histories are sound."

"For now. Have you told our two new friends everything about Sidara?"

"No."

"Do you *plan* on telling them?"

"I do."

Bremer brushed the back of his hand across his mouth. "Well, I wouldn't worry too much about it. Sidara made her choices and there can be no undoing them now. Speaking of which, I wonder if she plans on sending her forces to Acttun?"

"That would be a bold move. If Marlay Bonicle decided to leave his island fortress, well, who's to say what would happen?"

"I wonder if our play queen up north has heard about the attack on Hammerclaw," Bremer said.

"The High Queen of Dwenlin Thah is certainly aware."

Bremer pushed his plate away and wiped his mouth with a large cloth. "That family has brought this on themselves."

"True. But imagine if all our transgressions brought about this sort of carnage."

Bremer idly picked up the knife from the table, tested the edge with his thumb, then set it on his plate. "Maybe they do."

Rowe stared at Bremer, waiting for him to say more, but he changed the subject.

"And what of the Shadowfallen?"

Rowe sighed. "Uluk remains in the west destroying everything in sight. Sidara has extended his leash. It would not surprise me if she eventually grants him full command of her entire army."

"If Sidara intends to attack Dwenlin Thah, an army under Uluk's command would be unstoppable. Shades! He leads his brigades for days out of the way only to level small villages."

Rowe turned his gaze to the front window. A trace of morning light seeped through the dirty glass panes. "Dark days await the Fourwinds."

"Darker, you mean." Bremer yawned. "I best get some sleep. Those two little kittens played havoc with me."

Rowe sighed. "Haven't changed much."

Will felt more refreshed than he had in weeks. He released a contented sigh, realizing the last of his headaches had subsided. Morgan lay fast asleep. He wondered if she was dreaming of home as he had.

Rowe's bed was empty. Will suspected he was off somewhere preparing for the next leg of their journey. He wondered if Bremer would join them. That thought brought a mix of emotions. The man had single-handedly killed dozens of holgs and saved Will's life, but even so, the rogue terrified him. At times, Bremer watched him with penetrating eyes; it unnerved Will to no end.

Morgan poked her head over the edge of the top bunk. "Whatcha thinkin'?"

"My headache's gone." Will yawned. "Totally gone. I slept the entire night and even dreamed of home."

"No black horse or waterfalls?"

"Nothin'."

"Do you think the dreams are gone, or are you feeling better about things?"

"No idea, but I know my head's clearer than it's been in years. I feel good about being here. I feel positive, hopeful."

"That's encouraging to hear, Will. I was worried about you. Having your life threatened sure helps you appreciate what you have." Morgan pointed to a small bowl of fruit next to the bed and inhaled. "That smells delicious."

"Those green ones are as sweet as strawberries," Will said. "And that sliced red fruit sorta tastes like cantaloupe. The other ones are a little on the tangy side and quite filling."

"You're becoming a local," Morgan said, reaching down for a piece of green fruit.

"It's certainly a different way of life here."

Morgan bit into the fruit. "A place you'd like to visit, or stay?"

"Who knows? I never thought I'd ever say this, but as much as I wanted to leave Cochrane, I miss it."

"Imagine how different it would be to live here? There's something about getting back to basics. If it wasn't for…" She trailed off.

"An evil Dark Queen?" Will suggested. "And holgs and harvesters?"

"Not to mention witches, sorcerers, dragons, casualties of war, and who knows what else lies ahead?"

Will chuckled, but his laugh faded almost immediately. "If Rowe has his way, I suspect we'll soon find out."

Morgan left the room for a bath, and Will lay in bed, staring at the narrow gap in the curtains. He was tempted to peek at the busy street below but remembered Bremer's warning. He rolled over, hoping today would be different because cabin fever had already settled in. As far as he was concerned, they couldn't leave Acttun soon enough.

He must have drifted off to sleep again because, the next thing he knew, Morgan was back in the room drying her hair.

Rowe had also returned. His eyes were drawn and dark-circled as he nodded a wordless greeting to both of them. He flopped into a plush chair.

"There is something you both need to hear," he said.

Will sat up. "That doesn't sound good."

"Morgan, you remember the small island we passed yesterday, the one with the dwelling void of windows and doors?"

She nodded nervously.

"That is the home of a wizard named Marlay Bonicle," Rowe explained. "Many years ago, he and his brother, Addolay, operated the Academy. Students came from all over the Fourwinds to study magic under the two most prominent fellows alive.

"One day, a student arrived, and although she was only six years old, they all knew she was special. So measured and filled with understanding was she that Addolay brought her into his inner circle for…*advanced tutelage*—or so he said. In truth, he had singled her out for nefarious purposes.

"Almost five years later, Marlay discovered the vile things his brother had been doing to the child. Their confrontation lasted several days. Brother against brother, the magic they unleashed against one another destroyed the Academy and most of the island. In the end, Marlay had proven the stronger, but even after killing his brother, he could not live with the grief of what Addolay had done to the child. And so Marlay shut himself away on the island and has never been seen since."

"That's…that's awful, Rowe," Morgan said. "Did he…was he able to help the child?"

"I am afraid not. She ran away. Some say she ran into the arms of Natas."

"What do *you* think?" Will asked.

"I believe it to be true," Rowe said.

"I thought you said Natas was a creature of myth?" Morgan asked.

Rowe was quiet, studying their faces. He exhaled. "The young girl's name was—"

"*Sidara*," Will breathed.

Rowe bobbed his head. "It is a terrible thing that happened to Sidara. Some Callum Sages tried to help, but they were not well received, to say the least. We all have choices to make, and she has made some dreadful ones."

Will stood and ran a hand through his hair. "Not like the good choices *we* would have made had those things happened to any of us."

"Will, I have spent many hours contemplating what she has become. I cannot express the sorrow I feel for her. But she needs to be stopped. At this point, I cannot see how that is possible without—"

"Without *murdering* her," Will interrupted.

Rowe held Will's gaze but didn't deny Will's blunt statement.

Morgan stepped between them. "Rowe, you made it sound like, like...I don't know, but it's terrible what happened to her. Why didn't you tell us earlier?"

"Because he wasn't sure if we would be so keen on killing someone with that kind of past," Will suggested.

Rowe leaned forward and sighed. "There is something you should know about Callum Sages," Rowe said. "I should not assume you know more about our history than you do. I'm sorry.

"The first Sages were followers of a man named Callum who lived when the Fourwinds formed after the breaking of the old world. Callum had the favor of the kings and lobbied for better conditions for orphans, helping many find new families. He taught people sustainable ways to care for others. He stood strong against vile creatures that had the power to take a dash of evil in the smallest child and manipulate it until it consumed their innocence."

Rowe's voice softened. "Although we live in violent times, it is not within my power to decide who should live and who should die. I have tried to imagine a way to help Sidara, but we are dealing with someone determined to destroy two worlds."

"I know there's a war going on," Morgan said. "But I can't help thinking there was a time when Sidara was an innocent victim like Lillie. Even if Lillie grew to become an evil witch, I would have a hard time killing her."

"I apologize for not being forthright about Sidara's roots. I have always hoped she would remember her past and stop this madness." Rowe straightened in the chair. "But the fact remains that she has already developed a powerful weapon to use against the city of Hammerclaw. And now, she is close to unleashing that elixir she calls Phyriad. If ending her life is the only way to stop the war and destruction, what choice do I have?" He paused. "Although Raric may know a better way."

"Won't rescuing the general be pointless if Sidara unleashes Phyriad?" Will asked.

"If we can free General Raric, I am holding to the hope that he will lead us to the restoration of peace. But hope is an unpredictable friend that does not come around often these days."

A knock at the door cut Rowe short. "Speaking of…" He rose and pulled the door open.

Bremer strolled in and sat in the chair Rowe had been sitting in. He lifted his legs and thumped his boots on the small table as he leaned back with his hands behind his head.

"Is there agreement?" he asked.

"About *what?*" Will asked.

"Not what but *who*," Bremer said.

"Wow. Just like that, eh?"

Bremer scowled at him.

Will sat in a small wooden chair. "I wonder what *your* life would be like if you'd walked in her shoes as a child!"

Bremer was on his feet as fast as a snapping dog. Had Rowe not stepped in front of him, Will might have found himself concussed again.

"He is without understanding, Bremer," Rowe said.

Bremer stopped his advance and looked past Rowe to where Will cowered in the chair. The electrified air lingered for a moment before Bremer stepped back.

"That came out all wrong," Will said, still holding up his hands in defense. "It's just…I can't imagine what I would have turned into had I walked a mile in her shoes as a child."

"We all have choices to make in life," Rowe said. "The most heinous act done to a child cannot determine an evil course for one's life. In the same way, the kindest act cannot guarantee a child will grow up to be good. We choose our responses to evil and good. Sidara has made her choice."

"As I've made mine." Bremer sat down and folded his arms.

Will cleared his throat and swallowed hard. "I understand we all have choices to make, but if it hadn't been for Joe and Morgan showing up one day…well, I had been planning to kill myself."

Morgan gasped. "*What?*"

"I couldn't handle it anymore," Will continued. "Losing my parents, the intense loneliness of being an outcast in my own community, seeing strange creatures no one else could see… I'd given up. I thought I could make things better by making lots of money and leaving Cochrane. But the kind words of a friend changed everything."

Morgan sniffled. "I—I never knew that, Will."

"I had a choice to make, and I almost made the wrong one.

Sure, my life was nothing compared to what Sidara endured as a child, but I think unfortunate events and the unkindness of others reduced the odds of me making good choices. The simple kindness of friends made the difference for me."

"What are you suggesting, Will?" Rowe asked.

"I'm not sure." Will slouched in the chair. "But we're talking about killing someone as though we're talking about killing a harvester. Sidara is not an evil creature. No matter what she's become, something inside me feels sorry for her. I don't know, but can we at least acknowledge she's a human being and that life dealt her a bad hand?"

Bremer frowned at Rowe. "He is indeed without understanding."

"My dad used to say that violence breeds violence," Morgan said. "And that the cycle of vengeance never ends."

Will nodded slowly. "You're right. Back in our world, Rowe, there are wars that have been going on for generations. We've tried everything to stop the cycle: bigger, smarter bombs; better-trained forces; drones; spies; propaganda; fear." He looked at Morgan. "We've tried everything except forgiveness."

"I do not understand how forgiveness will help in our current plight," Rowe said. "I would be surprised if Sidara even *desires* forgiveness."

"I don't understand it either," Will said. "But I think that unless a person's heart changes, you'll always have enemies and war. And you'll keep making wrong choices." He shrugged. "Maybe the path to peace starts with forgiveness."

Rowe opened his mouth to respond, but Will interrupted.

"You guys believe Natas is behind everything, right? What if Sidara had a change of heart?"

Bremer huffed. "That would make ending this war a lot easier.

We could march into the Waerdreath, give Sidara a hug, rescue the general, join armies, and destroy Natas." He glowered at Will. "*That's* your plan?"

"All I'm saying is, maybe Sidara is not our real enemy." Will flashed a brief smile at Bremer. "Besides, have you ever received a hug at the right time?"

"I'll give her a hug, but only to get close enough to get a knife into her." Bremer glanced darkly at Rowe.

"*Not our real enemy.*" Rowe was staring at Will. "That's the second time someone has suggested that to me."

CHAPTER 23

TRAVELS

The next morning, Will and Morgan conversed alone in their room before the small flickering fireplace. Rowe must have lit the fire while they slept, but when they awoke, his bunk was empty once again. Will wasn't surprised to see him gone, but he had hoped Morgan might sleep longer. She didn't have as much time to recover as he had. Regardless, he was grateful for her company.

"It's hard," he said, stretching his legs. "I mean, how could a person with so much anger and hate ever change?"

"Lord knows," Morgan said. "My dad used to preach that anyone can change, that it's never too late…" Her eyes glistened as she stared at the floor.

Will remained quiet, remembering the beast her father had transformed into. Was it too late for him to change?

Morgan sniffed and lifted her head. "Whatever happens to Sidara, I'm committed to helping Rowe rescue the general. Anything beyond that…well, let's just say I'll be praying like I've never prayed."

"Think it'll help?"

Morgan stared at the ceiling. "It's what my family does. I often wonder how much my faith impacts situations like this. I mean, does it really change things or just influence my responses and choices?"

"And?"

"I dunno, but the way you defended Sidara last night seems more in line with what Dad used to preach about forgiveness. And you're..." She stopped herself.

"A heathen?" Will chuckled. "I was only saying what I thought, Morgan. And remember, it was *your* choice to be kind to me that started all this. So, don't question your upbringing too much. I was up half the night thinking about what Sidara's childhood must have been like."

"I think Rowe waited to tell us the full story because we needed to see more of this place before making up our minds. Imagine the pressure he feels."

"Yeah, I guess he has the weight of *two* worlds on his shoulders," Will agreed. "Do you think that magic potion she created is powerful enough to kill so many people?"

"If it does what they say, I can't see how humanity could survive that kind of pandemic."

"Have you ever read *The Stand* by Stephen King?"

"No, but I've heard of it."

"It's about a virus that's accidentally released from a military lab. The virus kills almost the entire population of the world."

Morgan stared at him. "That's terrifying."

"It was just a story, but what if it could really happen?" Will stretched his back. "That's why I'm committed to helping Rowe stop Sidara too."

Within the hour, Will and Morgan sat in the otherwise empty pub, finishing their breakfast. Will shivered and rubbed his arms. The room was chilly, but it looked worse outside.

Rowe stepped through the front door, shaking the rain from his cloak.

"Meagan just went into the kitchen," Morgan said as he sat down.

"Already ate," Rowe mumbled.

"When do we leave?" Will asked.

Rowe's face softened. "You are with me, then?" He exhaled slowly. "That is good news."

Morgan reached across the table and squeezed Rowe's hand. "I understand why you waited before telling us about Sidara. But from now on, please, no more secrets."

He hesitated for a brief moment, offering only a glance at Will before smiling at Morgan. "We are in agreement."

Thunder rattled the front window, and rain spilled over the deluged gutters in a steady waterfall. "So…are we heading out in *that* weather?" Will asked.

"I am afraid so."

Will slouched. "On horseback?"

"We cannot walk all that distance."

"It freaks me out the way they all look at me like they know me," Will said.

"Me too," Rowe said. "I suspect this is one mystery that will not be solved within the pages of the Histories but by experience. Come."

The crisp predawn air and steady rain almost persuaded Will to return to the warm, dry inn. He groaned and pulled his hood over his head. The chill subsided quickly as the magical warmth of the Trannalun cloak radiated around him. Morgan shivered and pulled up the hood of her heavy leather riding cloak.

Within twenty minutes, they crossed the main bridge and were riding out of Acttun along a mucky road that traversed a dense forest. Huge branches stretched high above the road but provided little relief from the rain. The way ahead was shrouded in misty gloom.

The three travelers trudged along as daybreak peeled back the semidarkness, revealing cheerless shades of gray. Rowe maintained a steady pace, somehow keeping his mount in the center of the road. The pace was too tedious for Will, and he found himself missing the comfort of his room in the Cauldron's Stew.

Gradually, light pierced the mist to provide a clearer view of the surrounding forest. Will raised his head, but the dark clouds looming above the trees dampened his spirits. The land was socked in by low cloud cover, and it looked as though they would spend the rest of the day in the rain.

About an hour later, a large group of people appeared through the mist. There were hundreds, all hunched over and wearing tattered clothing that provided little protection from the elements. They walked as a tight group, and soon Will understood the reason, which broke his heart. All the adults were elderly and frail but did their best to keep the children as protected as possible from the damp wind.

As they drew near, Rowe bent in his saddle to hand food down to an old man who should have been safe at home under the care of his grandchildren. Rowe kept one hand inside his cloak, and Will imagined he was gripping the hilt of his sword. After scanning the crowd, Will exhaled slowly, relieved to not see any harvesters.

Morgan threw back her hood and handed out three loaves of bread and all the dried meat in her saddlebags. She spoke to each person with a strength that surprised Will.

"Thank you, my lady," was repeated by many as they divided the food and gave it to the young.

After the crowd dissipated, Rowe picked up the pace. They continued almost due west throughout the morning, following the banks of the North Serpentine River until they reached a main junction.

"That thoroughfare leads through the Upper Plains of Ashron," Rowe announced. The straight road north disappeared behind large rolling hills dotted with rocky outcroppings. "The southern thoroughfare leads to the Lower Plains of Ashron."

The road south was narrow and congested with another large group of refugees trudging north. Without slowing, Rowe led them south, into the crowd of refugees. The road was more compact and much easier than the muddy trail they had been on all morning, yet the despondence reflected in the faces of the refugees made the journey more onerous.

Will followed Rowe as he turned his horse several yards off the narrow road through knee-high grass. A shiver ran down Will's neck and across his shoulders. It was chilling the way the refugees traveled in such silence. This group was larger than the first they had passed, and, like the first, the people traveled without wagons or horses. All their earthly possessions were in their hands or on their backs.

Rowe pressed on for several hours, leading down a narrow muddy road that cut a path through a sea of green grassy plains swaying in the gusting winds and relentless rainfall. Morgan kept her head covered against the biting wind rushing across the plains.

Will grew so accustomed to the flat scenery that when a small copse of firs came into view, it seemed oddly out of place.

Rowe brought his mare to a stop. Morgan raised her head for the first time since passing the refugees on the road. Her chin trembled. Rowe pointed to the small forest, and she sat upright.

"What is it?" she asked.

"Bremer."

Will stared at the forest but could see nothing but odd-shaped trees.

"Are you sure he's there?" Morgan asked.

Before Rowe could respond, someone stepped out from the forest to wave them over.

Rowe nudged his mare forward and motioned for Will to pull up beside him. "Is that still Bremer?"

Will trembled at the possibility of seeing a harvester in Bremer's likeness. He squinted against the rain. After a moment, he identified the person as Bremer before he disappeared back into the trees.

"What's he doing out here?" Will asked.

"Let's find out." Rowe spurred his mount into a fast trot.

He stopped at the tree line, slid from his saddle, and tied the reins to a small tree trunk. Will and Morgan followed suit, albeit slower due to cramped legs and sore backsides. They followed a path through the trees that was wide enough for a small wagon and soon reached an opening to a well-used campsite. A covered carriage was parked on the other side of the clearing. Strange red runes were inked into the wood, and dark coverings prevented any attempt to see inside.

"Sidara's emissary," Rowe hissed.

They took a few steps closer, and Will and Morgan gasped. Four headless death knights, two headless scribes, and a headless emissary lay sprawled on the ground behind the wagon. Bremer stood among the bodies, inspecting the harnesses of two massive steeds. An eighth body—a partially transformed harvester—lay dead a few feet away in the trees.

"Came upon them before dawn," Bremer said as Rowe helped secure the last buckles.

"Were they dead when you found them?" Morgan asked.

Bremer ignored her question. "I put their heads inside and was about to tie their legs to the back of the carriage before sending it back to the Waerdreath."

Will and Morgan turned away from the gruesome sight.

Rowe helped Bremer tie his victims' ankles to the carriage. "Hopefully, this message gets to the Dark Queen."

"From me to you, Sidara!" Bremer slapped a steed on the hindquarters, sending them both into a fast trot out of the trees.

"I wonder why they were heading to Acttun," Rowe said.

"The things I did to them, Rowe, and not one revealed a word of their plans."

Will stamped his feet, trying to send warmth to his numb toes. Morgan rubbed her hands together and paced around the clearing. The rain had slowed, and the trees sheltered them from the wind, but Morgan was shivering.

"I can't get my core temperature high enough to stop my teeth from chattering," she said. "And chilled nerves don't help."

"This is probably a stupid question, Rowe, but why not ride the carriage back to the Waerdreath?" Will asked.

"Sidara would know the moment we got close, if not sooner," Rowe answered. "Her magic is far-reaching."

Will stepped close to Bremer and cleared his throat. "Can I ask you a question?"

Bremer wiped his head dry with a dirty kerchief. He nodded with a piercing gaze that caused Will to reconsider.

"Um…how did you manage to kill them all *and* the harvester?"

"You wouldn't believe me if I told you," Bremer answered in a flat tone. "How can you see harvesters?"

"No idea. I first saw them a few years ago while I was playing basketball in my parent's driveway with my friend Todd."

"Do you have to summon magic?"

"Not that I'm aware of."

Bremer studied him.

"Do you enjoy killing?" Will instantly regretted the question.

Bremer's eyes flashed but softened as Will cringed. One side of Bremer's lip curled upward. "No one has ever had the stones to ask me such a question."

Will swallowed hard. "I figure if you wanted me dead, well, I'd a been pickin' carrots with a step ladder a long time ago. So, I think I will stop being so scared of you—for the time being anyway."

Bremer scowled. "How's that working out for you?"

"Not that great. I can hardly breathe right now."

Despite being nestled within the wooded encampment, the group found it difficult to defend themselves against the cold. A small fire provided a measure of heat but was hard to maintain as the rain sprinkled them throughout the night, leaving the area damp and dismal. They had hung a large canvas from the tree branches above, but it did little to shield them from the gusting wind.

Will and Rowe bundled themselves in their Trannalun cloaks, and Morgan shivered in her bedroll between them. Sometime in the night, Will peeked out to see Bremer crouched close to the fire with a steaming, wet blanket around him. Morgan's teeth were chattering. She rolled closer to Rowe, and his eyes opened. Without a word, he opened his cloak, and she slid in next to him with her back against his chest and her head resting on his arm. His other arm wrapped around her, and she disappeared beneath his cloak.

Will drifted off to the sounds of peaceful breathing and Bremer poking the crackling fire.

CHAPTER 24
SLAVE RUNNERS

Will peeked through the morning mist to see Rowe sitting alone by the fire. Morgan was slowly waking in her bedroll, and Bremer was nowhere to be seen. Will and Morgan rose and quickly packed before joining Rowe for a light breakfast from the dwindling supplies, then set out into another dreary morning ride across the plains.

They traveled with no sign of Bremer for three miserable days before catching the first break in the clouds. As the mist dissipated, a vast expanse of grasslands stretched in every direction. Rowe led them southwest toward distant rolling hills that stood in stark contrast to the pedestrian plains.

"Beyond those hills is the town of Fairbay," Rowe said, adjusting his weight in the saddle.

"Are there beds in Fairbay?" Will grumbled. "Three wet nights on the cold, hard ground is enough for me."

"Yes, they have beds."

"Elven mead?" Will pressed.

"Possibly." Rowe smiled for the first time in days. "If not, I'm certain we can find something to amuse your palate just the same."

"This isn't another crackpot place like Acttun, is it?" Will asked.

"I think you will find this village just as interesting, but in a good way." Rowe inhaled deeply. He had a distant look in his eyes as if the mere thought of the familiar town warmed his spirit. "It's a quiet fishing port on the southern shores of the Niasa Sea. It is also home to a dozen healers. I suspect they are busy tending to the injured soldiers from Hammerclaw."

"No sorcerers?" Morgan asked.

"No sorcerers."

"Good," Morgan said as she directed her mare beside Rowe's. "There's something about Acttun I've been wondering about."

Rowe cocked his head to one side as she pulled off her cloak. "Only one thing?"

Her eyes brightened. "You *do* have a sense of humor."

Rowe appeared more relaxed as she continued.

"In Acttun we saw the rubble that had once been the Academy," Morgan said. "It must have been a massive school. Next to it was an asylum that you said wasn't touched by the battle between the brothers."

Rowe nodded.

"Why was the asylum so big?" Morgan asked. "I mean…it seemed bigger than the Academy, by a long shot."

"An interesting observation," Rowe said. "The study of magic is a dangerous thing, no matter the form. It demands much of a person, and when those demands become unbearable for the wielder to satisfy, well…a person's mind can crack under the pressure."

"Are you telling me that place is full of students who cracked?"

"Yes."

"So…what's happened since the Academy was destroyed?"

"The asylum's caretakers were devout members of a sect called

Shalem priests. They lived like servants in a place most people could not tolerate more than a few minutes. The funding for the asylum came through the Academy. So, when the Academy fell, the city folk rushed in and built stone barricades against all the doorways and window openings, lest those inside escape. The Shalem priests had no choice but to remain inside with those they had pledged to care for."

Morgan closed her eyes. "How many were left to die?"

"The numbers vary depending on who you ask, but it was more than three thousand. And they might not all have died. To this day, people talk about the noises they hear coming from inside. These stories persist because the asylum has a constant water source from four deep wells, which might have helped them to create gardens for a seemingly endless food supply. But this is Acttun, and the Academy had some powerful alchemists and sorcerers. Some stories tell of more sinister methods of sustaining life."

"Ghost stories," Morgan breathed.

"Marlay Bonicle kept an office in the asylum with a massive vault attached to it. One can only imagine what he kept in such a place. There is no shortage of rumors. But in all this time, no one has set foot inside those walls—ghost stories or not."

After pressing hard for a few more hours, they approached a rocky ridgeline. Rowe stopped and shifted his head as if listening for something. A moment later, the wind carried broken fragments of sounds. Amid the confusing noise, Will heard metal ringing off metal.

They continued slowly and came to a riderless black horse.

Rowe slid from his mount. "It's Bremer's," he whispered as they drew near. "He must be up atop the ridge overlooking Fairbay."

Rowe left the path and scaled the rocky bank, trailed by Will and Morgan. Loose stones made the way difficult, and they had to use their hands to steady themselves in places where the terrain steepened near the top.

From behind a boulder, Bremer appeared and placed a finger in front of his lips to signal their silence.

Will groaned. So much for an easy entrance into a peaceful village.

They crested the ridge and crouched low, moving to the rocky outcropping where Bremer waited.

"The town's been sacked by slave runners," Bremer whispered.

"How can that be?" Rowe asked.

Bremer lowered his spyglass. "I believe I saw Onathe Wyeth by the tree line."

Rowe stood slowly and peeked over the rocks, then turned to Will and Morgan. "Stay close and keep quiet," he said. "If Onathe is here, his warding magic will be difficult to evade."

Will followed Rowe and pulled himself up on a rock for a clear view. Beyond the ridge, a large teal-blue sea stretched north almost as far as the eye could see.

"Fairbay is under attack," Rowe said.

Nestled beside a white-sand beach on the closest shore was a small port village. A ten-foot-high wall of fire spanned the entire length of the shoreline, cutting off access to the sea. Dozens of armed men moved from house to house, kicking in doors and carrying away small children. In the center of town was a growing crowd of shackled children, linked together. Their desperate cries reached the high ridge. At the southern edge of town, a row of medical tents lay in tatters around several motionless bodies.

Rowe slid down between Morgan and Bremer. His jaw flexed as he glared darkly at Bremer. "Definitely Onathe," he said.

"Are you certain?" Bremer asked.

"Absolutely."

"Who's Onathe?" Will asked.

"A dark elf," Rowe explained, spitting out the words. He buried his face in his hands. "His warding magic is always prodding the surrounding air. Shades! I don't see how we can reach him from up here without him sensing our presence."

"Then how do we get to him?" Bremer asked.

Rowe thought for a moment. "Do you have that quiver?"

Bremer rushed to his pack hidden within the rocks. He returned with a longbow and an empty quiver with dark runes inked into the leather.

"Hit him from above with a seeking arrow," Rowe said. "It might give us time to reach him before he can recover."

"That will be an interesting foot race," Bremer said.

"Why?" Will asked.

"Because if he recovers before we reach him, he will scatter our ashes to the wind," Rowe explained.

"I guess some elven mead and a bed was too much to hope for," Will muttered.

Bremer traced a finger along a particular symbol in his quiver, speaking something incoherent as he did.

"Those slave runners will take the children back to Sidara to be twisted into something terrible," Bremer said, gesturing beyond the ridge. "Still don't think she deserves to die, Will?"

"Hide your eyes." Rowe positioned himself between the quiver and the village. "My cloak should protect the quiver's magic from the dark elf's vision."

A bright flash left the quiver with a single arrow that looked like it was carved from ice.

"What is *that*?" Will asked.

"Seeking arrow," Bremer said. "The magic will direct the arrow as necessary, hopefully catching Onathe by surprise."

Will backed away and suddenly noticed that Morgan was gone.

He climbed a short rock and found her watching the unfolding horror below. The massive wall of fire on the beach was frightening, but the men ravaging the village presented a greater threat. Armed with swords, they chased children and kicked down doors. Each child they caught they shackled to a growing chain of captives. Skirmishes raged between a hodgepodge of buildings, but it was obvious the villagers were ill-equipped and untrained as they threw themselves into the fray, desperate to rescue their children.

Morgan was wide-eyed. "Rowe told me about slave runners and a small boy who once defied them. We have to do something, Will."

"Bremer and Rowe have a plan. Just wait for—"

Morgan snapped. She leapt over the rocks and ran down the steep slope toward the village.

"Morgan!" Will shouted as she disappeared over the rocks.

He was about to climb after her, but Rowe caught him by his cloak and jerked him to the ground.

Bremer sat back, raised both his feet, and braced them against his bow. Nocking the arrow, he extended his legs until the bow came close to snapping. The bowstring hummed, and the arrow flew into the sky at a sharp angle.

Rowe held Will, who was fighting to get up. "Wait!" Rowe snapped. "One more second!"

The arrow started to descend, and Bremer pounced over the ledge.

Rowe and Will followed him down the hill. As they ran, the

massive wall of fire vanished. Will followed Bremer, and Rowe chased Morgan.

Will's momentum sent him rolling a few times as he tried to keep up with Bremer's huge strides. At the foot of the hill, Bremer raced across a dirt road and into a clearing past several shanties. One sword, then a second, appeared in his hands as he sprinted toward the tree line. A hand moved in the tall grass ahead, and Bremer leaned into longer strides.

Will soon caught up as Bremer stood over a small creature that Will assumed was Onathe Wyeth. The dark elf lay in a small pool of blood. Bremer's arrow had nicked his prominent, pointed right ear before plunging into his neck. The sharp tip stuck out from his groin. The arrow would have killed anyone else, but Onathe showed his magical power by stopping the bleeding and forcing the arrow out.

The elf glared at Bremer. His mouth moved, but his dark lips fashioned no words. He raised one arm in front of his face as Bremer's first blade whistled down. Onathe's forearm sparked as if a magical force field prevented the blade from cutting through the bone, but it could not ward off the second blade that severed his arm at the elbow.

Bremer shouted a vicious battle cry and brought his blades up and down again in a blur, this time directed at the dark elf's neck. Will shielded his eyes from the dazzling sparks as Onathe's magical defense flashed with every strike.

"Now, Will!" Bremer shouted.

Terrified of what would happen if the elf—who was somehow still alive—started fighting back, Will did the only thing he could think of. He whipped his cloak to the side, drew his 1911, and stepped clear of Bremer's unfaltering assault. The shaking barrel pointed at the dark elf's exposed head. Will wavered, afraid to pull the trigger yet terrified not to. He aimed, closed his eyes, and squeezed.

The bullet blew a hole in the dark elf's high cheekbone. Bremer jumped back, and Will stumbled and tripped over something.

Bremer tugged his ear and blinked hard, trying to recover from the gun's blast. He slashed his sword down again. This time, Onathe's magic was not enough to repel the blade.

Bremer let out a satisfied huff as a rare smile spread across his weary face. A sheen of sweat covered his head.

"Over six hundred years old," he panted. "The most feared dark elf ever to walk the Fourwinds, dead at my feet!"

Will stared at a longbow in his hands.

Bremer ceased his gloating. "Where did you get that?"

"I…I tripped over it."

"That was Onathe's longbow. It was carved from bloodwood hundreds of years ago."

"It's…it's magnificent." Will found it difficult to take his eyes off the weapon. The bow was an aged burnt-orange color with detailed bright-red scrolls etched into the wood. If the markings were actual letters or words, they were unlike any language Will had ever seen.

Bremer stepped closer. "That string is fashioned from the mane of Thaudas, the infamous winged unicorn. That's the part you can see; imagine what sort of magic was used in its creation."

Will shuddered at the headless elf lying a few feet from him. Although he didn't understand what Bremer was talking about, he knew they had just killed something evil.

Rowe stopped running when he heard Morgan's scream. He knew at once it was not a scream of fear but a battle cry. He had to find her.

As he ran between two small cabins, Rowe bowled over an old man before he could break out into the open street. He caught the man before he fell, noticing he was probably close to eighty years old. The man stood in front of a group of seven young children, brandishing an old fishing knife.

"Easy, old friend, I'm here to help," Rowe said. "Take them inside until we're done."

Two slave runners appeared behind the children.

Rowe stepped out from between the buildings, his sword flashing in the late-afternoon sun. The first slave runner was a brute with a morning star, but before he could raise it to attack, his fingers were cut free from his hand. Rowe's sword came around a second time, cutting the brute's throat wide. Without slowing, Rowe lunged forward as the second slave runner swung his crude, rusted sword. Rowe's blade shattered the feeble weapon and followed through, opening the man's chest.

The last of the seven children disappeared into a cabin as the old man held the door. Rowe nodded to the man and dashed between two cabins, responding to another of Morgan's battle cries.

***

In the center of the village was a large open-air market lined with empty carts and tables. Three narrow streets opened into the market, providing the perfect staging area for the slave runners. They only needed to guard two streets because any possible escape toward the sea was blocked by Onathe's wall of fire. This once-peaceful village had been easily sacked.

Morgan reached the market and saw the screaming, shackled

children. Some were barely old enough to walk. She rushed forward, heedless of the gang of slave runners.

The first man to see her drew his short, dented sword and stepped forward, grinning at the striking young woman coming his way. His smile revealed chipped, rotting teeth as he brought his sword up, preparing to knock the sword from her hands.

Morgan ran at him with her sword in attack position, gaining momentum. The man took a few nervous steps backward. Morgan's arm snapped forward as she launched into a flying lunge at his chest. He parried a heartbeat too late as her blade disappeared into his chest to the hilt, driving him back several yards. A final shove sent him tumbling awkwardly onto his back, drawing the attention of sixteen slave runners in the market.

"What are you doing?" Morgan screamed. "They're just kids!"

The slave runners glanced around the market, and Morgan realized they had her trapped. Weapons—from maces to morning stars—flashed, but before anyone could move, Morgan closed the distance with two extended strides and attacked the nearest man. He raised a tall wooden handle topped with a spiked iron ball, trying to block her sword as it came whistling down. Coursing with magic, Morgan's blade easily sliced through the handle, opening his face in a terrible bloodletting.

Morgan sidestepped to avoid another iron ball at the end of a short chain. She brought her sword down at a sharp angle and caught her attacker high in the shoulder. His arm hit the ground, hand still clutching the weapon.

A few quick strides carried her to the middle of a line of about three dozen children shackled together at the wrists. Their frantic eyes stared at her as though she were their last hope in this world.

The slave runners formed a semicircle around Morgan. She

struggled to catch her breath. There were too many to fight alone. She glanced at her sword, knowing it had already done extraordinary things. Adrenaline surged within her, stronger than at any championship tournament, as if it were magic infused. It threatened to overwhelm her, but she had an intense desire to expend the energy. She lunged.

The blade hummed, and the dry ground whipped up in front of her. Each slave runner's head snapped back as dirt flew into their eyes. Morgan cried out and almost dropped the sword. She longed to control it, but it was as if the magic had a will of its own.

Momentarily blinded, the men stumbled backward, failing to notice the dangerous man behind them. Four fell dead at Rowe's sword. His powerful blade cut another slave runner in half and then buried itself into another. Stabbing one in the throat with his long knife, Rowe kicked another's legs out from under him, followed by a quick jab to the chest.

The other slave runners cleared dust from their eyes to see what was happening. Panic erupted. Those able to stand scattered, but two more died as Rowe pursued the survivors into the village.

Morgan dropped to her knees and removed a heavy iron key ring from the belt of a dying slave runner. As her heart rate slowed, she fumbled with the first shackle before noticing the child's skin. It was nearly translucent with a tint that reminded her of the teal waters of the Niasa Sea. She gazed at the boy's eyes, which were soft and blue as a glacial lake. She wiped her eyes, leaned back, and stared at the long row of children. One in five had features similar to hers, but the rest had teal skin and brilliant-blue eyes.

As Will examined Onathe's bow and Bremer rummaged through the dark elf's possessions, forty of the meanest, wildest-looking men Will had ever seen approached from the main village road. Most carried swords, and a few called out Onathe's name. Will's heart sank. If this brute squad was looking for their master, they were about to be disappointed and angry.

Bremer rose to his feet. "Go through those trees, circle around by the beach, and find Rowe."

Will stared at him.

"They are thugs, Will. Nothing more. Now go, so I don't have to worry about you."

"But—but what happens if I don't find Rowe in time?"

"In time for what?"

"To help you."

Bremer laughed. "I don't want you to bring him back; I want you out of here! If I needed help against this lot, well, I suppose I wouldn't be *me*."

He grabbed Will by the shoulders, turned him in the direction of the village, and pushed him into motion.

Will ran to the trees and turned to see Bremer reach down and grab a handful of the dark elf's hair before going out to meet the advancing mob. Will hid behind a bush. He knew he'd be useless in a fight against so many, but he couldn't leave Bremer alone.

The slave runners slowed to an unsteady halt.

Bremer strolled out from the long grass to the road and tossed Onathe's head. It stopped rolling a few feet in front of them. There was no mistaking their recognition.

"That who you're looking for?" Bremer adjusted a sword at his back, keeping the hilt below his belt. Sunlight hit the brace of knives across his midsection and reflected back into the anxious mob. "Seems your day has taken a turn for the worse," he added.

He reached behind his back and pulled out a small round piece of wood. He twirled it over his palm while sliding a short, flat knife from the brace.

"Bold words," growled an older slave runner. "Ayne here has heard it all." He pointed back to a bear of a man as a short knife slammed into Ayne's throat. Blood splattered as he choked and tumbled backward.

"I would say Ayne has heard his *last*," Bremer said.

He twisted the round piece of ash in his hand, and the wood expanded into a five-foot staff with thin curved blades extending from both ends. With all eyes on Ayne's dead body, Bremer slid the staff over his shoulder and strode into the crowd. He spun once, then twice, sending the staff out in a blinding arc. The sweeping violence was precise, cutting deep across the back of three necks before cutting a head off altogether. Bremer drove his feet down to stop his spin as he brought the staff over his head and around to his side before snapping it forward, burying it deep into flesh.

Those closest to him tried to scatter. More bodies hit the ground while Bremer spun low on the ball of his foot. He raised his staff sharply, slicing a chin in two before the trailing end of the staff carved a chest plate in half. Blood sprayed across the victim's face.

Bremer shifted sideways to avoid a flying mace and a sword. Two men threw their weapons and joined several others running in various directions. Bremer dove, somersaulting over three of them, striking two dead before landing in a crouch. He spun again and severed the back of an ankle. A spiked iron ball whooshed over his head. He ducked to avoid another sword, then snapped the staff up between the legs of the sword-bearer. Kicking the legs out from beneath the one holding the mace, Bremer stabbed both men with the ends of his staff.

Bremer moved with fatal finesse as the thugs pressed against him en masse. He elbowed someone behind him, crushing his nose to create space before spinning around to block a sword. He spun back again to deflect a spear that shattered in two by the force of his parry. The staff shot out, killing the one holding the broken spear as the remaining thugs scattered. Bremer twisted the staff, and it withdrew into itself. He tucked it into the back of his belt and pulled two flat knives free from the chest brace. Two men stumbled to the ground with the knives deep in their backs. Bremer withdrew two more knives. He threw one to his right, then pivoted to throw the second straight ahead, catching one thug in the back and another in the side.

The last of slave runners were out of range, fleeing for their lives. Will knew that some might escape, but most were about to be hunted. Either way, he dared not let Bremer see that he hadn't followed his instructions. He turned and raced toward the beach as the rogue had ordered.

He stopped at the edge of a grove of unfamiliar trees. Tall, smooth trunks topped with six-foot-long leaves towered above the deep-green foliage where he stood. Before him was the Niasa Sea and a beach of fine white sand. Three massive piers stretched out several hundred feet, each one lined with docked fishing boats. A large fishery warehouse stood back from the center pier. Dozens of gulls squawked overhead.

"Don't miss this," he told himself as he wiped sweat from his brow. It would be an ideal vacation spot if not for the present danger threatening Fairbay.

A scuffling sound beyond the trees to his right caught his

attention. Three slave runners darted behind a large shop with smoke billowing from two chimneys. Next to the shop was a low barn with a pitched roof and no windows. Its enormous front gate was closed, but a set of double doors beside them was partially opened. A young woman leading four small girls appeared from the far side of the barn and quickly corralled the children through the double doors.

Will hid behind a bush, transfixed. His pulse throbbed in his ears. He held a shortened breath in his throat as if keeping it there could capture the stunning image. Despite her youthfulness, the woman's waist-length, wavy hair was as white as snow. She wore tight pants to her knees and a sleeveless shirt. Her striking teal skin and slender legs left Will blinking in disbelief. Something so beautiful looked incongruous with the ugly violence of the moment as if a single flower had suddenly bloomed in the eye of a hurricane.

The woman helped the last of the young girls into the barn as the three slave runners reappeared from around the shop. They sprang forward like wolves to their prey. The woman shrieked and turned away from the barn as they pursued her.

She ran past the barn and was about to disappear around a small, narrow stable but collided with a fourth slave runner who caught her up into a bear hug. He lifted her off her feet. Despite her desperate thrashing and kicking, she was helpless with her arms pinned against her sides. The big man grappled with her beside the narrow stable while the other three opened the door, grinning.

Will tried to think of someone he could reach for help. He knew Bremer was near the end of his fight, and he didn't know where Rowe and Morgan were. He was alone.

The woman screamed again and fought in vain as the big man carried her into the stable.

Will knew he had to act, but fear held him in place. He thought of the Arden Forest, of watching Joe and Morgan fighting bravely. He thought of Rowe slaying harvesters in the Crow's Nest and Bremer standing against forty thugs. "That's it!" he said aloud as he stepped away from the bush. "I'm sick of being scared!"

With clenched fists raised to the clear blue sky, he reeled against his familiar sense of helplessness. *It's just me now,* he thought. *But if you're truly there, God, like Morgan says, save me from this crippling fear! Please!*

Out of the corner of his eye, he noticed a sudden movement on a roof about twenty yards away. With only its head visible, a dark creature quietly perused the scene below. A dozen eyes covered its broad, flat face. Massive wings rippled and folded behind the creature's shoulders. As it shifted on the roof's peak, Will ducked back behind the bush.

Just great, he thought. And this is supposed to help my fear?

Another muffled scream from within the stable snapped Will back to the task at hand. The creature on the roof slithered out of sight, and the knot in Will's stomach loosened. His spirit calmed as a wave of courage crashed against his binding fear.

With his 1911 in one hand and Onathe's bow in the other, he sprinted toward the stable. Without considering the consequences, he turned his shoulder and leapt sideways, striking the doors with his full weight. Something cracked on the inside from the impact. The hinges buckled, and the wall shuddered. The only thing that did not give was the large iron latch that held the doors together.

As if he had crashed into a Mack truck, Will bounced off the doors and landed on his back. Undeterred and reenergized, he gained his feet and jerked the dented latch. As both doors opened, he kicked them as hard as he could.

He stepped inside the shadowy barn, gun raised. As his eyes adjusted to the dim light, the first thing he saw was three men holding the woman down on a table. The big man who had caught her outside was trying to tie her down. He glowered at Will and dropped the rope, then drew a dented sword. His long legs quickly closed the gap between them.

Will pointed the 1911 center mass and pulled the trigger. Click!

He glared at the gun. The brute, standing over six feet tall with a large round midsection and a mess of greasy hair, flashed a yellow-toothed grin. Without pausing to determine if the gun had jammed or misfired, Will slammed it into his holster and drew his sword the way Dench had taught him.

The brute struck Will's raised sword so hard, it broke from his grip and hit the far wall. Will jumped back and barely had the wherewithal to close his cloak when the man's blade came around faster than he believed possible. The sword struck his cloak high in the shoulder, and Will let out a short yelp. The red flash of magic absorbed the blow and momentarily blinded the brute. Will kicked him between his legs. The man grunted, doubling over. Drawing his 1911, Will raised it above his head and drove it into the man's skull.

Will's chest heaved as he choked in the musty air. He met the woman's dazzling blue eyes for a brief second and detected a glint of hope…and something else that he read as gratitude.

She thrashed, trying to free a leg, but the brute at her feet had his weight across her knees. Another man was stretching the woman's arms straight back over her head. The third man drifted toward Will, sword raised.

Will whacked the gun twice against a wooden beam and jerked

the action back. The jammed slug flew from the chamber, and he gripped the handle with both hands. The unexpected explosion left everyone with hands covering their ears—everyone except the thug now lying in a bloodied mass.

The woman sat upright, and their eyes met. A profound sense of calm washed over Will. She was the most stunning, exotic woman he had ever seen. He would have done anything to freeze this moment in time. Besides her beautiful high cheekbones, narrow chin, full lips, smooth teal skin, and flowing white hair, something in her eyes drew him to her. Her slender arms pulled her knees tight against her body. She was trembling.

Will faced the two surviving men still covering their ears and shifted his aim. Again, the gun clicked when he pulled the trigger. The thugs glanced at one another as if trying to agree on who should rush Will. They moved in unison.

"Go!" Will shouted at the woman, pointing to a small door at the back of the empty stable.

She slid off the table as one man lunged at her, catching a handful of her hair.

Will jerked the action back, ejected another faulty slug, and fired at the man. The woman was instantaneously freed, and she dashed off through the door.

"Last one," Will said as he shifted the barrel and squeezed the trigger.

The gun kicked, and the slug struck the brute now less than five feet away. Before the man had hit the ground, Will was pursuing the woman.

Outside, he saw no sign of her. Despite his disappointment, he believed himself fortunate to have been in her presence. And those eyes, he would never forget those brilliant-blue eyes.

CHAPTER 25

FAIRBAY

By the time Will found Rowe, most of the inhabitants of the fishing village were emerging from their barricaded dwellings. Will had no idea where he was going but assumed he'd find Rowe and the others eventually. He turned down a path between timber-framed cottages, whistling casually.

"Will?" Rowe called as he ran to catch up.

Will smiled. "Hey, Rowe!"

"I heard the explosions, and I thought—"

"Nothing but a few bad guys in a barn over by the docks."

Rowe scanned Will from head to toe. "Are you hurt?"

"Mostly my pride." Will rubbed his left shoulder. "I tried to bust through a door and ended up on my back. I drew my sword, and it ended up on the ground too."

"What happened?"

"I saw a few guys carry this—this stunning woman into a barn." One word tumbled into the next. "Her eyes, Rowe…there was something in her eyes that—that stopped time."

"Hmmm…What was her name?"

Will shrugged. "I didn't get a chance to talk to her."

"Can you describe her?"

"I'm not gonna lie, Rowe: she was smokin' hot. Teal skin and all."

Rowe's eyes widened. "What color was her hair?"

"White—but not old-lady white. Exotic-to-the-moon white! And her eyes, Rowe, they—they were…" he stammered. "I dunno, but they were full of life—so much life. I've never seen anything so beautiful and so alive."

"I heard three explosions," Rowe said.

"My gun first jammed, then misfired—probably from all the water and dirt. If not for this cloak and a boatload of luck, I'd be dead right now instead of those other guys."

Rowe eyed him suspiciously. "The encounter has certainly changed you."

"To be honest, Rowe, there's more to it than the girl. I was terrified—like you saw me back in the Crow's Nest…like I usually am when you step in to save us. But you and Bremer weren't around, so I looked up into the sky and prayed for help. And you know…I can't explain, but something happened. One second, I was shaking and almost in tears, and the next, I wasn't."

"Being thrown into situations like that can change a person. I am sorry I was not there to help. So, then what happened?"

"The best I can say is…well, it was like I wasn't alone anymore—even though I was. Since the first day I saw Lessers coming from the Arden Forest, a giant anchor of fear has been chained to my neck. Well, it's like the chain broke today. I can't tell you how it happened, but instead of crushing fear, I felt…raw courage."

"It is good to see you smile, especially after what you went through."

"And then there's this," Will said as they turned down another street.

Rowe whistled softly. "Onathe's bow. Did you have to fight Bremer for that?"

"No, I didn't even ask if I could keep it after I found it. Guess I should talk to Bremer about it."

"No need. If he had wanted it—and I cannot believe he did not—he would have it."

Will examined the markings, turning the weapon in his hands. "What's the big deal with it?"

"You could trade it for a fully stocked castle."

"Humph! I'd settle for a warm bed and a couple bottles of elven mead." Will laughed. "Listen to me. I sound like a local, eh?"

"Let's head over to the beach where everyone is gathering. Morgan is waiting for us there. But we have time for a quick stop."

They turned left at the next lane. Rowe pointed to a tall, narrow building with an old wooden sign hanging from the weathered barn board: *The Recovery Ale House and Inn*. Against the wall lay the bodies of three dead slave runners.

People thronged the street, heading for the beach, but Rowe led Will to the inn.

"Let's see what I can trade for this bow in here," Will said with a wink.

"Did you recently develop a sense of humor too?" Rowe chortled.

"I don't know what to tell you, Rowe, but the knots in my stomach are gone, and the world has taken on color. I have a feeling that after a bottle of elven mead, I'll inform you that I've recently fallen in love."

Rowe clapped Will's shoulder as they stepped through the narrow doorway. "Quite the day you've had."

Inside the Recovery was a U-shaped bar to their right that curved from near the entrance to the back wall. Tall wooden stools lined the bar that occupied one side of the room, and six tables were set neatly on the other side.

The fishing spirit was strong in this place. Old ropes looped around two huge pillars supporting the massive bar top. The wall behind the bar was lined with shelves of glasses, steins, and old bottles in various shapes and colors. Sturdy bookcases framed the large window facing the street. Between the well-used volumes were dozens of carved fishing boat models that acted as bookends. On the other walls hung countless old fishing lures, poles, oars, and paintings of boats and marine life. Will thought it curious that many paintings included mermaids.

The place was empty until three husky, longhaired men with bushy beards followed Rowe and Will in. Each man wore a dirty apron and carried a bloodied war hammer over his shoulder.

"Red cloaks," shouted the tallest of the three as he walked behind the bar. "Must be the lads!"

"That a good thing?" Will asked cautiously, staying close to Rowe.

"Aye!" said the second.

"Heroes ya be!" said the third.

"Oh right, we're heroes now?" Will placed the bow on the bar and stepped up to the nearest stool.

"Name's Jessman," said one man. "This here's Hansla, and the wee one's Homas."

"Do you have elven mead?" Will asked, licking his lips.

"Aye, that we do!" Hansla said, turning to Jessman. "The lad has a palate, he does."

"Three bottles sittin' in me cellars," Jessman said. "And they be the only three within a ten-day ride, I might add." He nodded, and Homas slipped through the door behind the bar.

Rowe stood beside Will. "My name is Rowe of the Nest, and the thirsty one here is called Will Owens."

"Pleased to be meetin' ya. And for you, lad? Fancy the mead or shall we fetch ya somethin' else?"

"Whatever ale you have on tap will be fine; besides, Will here did most of the heavy lifting today."

"Bring up some of the Whistlin' River Extra Special!" Jessman shouted in a thundering voice.

Rowe held up his hands. "No need. I'm happy with what you have out."

Jessman scowled, so Rowe conceded.

"And for the bellies?" Hansla asked. "We have the best fish stew you'll ever taste!"

"There's someone waiting for us at the pier, so just the drinks for now," Rowe said.

"Aye," Jessman said. "The evenin' stew is about ready, so we'll bring bowls out to ya soon."

"How many are ye?" Hansla asked.

"Four," Rowe answered. "And the bowls would be much appreciated."

"Beggin' yer pardon?" Hansla glanced at Jessman. "How many?"

"Four," Rowe repeated.

"But how is that possible?" Jessman asked. "There be a hundred slave runners if there be one, and what of the dark elf?"

"Like I said, Will did most of the heavy lifting."

Will started to correct Rowe. "Well, actually—"

"Shades, lad!" Jessman examined Will as if Rowe had introduced him to royalty. "What manner of man are ya?" He laughed heartily.

Will flexed one of his slender arms and grinned. Everyone joined the laughter.

Homas returned through the door with a heavy mug in one hand and a tall bottle in the other. "What's all this?" he said, sliding the bottle to Will and the mug to Rowe.

"We have us a spirited lad, we do!" Hansla shouted, reaching for a goblet.

"Won't be needing that." Will brought the bottle to his lips.

Hansla chuckled. "How many rooms will ya be needin'?"

"Do you have one with two bunks?" Rowe asked.

"Certainly do!" Jessman said.

Rowe started for the door. "Have any injured arrived from Hammerclaw?"

Jessman's broad smile disappeared. "Not yet heard, have ya?"

"Please tell me what you know."

"The Dark Queen, Sidara, arrived at Hammerclaw two days ago with the vilest o' spells. Our last caravan of food saw it happen when they were a mile from the castle. But we can't get a straight story from them. They agreed that one moment, everythin' was as it should be, then in the next, a terrifyin' roar shook the earth. One wagoner said everythin' in Hammerclaw flew up into the air—up to the clouds, if you can believe it. Everythin'—people, animals, anythin' not nailed down was sucked up. He said as quickly as it started, it was quiet again, save for the screams of people plummetin' to their deaths.

"Another wagoner denied that story. He said there was a great cloud o' fine dust or vapor that blew through the city, turnin' everythin' to dust." Jessman's voice caught in his throat, and he cleared it gruffly.

"Have mercy," Rowe whispered.

"I understand how crazy this sounds," Hansla said, "but we heard the same two stories repeated by others who traveled with the caravan—people we've known for a lot o' years. All we know for certain is that Hammerclaw was sacked, and the city is no more."

"Will Sidara's army be heading this way?" Will asked.

"No, lad," Jessman said quietly.

Rowe agreed. "They will journey east to attack the Crow's Nest. But I suspect they will first hold up outside Hammerclaw to establish new supply lines."

"I do hope our fair queen up in the capital city can pull her head out from her beloved nether regions before all's lost," said Homas. "If Dwenlin Thah falls, well, I suppose that'll be the end."

"Do not lose hope," Rowe said as he pulled the door open. "There are many good men in the fight."

"Aye," Jessman said. "And you've proved that today. But Sidara's army just breached Hammerclaw—somethin' no one thought possible, not to mention that cursed Shadowfallen doin' her biddin'."

"One victory at a time, boys." Will enjoyed a long pull from the bottle.

"Aye, lad!" Jessman's smile returned. "We'll bring another with the stew, if it pleases ya."

"Consider me pleased." Will raised the bottle in thanks as he slid from the stool.

"Is there anythin' else we can do for ya, lads?" Jessman asked.

Rowe sipped his ale. "Well, we came in off the plains south of the crops. Our horses are beyond the East Ridge, a couple hundred yards in. Would you have them brought over and stabled?"

"Consider it done!" Jessman said. "Homas!"

On their way down to the Niasa Sea, Will and Rowe searched

the growing crowd for Morgan and Bremer. It didn't take long to find them.

Morgan leapt and ran toward them, waving her arms. "They're mermaids and mermen, Will!" she shouted.

"Whoa, what?" Will held up his hands as she slid to a stop.

"The ones with the teal skin—they're mermaids. That's why they went into the sea!" Morgan spoke so quickly, it was difficult to understand her.

Will turned to Rowe, who was smiling.

"Merpeople," Rowe explained. "Remember the healers here in Fairbay I told you about? Merpeople have always been natural healers. Those who study the healing arts are among the best in the Fourwinds. Unfortunately, this little town is the only place they spend time ashore."

"So, that woman I saw was…a—a mermaid?" Will tried to mask his surprise, but the grin on Rowe's face told him he was unsuccessful.

"She is."

Morgan pointed excitedly at the water. "Come on, they're returning from the sea!"

By the time they arrived at the beach, hundreds of people had gathered around the piers. Lingering tears mixed with beaming smiles and hugs as the reality of death and trauma mingled with a deep sense of freedom and relief. A celebration was brewing. People exchanged stories about how all hope was lost until four strangers came and saved them from the hands of the Dark Queen.

"Why are people so happy?" Will asked Rowe. "Those thugs must have murdered dozens of their friends and family."

"Not so," Rowe explained. "The slave runners need their victims alive and usually prey on vulnerable communities, so they do little killing. They prefer to spare the adults so they can produce more children for them to steal. And the people of Fairbay are not soldiers, so they posed little threat anyway. The key to the slave runners' success was Onathe Wyeth's wall of fire. The dark elf was correct: once the merpeople were cut off from the water, there would be no danger. Mer children would have brought an unimaginable bounty from Sidara. Onathe was famous for his greed as much as his dark magic. I'm sure he was fantasizing about earning Sidara's favor at the exact moment Bremer's arrow tore through his corrupt heart."

Will and Morgan listened as the crowds continue to expand.

"See that large structure over there?" Rowe pointed beyond the piers at a giant igloo-like building made of coral rock. Just beneath the surface, a winding passage of bright-orange coral disappeared into the depths of the lake. On the other side of the building, a steady procession of merpeople flowed through a large door.

"What is that?" Will asked.

"When merpeople emerge from the water, their tails form into legs like ours," Rowe explained. "The transformation happens so quickly that they can be swimming one moment and walking the next. They wear no clothing in their natural habitat and emerge naked—which is one reason they rarely cohabit with humans. Since they swim most of their lives, their bodies are lean and alluring. Humans have gone to unimaginable lengths to capture one. To help curb the temptation here in Fairbay, the merpeople surface inside that structure and clothe themselves before coming into town."

"If they're all like the woman I saw, I'd just as soon go back to the Recovery and get another bottle of this mead," Will said. "I don't think I could handle it."

Rowe laughed.

"Typical men!" Morgan huffed.

"You may have trouble going back to the Recovery soon," Rowe said. "There will be a celebration this evening, and we will find it difficult not to be pulled into the center of attention."

"I can already feel it starting," Morgan said.

Seconds later, someone on the beach noticed the two red Trannalun cloaks. A cheer thundered through the crowd. Will stood stationary as people converged upon them.

"Come, Will," Rowe said. "You have earned this."

Will noticed a few merpeople in the crowd but could not find the woman he had seen earlier. Reluctantly, he followed Rowe.

An elderly man elbowed his way through the crowd. "Please, room, give 'em room," he shouted, receiving several bumps before reaching Rowe. "Come, let's get you kids up on the pier so everyone can get a look at ya."

With considerable effort, they squeezed past people to the eight steps leading up to the center pier. Some tried to follow them up, but the aged man turned and stopped them. Once they reached the top, he raised his hands to quiet the townsfolk and turned to Rowe.

"I'd like to introduce myself to our new friends. My name is Akia Tibers, one of three elders who govern Fairbay. What you have done here today is somethin' that will become a bedtime story for a new generation."

The crowd erupted into cheers that slowly subsided as Akia raised his hands again.

"Thanks to you," he continued, "our little town has much to celebrate. So, on behalf of everyone, may I humbly ask you to join us?"

Rowe nodded, which sparked another round of cheering.

Akia worked at quieting the crowd as Rowe removed his cloak and rolled up his shirtsleeves. When the applause settled, Rowe cleared his throat and addressed the crowd.

"It was our honor to fight alongside you today. There are many battles being fought throughout the Fourwinds. Despite what many of you have heard, victories have been and will continue to be won in the months ahead. We need to cling to the hope these victories bring. Let us allow hope to carry us on through both the good days and the dark days ahead."

"But Hammerclaw has fallen," someone yelled from the crowd.

"Our men in Hammerclaw were prepared to thin Sidara's ranks and prolong the battle. In that regard, they were successful. When they lost the bridge, the plan had been to withdraw and join our forces to help prepare for the next stand. Unfortunately, they were not ready for Sidara's merciless plan."

Someone else began a question, but Rowe raised a quick hand, and the question fell short.

"If our queen in Dwenlin Thah ordered our army to engage Sidara's army on their terms, it would not end well for us. At the moment, we must give up ground and engage Sidara on *our* terms. In doing so, we stretch her supply lines, which makes her army vulnerable. Not an easy task, I can assure you, but a necessary one."

"Who's leading our army?" came another shout. "Certainly not that spoiled brat of a play queen we ended up with!"

Akia was about to intervene, but Rowe patted him on the shoulder and responded.

"We have all had our frustrations with the crown. They have made a mess of governing and, in doing so, plunged the Fourwinds into a war that will take everything we have to win. Thankfully, our queen is uninterested in the affairs of the military, so the war is being run by those most qualified."

"We heard that all the Callum Sages had been hunted and killed," said another.

"Partly true. Sidara sent out hunting parties to exterminate my order, and we have made her pay dearly for her futile efforts. We are a peaceful lot until pressed."

A cheer rose from the crowd.

"A final thought about the war," Rowe said. "Your contributions have been invaluable. The amount of fish and vegetables you have been providing to those at Hammerclaw has kept our soldiers nourished while our enemies scrape by with barely a meal a day. We need you to continue that work."

Will noticed more people with teal skin in the crowd. Each one was intriguing, but he could not forget that one woman. A smile crossed his lips as the spirits of the elven mead danced in his mind. But the gentle buzz only relaxed his body a little, and his mind remained sharp and energized. It was then he noticed the bottle was empty.

I need to do something about that, he thought.

Rowe concluded his speech. "For now, we will get cleaned up and eat before joining you for what I hope to be a great evening."

With that, he and Will followed Akia through the crowd back to the pub. At a clearing, Rowe stepped close to Akia and lowered his voice.

"Where is Ryodan Ayoust?"

"That's an interestin' question, Rowe. The dark elf could not have picked a more opportune time to attack. Somethin' to do with the Shadowfallen reopenin' the iron mines along the northern shores. Ryodan and his army left an hour before Onathe attacked. Addin' to his timin' was the fishin' boats all went out at dawn today and are not due back till the morrow before sundown."

Rowe rubbed his chin. "Interesting…"

"Will ya be stayin' with us long?" Akia asked.

"Just passing through," Rowe said.

"Where will your journey carry ya?"

"The winds blow where the winds blow."

Akia studied the sage's face. "You were surprised to hear that Hammerclaw had been breached, so I suspect you'd been plannin' to head south." Akia paused. "Now ya must make new plans."

Rowe raised an eyebrow.

"I am a politician, Rowe. My job is to pay attention and to be discernin' with what I see. For instance, a Callum Sage arrives in my wee town from…the Crow's Nest, I would guess? You were either headin' south to Hammerclaw or beyond, near Bayou Sorral. That's the route I would have taken if I were goin' to the Waerdreath. And if that were the case, your first choice would be the main road, but that is likely overrun with gnome soldiers. Your second choice would be to cross the Bull River and travel through the Hollowtangle forest—which would be difficult…unless you know your way."

Rowe said nothing and gave nothing away.

Akia nodded slowly. "I can understand the need for secrecy, but if ya mean to travel through the Hollowtangle, I know of a guide who could take ya through."

Akia entered the pub and left Will and Rowe alone on the street.

"Who's Ryodan Ayoust?" Will asked.

"King of the merpeople," Rowe answered. "That wall of fire would not have gone unnoticed. I expect he will be here shortly. In the meantime, keep your eyes open."

CHAPTER 26

REPRIEVE

The sun dipped beyond the distant shores of the Niasa Sea, offering gentle good-night kisses to the cheeks of those gathered on the beach. The sun was leaving for the day, but the crowd showed no sign of retiring so early.

Morgan and Rowe left the Recovery Ale House and Inn to enjoy the sun's parting gift of soft pinks, oranges, and blues painted on the evening sky. It was a beautiful ending to an ugly day.

Morgan had slipped into a pair of loose-fitting light-brown linen pants Meagan had given her before they'd left Acttun. The sleeves of her simple white shirt were too long, so she had rolled them to the elbow. She was barefoot, clean, and content. To match her relaxed mood, she had gathered her hair in a loose ponytail. She sipped the delicate spiced wine Jessman had recommended and turned her face to take in the amazing sunset.

Rowe had shed his Trannalun cloak. He wore a pair of light-weight linen pants and a sleeveless chemise with three bottom hooks in place, leaving it partly opened at the chest. Despite his apparent interest in the harmless celebration growing all around, he was armed with a sword that hung loosely at his hip and a long knife tucked into his right boot.

"Boy Scout," Morgan muttered as she took another sip.

"That didn't sound very nice," Rowe said.

Morgan smirked. "A Boy Scout is someone who's always prepared."

"Well, that sounds a little better." Rowe swallowed a mouthful of dark ale. "I think we should wait for Will."

"How many times did he say he would meet us down on the beach?"

"I know, but—"

"But nothing, Rowe. We've been traveling in tight quarters for days, and he simply wants some space. He'll be fine."

"I suppose so. He was in the soaker," Rowe said with a small laugh as they strolled down the road.

"What's that about?"

"He had one arm hanging over the side with a bottle of mead in hand. That was number two, and he was headlong into it."

"Good for him," Morgan said. "I think we all deserve an evening of fun. You *do* know how to have fun, don't you, Rowe?"

•••

After soaking in a giant cast-iron tub for nearly an hour, Will slipped into some clean clothes someone had provided and headed down to the empty pub. Halfway down the stairs, he noticed Onathe's bow resting loosely in his hand. He knew he was feeling the effects of the mead, but he could not remember picking up the weapon. *Strange.* He went down a few more steps and realized he had left his 1911 back in his room, wrapped in his Trannalun cloak. *Very strange.*

As he crossed the dimly lit room, Jessman casually turned and slid another bottle of elven mead along the bar.

"What are you still doing here?" Will asked.

"Waitin' for you to come down before headin' out. I found some lilac wine for Morgan and some of the darkest ale we have for Rowe. And for you, lad, I managed to get me hands on another bottle. It's chillin' in the cellar right through there and down the stairs whenever you wish."

"That was very thoughtful." Will couldn't stifle his smile. The effects of the first two bottles provided a wonderful sensation he wanted to last all night.

"I risked nothin' in this. Hear me, lad, when I tell ya that you'll never pay for anythin' in Fairbay—ever."

"Well, that sounds like something worth drinking to!" Will grabbed the bottle.

"There'll be a bard on the pier with two fiddlers you'll not want to miss." Jessman picked up a small splintered crate filled with bottles. "I imagine they'll be startin' shortly."

Will held the front door open for him. "I'll see you down there."

Jessman nodded and walked down the street toward shouts and laughter. Already, the glow of a beach fire was lighting up the darkening sky.

Will leaned his head back and breathed in the fresh air. He relaxed for the first time in days and welcomed the feeling with open arms and a fresh bottle of elven mead. To avoid the crowds, he wandered down a road that ran parallel to the beach, listening closely to the sounds of night. Near the last of the homesteads, he turned down a quiet path that led to the beach and stopped.

Someone was talking out near the trees. The light was faint, but after staring intently, Will discerned the outline of a man in the shadows. The single figure appeared to be talking to a tree.

Will moved sideways and crouched quietly beside a small woodshed. He rubbed his clammy palms over his knees. Everything in his being was telling him to slip away, but curiosity held him fast. He tilted his head and strained his ears but could not understand any words. But the voice was definitely male and somewhat familiar.

From a tall branch above the man, something slid down. Little by little, the lanky torso came into view before the creature flipped itself upside down, hanging several feet from the ground. It said something incoherent, in a voice that caused Will's skin to crawl. Moonlight peeked behind a cloud, revealing the same flat-faced creature he had seen on the roof before he'd rescued the beautiful teal-skinned woman. Below the numerous eyes, a narrow mouth clicked as it spoke.

Before Will could get a clearer view, the creature pulled itself back up into the tree and leapt from a branch. The tree shook as the creature spread its wings and took to the sky with a low swooping sound. Bright stars flickered as the unusual beast darkened the sky and quickly disappeared over the trees.

Will flattened himself on the ground, holding his breath and listening as soft steps grew closer. He was certain the man would see him or hear his heart thumping, but he risked a quick look. With his cheek against the cool earth, Will recognized him immediately: *Akia Tibers*.

The old man passed by silently, failing to acknowledge Will.

Moments drifted by before Will slowly climbed to his knees, brushing off his arms and adjusting his short-sleeved tunic. He stood, took a quick sip from his bottle, then hurried to the beach. He had to find Rowe.

He was about a hundred yards from the center of the festivities at the main pier when dozens of mermen exploded from the water. Will fell back in the sand, stunned. They flew about twenty feet above the surface, tails transforming into powerful legs before landing in a wide semicircle on the beach. Each one carried a long, menacing trident.

Before Will could catch his breath, something else breached the water. Turning, he found himself gawking at the tallest person he had ever seen. Clad in dark-blue armor made of rough coral, the teal-skinned merman had a shock of white hair and a face contorted into a foreboding glare. He drove his trident into the sand and surveyed the area. His eyes settled upon Will.

"That is the bow my sister spoke of," he said.

Will searched in vain for help. Unfortunately, he was far from the light of the bonfires, and no one seemed to notice the sudden invasion.

"Well, this is just great," Will muttered. Despite the imminent danger around him, his heart rate slowed from the initial fright. He had fallen awkwardly but noticed the bow in his lap and the bottle of mead in his hand. That was something.

The tall merman's teeth were clenched so tight, Will could see his jaw muscles flex ten feet away. Bulky shoulder and arm muscles rippled as a massive hand wrapped around the shaft of the trident, pulling it from the sand. A cluster of silver spearheads suddenly filled Will's vision, and he shut his eyes.

The merman growled. "No man will ever—"

"Easy there, flipper fish," came a voice from the trees.

Will opened one eye and turned to see the outline of Bremer materializing from the shadows. The warriors redirected their tridents to him but did not attack; the brace of knives catching the moonlight were enough to deter any soldier.

"Bold words for a—" the tall merman said before Bremer cut him off again.

"I wish I could say the same of you." Bremer moved forward. "Didn't know it took so many mermen to kill one *human*."

"Come closer so I may see the face of the coward who dares address me."

Bremer stepped between the two nearest warriors and stopped. Tridents brushed his sides, but Bremer simply scratched his head and yawned. "Best step back from my friend before I beat you to death with that toy you carry."

A deep, thundering voice shattered the tension. "Wrathan, my son, what is the meaning of this?"

The large merman held his ground while the others lowered their tridents, bowed their heads, and spoke in unison: "Hail, Ryodan Ayoust!"

"My father, this is the one Ryowyn spoke of," Wrathan said.

"The one who *rescued* her?"

"Search your heart, Father. He is a human who planned to take Ryowyn as his own. You know this to be true."

"Wrathan, it is time to lower your trident."

Will was acutely aware that one simple thrust would end his life.

"Sounds like good advice," Bremer said.

Wrathan snapped his head up and glared at Bremer. "Your words mean nothing here, human!"

"That may be," Bremer said, then lowered his voice. "But I can assure you my steel does, and if that trident drifts forward any more, it will speak for me."

"My son, I was not asking you," Ryodan said.

The warriors all raised their tridents, spears up, and drove the handles into the sand in unison.

Rowe appeared suddenly, skidding to a halt in the sand between the mermen and Will. "What is the problem here?" he gasped. One glimpse at Wrathan's fiery eyes answered his question. "Please, Wrathan, there's a misunderstanding here."

Wrathan held fast. "No misunderstanding. Ryowyn came into this world with her freedom, and she will remain free."

Rowe gestured at Will. "He is a traveler from a distant land and does not understand your customs. He simply saw someone in trouble and did what you would have done."

"My son," Ryodan said. "I have looked into him. There is no ill intent."

"The bow, then!" Wrathan snapped. "How does someone steal a weapon such as this without evil in his heart?"

"He didn't *steal* it," Bremer offered quietly. "He removed it from Onathe Wyeth's cold dead fingers…*after* he killed him."

Almost every merman's jaw dropped.

"Is this true?" Ryodan asked.

"It is, my lord," Rowe answered. "He and Bremer killed Onathe earlier today. Had it not been for that, no one would have left this village with their freedom."

"Including Ryowyn," Bremer added.

"And is it true this man is unaware of our customs?" Ryodan asked.

"It is, my lord," Rowe said. "He is a Callum Sage, but he has traveled from beyond the Hillron Mountains to aid in our fight against a common enemy. Please, Wrathan, what he did today, he did with purity of heart."

Wrathan spat in the sand. "Very well. Father, explain to this human what he has acquired."

"No need for this," Rowe said quickly. "We are passing through this land, and you will never see him again after this night."

Wrathan glared at Rowe. "If you are so certain of the purity of his heart, we *must* tell him. This is our custom as it has always been."

"My lord," Rowe said to Ryodan. "We have had a great victory this day in a time when victories are hard to come by. Please end this and join us in celebration."

"Or allow me to take Wrathan behind a fish shack and beat him like the spoiled child he is," Bremer said.

Ryodan quickly placed a restraining hand on Wrathan's shoulder and addressed Will. "What is your name?"

"Will," he answered with a dry voice. He swallowed hard. "Will Owens. Uh…my lord."

"Please, Will Owens, drink so you may speak freely," Ryodan said.

Will put the shaky bottle to his lips. Despite the mounting tension, he smiled as the cool liquid soothed his throat.

"When you save a life," Ryodan continued, "that life becomes your own. This has always been our custom."

Will blinked several times. He would have been happy with one more minute with her, but this was overwhelming. He was speechless.

"Do you lack understanding?" Wrathan snapped.

Bremer stepped between Wrathan and Rowe and sat beside Will. "That elven mead?"

Will's mind reeled as he turned to Bremer. "Want some?"

Bremer accepted the bottle from Will's shaking hand, took a sip, and handed it back. "I have to tell you, Will, your fortunes are greater than you could ever fathom."

"I don't feel very lucky at the moment."

Bremer lowered his voice to a whisper. "That bow you hold is more valuable than anything Wrathan has ever touched—and he is the son of a king. You won it from someone they have been trying to kill for years, and that infuriates these warriors. They have dreamed of being the one to kill Onathe Wyeth, not to mention winning the king's favor and bedding Ryowyn. And now you hold the sum of all their desires."

"I don't know what to do, Bremer."

"What?" Bremer placed a firm hand on Will's shoulder and joggled him. "Did you not get a good look at her? Shades, lad! Men fall for her like wheat before a sickle's blade."

Will nodded. "I've never seen anyone like her."

"You do not know the first note of the music that moves her," Wrathan said.

Will simply shrugged.

"You fail to understand!" Wrathan snapped. "She is bequeathed to you for the remainder of your days, and it will be her heart's desire to fulfill your every need."

Everyone stared in silence at Will.

"I get that part—like a life for a life kind of thing," Will said. "But I don't want that for her."

Wrathan tightened his grip on the trident. "I do not know what type of false iron you're peddling, but this means nothing!"

Ryodan gripped his son's shoulder and pulled him back a step.

"I—I don't want any part of turning her into a slave," Will said.

All the mermen stared at Will. After a moment, Ryodan raised his deep voice in proclamation. "This is why we will win the war! People of such virtue cannot be stopped!"

The mer soldiers all raised their tridents and slammed them back into the sand in perfect unison. Wrathan left in a fit of anger, and the others followed him into the water. The mer king remained, staring at Will.

Music suddenly filled the air as the bards and fiddlers broke into song. The majority of those gathered on the beach were too busy celebrating to notice what had taken place. Those who had come to see what was going on now headed back to the pier.

"Rowe of the Nest," Ryodan said. "It is good to see that rumors of your demise were untrue."

"As with most rumors, my lord."

"Come, walk with me. We have much to discuss."

Bremer stood, folding his arms. "Do you have nothing to say after what you just allowed Will to go through?"

Ryodan turned. "A man such as this does not require prestige, prosperity, position, or plaudits," Ryodan said. "His face is set, his gait is sound, and it has been my honor to have been in his presence!"

The mer king walked away with Rowe, leaving Bremer and Will gaping.

Despite the alluring music and celebration a few hundred yards away, Will was content to lie on the sand long after Bremer had slipped away. He gazed at the ocean of stars. This could be their last friendly stop on the journey that would take them through lands controlled by the Dark Queen. He traced a finger along the bowstring, enjoying the effects of the mead and resting in the moment.

He was suddenly aware of someone watching him. He lifted his head slightly and saw the head and shoulders of the woman he'd rescued surfacing from the sea. *Ryowyn.* The delightful effects of the elven mead paled in comparison to the enchanting sensation that now flooded him. In the milky light cast by the moon and a myriad of stars, her naked form rose from the water and glided across the sand toward him. Time stood still.

Ryowyn stopped at his feet, and beads of water rolled down her sylphlike form. She brushed a few hairs from her face and placed her delicate hands on her hips. Will gazed into her admiring eyes and reveled in their alluring charm. Had she not spoken first, he would have remained forever silent.

Her voice danced softly in the night air. "Why?" she asked. The sweetness of the sound was intoxicating.

Will continued to stare into her wide, luminous eyes, stumbling over his words, though he understood her question. "I…we left…I mean…we leave tomorrow."

"Your journey is now my journey."

Will summoned every ounce of strength just to shake his head. "I spoke to your father. You are free from any obligation your customs place upon you."

"What I feel has nothing to do with obligation."

"Maybe not now, but—" Will sensed his words had stung. "I'm sorry. But I'm heading west, Ryowyn."

"I know, Will Owens."

"And from there, I have no idea where the war will take us."

"I wish to be with you this night, and when the road leads you back, I will be waiting."

"I'm not ready for what's ahead. It's unbearable to think of leaving this place, but we have to. If we're successful in the days ahead, Rowe said the tide of the war could change." A rush of emotion choked his words, and he lowered his eyes.

"Would you like me to clothe myself?"

"No. Yes. I mean…no. But…would you?"

"Will you be here when I return?"

"I'd love to sit here with you until dawn."

"Please stay, Will." She returned to the water, glancing once over her shoulder before disappearing beneath the surface.

Will released his held breath and dropped back onto the sand. He pinched his forearm to be sure he wasn't dreaming, then closed his eyes and smiled. His life had changed so dramatically since leaving Cochrane. He thought of his parents and the possibility his mother was still alive, of the harvester and the Lessers, of Inspector Joe Cheechoo, of the cabin in the Arden Forest, and of all the death and evil he had faced since arriving in the Fourwinds.

All those thoughts drifted away like a dark cloud, leaving his mind as clear and bright as the starry night. It was as though a warm breeze had blown in from some unexpected place, filling him with profound joy. He felt unworthy to receive it but opened his heart to it anyway. Morgan had called it *grace. Yes,* Will thought, *grace. What an amazing word.*

"Don't miss this," he told himself.

Deep in the night sky, something caught his attention. He blinked once, saw the same thing, and blinked again, this time rubbing his eyes.

"What the—" he muttered, scrambling to his feet without turning away from the night sky. "That can't be!"

He lowered his eyes to the massive beach fire in the distance and blinked again to make sure he was seeing clearly. This time, he slowly raised his head and again saw the same thing in the night sky.

"What does that mean?"

"What is it, Will?" Ryowyn called as she ran toward him. Not yet dry, her clothes clung to her body. She tied her long hair back in a wet ponytail and stepped close to him.

"What is it?" she repeated.

"Look up there," he said, pointing. "You see those three bright stars forming a slight arch?" He was cheek to cheek with her to ensure she was looking in the right place because there were millions of stars.

"You see: one, two, three stars, the bright ones, then there are four stars forming a square. Picture those three stars as a handle and the other four as the pot."

Ryowyn smiled. "We call it the Ladle."

"That's it! We need to find Morgan!"

As they approached the fire, Will slowed to watch the bard strumming his instrument on the pier. Short and skinny, the bard danced up and down the smooth wooden planks, working the townsfolk. Most people seemed to know the tune being played by the masterful blur of fingers on the narrow fretboard.

Some people were dancing in front of the makeshift stage while others frolicked around the fire. With hands raised and bodies twirling everywhere, people sang along as they gave themselves to the spirit of celebration. Those drinking at the outskirts of the party tapped their feet in the sand, enjoying the conversation of friends. Many carried large goblets. With three carts carrying kegs of ale, no one had far to go for refills. The excitement was irresistible.

Ryowyn's hand slid into Will's, and a grateful smile surfaced from deep within his heart. More than satisfied, he felt whole.

He and Ryowyn moved through the crowd toward Jessman, who was serving from a keg. As they did, Will overheard fragments of various tales of Onathe Wyeth's death. People spoke of the Callum Sage who destroyed the dark elf, freeing Fairbay and saving the beautiful princess of the Niasa Sea. Will was used to people talking about him back in Cochrane, but they never told hero stories.

Someone recognized him and Ryowyn, and the crowd pressed, raising goblets in salute while trying to get the young couple to join the dance. Ryowyn was gracious as men of every shape, size, and age asked in vain for a single dance. She smiled kindly and clung to Will's arm. It was becoming difficult to keep moving forward as more people joined them in what was becoming a party within a party, but Will focused on Jessman.

A single voice cut through the music, singing, and laughter. "Will!"

He searched the crowd and saw Morgan dancing near Jessman's cart.

"Morgan!" he shouted back, waving her over when he realized he couldn't escape the enthusiastic crowd.

"Back up!" Jessman shouted as the crowd pressed in closer to his cart.

People bobbed and twirled and sang their way back to the fire, allowing Will and Ryowyn to reach Morgan.

"Take a look at that!" Will pointed excitedly to the sky, but Morgan was staring at Ryowyn.

"You're beautiful," Morgan said with a hiccup.

Ryowyn smiled. "You're sweet—and a hero. I have heard stories of what you did today for our children."

"Hold on a second here," Will interrupted, pointing to the sky again. "Morgan, look up there!"

Morgan giggled and leaned her head back as she swayed to the music.

"Whoa. So many stars," she said. "Reminds me of camping up at Mistango."

"No, Morgan." Will moved his arm closer to her and pointed again. "*There.*"

Her body stiffened.

Rowe stepped around the cart. "What's wrong?"

Jessman handed him a mug of ale and he took a few gulps.

"That—that can't be," Morgan said.

"It's the Big Dipper, Rowe," Will said, pointing.

"Yes," Rowe said. "The Ladle."

More than a dozen people now joined them, dancing and gazing at the stars. Rowe stepped beside Morgan and slid his arm around her back.

"We have the same constellation, Rowe," Will said. "Many things in the Fourwinds are different from our world…but it's the same sky!"

Rowe and Morgan laughed softly and walked across the sand until they were lost in the crowd. Everyone seemed too caught up in celebration for serious conversation, and Will couldn't blame them. But he surveyed the familiar stars again, his mind reeling. Were they on earth? If so, were they back in time, or forward in time? Or was there another option?

"Indeed," he whispered. "What *does* it mean?"

After a moment, Ryowyn gently pulled him away from the festivities.

Hours later, the first traces of sunlight glowed over the eastern ridge. Will lay on his side next to Ryowyn. Lost in each other's gaze, they barely heard the early songbirds. Despite his deep desire for the night to last forever, he realized a new day was dawning and, with it, the inevitable parting of ways.

"You are worried about the days ahead," she whispered.

"I can't imagine standing against someone like the Dark Queen."

"My heart tells me her end will come in your presence."

Will sat up on one elbow. "How can you say that?"

She smiled. "My father told me he would rather face an army than stand against you."

Will was at a loss for words. He rolled onto his back and placed one hand behind his head. The sand beneath him cooled his body as dawn's first light warmed his face.

Ryowyn slid close and rested her head on his shoulder. "There is a fire inside you, Will, that will not be denied. This I know to be true."

"You make me feel like I can do anything, Ryowyn," he whispered.

"You can, and you will."

He lowered his eyes. "You don't know that."

"I can only say what my heart knows to be true."

She sat up and reached behind her neck. Pushing her hair to the side, she unfastened the clip of her necklace. The cord was woven from strands of seaweed but was almost as fine as a spider's silk. Almost translucent save for a soft green hue, it was a marvel to behold. Dangling from the tiny thread was a pendant shaped like a small drop of morning dew.

"I want you to have this," she whispered.

Will sat up and examined the necklace. He knew instinctively it was something extremely special.

Ryowyn reached around his neck and carefully fastened the locket. After she drew back, her warmth lingered as if she remained pressed against him.

He gazed at the dewdrop and she seemed pleased by the way he admired it.

"What is this?" he asked.

"I think you know."

Will returned to the Recovery to find Rowe talking with Bremer. Rowe stopped midsentence and pointed to the necklace.

"Incredible," was all Rowe could say.

"And he has no idea what it is," Bremer added.

Ignoring their comments, Will described his encounter with Akia Tibers and the strange winged creature he'd seen before last night's celebration had begun.

"How many eyes did it have?" Rowe asked.

Will was uncertain.

"Thirteen?" Rowe pressed.

"That would be close."

"Aamon."

Bremer brooded.

"What was that thing?" Will asked.

"One of Sidara's minions," Rowe said. "Its numerous eyes and speed in flight make it ideal for overseeing a network of hunting parties."

"Sucks that Akia was in cahoots with it," Will said.

Rowe rubbed his chin in silence.

"So…will we be followed?" Will asked.

"It is difficult to tell," Rowe said.

"What do we do now?"

"We have few options ahead of us."

"Our best hope is to head deep into the Hollowtangle," Bremer suggested.

"That *would* make it difficult to be followed from the air," Rowe agreed, arching an eyebrow.

"I wouldn't worry about it, Rowe," Will said.

"Why not?"

"This trip has been one train wreck after another, yet here we are. Someone's watching out for us. Man, if I could get back home, I'd head straight to Vegas with the luck we're having."

"You are a strange man," Bremer said.

Will folded his arms and grinned. "Maybe so, but would you wager against me?"

Bremer scowled. "In my experience, luck has a habit of abandoning you when you need her most."

CHAPTER 27
FALLEN

After a hearty breakfast, Will helped Rowe and Bremer prepare the horses and secure their replenished saddlebags for the journey. Within the hour, they were ready to leave Fairbay. Rowe, Morgan, and Will mounted their horses, but Bremer returned to the Recovery, claiming he had something to take care of and that he'd catch up with them later. As the rogue entered the inn, Will tried not to imagine what he was up to.

As expected, many villagers gathered to see them off. Surprised murmurs rippled through the crowd when they learned the heroes were leaving so soon. They had hoped the celebrations might continue for many days. Avoiding a barrage of questions, Rowe had told them it was important for them to "investigate the happenings at Hammerclaw" and that they must do so alone, without guides.

So, amid much fanfare and well-wishes, they struck out on the wide, winding road that followed the eastern shore south toward the Bull River.

It did not take long for each to become lost in thought. Will had cringed when Morgan vomited twice before they left, and he kept an eye on her as they rode. Apparently, too much spiced wine mixed with tasty but unfamiliar fish stew made for an unsettling combination. A day in bed would have helped, but Rowe had insisted they reach the Bull River bridge before Sidara sent scouts north, and before her minion—the multi-eyed creature named Aamon—could orchestrate an ambush. If the bridge were cut off, their options would be reduced significantly.

Morgan groaned off and on as if struggling to scrape together an ounce of energy, but Will's spirits were high. Despite having to leave Ryowyn, he was grateful for the time they had shared. As he traced a finger along the necklace that she had given him, he breathed deeply, confident her memory would carry him through the dreary days ahead.

He gazed at the dazzling sea and lush trees, then glanced at the sky. "For whatever it's worth, I appreciate everything," he whispered. Like the transforming beauty of sunrise after a long night, his life had turned from murky gray to a multicolored mosaic filled with wonder and hope.

Morgan rubbed her eyes and grumbled at Will. "You seem wide awake this morning."

"I can't explain it, Morgan, but I think my prayers have been answered in ways I never expected."

Morgan's mouth moved silently as if a jumble of thoughts collided in her mind, but all she could say was, "That's nice."

After six hours of steady riding, they crested a steep ridge and rode into a small clearing atop a rocky bluff overlooking the Niasa Sea. Rowe slid from his saddle, and Will and Morgan quickly followed. The long ride without a break had left Will's muscles aching in places he never thought possible.

The vista was so breathtaking, Will temporarily forgot he could barely walk. He scanned the smooth waters hoping, even at this distance, for one final glimpse of Ryowyn.

"Do you see how the forest splits into two valleys past the southern shoreline?" Rowe asked.

Will nodded while Morgan stretched and breathed the fresh air.

"We will cross the Bull River at the first valley. Then, we will follow the second where we will come to some waterfalls that I suspect you are eager to see."

"I don't know, Rowe," Will said. "I think I need to find the black horse first, for all the sense that makes."

"You have not experienced the dream for some time now. Maybe you should speak of it again since you have had time to consider the matter without the emotion of it." Rowe climbed back into his saddle. Will and Morgan mounted their horses, and they continued onward.

"I'm standing on a high ridge looking down into a canyon with seven waterfalls," Will began. "There's some kind of tower behind me to my left. I could never see it in my dreams, yet I know what it looks like. And it's old—older than the Crow's Nest, I think. Before I can get a handle on it, the large black horse appears behind me to my right. Its presence overwhelms me, yet there's a connection between us, and somehow, I know that something important will happen in the next few moments. Then I wake up."

"Why did you think you'd find something like that in a stable?" Morgan asked, her first words in hours.

"That is an insight I had not considered," Rowe said.

"What do you mean?" Will asked.

"Well, did the horse give you the impression it could be locked away in a stable?" Rowe asked.

Will was quiet before shaking his head. "There's no way. It's too wild to be controlled."

"Have you ever been inside the tower, Rowe?" Morgan asked.

"I have only seen the Maidstone from a distance as I passed through the canyon. So little is written about the tower, and most of it is hearsay. One thing for certain is I have never read about anyone venturing close to it and living to recount the endeavor."

"Why is that?" Will asked.

"I don't know, but all who have seen it share a deeply rooted fear."

"Were *you* afraid?" Will asked.

"I do not understand, but as I traveled through its shadow, I was more unsettled than I ever remember being."

"Maybe that's why I need to find the horse before we go there."

For the rest of the day, they followed a winding road downward through the forest. As the sun neared the end of its journey west, the road led them back to the southern shore of the Niasa Sea, where they stopped for the second time.

"We will cross the river after dark, but we should eat something first. This is also where we part company with the horses."

After a light meal, Will and Rowe lifted their heavy packs over their shoulders. The magic within their Trannalun cloaks would help support much of the weight, Rowe explained, so Morgan could carry a smaller leather pack. Jessman had provided a quiver of arrows that Will secured to his belt behind the 1911. He held his bow loosely in one hand and a strip of dried meat in the other. With his sword at his left hip and a fresh confidence in his heart, he felt like a seasoned fighter, prepared for anything.

Over the next few hours' journey, the road often strayed from the Niasa Sea. At various points, the darkening forest of fir trees threatened to overtake the road with great drooping branches.

Sawdust covered the road. Rowe explained that many large branches had been cut back to allow the regular procession of wagons, heavy-laden with fish and vegetables, to pass through unhindered.

Each time the group emerged from the gloomy forest, moonlight greeted them anew, reflecting off the vast expanse of the sea.

"That sight could raise the spirits of a goblin," Rowe remarked.

Will caught Morgan's confused expression and shrugged. An image of Urk, Bremer's goblin friend, flashed in his mind. He scanned the forest, hoping they wouldn't encounter such dangerous creatures.

Time seemed to pass slowly after sunset. Occasionally, they would catch a glimpse of stars through the canopy of billions of small green needles. Somewhere during their relentless march, Will became keenly aware of someone following them. His confidence flickered as he struggled to stay in step with Rowe.

The river crossing proved uneventful. Will continued to search for signs of followers, but they seemed to be alone as they crossed. Once safely on the other side, they found a place to camp for the night near an outcropping of rocks in a large meadow. Rowe sat heavily on a small ledge and caught a chunk of cheese that Morgan tossed him.

"I'm starving," she said, breaking off another chunk for herself.

"Long day," Rowe said with a yawn.

"I'm feeling pretty good," Will added. "My feet hurt a bit, but I'm up for first watch."

※❦❧

Over the next two days, they traveled farther southwest along a swiftly flowing river. Bremer joined them somewhere along the trail during the second day. But while he traveled with them physically, he was aloof.

A steady, distant thunder rumbled ahead of them and grew louder with every step. Rowe waved Will to his side.

"That is the sound of the seven waterfalls." He pointed to a series of steep ridgelines. "That trail leads up a series of treacherous switchbacks to the Maidstone. My offer to take you there stands."

"No. Nothing feels right, Rowe. It's not time."

"How did you feel in the dream?"

"Extremely sad, like I was mourning the loss of someone," Will said. After a moment, he looked up and winked at Rowe. "Let's hope it's Bremer."

Bremer shook his head but didn't comment on Will's joke.

The granite walls closed in on them. Tension rose as they journeyed closer to the rolling currents of mist created by the waterfalls. Will's sensation of being watched increased, but Morgan was first to mention it.

"Why does it seem like someone is looking right through me?" she asked, wiping wet hair from her face.

"It is always so when traveling beneath the eye of the Maidstone," Rowe said.

He slipped the pack from his shoulders and pulled out a length of rope. He had Will hold it near the middle, with Morgan a few feet behind him. Rowe took the leading end of the rope while Bremer held the other end.

"When we enter the canyon," Rowe explained, "there can be no stopping or turning back. It will feel like you are walking through a hurricane. You will see very little, so do not let go of the rope—no matter what happens."

"And here I was expecting a nice view of a waterfall," Morgan muttered.

"We will enjoy the view from the other side. Until then, it will be a nasty stretch of trail," Rowe advised. Without another word, he adjusted his pack and gripped the rope.

Spaced along the twenty-foot length of rope, the four hikers followed the treacherous path into the heavy mist. Low-lying clouds shrouded any view of the cliff walls beyond a hundred feet up, but Rowe regularly scanned the heights, nonetheless. Will followed his gaze, searching for a glimpse of the Maidstone. He could not see the tower but felt the eyes upon him. It was an eerie, unmistakable feeling as if someone—or something—were searching his soul. The thundering continued and the heavy mists pressed closer as the white-knuckled group clung to the rope and moved forward.

After they had advanced for nearly an hour, the first waterfall rose before them, roaring over the cliff and down through torrents of mist like ten steam trains hurtling through a canyon. The deafening roar drowned out even their loudest cries. At times, Will could not see Rowe through the vortex of water-soaked wind currents. Across the narrow canyon, another waterfall was crashing over three ledges.

Shielding his face from the spray, Will noticed a large, smooth metal object by his feet, like a section of railroad track. It was impossible to get a clear view, but as he continued, several more sections appeared on the trail before disappearing beneath the ground. He supposed he might be hallucinating, but the trail took on the distinct appearance of a railbed. Dumbfounded, he tried to widen his eyes against the mist. With little effort now, he discerned two rails and four railroad ties as plain as he could see his feet. He could barely see Rowe's outline several feet ahead, so it would be futile to call out over the roaring water. Too afraid to stop, he kept his eyes fixed in front, but the tracks had disappeared again beneath the shale.

As they crossed the first of three natural bridges, Will gasped at the sight of a railcar partially submerged in the raging river below. It was leaning on its side and rusted beyond hope of being restored, but it clearly resembled the coal trains he had often seen back home.

Before reaching the end of the bridge, he saw a second railcar. He wiped his soaked face and sputtered as he considered the ramifications of what he was seeing. His father had worked for the Canadian National Railway his entire life. Those were railcars, without a doubt. Will tried to calm himself. The Big Dipper had led him to believe they were on earth, but this confirmed his theory. But where and when?

The path veered to the right before descending for a distance. It curved right a second time, and they ascended sharply, leaning forward to keep their footing on the slick, uneven path of broken shale. But the moment they started climbing, the chaos subsided as they left the seventh waterfall behind. The trail led to the left, where the visibility cleared dramatically. Everyone stopped and released their desperate grips on the rope. They examined one another to make certain they were all well, and Morgan laughed at how soaked they were.

Rowe pointed behind them. "There's the view I promised, Morgan."

Morgan and Will turned around and gasped. They had traveled up several hundred feet. The bright-blue sky contrasted with the dark-gray torrents of waterfall mist. Multiple rainbows stretched across the valley. No two were the same. Each was a different size with colors they had never seen in a rainbow. But unlike the rainbows they were familiar with, these skipped along the currents of wind as if alive and free.

"It's so beautiful," Morgan breathed.

"Yes," Rowe said. "But from here, you can also see how treacherous our path was. The waterfalls supply those two branches of the river running along the edge of each cliff face. See that point where the valley narrows? We were literally walking between the river on a narrow path less than ten feet wide."

"That's the patch of high ground that resembled a railbed," Will said. "Morgan, did you notice the railcars?"

"What?" She smiled slightly as if he were joking.

"I noticed pieces of train track on the path, and when we crossed the first bridge, I saw a railcar as clear as day beneath the water!"

"But—but how could you see *anything* clearly with all that mist?" Morgan asked.

"I saw it, Morgan, as clear as those rainbows! The river must have uncovered it, and that can only mean one thing!" Will could not contain himself.

"What?" Morgan asked.

Will nodded. "The future. The Gateway took us into the future."

Rowe seemed skeptical. "Are you certain of this?"

"No question."

"I didn't see anything like that," Morgan said.

"Let's go back; I can show you!"

"That would be ill-advised," Rowe said.

"But, why would there be an old railroad around here?" Morgan asked.

"First the Big Dipper and now this," Will said, raking back his wet hair. "Imagine if our world as we know it ended—all because the Dark Queen unleashed her poison back in Cochrane."

Morgan stared at him. "I always assumed that if the world were going to end, it would be a nuclear war or—or Armageddon."

They followed the trail out of the valley and into a forest of stately cedars. Will was exhausted. The others looked as bad as he felt, but Rowe pushed onward until the sun had almost set.

Will was about to ask if they were planning to continue all night when they strode into the ruins of an ancient village. Past the remains of two small stone buildings, they stepped into an overgrown courtyard surrounded by a two-foot-high stone wall. Behind it was the only structure in the area with a roof intact.

"What was this place?" Morgan asked.

"A hamlet called Pittbrire," Rowe answered. "The Hollowtangle was once a well-populated forest. Ruins like this stand as painful reminders of a history marred by war."

"Is that why we haven't seen anyone?" Morgan asked.

"Well, we've been staying off the main trails through the Hollowtangle to avoid Sidara's messengers," Rowe answered. "Since her army passed through the Stoneberg, Sidara has sent heralds throughout the lands to proclaim the ushering in of a new queen. I would prefer not to meet them on our journey. The problem for us is that her heralds are difficult to discern from common folk. They act first as spies when they enter a new area."

"Could Akia and that flying demon be Sidara's spies?" Will asked. "Are we worried about them?"

"I'll be worried about them until we win this war," Rowe said.

Bremer dropped his pack and rummaged through it for a chunk of dried meat before moving to an opening in the wall. "I wouldn't worry so much about Akia," he said.

"Why not?" Will asked.

"I killed him."

"What?" Will was stunned.

"I poisoned him after you told me about his conversation with Aamon. I expect he would have died in a way that would have appeared as though he had choked on a fish bone or the like, long after we all left."

Before another word was spoken, a large dark object dropped from the sky with a terrific thud beyond the short stone wall.

Everyone jumped, and Bremer spun around with both swords flashing.

A creature with two large dark-gray wings folding behind broad shoulders rose to its full height, dwarfing the tallest of humans. A wide, flat mouth opened and closed several times, exposing short, pointed teeth. A thin gray membrane of skin covered its face so tightly that veins bulged beneath it. Thirteen wide slits blinked, and two tiny flat nostrils flared, testing the air.

"Interesting timing," Bremer said in a low voice. "We were just talking about you, Aamon."

Despite the width of the creature's shoulders, its arms were disproportionately long and lanky, with sharp, sturdy claws. Its chest narrowed into a small waist. Dark skin stretched over the bones, muscles, tendons, and veins of two spindly legs. The creature wore no clothing and carried no weapon.

Something tickled Will's hand. He lowered his eyes and saw an arrow in one hand and Onathe's magical bow in the other. *How on earth did these get there?*

"All but dead," the creature growled in a raspy, nearly unintelligible voice.

"Not yet, Aamon," Rowe said, raising his sword. Morgan drew her sword and stood next to him, looking ready to attack.

Aamon made a clicking sound with its teeth that made Will's skin crawl. The noise grew louder and distorted as it echoed off the surrounding structures.

Bremer shot forward over the wall in a single bound as Rowe yelled at Will to shoot.

The creature's wings stretched out, creating a whirling dust cloud in the small clearing. Before it ascended, Bremer leapt off the wall with a terrific grunt, swords swinging. Aamon's wings came down, propelling its body upward, but not before Bremer stretched to his limit, severing the creature's foot at the ankle. Aamon shrieked and rose a dozen feet.

Will's left hand shot up as he nocked the arrow. A great rush of unfamiliar energy flowed through him, forcing the bow up and the string back.

The bowstring loosed with a deep thump, and the arrow whistled through the air. It struck Aamon high in the chest, slamming the creature back in a series of somersaults. Black ichor sprayed as Aamon crashed through the trees. By the time it hit the forest floor, little of Sidara's favorite minion remained.

A powerful wind rushed from Aamon's body and blew across the clearing. Will's Trannalun cloak opened and flapped behind him, exposing his body, but the main brooch held tight at his neck.

At the same moment, four small creatures resembling younger, meaner versions of the gnome healer Ellywick broke from the forest, firing small bolts from crossbows.

"Bush gnomes!" Rowe shouted.

A single bolt deflected off Will's cloak. He staggered backward as he struggled to close his cloak. But before he could protect himself, a second bolt struck him in the side beneath his armpit. The bolt plunged deep into his chest, and he collapsed. He tried to cry out but couldn't find his voice. Each breath was shallow and strained. As gnomes invaded the area, Will watched helplessly as his friends engaged the attackers.

Bremer dropped onto his back as four bolts whooshed over his head. Casting aside their crossbows, the gnomes drew short swords and attacked, but Bremer rebounded to his feet as quickly as he had hit the ground. He lunged forward. His first sword slashed across the lead gnome's exposed chest, slicing through layers of ragged green clothing. The gnome fell to the ground. Bremer's other blade hacked the shins of the second gnome. It dropped awkwardly to its knees as Bremer slid to avoid the short blade of the third gnome. The momentum carried the gnome stumbling sideways, and Bremer's sword opened its exposed neck.

The fourth gnome brought its sword down in a high arc. A moment sooner, it would have cut Bremer in half. Instead, the rogue slid a half step back as the sword whistled past his face before sinking into the dry ground. The gnome jabbed with a knife that just missed plunging into Bremer's chest. In one fluid motion, Bremer cut off the gnome's hand with his sword while driving his second blade deep into the gnome's chest.

As Bremer fought the four gnomes, two more sprang at Rowe and Morgan from behind a large rock. The small creatures' forest garb flowed as they fired crossbow bolts before drawing short swords.

Rowe raised his sword to block the first attack and kicked the gnome in the chest while sidestepping the second blade that came down in a high arc. With a quick jab, he drove the hilt of his sword into the gnome's face, and its head snapped back with a shattered nose. Rowe plunged the blade of his boot knife through its heart.

The gnome he kicked recovered its footing and clashed blades with Rowe. The creature lunged, and its short sword bounced harmlessly off Rowe's cloak. The gnome's eyes opened wide with the revelation of its fatal mistake. Rowe slashed open its chest.

Another gnome rushed past Rowe. Morgan raised her sword, bent her knees, and assumed the en garde position. The creature attacked, its mouth opened in a nearly toothless grin. Shorter and leaner than Morgan, it moved with surprising agility despite layers of loose clothing. The gnome tried to slap Morgan's blade from her hands, but she whipped her sword around, and the gnome's sword flew from its hand. The gnome's confident grin vanished. Morgan lunged, and her sword cut clean and quick, exiting through the gnome's back.

Almost as quickly as they had attacked, the few surviving gnomes retreated into the forest. One by one, Bremer, Rowe, and Morgan came to Will's side. He was vaguely aware of their presence.

Morgan fell to her knees beside him and sucked in a sharp breath.

Will followed her gaze to his bloodied side and the small dark pool saturating the soil. He met her eyes for a second before his eyelids closed against his will. All sound was fading. His breathing became slow and staggered.

Seconds later, his eyes flickered open. He could see Rowe's lips moving but heard nothing. His eyelids drooped again. Try as he might, he could not keep them open. He wanted to ask what was happening but realized something had gone terribly wrong. The worried faces of his friends faded into darkness.

✦

Panic battered Morgan's chest like unremitting waves in a winter storm. She cast desperate looks at Rowe and Bremer.

Rowe dropped to his knees and examined the end of the bolt protruding from Will's bloodied side. Only four or five inches were visible. "Get his cloak around him!"

Morgan helped him pull the cloak from under Will's body and spread it on the ground. Together, they rolled him onto it and wrapped him in it. Rowe jerked both sides tight and pressed down on the garment.

Nothing happened.

He pulled it tighter and waited.

Nothing happened.

With trembling hands, he tucked the cloak around Will's body, pushing and wrapping down to his feet.

Nothing happened.

"What are you waiting for!" Morgan cried. "Why isn't it working?"

Rowe threw up his hands. "The cloak…it—it…the magic should be… It should be warm, but…" He pressed the garment gently against the wound and held his breath.

Nothing happened.

Bremer placed a finger against Will's neck and waited. After a moment, he slumped.

Rowe opened Will's cloak and grasped the end of the bolt. He inhaled deeply, pulled the bolt free with a single tug, and promptly pushed the cloak down over the gaping wound.

Still, nothing happened.

Rowe slouched, released a deflating breath, and stared at Morgan's ashen face.

CHAPTER 28

SACRIFICE

Will opened his eyes, but his vision was slow to return. He squinted against the bright sunlight as his mind cleared. The sound of gentle waves lapping the shore reached his ears. He turned his head to see more, and warm, soft sand fell from his cheek. He blinked and raised his head slightly. *Is this a dream?*

Ryowyn lay next to him, her captivating eyes glistening in the sunlight. Contentment spread over him like a cumulus cloud on a hot, sunny day: the shade offered relief but foreshadowed an unwelcome change. Ryowyn brushed her fingers through his hair. It certainly felt real. As she leaned in to kiss him, her smile faltered. Will's heart lurched. Something was wrong.

He tried to sit up but found he could not move. A tear formed in Ryowyn's right eye and rolled down her cheek in slow motion. She wiped the tear, trying in vain to recover her smile.

Will attempted to collect his muddled thoughts that ebbed and flowed in rising waves of panic. He could not remember the moments leading to this one.

"Shhhh," Ryowyn soothed. "Everything is as it should be, my

Will. My tear was that of joy at having you near, if only for this moment."

He tried to speak but had no command of his voice. Again, her fingers combed his hair and brushed his cheek with a gentleness that calmed his racing mind.

"I wish we could remain here forever, but there is much that is required of you. I must let you go."

Will tried desperately to shake his head but failed. Every muscle resisted movement.

"I will always be with you, my Will. No matter how bleak the path ahead becomes, I will be your light."

Suddenly, everything went dark as if someone had flipped a switch. Will was cold and alone. He tried to scream, but he could neither move nor speak. Seconds later, Ryowyn's hand rested on his heart and he drew a deep, desperate breath of air.

Morgan wept, staring at Will's lifeless form. Rowe knelt in silence with his arm around her. Bremer had disappeared into the forest.

"I've sat with many soldiers and friends as they died," Rowe said, "but this…"

Morgan squeezed his hand, wishing she could have done something different over the past few hours, something that could have altered Will's fate. Her other hand rested on Will's chest as hope for a miracle withered. She closed her eyes.

After several minutes, she blinked. Something was different. Will remained motionless, yet something had changed that would have been easy to miss. Her hand warmed.

She turned to Rowe, who was gazing at the necklace around Will's neck. His face brightened. He reached down and gently pulled the thin cord from beneath Will's shirt. In the otherwise flawless dewdrop-shaped pendant was a tiny dark speck.

"What's happening, Rowe?"

"Ryowyn's pendant," he said. "I didn't have a chance to discuss the implications of her gift with Will. I would do anything to have him back, but…I did not expect this." His voice caught in his throat as if a terrible pain stabbed his heart.

Shattering the somber stillness, Will drew in a sudden breath of air. The Trannalun cloak shimmered. Will's eyes flew open. He sat up, and Rowe grasped his shoulders to steady him. Morgan stared with lips partly opened in shock.

"It's good to have you back," Rowe said, masking his concern about Ryowyn's pendant.

Bremer rushed from the forest. "How can this be?"

"The…cloak has healed his wound," Rowe answered.

"How do you feel, Will?" Bremer asked.

"Thirsty." Will rubbed his neck, then lowered his hand until he found the necklace.

"What's wrong?" Bremer asked.

"It must have been a dream," Will said. "I was with Ryowyn."

Rowe wore a pained smile, and Morgan noticed a hint of recognition in Bremer's face. As if anticipating a question, Rowe raised a hand to silence him.

Morgan snapped out of her shock and hugged Will.

"Was I knocked out or something?" Will asked.

"Something like that." Rowe handed Will a waterskin. "What's the last thing you remember?"

"I—I dunno."

Rowe stood. "Bremer, let's do a wide sweep of the area to make certain the gnomes have all tucked tails. Morgan can stay here with Will until we return."

Rowe spun on his heels and disappeared past the ruins while Bremer ran in the opposite direction.

"Why is Rowe acting so strange?" Will asked. "And why were you crying, Morgan? What did I miss?"

Morgan smiled and hugged him again.

⚜

After a light meal the next morning, Morgan helped Will with his pack. He appeared weary and sad to her but seemed as ready as the others to continue their journey. Considering the trauma he had experienced, she was amazed he could even walk so soon.

They pushed hard all day and slept little the following night, each of them agreeing that they needed to make up for lost time. As the sun warmed their backs, they climbed a steep hill that was a patchwork of trees, wildflowers, and rocky outcroppings. The crest of the hillside led them over a narrow ridgeline, and a cool wind soothed their flushed faces.

To the south were some of the largest mountains Morgan had ever seen. Dark-gray granite rose several thousand feet to form thirteen snow-covered peaks.

"Those are the Thirteen Sisters that form the Border Lands," Rowe said. "We are getting closer."

He led them along the ridgeline until they came to a trail that followed a series of wide switchbacks that cut through a jagged reddish-orange cliff down into a canyon.

"This trail is the only way in," Rowe explained.

They were about to descend when Rowe turned and stopped. Less than two miles east of them was the trailing end of a supply caravan. Hundreds of horse-drawn wagons, heavily laden with food and supplies, flowed eastward like a murky river.

"Our timing could not have been better," Rowe said as they ducked from view. "They must have passed by this very spot less than an hour ago. This canyon is the primary passage through the western mountains. Those wagons are traveling east between the Hollowtangle and the wetlands of Bayou Sorral. I imagine they are going to supply Sidara's army at Hammerclaw."

"So, we're heading *that* way, right?" Morgan pointed west in the opposite direction of the caravan.

"Yes, around that ridge." Rowe pointed in the same direction to where the canyon narrowed and disappeared around a bend. "We will find shelter there for the rest of the day."

"Where's Bremer?" Morgan asked.

"He spent the night backtracking in wide circles to ensure nothing picked up our trail."

Without waiting for Rowe's lead, Will trudged past them along the first switchback as if too exhausted to stop or afraid of not being able to continue.

Morgan watched him shuffle along. She cleared her throat and lowered her voice. "What are you not telling him about the necklace, Rowe?"

Rowe was quiet for a moment. "The necklace Ryowyn gave him…well, the pendant… it connected them."

"What do you mean, *connected*?"

Rowe folded his arms across his chest and huffed. "There's no easy way to say it: Will died back there, and Ryowyn came to him. *She* brought him back to life, not his cloak. I know that because when a Callum Sage dies, the magic within the cloak dies with him. It was cold and lifeless."

Morgan licked her dry lips and swallowed. "How was she able to bring him back to life?"

"According to mer folklore—which I used to think was mere romantic legend—she offered her life for his."

A terrible ache replaced the relief Morgan had been enjoying since Will's recovery. "He said she came to him. Do you think he knows what happened?"

"I believe he senses something is wrong. His soul is mourning her loss, and soon he will make that connection."

"That's why he seems so sad." Morgan noted the change in Will's gait as he continued along the trail. "Like the sadness he described in the last few dreams of the Maidstone and the black horse."

Rowe sighed heavily. "I wish I knew what it all meant."

When the last caravan wagon faded from view, Rowe and Morgan followed the first switchback and soon caught up with Will.

"We must watch for stragglers in the canyon," Rowe advised. "They might have left behind a few gnome scouts."

Will yawned loudly. "Is there any cover once we get down there? This canyon looks like a frying pan, and I need a rest."

"I believe there is a small grove ahead, but we must keep moving. Stay close. If we push hard, we will reach the trees in an hour. We can rest there."

"What about Bremer?" Will asked. "Shouldn't we wait for him?"

"I think you know better than to worry about him," Rowe answered.

When they reached the canyon floor, they kept close to one wall. It was better than walking through the middle of the canyon, but if there were stragglers from the caravan, there would be nowhere to hide should trouble appear. Fortunately, after nearly an hour, the only remnant of the caravan was a few dead horses, probably forced to pull wagons until they had collapsed from exhaustion.

They rounded a bend and stopped to marvel at a massive gray wall spanning the canyon far ahead.

"That is the Stoneberg," Rowe announced. "This canyon is the closest passage between Sidara's lands and our own."

"I thought that was a mountain range, but it looks man-made!" Will exclaimed.

"It is. Our current queen's great-great-grandfather commissioned its construction after years of fighting to hold the valley. Upon completion, a garrison of hundreds replaced an army of thousands."

"What's all that in front of the wall?" Morgan asked.

"The remnants of the town of Longcross. Until recently, when the wall was breached, a few hundred people had called it home. Most were defenders of the Stoneberg…and their families."

"But how could anything breach that wall?" Will asked.

"The Stoneberg has but a single iron gate that allows passage between lands. Ten feet thick, the gate was fashioned from a blend of alloys, making it virtually indestructible."

"Virtually?" Will said.

"Sidara was careful in preparing General Raric's ambush," Rowe explained. "Not only had she wanted him as her prisoner, she also wanted the key he carried around his neck—the key to the Stoneberg gate. She orchestrated an act of treason, and…here we are."

"Did the people of Longcross escape?" Morgan asked.

"Possibly. But remember how long the canyon is."

"It must have been awful." Morgan stared at the ruins. "Women and children running for their lives…"

They arrived at the grove Rowe had referred to, a half-acre forest of spruce trees two miles from the Stoneberg. Before they entered the shelter of trees, Rowe pointed to something moving about halfway between them and the wall.

"What is that?" Morgan asked.

"There's a… It's a wagon. And it's…it's being pulled by something huge."

"Let's have a closer look."

Morgan flinched at the sudden sound of Bremer's voice. She had been so focused on the Stoneberg and the fate of Longcross that she hadn't noticed him approaching from behind.

Bremer stood beside Rowe and gazed at the wagon in the distance. He retrieved a small spyglass from his pack and held it to his eye.

"A couple of rhinos pulling a heavy wagon, with one big rider," he said.

Rowe squinted. "Not the kind of straggler I expected. Can you see the payload?"

"No. There's some type of frame on the wagon. And I think the rider is a giant, but I can't tell what kind."

Morgan exchanged a surprised look with Will, who mouthed the word *giant*.

"Can you—" Rowe began before Bremer cut him short.

"There are two hellhounds walking beside the wagon."

"Not good. The breeze is flowing from the wall," Rowe said. "They will have our scent soon after they pass."

"I want to know what's in the wagon," Bremer said.

"As do I," Rowe added.

"Hellhounds?" Morgan asked. "What's that?"

"Shouldn't be a problem," Rowe said.

"How's that?" Will asked. "I've come to assume everything's a problem in these parts."

"They're traveling with that wagon—or more accurately, with the payload," Rowe said.

"With that kind of escort, the payload will be worth getting our hands bloodied," Bremer said.

"Great," Morgan groaned. "Now I definitely don't want to know what a hellhound is."

Rowe took the spyglass from Bremer and held it to his eye. "It's moving extremely slow. At this pace, the wagon could be an hour or two before it passes us." He folded the spyglass. "Get some rest back in the trees, and I will keep watch."

CHAPTER 29

DISCOVERED

Will and Morgan were asleep the moment their heads hit the soft bed of spruce needles beneath the trees. Rowe sat with Bremer and watched in silence as the scene unfolded before them at an excruciatingly slow pace.

Both rhinos had massive horns protruding from broad, flat heads. Enormous dark-gray plates covered in loose, cracked hide shielded their bodies like exoskeletons. Their wide feet left deep indentations in the hard ground.

Thick chain harnesses clinked and rattled behind the rhinos, connecting twelve-inch timbers to a single hitch. The flat deck wagon was reinforced with thick iron slats. Fastened to the deck was a rectangular frame made of twelve-inch timbers six feet high. A large round flagon made of thick frosted glass hung from heavy cords wrapped tightly around all four corners of the timber frame. At over five feet in diameter and with no visible opening, the glass container must have held at least two hundred gallons of liquid that swirled back and forth as the wagon plodded along.

On a tall bench built into the front of the wagon sat a giant.

When standing, he was probably over fifteen feet tall. A loose brown tunic cinched at the waist with a wide belt was open in front, revealing an expansive, muscular chest. The only weapon visible was a large, burnished oval shield that hung outside the wagon's frame.

Two hellhounds roamed nearby, giving the wagon a wide berth. Their snouts were low to the ground. With bristling black fur, each stood over four feet high at the shoulders. Despite their considerable weight, the hounds seemed capable of running down anything they attacked.

Set back among the spruce trees, Rowe studied the wagon and its driver. Bremer lay next to him beneath a low-hanging branch, his bow out in front with the empty quiver humming gently in response to the danger. Both swords and a full brace of knives were within reach.

"Storm giant," Rowe said darkly.

"And the hellhounds are widening their circles around the wagon," Bremer said. "If they pick up our scent, we'll have our hands full."

Rowe examined the blanket of dried spruce needles. Hell-hounds—especially those as big as these two—could breathe fire across a great distance, so it would take little for them to turn the trees into a firestorm.

The gentle thumping of the rhinos' footfalls grew louder, and the reinforced wheels groaned under the wagon's weight. The sound awakened Will and Morgan, and they scrambled to find their weapons.

Will was several feet behind Rowe and Bremer with wide eyes, and his hands clutched his bow in a tight grip. He found an arrow, but Rowe held up his hand, signaling for Will to hold fast. He was concerned that the lure of the elven bow might overpower him as it did in the Hollowtangle.

As the wagon drew closer, Rowe pulled his cloak tightly around his chest. Morgan quietly moved next to him with her sword ready.

The storm giant glanced at the trees a few times but paid it little heed. Behind him, the precious liquid within the giant flagon swished and sloshed as the wagon rocked gently.

The hellhounds rushed about, sniffing rotting carcasses and debris left behind by the war supply caravan.

As the wagon came closer, a hellhound ran to the remains of what might have been a small dog about thirty yards from the trees. The other hound circled around the wagon and started to run to the far side of the canyon. The storm giant, who to this point had sat stone-still, pointed at the trees. Both creatures regrouped at the small carcass, sniffed it once more, then continued toward the trees.

The four humans tensed.

One hellhound approached with its head down, nose to the ground. It looked up as though seeing the tiny forest for the first time. Its head tilted slightly as its snout tested the air. A low, guttural growl reverberated from the depths of its being. The other hellhound trotted over. Fortunately, the steady breeze carried the humans' scent farther down the canyon, making them undetectable from where the hellhounds stood. But something had caught their attention, although it was impossible to tell where the creatures were looking because their eyes were a solid red.

Beneath the dense overhanging branches, Rowe and the others were completely shrouded within heavy shadows cast by the trees. But they would not remain protected for long. All the while, the wagon rolled slowly past.

Suddenly, the storm giant let out a sharp whistle. Both hellhounds spun around and returned to the wagon that was now as close as it would come to the group hidden in the trees.

For a brief moment, Rowe thought it would pass uneventfully until one of the hellhounds jerked its head up, sniffing the air. Both creatures caught a scent, spun around, and ran to the trees. Heavy snarls filled the air.

"We need to get to the downhill side of this, and *quick*!" Bremer hissed.

Across the canyon, something caught Rowe's attention. At the base of the rocky bluffs the light bent, making most of the rock appear out of focus. The illusion vanished, and an elvish battle cry rang out as twenty riders on horseback charged into the canyon toward the wagon.

The hellhounds reared and filled the canyon with heinous howls. Changing course, they sprinted to intercept the riders.

The storm giant grabbed his shield and a whip that was curled in a tight circle at his feet. He stood to his full height. The whip cracked like a streak of lightning above the rhinos, and they turned slowly to face the approaching riders. The sharp sound of the snapping whip echoed off the canyon walls, and everyone's hair charged with static.

"What is that?" Will rose to one knee.

"We need to move…*now*!" Rowe said.

Morgan scrambled to her feet.

"Wait!" Bremer said as he rose into a crouch. He traced a rune embedded deep in his leather quiver. After a small flash, a single arrow appeared as thin as a blade of grass at the point, widening all the way down the shaft to nearly an inch thick at the nock.

"No one is leaving the canyon alive while that storm giant has enough breath to stand." Bremer handed the translucent arrow to

Will and raised a finger. "Wait for my signal. I have no idea how the magic in the bow will respond to the magic in the arrow, so keep your cloak about you."

The elves continued their charge. They all wore the same thin leather armor, but some carried bows while others held long spears. Fine blond hair trailed behind each rider as their horses galloped as one. In the next second, they broke into four groups. One group veered right, and another left, as the two remaining groups sent a volley of arrows whistling toward the wagon.

The storm giant brought his massive arm up and snapped it forward. A bright streak of lightning flashed as the whip cracked in front of the rhinos, shattering the hail of arrows into a thousand shards of wood that floated to the ground like harmless toothpicks.

The lightning whip came back in a high arc before the giant sent it forward a second time. An elf rider dove from his mount to avoid the whip that struck his mare in the forehead. A violent crackle electrified the air as the mare's skull exploded from the impact. Arcs of lightning lanced out, catching the rider in midflight and burning him to ash before he hit the ground.

The first hellhound to reach the wagon leapt up beside the giant flagon and sent a blast of flames into three riders. Elvish cries filled the air as the two who narrowly avoided the flames launched their spears before turning their galloping steeds away. One spear caught the hellhound in the shoulder while the other clipped the creature's back and deflected loudly off the flagon. The storm giant spun around to steady the flagon, then raised the whip above his head for another attack.

The second hellhound bounded around the other side of the wagon as a group of five riders galloped past. It leapt up and, finding flesh, pushed the rider from his saddle, but not before the elf drove a long knife into its stomach. A savage twist of the blade and a frantic shove parted the two as a pair of riders bore down. The creature faltered as if trying to summon its fiery breath. Before the hellhound could defend itself, the riders drove their spears deep. The beast roared and erupted into an explosion of flames.

An elvish arrow struck the storm giant's arm. He pulled it out and tossed it aside, bringing the whip around in a high circle once, then twice, before lashing out. The end of the whip came around and cracked a few feet above five riders who were making a wide circle around the wagon in an attempt to get to the flagon. The whip snapped loudly, and the tip erupted into a burst of lightning that tore through the five riders and their horses.

Will held his bowstring completely taut.

At the sight of the nocked arrow, Rowe yelled at him to stop but was too late. A second before Will released, Rowe grasped a tree trunk, anticipating a gust similar to the one that followed the arrow that had killed Aamon. But this one was worse.

The resounding blast whipped through the trees. Rowe's cloak bore the brunt of it, but the gust slammed Will against another tree and sent Morgan tumbling to the bluffs. Bremer had slid behind a boulder at the last second.

The arrow's path was silent, but rocks loosened from the canyon walls. In flight for less than two heartbeats, the arrow struck the storm giant in his lower back and exited through his stomach. The velocity created a vacuum that sucked out most of the giant's insides, sending them splashing to the ground.

Now without a driver, the wagon rolled forward. The flagon swayed but appeared sound.

Rowe pulled himself to his hands and knees and crawled out from the trees, waiting for the dust to settle so he could see the wagon. Initially, he thought they had been lucky but noticed something leaking from a small crack in the glass.

A translucent green gas spread so quickly, it caught the rhinos unaware. Both creatures reared before their bodies disintegrated. As the wagon crumbled, the flagon shattered. Panicked cries filled the air.

"Run!" came the distant shout from an elf who was pulling himself onto his horse. Several others saddled up and galloped back to the main switchback trail.

"Move!" Rowe yelled as he grabbed Will by the cloak, jerking him to his feet. *"Go!"* he yelled again, pushing a stunned Will out from the trees. He turned back to search for Morgan, and she stumbled from the trees with Bremer close behind.

"Oh, thank goodness!" she cried. "I thought you were all dead!"

"We will be if we don't get going!" Bremer pushed her after Will, and they all raced along the bluffs toward the Stoneberg.

Bremer sprinted ahead of everyone, and after a long run, he stopped and turned, spyglass in hand.

"What do you see?" Rowe shouted as he caught up.

"The wind is pushing the cloud east!"

"Are you certain?" Rowe wiped his sweaty forehead as Morgan and Will joined them, breathing heavily.

Bremer nodded. "It's clear across the canyon and getting higher. The grove we were in is gone."

"I've never seen such a thing," Rowe said, fighting to catch his breath.

Bremer lowered the spyglass. "Imagine if that flagon was meant for the Crow's Nest?"

"I was thinking the same thing."

"Which begs the question…"

"Where was it being taken?" Rowe finished.

"Somewhere to turn a castle into a graveyard."

Rowe sighed as they continued at a fast walk. Will and Morgan followed in silence, clearly shaken by the encounter. The brisk pace made conversation with Bremer somewhat stilted between breaths.

"I would love to know how many more of those flagons Sidara has."

"Best hope that was the only one."

"How far do you think the poison will travel before it dissipates?"

"No telling," Bremer said with a shrug.

"How did Sidara create such a thing?" Morgan asked.

"Rumor has it that nearly half the Waerdreath was set up for the study of alchemy," Rowe answered.

"I'd say her alchemists have been busy," Bremer said. "Makes me wonder if the rumors about Phyriad are true."

Rowe huffed. "After what we just saw, I'm assuming Phyriad is a genuine threat. But good to know we are not alone in trying to stop Sidara."

"Interesting," Bremer said. "Did those elves break cover to save us, or were they going after the wagon?"

"I would have given much for a brief word with them." Rowe shook his head. "Were they a small hunting party working alone, or is there more going on here than we know?"

"Think they were sent by Cinhalla?" Bremer asked.

"I believe so."

"Bold move…for elves."

"I wish I knew if they were alone," Rowe said.

CHAPTER 30

THE STONEBERG

The closer they came to the massive stone wall stretching several hundred yards across the canyon, the more Will longed to be back in Fairbay. Since the encounter with the gnomes in the Hollowtangle, he had the growing sensation that something bad had happened to Ryowyn. The loneliness that was a regular part of his life in Cochrane was knocking again at his heart's door, but he refused to let it back in.

Rowe stopped everyone at the outskirts of the charred remains of Longcross. Almost everything in the small village had been burned, including bodies. Human and animal remains littered the ruins. The sheer extent of the destruction left little evidence of what had once been a peaceful community.

Morgan wept at the horrific scene. Rowe put his arm around her and led them all to a huge keep built out from the middle of the massive wall. Ghostly quiet, the keep was a marvel to behold. On either side of the structure was a tall tower topped with an overhanging conical roof. At the center of the keep was a wide tunnel leading to the Stoneberg gate.

"The entire structure, including the towers," Rowe explained, "was constructed as part of the Stoneberg wall. Its sole purpose: to defend that tunnel."

Giant curved staircases rose high above either side of the tunnel and joined at the keep's fifteen-foot-tall front entry. An enormous wooden door lay at the base, and another hung precariously on a single hinge. Both doors were badly burned. Rowe stopped at the bottom step and pointed to the entrance.

"What you see are the remains of the infamous double door. They were carved by a descendant of the dwarf craftsman Maxhan Barak as a gift to solidify the truce between King Celthric and the dwarven nation of Thanktharkus. One door displayed the king's crest of a timber wolf's head, and the other the great ax of Thanktharkus."

"Looks like Sidara's not interested in a truce," Will said.

"Not at all." Rowe pointed up and to his right. "We will bed down in the Upper North Tower."

"We're *staying* here?" Will said, thumbing the shoulder straps of his backpack.

"The north tower has a secondary secret passage. We can lock ourselves in there to get some rest. This place is deserted, and it will be the last place we will find safety for the foreseeable future."

"Great," Will mumbled sarcastically. "Looks nice and cozy."

"Aren't you exhausted, Will?" Morgan asked. "I could sleep upside down in a closet right now."

They followed Rowe up the scorched stone steps into the keep. The burnt doors made the keep inhospitable enough, but the Mark of Natas etched across the crown of the entrance made it worse. Inside, however, the smell of fresh air flowing through the keep eased Will's fear of what they might find inside.

He took a shaky breath and followed the others through the elevated foyer that branched into four smaller hallways. Broken furniture lay scattered everywhere. Each footstep echoed off the barren walls that once held the colorful tapestries now piled at the base of the walls.

The dreary walk through empty hallways and up tight spiral stairs drained the last of Will's energy. At the top of the stairs, they reached a narrow hallway that spanned both towers. There, they turned left and passed a dozen embrasures before the hallway ended at another spiral stairwell. Will took a deep breath, summoning a small reserve of strength.

At the top of those stairs, they entered a wide circular room. The shutters here were all closed, leaving the room shrouded in shadows. Morgan instantly dropped her pack, spread out her bedroll, and lay down.

The sparsely furnished tower room was somewhat cleaner than the rest of the keep. Three plush leather chairs sat against the far side of the room next to a round table with five wooden chairs around it. Near the embrasures were tall stools that Rowe explained were positioned to allow a high perch for those on watch duty.

Will sunk into a padded leather chair and stretched out his legs. Rowe crouched beside him and pushed a knot in a floor plank that released a narrow trapdoor. Below the door, an iron ladder disappeared down into the darkness.

"How could you have known about that?" Will asked, peering over Rowe's shoulder.

"I have been planning this journey for some time," Rowe said. "Get some rest while I go down to make certain the way below is passable."

"I'll go," Bremer said and, without waiting for a response, started down the ladder.

"Left leads to the kitchens," Rowe explained. "At the end of the passage, there should be a latch down by your feet to open another door. Right leads to the main quarters. There you will see the peepholes; look for the latch up above them."

Rowe closed the trapdoor behind Bremer and turned to Will. "Do you have elves where you are from?"

"No," Will answered. "Only in stories."

"Judging by your reaction earlier, I thought not. This land must seem quite foreign to you."

"I feel like I'm getting pretty close to my wits' end," Will said, prompting a slight smile from Rowe. "That glass container was something else."

"As was your shot." Rowe dropped his pack and stretched.

"This bow has a mind of its own."

"Magic always does."

Morgan propped herself up on her elbows. "So, were those elves on our side?"

"Rarely do elves get involved in the affairs of men. I cannot say what their purpose was."

Will closed his eyes and leaned his head back, tracing the length of his necklace with his fingers. "Let me keep first watch," he said, opening his eyes.

"There's no need for a watch tonight," Rowe said. "Besides, you're exhausted."

"I am, but I need some time alone to think."

"I believe all will be revealed as it should, Will. I leave you to your thoughts." Rowe bent to untie the laces of his leather boots. "But please, get some sleep."

He rubbed his feet before slipping off his wool socks. Standing, he pulled off his shirt and scratched a long scar across his lower back. He lay down on his cloak next to Morgan and kissed her forehead. She reached out from beneath her blanket and squeezed his forearm. Within a few minutes, they were both breathing heavily.

Will stood and went to a window facing east. He scanned the canyon they had walked through, thinking about the storm giant and the deadly cargo it had been carrying. He walked around to the other side and sat up on a tall stool. Looking down, he gasped loud enough to awaken Rowe, who was by his side in an instant.

In the canyon, several large crosses, crudely made from enormous timbers, formed three uniformly spaced rows a hundred yards from the Stoneberg. His stomach churned at the sight of so many crucifixions, a practice he had thought died with the Roman Empire.

"Are they…dead?" Will asked.

Rowe sighed. "No way to say from this distance. It's the Dark Queen's way of warning those who wish to travel west. It gives them a tangible reason to turn back."

"Are we gonna see more of this?" Will asked.

Rowe returned to his bedroll. "I wish I could promise you otherwise."

Someone was strolling between the crosses. It was impossible to discern what the person was doing, but Will assumed it was not good. He traced his fingers across the bow—which, once again, he could not remember picking up—and considered the possibility of hitting the person with an arrow, even at this distance. Since the bow was magic, he assumed the shot would be successful. Taking the thought a step further, he considered firing arrows at all the people on the crosses to end their suffering.

Far from the crucifixion scene, something else caught Will's attention. Three figures ran through the canyon near the cliffs as though chased by a wild animal. They appeared to be working their way toward the Stoneberg. Will gazed at them for a moment, then another person approached the crucifixions. But Will knew this man, and he guessed his intentions.

Bremer found the tunnel leading out of the keep and surveyed the outside area west of the wall. Appalled but not entirely surprised to see the crucifixion scene, he marched toward them, barely able to contain his indignation.

Between one row stood a tall lanky gnome with a long spear. The gnome stabbed at a person nailed high above the dry ground, inducing the muffled cries of a man in the final terrible moments of his life.

"Hey, ugly!" Bremer's booming voice cracked.

The gnome whipped around in surprise but quickly regained his composure. The trace of fear in his large eyes quickly vanished.

Intricate runes tattooed the gnome's light-brown skin, including his shaved head. Large metal piercings hung from his face: some above his glaring, bulbous eyes; one through his flat nose; a few in his high cheeks; and several in his droopy ears. Even his thin lips were pierced. His only piece of clothing was a pair of torn and dirty britches. The creature was lanky, but Bremer was taken aback by the gnome's height.

Despite efforts to hide it, the gnome had been caught off guard and was taking his time assessing the intruder. Bremer despised the merciless bush gnomes, and this one seemed especially void of grace and full of evil intent. The filth and blood on the gnome made Bremer wonder what it would be like to see ten thousand gnomes organized under Sidara's banner. Their devious minds made them formidable in battle, and with such a high birth rate, they were the perfect race to fill her ranks.

The gnome lowered his spear and wandered over to his pack, his eyes locked on Bremer. He buckled a belt and scabbard around his waist, adjusting a sword at his side. Grabbing the spear, he hastened toward Bremer, who was nearing the first row of crosses.

"Halt! Unholy ground this is," the gnome called out, quickening his pace to meet Bremer before he reached the crosses.

"Final words," Bremer growled through clenched teeth as he gazed at the crucified men. He knew enough about war to know that those nailed to the crosses were all captured human soldiers, possibly the defenders of the Stoneberg. The few eyes that were open reflected a delirious sense of hopelessness. In that moment, Bremer realized none could be saved.

The gnome rushed past the first row to intercept Bremer. "*Halt, I said!*" He jabbed the spear with a dangerously long reach.

Bremer spun his upper body sideways and leaned back, narrowly avoiding the bloodstained blade. He grabbed at the shaft, but fresh blood caused it to slip through his fingers as the gnome wrenched it back.

The gnome thrust the spear again, and this time, the blade cut Bremer across the shoulder as he shifted out of the way half a second too late. The gnome shuffled back, sliding the spear through his fingers until he brought the blade to his lips. He licked the blood with a long dark tongue, but Bremer saw fear in his eyes.

"That'll be the end of you," Bremer said, taking a few quick steps forward.

The spear came down fast, but Bremer caught the shaft with

his left hand and spun around so quickly, he jerked the gnome close. With his back momentarily to his foe, Bremer slammed his elbow into the gnome's face, snapping his head back. Blood erupted from the shattered nose. Bremer spun around again and, keeping a firm grip on the shaft, sent the spear back as quickly as he had pulled it.

The gnome somehow kept his hands on the weapon until Bremer's boot came around in a high arc, catching him across the cheek. The impact drove the gnome to the ground, and before he could recover, Bremer tossed the spear to the side and drew a sword. In a quick, fluid motion, he sliced the scrambling gnome's Achilles tendon. The gnome's cry echoed off the canyon walls.

Bremer bent low. "By the time death overtakes you, you'll be begging for it."

A gruff coughing sound from beyond the crosses drew Bremer's attention away from the gnome. He stood slowly, shielding his eyes from the late-afternoon sun, squinting at three strangers approaching on foot. He swallowed dryly, trying to comprehend what he was seeing.

Tattered clothing flapped from their scrawny forms as they leaned into a frenzied gait. Ash-gray scales covered their bodies. Their legs were unnaturally long, their heads disproportionately large. Muscular arms with huge clawed hands swung frantically as they ran.

Alarm bells sounded in Bremer's mind: these creatures were anything but human.

"I should leave you to suffer, you sack of rot," he said to the gnome. "But I've got bigger problems now." He thrust his sword into the gnome's chest and readied himself for the next threat.

The first scaly creature scrambled up a cross. Its claws dug deep into the timber, allowing it to climb without slowing. Its feet were oversized and lizard-like, with talons that propelled it upward with breathtaking efficiency. A row of small horns ran down its spine, surrounded by rippling back muscles. Bremer gasped aloud at the frenzied desperation with which it moved. Its head turned suddenly to face him, eyes blazing red.

Amid the terrifying screams, the creature leapt up, driving its claws into the crucified man's legs. Without a firm hold, it fell, tearing tendons and muscle to the bone. After landing with a loud thud, the creature immediately sprang toward the next cross.

Bremer had faced harvesters, holgs, and wild animals, but this beast was unlike anything he had encountered across the Four-winds. Remembering something Rowe had said about the elixir Sidara was working on, Bremer was struck with the possibility that before him were three men infected with Phyriad. *Were these creatures once human?*

Those nailed to the crosses stared at Bremer, their eyes pleading for mercy.

Sliding two knives free from the brace across his chest, Bremer bounded forward and threw the first knife. While the creature was in midflight, claws about to dig into the next cross, Bremer's knife struck its side. The blade plunged deep, knocking the creature sideways. It careened into the massive timber, and before it could recover, Bremer severed its head.

The second creature climbed up the backside of another cross. Reaching around, it drove its claws into the screaming man's waist. Bremer rushed forward, throwing his knife into the creature's neck. The impact drove it from the cross, but not before its claws tore through more flesh. Bremer followed with another deadly knife.

The third creature had kept its distance from Bremer, working with greater stealth but no less violence. Within moments, those hanging from the farthest row of crosses were bleeding profusely from deep wounds. Bremer's stomach churned at the sound of gnashing teeth as the third creature sought its next victim.

Distraught and infuriated yet spurred by something greater than himself, Bremer launched forward.

The third creature was about to climb another cross until it met Bremer's eyes. There was something different about this one, Bremer realized. Its actions were slower and more calculating, but there was something else. As he sized up his final opponent, Bremer noticed its eyes. Unlike the fiery red of the first two creatures, this one's eyes were as radiant and blue as those of a girl he once knew in Hammerclaw. Captivated for an instant, he lowered his sword.

The creature shifted suddenly and pounced toward Bremer, arms and claws outstretched. Its maw opened unnaturally wide, flashing ferocious jagged teeth.

Bremer acted instinctively. One sword came up, severing both of the creature's arms at the elbows. He kicked at its chest, and several ribs cracked. The creature drove its arm stumps into the ground and struggled to its feet, undeterred by pain or loss. Bremer gaped in horrified disbelief before cutting the creature's head clean from its shoulders.

With practiced precision, Bremer reset his stance, heeding the details of what he was seeing. Feeling many eyes upon him now, he gazed up at the crosses. The soldiers' silent, terrified expressions spoke of a final, agonizing request. Many had been hanging a long while, two were already dead, and those alive were too weak to be saved. Those that had been clawed writhed and moaned.

Bremer felt his shoulders slump. His mind reeled against the weight of what he needed to do. Unable to look at those nailed to the crosses any longer, he walked over and grabbed the gnome's spear lying at the base of one of the crosses.

After caring for those in the first two rows, he walked toward those who had been clawed in the farthest row. Something about the first crucified soldier that had been attacked stopped Bremer midstride. The man was foaming at the mouth, and sweat covered his body. His eyes were dark and drawn as his head shifted from side to side. He opened his mouth wide, then bit down so hard, Bremer heard the cracking teeth a dozen yards away.

The crucified man noticed Bremer and jerked his entire body until he pried one hand from the massive nail. Thrashing wildly, he pulled his other hand free and fell forward. Bremer cringed as both of the man's ankles snapped loudly before tearing free from the final nail through his feet. Bleeding and broken, the man crunched to the hardened ground and rolled onto his stomach, writhing in what Bremer knew was more than agony.

The man's skin turned ash gray. Long moments later, a layer of dried skin flaked off in large sections. As he convulsed in the dirt, his physiology slowly changed before Bremer's eyes. His feet and hands were shattered, bones exposed from tearing free of the cross, but now talons protruded from his feet and dark claws pushed out his fingernails, easing out from every digit. The man screamed and thrashed.

Terrifying minutes drifted past as clumps of hair fell away from his head. His skin—beneath what had flaked off—hardened into a thick, scaly gray hide. In a final cry, the man's jaw dislocated, opening unnaturally wide to reveal large, sharp teeth.

For nearly twenty minutes, Bremer watched all three infected soldiers transform in a similar fashion. The scene repulsed him, but he wanted to see how it ended. Eventually, the process slowed, and the first transformed man shot an angry look at Bremer. He rushed forward, swinging his sword harder than necessary, sending the head rolling across the dirt.

The final two soldiers floundered on the ground. It was the most horrific scene Bremer had ever witnessed. Without waiting for them to attack, he ended their misery.

※◆※

Gape-mouthed, Will stared at the violence below, and what followed broke his heart. Not wanting Bremer to endure it alone, he started for the trapdoor, but Rowe placed a hand on his shoulder.

"You'd get yourself lost if you tried to get down there, Will."

"What if you gave me directions?"

"It would all be over before you reached him."

"But…we have to do something." Will struggled for something to say, something to do.

"It would have been better if you hadn't watched," Rowe said. Will slumped.

"Take heed, my friend. Events have become far more complicated."

Will stared. "Those that were clawed…they were infected with Phyriad, weren't they?"

Rowe gave him a thoughtful nod.

"But that man transformed so quickly. Imagine if that—whatever that sickness is—reached a large population?"

"Hopefully, those three had somehow escaped alone. If we're not too late, there could still be a way to stop it from spreading."

"And if we can't?"

After a moment, Rowe sighed. "There will be a way to stop it. Has to be."

Will walked across the tower on legs that barely cooperated. Tracing Ryowyn's fine necklace with the tips of his fingers, he tried to draw strength from it but found none. His hands shook uncontrollably.

By the time Bremer shambled back to the stronghold, all the crucified soldiers were dead. His head was low, and his arms hung loosely at his sides as he trudged along. Will wondered if any magic was powerful enough to erase the memory of that brief but horrific moment.

CHAPTER 31

THE GREAT BEYOND

Will stared numbly as the sun dipped below the horizon. The beauty and simplicity of the changing colors in the sky distracted him from the horrific scene below. An eerie calmness settled over the canyon like a weary sigh after Bremer ended the suffering of the crucified soldiers. The peaceful sounds of Rowe and Morgan sleeping eventually settled Will's mind, if only a little.

Before retiring to his bedroll, he peered again into the deepening blue sky. In the distance, he thought he saw an airplane but realized that was unlikely. But the dark object was moving. Riveted to the stool, Will watched in awe as the shape grew larger and more defined. He was beginning to see some detail in the object's wings when it dropped behind a vast granite ridgeline.

A moment later, soaring on unseen currents, an enormous iron-gray dragon glided silently above the canyon. A bead of sweat tickled Will's temple, but he dared not move to wipe it away. Everything inside him screamed to wake the others, but he found himself fixated on the dragon.

The massive wingspan spread like a thick curtain in front of the sunset as the dragon descended into the canyon. It banked lazily, tail snaking behind, then flapped its wings, rising several hundred feet. The dragon leveled out and soared between the canyon walls, ever closer to the Stoneberg.

Will started and turned his head briefly. Behind him, Rowe leaned over a wide-eyed Morgan with his index finger pressed against his lips. Will had been so focused on the dragon, he had not heard them rise.

With a sudden flurry of stone and dust, the dragon flared its wings before settling its enormous, scaly mass upon the wall, talons stretched across the battlements. Its strong neck lowered a large head covered with innumerable horns and scales. Nostrils flared as its eyes, flashing like two small suns, scanned the canyon floor east of the Stoneberg.

With a powerful huff, the dragon leapt from the wall. It swooped down near the area where the small grove had been, circled once, then rose above the canyon heights and disappeared into the eastern sky.

"And there it is," Rowe whispered.

"Was that—" Will began, too afraid to speak the name.

"Natas, the Iron Dragon."

"How did it miss all the dead people on the crosses?" Will asked. "And the dead gnome?"

"It didn't," Rowe replied.

"So…where did it go?"

"I suspect it is on its way to see what happened to the contents of the flagon."

"How are we supposed to stand against something like that?" Morgan asked.

"Not our intention," Rowe said.

"Why not?"

"As far as I know, Natas cannot be killed by any ordinary weapon. That is why we are going after Sidara and rescuing the general."

They were quiet for a long while before Will spoke.

"Those three creatures that attacked the crucified soldiers," he said, "and even the man on the cross that had transformed… They all had skin that looked a lot like dragon scales."

"I noticed that too," Rowe said.

"Is Natas wanting to turn everyone into…" Will fell short.

"His likeness?" Morgan finished.

The next day's journey was arduous. Will focused on the narrow, rocky trail. The effort provided little distraction from images of the Stoneberg crucifixions that weighed on him as if someone were adding bricks to his backpack. Rowe had promised that tonight they would rest by the peaceful Ellerly River, but it was small comfort: each step brought them closer to the Waerdreath.

Billowy cumulus clouds drifted past as Will's thoughts once again returned to Ryowyn. Despite being from different worlds—not to mention their preferred natural habitats—he yearned for another moment with her. He knew she felt the same, yet something unsettled his spirit and made him physically nauseous. The same feeling had plagued his dreams, and now he feared what he would find at the Maidstone—if they survived the Waerdreath.

As the Ellerly River came into view, Bremer rejoined them. Will made room for him on the narrow trail and was surprised to see the rogue walking beside him.

"I wish I could trade you in for Ryowyn right now." Will yawned as he struggled to keep one foot in front of the other.

Bremer cast a weary sidelong smirk. "I can think of a few women I would gladly trade you in for."

"A few, eh?"

Bremer was silent a moment. "I've had women at every stop across the Fourwinds, kid, but at times like these, I wish I had one to come home to."

"Haven't found the right one yet?"

Bremer frowned. "You saw what I did to those men nailed to the crosses. They were husbands and fathers."

Will's stomach tightened.

"Can't imagine a 'right one' able to handle that kind of history," Bremer added. "So, that leaves women who like to burn up the sheets."

Feeling awkward but wanting to continue any conversation, Will said the first thing that came to mind. "I've never had much luck with women."

"No kidding? I would have guessed someone with two left feet would be popular in any port."

"My life back home was hard," Will said, ignoring the sarcasm. "What you all see here as an asset cost me everything in my world."

"So, why go back?"

"How do you know I will?"

Bremer slowed and met Will's gaze. "Whatever you do, I have a feeling that books will be written and songs will be sung about your life."

Will offered him his best skeptical look.

"The fact that this surprises you, I find bewildering." Bremer shrugged. "But I guess most heroes throughout the ages would have been equally surprised."

"I—I hope I'm around to read the books and sing the songs."

Will shifted the weight of his pack as if someone had recently removed a brick.

"You will live to see a litter of great-grandbabies at your feet," Bremer said.

Their night by the Ellerly River was exactly as Rowe had promised. Sheltered under a canopy of firs near a large boulder that had absorbed the sun's heat all day, Will relaxed for the first time since Fairbay and rested his tired muscles. The gently flowing sounds of the clear mountain stream had soothed him to sleep. Rowe and Bremer shared the night watch so Will and Morgan could sleep longer than they had in many nights.

"I hope you rested well," Rowe said as they left their small campsite.

"Best sleep I've had in a while," Will said. "Where to from here?"

"We travel due west through a forest of Alerce trees until we reach the Habina Ocean. After that, due south until we reach the Waerdreath."

"How long will that take?" Morgan asked.

"Three, maybe four, hours to the coast, then a few more south to the Waerdreath."

"Why are we doing the final leg in daylight?" Will asked. "Won't we be seen?"

"Being out after dark in these parts is too dangerous. Besides, we need daylight to find an old ladder that leads from the bluffs to the beach."

"Then what?" Will asked.

"I've studied the Histories in detail and have committed to memory every stone of the castle, including the secret passages."

"How much was there in the Histories about the castle?" Will asked.

"The original plans, actually. I suspect Sidara knows little of the extensive labyrinth of secret passages all around her. If not for our ability to move freely through those passages, I would never have embarked upon such an adventure."

After a few hours of steady hiking, they stopped for a short break at the foot of a lofty Alerce tree. Will sat down and unlaced his boots. "Do you smell that?"

Bremer closed his mouth and inhaled deeply. "Salt."

"The wind's picked up too," Rowe said.

"What is it?" Will asked.

"The ocean is not far from here," Rowe answered.

Leaving the forest behind, they spent the next hour climbing a rocky shelf. The terrain was different from anything they had seen thus far. As black as coal, it was coarse to the touch, forcing them to take extra care with their steps. At the top of the shelf, a series of similar rocky shelves descended to the water's edge. Everyone stopped.

Will stared in awe at the vast Habina Ocean. It was the first time he had ever seen an ocean, and he breathed deeply, soaking it all in as a deep sense of calm washed over him. The crashing of breakers far below and the dissonant cries of thousands of seabirds living in the crannies of the cliffs filled his ears.

"I wonder what ocean that is back in our time, Will?" Morgan said.

Will shrugged. "Whatever caused our world to evolve into this one, well…who knows?"

"You mean you haven't developed your theory further since

seeing the Big Dipper and the railcars at the seven waterfalls?" Morgan flashed a smile. "Seriously, what do you think happened?"

"I've been trying not to think about it, Morgan. Still, I can't help but think it had something to do with Sidara and all these weapons she's developed."

"So, you think she found a way to get Phyriad through the Gateway?"

Will held up a hand. "Don't go down that rabbit hole, Morgan. You'll go nuts." He stretched. "One thing at a time; let's get through today."

Will scanned the landscape as Rowe led them across the strange rock formations, some so large they had to walk around. "This place is desolate," he muttered. "Like the moon."

Morgan pointed to a distant harbor where about two dozen tall ships were anchored. With sails folded tightly beneath their masts, they looked like skeletons in the mist that spread inland for miles. "What is that, Rowe?"

"The Waerdreath lies within that fog."

"Do we need it to lift before we get there?" Will asked.

"Impossible. That fog has been there since Sidara arrived."

"Where is everyone?" Morgan asked as they crossed the barren landscape. "It appears to be deserted."

"Most people live in the city of Gilesonia, which lies in that valley south of the Waerdreath."

After about an hour of hiking down the rocky landscape, they noticed three tall ships sailing in from the northwest. Bremer pulled out his spyglass from a pocket below his knee and handed it to Rowe, then walked away. Seconds later, he had disappeared through a craggy section of rock.

"What are those ships?" Will asked.

"They do not appear to be flying any flags," Rowe said.

Extending the narrow spyglass, he sat down and rested his elbow on a raised knee to steady his hand. He brought the spyglass to his eye and sat motionless.

Will took the opportunity to slide off his boots and rub his feet while Morgan sat on a rock and ate some nuts and dried berries.

Rowe described what he saw through the spyglass. "There are no identifying markings on the ships," he said. "All three figureheads are the same but unlike anything I've ever seen. They look like massive carved goat heads with horns at least ten feet long. The eyes are made of glass, and I can see fires burning within each head."

"That explains the smoke," Will said as the ships lowered sails and slowed their approach into the harbor.

"Wait," Rowe said. "There's a metal box dangling from heavy chains beneath the horns of the lead ship. It's a perfect square, about five feet across, and made from dark metal. It's completely covered with glowing red runes." Rowe raised his eyebrows. "Whatever is in that box is guarded by powerful magic. Not to mention the armed guards."

"What do you think it is?" Morgan asked, handing him some dried meat.

Rowe lowered the spyglass. "If we're lucky, we might find out when we get to the Waerdreath."

Will stretched out on the ground. "I feel like we've walked a thousand miles. Back home, I used to go for a walk around the lake, and on rare occasions, I would do two or three laps. But this…"

"A stroll around the Lake Commando sounds nice," Morgan said. "How about stopping by Nick's Confectionery for some soft-serve ice cream?"

"I'll take a large chocolate sundae with extra fudge and no

nuts," Will said, sitting up. "Screw the walking. Let's take my Land Cruiser."

Morgan laughed. "I could spend a week in my old bed, listening to music, watching movies. Too bad we didn't bring a camera; I haven't updated Instagram in a while."

Will smiled at Rowe. He was gazing at both of them as if they were speaking another language.

"What we need, Rowe, is a helicopter," Will said. "That's a vehicle that can fly and take you anywhere you want. It could carry the four of us *and* a complement of rockets to destroy the Waerdreath and have us back at the Crow's Nest by nightfall."

Rowe stared.

"Oh, that isn't the half of it, Rowe," Morgan added. "You know that beautiful moon we all like to look at? Well, back in our time, people have traveled to that moon."

"But…how—"

"Our home would be as foreign to you as this place is to us," Will said.

"It sounds unbelievable," Rowe said.

"I wonder if we could get Bremer to come?" Will chuckled. "I would love to get him in a helicopter."

"One thing at a time." Rowe climbed to his feet.

Will's smile faded as he laced up his boots. He slid on his pack and picked up his bow.

"I should tell you," Rowe said, "Bremer's thinking of trying to use poison to kill Sidara."

"Poison? Like he did to Akia?" Morgan said. "Never thought of that."

"That's because you're not a killer," Rowe said.

A moment later, Bremer materialized from a narrow fissure in the rock, sweating freely despite the coolness of the ocean air.

"The bluffs are about two hundred feet high," he announced.

"We don't have to jump, do we?" Will asked.

Bremer shrugged. "It would save us time."

"We need to follow the bluffs, probably into the fog," Rowe explained. "But we shouldn't have to jump. There will be an old iron ladder bolted to the bluffs that will take us down to a narrow section of beach. Unfortunately, we cannot use the main castle entrance. The Waerdreath was carved out of a volcanic island a few hundred yards from the mainland with a single stone bridge as its only access. There's a guard tower and gatehouse at both ends of the bridge to operate the portcullis and main gates. At the castle, the bridge is over three hundred feet of solid rock carved from a narrow cleft that juts all the way to the island."

Will frowned. "Sounds inviting."

Rowe continued, speaking slowly so they all understood. "The bridge begins on a large plateau across from the bluffs. The plans show that a secret passage lies under the bridge above the waterline and leads into a labyrinth of secret passages within the Waerdreath."

"Are you sure Sidara doesn't know about these passages?" Will asked.

"She might know about some, but passages such as these have a way of becoming forgotten through the ages. Sidara came here almost four hundred years after the castle was built."

"Even so," Bremer said in a low voice, "when it comes to Sidara, I wouldn't assume anything." He frowned at Will. "You ready to give her that big hug?"

Will shrugged. "I'm holding on to the hope that there's a less violent way, but after the Stoneberg, I'm not sure anymore."

"I'm praying for a better way," Morgan said.

"Praying?" Bremer snorted. "To who? The gods are either dead or they're silent."

"Well, maybe you're not listening for an answer."

Bremer lowered his voice. "If the gods are as powerful as some say, how can they watch idly as men mistreat children like the young Sidara or those soldiers at the Stoneberg?"

Morgan hung her head. "Well, I don't have all the answers." She looked up at Bremer. "But maybe God doesn't like the violence either."

Bremer huffed and shook his head. "Then why not put an end to it?"

Morgan shrugged. "I guess we're free to make our own choices, good or bad. Some choose violence, and others choose to stand against it. Dad used to say that free will comes with responsibility. People have made some terrible choices throughout history, and we live with the consequences." She held up her hands and sighed. "Like I said, I don't have all the answers."

"Pray all you like," Bremer grumbled. "As far as I'm concerned, I make my own choices, and I choose to fight."

"Well," Rowe said, "we will each have important choices to make inside the Waerdreath."

CHAPTER 32

EVERY JOURNEY MUST END

Morgan stayed close to Rowe as he led the small group over the craggy landscape of desolate lava rock. He had given instructions to search for any sign of the iron ladder but warned it would be a difficult task. The terrain was bad enough, forcing them to struggle at times for the next step forward. Often, they would have to leave the bluffs to avoid deep fissures or steep escarpments. With each passing moment, the dense fog closed in, screening the afternoon sun and pushing each of them closer to the ground for stability as they searched for the secret ladder.

After a few hours, Rowe called out in a raspy voice. "Found it!"

Morgan stretched out beside him as he leaned over the crest. Constructed from ten-foot lengths of iron, the ladder was rusty and deeply pitted. The rings were crudely fashioned cables secured to the iron sides through a series of holes. Several of the bolts anchoring the ladder to the bluffs had broken away over the years.

"Have mercy," Rowe whispered, reaching down to give the ladder a firm shake. He pulled himself onto his knees as the others huddled in close. "It's in bad shape," he explained. "I believe the first section will support us, but beyond that is anyone's guess."

"How far down?" Morgan asked.

"If memory serves, I believe it to be around two hundred feet."

Bremer knelt beside Rowe and peered over the edge. "I'll go first, Rowe. If the ladder fails, you'll have to find another way in."

"That would mean heading into Gilesonia. It would take some time and more luck than I care to admit."

"I figured there was a reason we were trying so hard to find this blasted ladder."

Bremer rubbed his hands together and inhaled. He leaned over the crest and shook the ladder. Without another word, he slid around and lowered a foot onto the second rung.

"When you get to the bottom," Rowe said, "and if the ladder is secure, give two short whistles."

Bremer nodded and started down the ladder, taking one precarious step at a time as he disappeared down into the fog. After several minutes, he whistled.

Will stepped onto the ladder. It shook slightly but held fast as he descended. Minutes later, another whistle signaled for Morgan to descend. She cleared her throat and stepped down.

"It is sound," Rowe whispered.

Morgan raised her head as he leaned down to help. His concerned eyes filled her vision. Without hesitation, she kissed him. Rowe reached a hand around the back of her neck, and for a second, she was somewhere else, wishing the moment could last. But her hair slipped through his fingers as she stepped down the ladder into the fog. Despite the gloom, the kiss lingered all the way down, bolstering her confidence.

When Rowe joined them at the bottom, the loud, high-pitched

sound of chains passing over steel rang out in the harbor. A moment later, the sound came a second and third time.

"The three ships have dropped anchor," Rowe said. "If the opportunity presents itself, I want to know what's in that crate."

He led them to the bluffs, and the moment they reached the vertical rock face, he pointed to the bridge deck above them. He moved his finger to his lips. Taking a few steps to the left, he slid his hand into a shallow cleft. He pulled with one hand and pushed the rock face with the other. A small doorway opened and greeted them with a waft of stale air.

Both Will and Morgan turned their heads and covered their noses. Rowe pulled out his sunstone and stepped into the darkness, motioning for the others to follow.

"Be careful," he said. "It's low and narrow, but it will open up as we go."

Morgan went first, her shoulders rubbing against the sides, followed by Will. Light glowed from behind, and Morgan turned to see that Bremer also had a sunstone. He pulled a small iron handle until the locking mechanism clicked into place, locking the door behind them.

Single file, they shuffled across the rough stone floor as quickly as possible given the tight confines. Shifting her shoulders sideways in places while walking with a low slouch, Morgan's muscles started to cramp.

After several minutes, Rowe stepped into some water, and everyone stopped at the splashing sound. His next few steps carried him knee deep but thankfully no deeper. The others followed. The dank air grew more pungent around the water. As the passage grew more cramped, Will stopped.

"Wait," he mumbled. "Give me some space."

The splash left little to the imagination as Will's deep retching echoed through the passage. Morgan and Rowe shuffled forward, and Bremer backed up several paces.

"Thanks for that," Bremer grumbled.

Will wiped his mouth with his sleeve. "How much farther?"

"Almost there," Rowe answered.

"Are you okay, Will?" Morgan asked.

Will nodded feebly, and Morgan waved Rowe onward.

They passed through the shallow water, and a minute later, Rowe stopped at a main junction. He stretched and groaned as he slid off his pack.

The junction was a large round area carved into a much smoother, lighter rock than the lava rock they had recently passed through. One by one, they emerged and stretched their backs. Morgan wiped the sweat from her forehead as she retrieved a waterskin from her pack. Will dropped his pack and inhaled deeply.

"Much better," he whispered.

"I hope that's the last passage like that," Morgan said.

"Those look much better," Will said, pointing at three passages that led away from the junction. Each one looked high and wide enough to allow them to walk without slouching.

"No one has been here in ages," Bremer said as he brought his sunstone down to the floor. He ran a finger through the thick and undisturbed layer of dust.

"We leave our packs here and carry only what is required," Rowe said.

"So, where to first?" Will asked.

"The dungeons are ahead. I would like to have a look inside them."

"Do you think we'll find the general there?" Morgan asked.

"Unlikely, but we must begin at the beginning."

"What else are you thinking?" Bremer asked.

"Something dangerous is in that crate the lead ship was carrying." Bremer nodded.

"Watch for it," Rowe said. "If I had gone through so much trouble to deliver a crate to the Waerdreath, I know I would want to inspect it upon arrival. If we stumble upon it, it could lead us to Sidara."

Bremer slid off his cloak and vest, leaving a black shirt and the full brace of knives across his chest. One sword he kept strapped to his back, but he unbuckled his second sword angled down across his back and attached it instead to the belt against his left hip. He took the empty quiver, dropped to his knees, and traced his fingers along a series of runes.

"Shield your eyes," he said before completing the pattern.

A light flashed, leaving a single orange arrow in the quiver. He attached the quiver to the back of his belt and slipped the bow across his back where the sword had been. Reaching back, he withdrew the arrow and handed it to Will.

"*This* is only to be used if all else fails," Bremer said.

"What is it?" Will asked.

"Hope you never need to find out."

"Why don't you keep it?"

"I can't use it without killing myself. Your cloak will protect you, but remember—"

"I got it. Only if the train has come right off the tracks." Will slid the arrow into his quiver, giving him a total of ten arrows.

After passing around a small sack of mixed nuts, Rowe led the way into the passage to the right of the one they had recently exited. Moments later, they descended a series of steep steps. The dankness grew heavier, and soon the sound of trickling water slowed their pace.

The moment they reached the bottom step, Bremer doused his sunstone, and Rowe's went so dim only faint outlines of one another remained. They all stood stiffly for a few seconds, and gradually a thin strip of light came into focus. Naturally drawn toward it, everyone approached and peered through the crack.

Morgan quickly realized they were looking down at a large, dimly lit dungeon. The passage they were in must have been hidden above the ceiling. In the limited field of vision, flickering firelight cast by wall-mounted torches bathed the dungeon in a soft glow that illuminated several metal bars. Rotting hay and the remains of a few blankets covered the stone floor.

Rowe moved sideways and found a short ladder. He tugged it, but it was firmly bolted to the wall. He climbed up the rungs and leaned forward. A small opening in a cleft of the dungeon's jagged ceiling illuminated his face as he peered down. He motioned for Morgan to join him.

The opening revealed six prison cells divided equally by a corridor that ran through the middle of the dungeon. At the far end was a closed, solid door. Iron bars, heavily reinforced with thick crossbars, spanned floor to ceiling in front of the six cells. Each gate bore a large locking mechanism. Various lengths of chain were anchored to the walls and floors of each cell. The stench of human feces was overpowering, and Morgan jerked back.

They climbed down the ladder, and Rowe stepped past Will to whisper instructions to Bremer.

"There's a short ladder a few paces up. Climb it and you'll find a small embrasure through which you'll see six cells. I could only see into one, and there's a prisoner in it. Keep watch while we go check other sections of the dungeon."

Rowe tugged the cloaks of Will and Morgan, whispering for them to follow. They climbed a few steps and followed a passage to the left. Rowe ascended another short ladder and, as before, the light from the embrasure lit his face as he looked down.

He climbed down the ladder and whispered similar instructions to Will as he had to Bremer. He then led Morgan farther into the passage. Together, they crawled up a flight of crude steps to another short ladder where they heard a muffled conversation.

Morgan squinted as they approached the soft glow of the embrasure. Below, two gnomes sat at a table in the light of a wall-mounted torch playing a card game. The longhaired, long-bearded gnomes were only about four feet tall but were well built and well armed. Behind them was a closed gate leading to the dungeon corridor. There were no other chairs around the table and nothing else to suggest that more guards were stationed at this post.

Rowe and Morgan retraced their steps to gather Will and Bremer before returning to an area where they could use the sunstones and speak more freely.

"I think the person in the cell I was watching is dead," Bremer reported.

"I saw five prison doors but couldn't see inside," Will said. "The corridor was empty except for a slant-back chair and a small bench. There're two torches on the wall. At the far end is a guard sitting by a closed gate, but he's sound asleep."

"On the other side of that gate are two gnome soldiers playing cards," Rowe added.

"I'd like to know what's behind the closed door at the far end," Bremer said.

"Do you think the general's in there?" Will asked.

Rowe shrugged. "Bremer, can you pick those locks?"

He nodded.

"How long would it take?" Rowe asked.

"Two, maybe three, minutes. What's on your mind?"

"I'm torn. If the general *is* in there, all is well in the Fourwinds. If he *isn't*, there's no telling what we could be stepping into."

"Regardless, our search begins there," Bremer said. "I'll go down and have a look."

"All right," Rowe agreed. "Will, head back to the second ladder and keep an eye on that guard sleeping in the chair. If he or anyone else comes our way, tap softly on the stone floor. Morgan, you wait here. If you hear Will tapping the stone, take a few steps down that passage and do the same. I'll be waiting for Bremer at an access point about fifty feet from here."

Will nodded and started down the dark passage.

"Use this to help Will to his post," Rowe said, handing Morgan his sunstone. "Then keep it close till I return."

After a few steps down a new passage with Bremer, Rowe turned. His strained smile faded in the soft glow of Bremer's sunstone.

⁂

Bremer and Rowe found another ladder leading to a small embrasure. Through it, Bremer examined the deepest section of the dungeon, close to the cell he had been watching earlier.

Lying on the cell floor, a form huddled beneath a frayed blanket. Bremer inspected it for a moment, but it remained motionless. He scanned the area but saw nothing that gave him cause for concern. The other cells were empty.

When he stepped down from the ladder, he found Rowe waiting, hunched low with both hands on a stone block in the floor. After a few seconds applying steady pressure, there was a muffled click, and a small section of rock opened before them.

Bremer lowered himself through the opening and dropped softly to the dungeon corridor floor directly between two cells. Bringing a kerchief to his nose to ward off the stench of rot and feces, he crept toward the cell containing the covered body. As he came close, the sight of rotting flesh confirmed his suspicions about the prisoner's condition.

Bremer continued to the end of the corridor toward the closed iron door and knelt before it. After laying out his pick tools on the floor, he examined the handle and the small keyhole. He was about to select a tool but stopped and tested the iron handle. To his surprise, it moved freely, causing the latch to release.

Makes sense, he thought. The way these prisoners are treated, why bother with locks?

He pocketed his tools and pulled the door open a few inches. The space within was dark and deathly silent. He withdrew his sunstone and placed it on the floor, nudging it inside with his foot. The sunstone glowed. His eyes adjusted to the faint light, and he soon noticed the outline of a person stretched out in the center of the cell. Bremer opened the door a little more and nudged the sunstone in to see more clearly.

Two chains from the ceiling held the prisoner's arms outstretched. His shoulders had obviously dislocated from the weight. Two additional chains separated his legs wider than humanly possible. Bremer shuddered. The man was naked except for a small blood-soaked cloth wrapped around his loins. His head slumped forward, and a tangled mess of long hair hung down and covered his chest. He appeared to be dead.

No one else was in the cell, so Bremer picked up the sunstone and stepped inside. He closed the door and lifted the light for a closer view. The man's head jerked up, and Bremer slid back with a start.

With a feeble flick of his head, the man shifted some hair from his eyes and squinted against the light. Tattoos covered his face. Bremer had seen the general twice before and knew in a heartbeat this man was not Raric.

"Who are you?" the man asked in a low, raspy voice.

"Your last hope in this world," Bremer replied.

"Are you here to rescue me?" he asked, slurring the words.

"I'm afraid not. What did you do to deserve this?"

"I will answer all your questions if you promise to kill me," he uttered through staggered gasps.

"That depends on what you tell me."

There was a long silence before the man spoke, gasping for breath between short sentences.

"What they have done to me…is not even the beginning of what they plan to do. Please, I beg you…promise me you will kill me…and I will tell you all I know."

"Start talking."

"My name is Fadua. I am…I *was* an alchemist…specializing in glassmaking."

"Why are you here?"

"I was the chief architect on a project that required giant flagons to carry a potion called…Guilliad."

"What's Guilliad?"

"When a flagon is shattered…the liquid comes into contact

with the air…it turns into a vapor that disintegrates anything living it comes into contact with…anything."

"Was Guilliad meant for Dwenlin Thah?"

"First for the Crow's Nest…second for Dwenlin Thah, as far as I know. We made two others… Don't know their intended purposes."

"But wouldn't the vapor destroy the Histories?"

"We made a special flagon for the Crow's Nest…enough Guilliad within to create a vapor to cover everything for two or three stories…leaving the Histories sound."

"Are these flagons mounted within the framework of a wagon?"

Fadua nodded.

Bremer shook his head, confirming the contents of the flagon at the Stoneberg. "Why are you imprisoned?"

"I refused to create a similar flagon for the project that preceded the creation of Guilliad," Fadua wheezed. "Called…*Phyriad*."

"Why did you refuse?"

"I discovered that Sidara was planning to use it on both human and gnome populations."

"Gnomes? Why would she destroy her own army? What does Phyriad do?"

"If the elixir is released into the general population, it would mean the end of human and gnome alike." Fadua coughed and spat blood. "The effects vary, but the end results are similar. When infected…you become dragon-like. No more racial wars…only one powerful species."

Bremer grabbed Fadua's sweat-soaked hair and eased his head up enough to give him a drink from his waterskin.

"Thank you," Fadua said. "That is only part of it. I am not sure how they accomplished this, but…my understanding is that once a person changes, they secrete a venom from their claws that will then infect others with even a tiny cut."

"Why would the infected just cut other people instead of killing them?"

"They become driven by the insatiable need to spread their condition. So, they cut and move on. But that's the part we know; the poison could morph and spread in other ways. We did not have time to test the possibilities."

"How has Phyriad not infected those working on it?"

"Sidara had cordoned off a section of the dungeons…turned them into a self-contained laboratory…with powerful magic to keep anything from spreading. Within were some of our most brilliant alchemists and two powerful magic users to assist with containment…even several healers, in case an accident occurred. They poured time and resources into the experiments…but then something terrible happened. Three men escaped. So, the entrance to the dungeon was cut off with a perpetual wall of fire to stop the spread."

Bremer rubbed the back of his neck, remembering the state of the three creatures he had killed at Stoneberg. "Does Sidara have access to Phyriad?"

Fadua nodded.

"How much?"

"Enough."

"How did the alchemists create such a thing?"

Fadua's head rolled to one side. "No one seems to know…but rumors suggest it was not created in the Waerdreath…but *found* in a place called the Maidstone. The work done here was only to develop a delivery system."

Bremer's eyes darted around the room, considering this new information. He gave Fadua another drink.

"Why do they keep you alive?" Bremer asked, questions flooding his mind.

"I am to be part of an important sacrifice…along with others being brought here."

"Do you know anything about a crate that was being brought in by ship?"

"No."

A small *tap* struck the door. Bremer spun around, realizing his time was short.

Fadua's weary voice had an anxious edge to it. "Please…please k-kill me quickly."

"How long before the sacrifice?"

"Two days," Fadua said. "Please…"

Bremer reached into his vest and pulled out a small leather sack. "Inside is a balso mushroom. It will—"

"Kill me in two hours with no pain," Fadua said, breathing easier.

"You won't feel anything." Bremer pulled Fadua's head back and raised the sack to his lips. He carefully shook the mushroom out without it touching his skin. Fadua chewed it slowly before taking a final drink from Bremer's waterskin.

"Thank you," Fadua said.

"I wish I could do more, friend."

Bremer rushed to the door and opened it a crack. A torchlight flickered at the other end of the corridor. He closed the door softly and stepped back to the corner of Fadua's cell, returning the sunstone to a pocket. He climbed the crudely carved twenty-foot lava rock wall to a small ledge near the ceiling. A moment later, a bush gnome walked inside.

"Fadua! Drink time!" the gnome said in an accented, nasal voice. He dropped the torch into a wall mount beside the door.

Bremer shifted slightly so he could observe without being seen.

The gnome grabbed a handful of Fadua's hair and jerked his head back. He slapped his face, then forced the end of a dirty waterskin into Fadua's mouth.

"Keep you alive a few more days we must," the gnome said. "Come now, drink!"

Fadua coughed loudly, gasping for breath as the gnome forced the contents of the waterskin down his throat.

Bremer narrowed his eyes and clenched his teeth but remained still.

The gnome stepped back and tapped Fadua between the legs with the waterskin. Pus squirted from what Bremer imagined to be an infected castration.

"For luck," the gnome murmured as he left the cell.

Fadua let out a gut-wrenching groan and his head fell backward.

Silence returned, and Bremer climbed down from his hiding place. He pushed the door open and noticed Rowe leaning out from the secret ceiling entry. Bremer raised a finger to signal that he would be another moment. Returning to Fadua, he pulled out the sunstone and saw pus and blood leaking from the reopened wound. He stepped close to Fadua and lightly tapped his face.

"It's me, Fadua, wake up," Bremer whispered.

With another tap, Fadua opened his eyes, and tears streaked his dirty face.

"I'm going to stuff some tevan root into your nose," Bremer said.

"Please," Fadua groaned.

Bremer produced another small sack from a pocket and removed a tiny amount of brown gel-like root extract. He separated it into two pieces, rolled them into balls between his index fingers and thumbs, then pushed the extract into Fadua's nostrils.

Fadua inhaled deeply, and immediately his face relaxed.

Bremer stepped back. "Slow down, friend."

Fadua opened his eyes and smiled. "We go through so much of this in the lab," he said, inhaling again. "I wish we could have met under better circumstances. I think I would have liked you."

"I hope our paths will cross in the next," Bremer said.

"Are you going to kill Sidara?"

Bremer nodded.

Fadua's eyes became glassy. "In violent times, you shouldn't have to sell your soul."

"Fadua, listen. I'm also here for General Raric."

Fadua let out a giggle. "Good for you."

"Do you know where he's being held?"

"Blue flowers and tall towers," Fadua mumbled.

"Fadua." Bremer shook the man's head. "Where is the general being held?"

Fadua looked at Bremer as if seeing him for the first time. "I heard they had him on the roof."

"Why would they have him on the roof?"

A broad grin spread across Fadua's dirty face. "You'll see."

Bremer realized he would get no more information from the dying man. "Enjoy," he said, patting his cheek lightly before he turned to leave the cell.

"Don't tell the girls I'll be home from work early today, Makayla," Fadua mumbled. "I want to surprise them."

Bremer opened the door but turned back for a final look. "Sorry I couldn't do better," he whispered.

Morgan leaned her head against the rough stone wall as she listened to Bremer's account of what had taken place in Fadua's cell. The four of them had regrouped and now spoke quietly around Rowe's sunstone.

"I'm sorry you had to go through that," Morgan said.

Bremer closed his eyes. "Fadua was a good man."

"And lucky to have met you," Morgan added.

"So, it's all real," Will said.

Bremer sighed. "Afraid so, kid."

"Can we stop Sidara from spreading Phyriad?" Morgan asked.

"As it stands, the Records of Time is sound, and so is the Gateway," Rowe answered. "Other than that, the Fourwinds is unprepared for something like Phyriad."

"What was it Fadua said about the Maidstone and the creation of Phyriad?" Will asked.

"He said it was *found* there, not *created*."

Rowe was studying Will's reaction. "Seems there are *two* paths now leading to the Maidstone," he mused.

"The path we need worry about is the one that leads us to Sidara," Bremer said, "so we can rid the Fourwinds of that cursed witch."

Rowe leaned forward. "We need to find the crate that was on that ship. I'm convinced if we find it, we find Sidara."

Bremer nodded.

"Where would we even begin to look?" Will asked.

"Where would you take something locked up like that, Bremer?" Rowe asked. "Especially if you meant to open it?"

"To an environment that offered me the most control."

"Exactly. Sidara derives much of her power from an altar in a place called the Unholy."

Morgan hugged her chest and shivered. "Bremer, you said that

Fadua referred to an important sacrifice that Sidara's planning. Could there be an animal or…a—a person in the crate, someone she means to sacrifice?"

Rowe stared at her. "Interesting thought," he said. "I was thinking the crate might contain some sort of weapon, but an important hostage…that's a possibility."

"What kind of sacrificial victim would warrant such magical protection, and to what end?" Bremer asked.

"Sidara already controls the gnomes," Rowe said. "And she already has an important human leader in the general. Who else could she add to her collection?"

Morgan was silent for a moment until a thought struck her. "An elf?"

"What would make you say that?" Rowe asked.

"Well, elves seem important. I know Onathe was a bad elf, but he seemed like a pretty big deal. And what were those elves doing by the Stoneberg? Rowe, you said they rarely get involved in the affairs of men, but they were obviously trying to stop the giant from transporting what Fadua called Guilliad."

Bremer shook his head vigorously. "There's no way Sidara would risk open war with both us *and* the elves at the same time."

Rowe thought for a minute. "There was a time I would have agreed with such sentiment, but now that Natas has returned to the Fourwinds, I'm not so sure. And with Guilliad and the mere threat of Phyriad, war is inevitable."

"I don't understand the need for a sacrifice," Will said.

"Sidara's power increases through sacrifices," Rowe explained. "The purer the offering, the more power she receives—at least that is the accepted theory."

"That makes no sense to me," Will said, shaking his head.

"Me neither," Rowe said. "But I believe we should head to the antechamber."

Will raised both eyebrows. "What's an antechamber?"

"It's the vestibule where sacrifices are prepared. If the crate is there, we can assume someone is inside," Rowe said. "And I know a way to get us close."

"What do you mean by *close*?" Morgan asked.

"The antechamber is in the center of the keep. We will have to leave the hidden passages to reach it."

"If they're preparing for a large ceremony, won't the place be crawling with bad guys?" Will asked.

"It will. And, if the gods have not abandoned us, the Dark Queen will be there too."

"Shouldn't we be heading to the roof in search of the general?" Will asked.

"*If* he is still alive," Bremer said. "Besides, maybe *he's* the guest of honor at the ceremony Fadua spoke of."

Morgan sighed. "So, we're off to find Sidara?"

"To the antechamber," Rowe said. "And into the depths of darkness."

CHAPTER 33

INTO THE
DEPTHS OF DARKNESS

Morgan lost track of time in the labyrinth of secret passage-ways behind the castle walls. It could have been morning or evening. The group walked silently in single file throughout the narrow passages around the keep, trusting that Rowe knew the way. Silence was critical, Rowe had advised, because there were likely hundreds of servants within the keep attending to their duties for the Dark Queen. To remain undetected, Rowe kept the group in virtual darkness, except at major intersecting passages. At such intervals, he used the light of his sunstone to study the thick layer of dust on the floor for signs of use. Fortunately, he found none.

Eventually, they came to a ladder similar to the ones they had accessed in the dungeons. Rowe climbed to the top and pushed a wooden slat sideways, opening a small hole. After a few minutes, he closed the hole and climbed down. Gathering the group in a tight circle, he explained what he had seen.

"There's a hallway on the other side of this wall. The antecham-ber is about twenty feet away." He sighed. "I thought it would be closer. The antechamber is blocked by a thick red curtain, so there's no way to tell what's inside."

"Do you think Sidara is in there?" Morgan asked.

"The Histories say the antechamber is one of the largest rooms in the keep, but it pales in comparison to the adjacent room where the ceremonies take place. Sidara built her imposing altar there, a powerful slab of rock known as the Unholy. We might find her there."

"What about the crate?" Will asked. "Is there anywhere else they would take it?"

"If it's anywhere else, I'm not interested in its contents."

"Does the hallway continue beyond the antechamber?" Bremer asked.

"No. To the right of the red curtain is a wide staircase leading down."

"I think we should keep watch for a time to get an idea of who comes and goes," Bremer suggested. "There's also the possibility that the crate has not yet arrived at the antechamber."

Rowe nodded his agreement. "Back where we came from, there is another embrasure that offers a vantage point to view a prominent intersection. I'll go have a look while you keep watch over this hallway."

"Should we come with you?" Will asked.

"You come with me," Rowe said. "Morgan, wait here with Bremer."

"When we're ready, how do we get into the hallway?" Bremer asked.

"Directly beneath the right side of the ladder is a shallow indentation in the stone, a handbreadth off the floor. Inside is a short lever that unlocks a small door."

After Rowe and Will had gone, Bremer located the lever for the entry into the hallway, then climbed the ladder. Morgan followed him up. There was just enough room for both of them to look through the hole. Bremer noted the details in a hushed voice.

"That thick hallway rug will muffle our footfalls, and those rune-marked red tapestries will also absorb noise. That will help us move around without drawing too much attention. See those golden wall lanterns? I estimate they will need refueling at least every three hours, so will only have a small window of opportunity."

For about a half hour, there were no signs of guards, lantern lighters, or any activity. Suddenly, the curtain opened, and a short man stepped out from the antechamber. He was naked, save for the tattoos inked into most of his skin. Stepping into the center of the archway, he remained motionless for several minutes before raising a hand. Morgan saw no one but heard the footsteps of someone ascending the stairs. The man grasped the curtain and walked backward slowly, opening the archway to the antechamber.

From the dimly lit room beyond, four similarly tattooed men walked into the hallway without a word. They stood in pairs, facing one another. The man who had opened the curtain started a strange clicking sound with his mouth, and at once, the four other men turned to face the walls.

The clicking sound had a distinct hypnotic rhythm, but Morgan remained alert, straining to see the stairs. After a moment, a person came into view, taking perfectly timed steps to the beat of the clicking sound.

"That's a temple cleric," Bremer whispered.

The man wore a long deep-purple robe that swept the floor behind him and a leather helmet that covered his head down to his shoulders. He held the end of a pole in purple-gloved hands.

As he walked toward the antechamber archway, another identically dressed cleric followed, holding the same pole.

Bremer exhaled slowly. "I think we found the crate."

Two other clerics carried the pole behind the crate, trudging forward to the beat of the clicking sound. The pole was fastened to the metal crate so the clerics could carry it without touching it with their hands.

Other than deep runes covering most of the surface and a large lock dangling from an iron latch, the crate was unremarkable. It was smaller than Morgan had imagined. If a person was in it, he would probably be crippled by now. There were no air holes, slats, or anything to reveal its contents.

"I could easily pick the lock, but the runes suggest a warding magic," Bremer whispered. "That's another matter altogether."

Hearing Rowe and Will below, Bremer and Morgan climbed down the ladder and joined them.

"It's here," Bremer told Rowe.

"I know." Rowe climbed the ladder. He watched for a moment, then returned to the others. "Any idea how many others were inside the antechamber?"

"One person opened the curtain, and four others came out," Bremer replied.

"I saw those four and the clerics leave down the stairs but not the one working the curtain. They must have left the crate in the antechamber."

"He could be the only one in there," Bremer said. "We need to go now."

"Are you serious?" Will gasped.

"That's why we came, kid."

"Wait here while Bremer and I check beyond the curtain," Rowe told Will and Morgan.

"What happens if you end up in trouble?" Will asked.

"Come and save us," Bremer said with a smirk.

Rowe reached for the hidden lever at the foot of the ladder. "Will, go up and make certain the hallway is clear," he whispered. "Tap once if it's safe for us to go out there."

Will climbed the ladder and a moment later tapped softly.

Rowe pulled the lever. Without a sound, he pushed the small doorway open, and he and Bremer crawled through on hands and knees. As soon as they stood, Bremer rushed the curtain. He reached out to open it but jerked his hand back as though he had touched molten metal. Rowe drew his sword quietly and used the blade to open the curtain a crack to peer into the antechamber.

There was no visible light source in the room, but a dim yellow glow flickered among shifting shadows. The antechamber was over fifty feet wide, with a marble floor and six stone statues standing guard on both walls. Each seven-foot statue was clad in plate armor with helm down, masking its face. Stony gloves clasped the hilts of huge swords whose tips were embedded in the statue bases.

In the center of the room sat the crate, apparently unguarded. The pole used to carry it remained attached, suggesting that the crate had not yet reached its final destination. The short, naked man who had opened the curtain for the clerics now stood with his back to the crate. He faced the curtain yet failed to notice the two men.

Bremer stepped back and carefully removed the bow from across his back. Reaching for his quiver, he traced the opening and a single arrow appeared. He took a knee on the rug near the curtain and drew the bowstring back in a single fluid motion.

Rowe moved the curtain open with the tip of his sword, allowing Bremer a clean shot.

The man inside turned with a confused look on his face. The arrow covered the short distance so quickly that before the man could react, he was struck high in the chest. His head bounced awkwardly off the crate, and his bleeding body crumpled to the floor.

Rowe swung the curtain open wider. Bremer raced inside and slid across the marble floor in front of the crate. He examined the lock.

Rowe stared at the statues. A red glow radiated from behind each helm. "I might need your help here, Bremer," Rowe said a little louder than he had intended.

"Not yet," Bremer said, reaching for his pick tools. He tapped the lock, but nothing unusual happened, so he probed the tiny keyhole. "You sure you want to know what's in here?"

"I am. Do you think the—" Rowe stopped midsentence as one of the statue's swords was slowly drawn from its base. "Best get on with it, Bremer."

The stone guard stomped a massive armored foot onto the marble floor and raised its sword. At once, several armored footfalls filled the air as all six statues left their posts.

While Bremer remained focused on the lock, exchanging one pick tool after another, Rowe shuffled close to him and turned to face the nearest knight. The creature clomped across the floor, quickly closing the gap. Rowe stepped forward, and the clash of metal rang out as he met the knight's attack.

The creature lifted its blade. Rowe shuffled forward under the knight's guard and brought his sword up with a quick thrust. He pushed the flaring blue blade through its chest plate with little resistance. Despite the searing magic of Rowe's sword, the knight lashed out with a powerful backhand before dropping first to one knee, then the other. Rowe leaned back, and the gauntlet narrowly missed his face.

"No time, Bremer, no time!" Rowe faced two more knights that had shed their stony shells, revealing their true identity.

Rowe whirled his sword in front of himself, summoning a tight collection of light particles. A magical round shield formed before him, bending the light as it hung translucent in the air. He raised his free hand and lunged at the nearest knight. It was about to slash at Rowe's exposed arm, but the light shield struck its midsection, sending it sprawling into the far wall in a high-pitched crash of flailing armor.

Rowe slashed the next knight across the hip. It shifted awkwardly but caught the sage in the forehead with the hilt of its sword. Rowe stumbled back but kept his feet beneath him as the knight attacked with a powerful thrust. He parried a second too late, but the knight's sword deflected harmlessly off his Trannalun cloak, sparing his life yet again.

The creature hesitated. Seeing movement all around him, Rowe swung his blade across the creature's neck, but a different knight blocked his sword. Another knight's blade bounced off the back of his cloak.

Rowe cried out, and Bremer leapt to his feet, both swords flashing. One knight's head hit the floor with a heavy clank. Another received a blade deep in its chest.

Rowe dodged to avoid another gauntlet to the face, brought his blade straight up, and thrust it through the knight's chin and out the top of its head.

Another knight stumbled, dropping awkwardly to its knees

before Bremer sent its head rolling. He sidestepped one attack and shuffled back to avoid a second. With both knights caught off guard, Bremer thrust at the chest of the first with one sword and slashed through the neck of the second with the other.

As the last knight dropped in a heap, Rowe and Bremer spun around to face each other, chests heaving.

"I thought you'd never exchange those lock picks for your blades," Rowe said.

"Well, they weren't doing much good. I can't get the lock open."

The far end of the antechamber was awash in shadows so thick, Rowe had not noticed a large black-curtained doorway that had opened during the skirmish with the stone knights.

Two tall individuals emerged, taking deliberate steps. At first, it looked like they were clothed in dark, skintight clothing but as they stepped into the half-light, it became clear that black ink covered most of their naked, hairless bodies. Except for the fact that one was at least six inches shorter than the other, they were identical.

In his study of the Waerdreath and its residents, Rowe had read about these rare human eunuch warriors called the Omasai. Taken from their mothers at birth, they were castrated two days later, and trained their entire lives in the art of combat with a staff. They touched no other weapon, including—and most importantly—edged weapons of any kind. Each Omas was trained in an arcane religious sect, making them ideal warriors as Sidara's personal guard.

<hr>

Will scrambled down the ladder, almost stepping on Morgan, who crouched below.

"What are you doing?" she gasped.

"We have to help them!"

As Will struggled to find the hidden lever, Morgan leaned against the wall and realized that the entry had not been closed tightly, so she gave it a tentative push. It opened wide, and adrenaline coursed through her veins.

"Are you sure about this?" she asked.

Will crawled through the narrow entry. "Not even close."

Morgan followed quickly and pushed the small door closed as a clash of metal filled the air. Had it not been for the curtain and tapestries muffling the ear-piercing sounds, the skirmish would have alerted half the keep to their presence. Unfortunately, a few *had* been alerted.

As Will ran to the red curtain, two storm giants appeared at the end of the hallway. The giants were identical to the one Will had killed in the canyon near the Stoneberg, and they carried the same type of whip.

Morgan's skin tingled from the rush of static emanating from the whips. She shrieked and grabbed the curtain, intending to flee, but jerked her hand back from the heat. She cast frantic glances from the giants, to Will, to the curtain, and to a small group of gnome soldiers that gathered behind the giants. Morgan and Will were trapped.

Will drew the slender arrow that Bremer had given him from his quiver. The shaft glowed with a swirling blend of fiery reds and oranges.

"I'd say this train is heading right off the tracks. As soon as I shoot, we have to get behind the curtain!"

Morgan drew her sword and used it to part the curtain.

Will pulled his hood over his head. He nocked the arrow and

drew the string back. Bremer's warning had been quite stern, but there was no other choice.

Will inhaled a shaky breath and held it for a tenuous moment before releasing the bowstring just as a giant cracked his whip. The bow bucked, and a deep swooshing sound roared into a powerful crescendo. An unseen force lifted Will off the floor, throwing him back into the curtain like a rag doll.

The arrow ignited the lightning-whip-charged air around it. A ball of fire sailed down the hall and turned everything to ash, including the giants and those behind them. The arrow struck a beam and erupted into liquid fire that splashed down the stairs.

Morgan had ducked behind the curtain and dared to look only when the brilliant flash from the arrow subsided. Will's faith in his cloak was rewarded once again: the magic woven into the fabric protected him against the force that would otherwise have broken his back.

Morgan turned to see Rowe and Bremer squared off against two strange-looking creatures. She ventured a few steps toward them, intending to offer her sword, but Rowe stopped her.

"No, Morgan! The Omasai are too powerful. Try to open the crate."

Morgan ran to the crate as Will recovered from the blast. Seeing the lock, she searched the seams of the crate for another way to open it.

"Ready to die, Omas?" Bremer said.

"Not before your defiling carcasses are dragged into the Unholy," the taller Omas said in a feminine voice.

Bremer advanced, but his hands began to tremble as if an overpowering force were pulling both his swords toward the Omasai.

Before his weapons slipped from his hands, Bremer spun around to maintain his grip. He sheathed them both in a single fluid motion.

Bremer glared at the Omasai with a vicious grin. "You are right to be fearful of my swords."

He reached behind his belt and retrieved a small piece of wood. He flexed his hand, and the handle flared into a full-length staff. He spun the staff in his hands, and the Omasai warriors let out soft, condescending sighs.

"Oh, see how delicately he holds his staff," the tall Omas said in a breathy voice.

"Like a child," said the other Omas.

Rowe held his sword ready. The force that had tried to pull Bremer's sword from his grip seemed to have no impact on Rowe's.

The Omasai stepped apart and spun their staffs in a blur. In unison, they raised them over their heads in a mesmerizing spinning motion before lunging forward. Bremer and Rowe were almost caught off guard.

Rowe crouched and shifted his head as the staff struck his shoulder, but his cloak absorbed the impact. He responded with a quick thrust, but the short Omas twisted his hips while snapping the staff sideways, striking Rowe on the ear and sending him stumbling. Rowe's blade cut across the short Omas's side, but the wound was superficial.

A second before the tall Omas attacked, Bremer tossed his staff at the spinning blur. The Omas knocked the weapon aside with little effort but gasped as Bremer shot forward, low and lightning fast. Bremer ducked under the warrior's guard and drove his shoulder into the Omas's waist. Locking his arms around his opponent's legs, Bremer lifted with a terrific grunt and used his momentum to drive the Omas onto his back.

Before the Omas could recover, Bremer pushed himself onto his knees and leaned in with a flurry of punches. The Omas's head bounced off the marble twice, and before he could get his arms up to protect his face, one eye was bleeding, and his nose was shattered. The Omas jerked onto his side and raised a muscular arm in self-defense. Undeterred, Bremer leaned over and reached around with another perfectly placed fist to the Omas's face. The Omas tried to turn onto his stomach, but Bremer drove his knee into the side of his head once, then twice.

"Bet you don't care how I hold a staff now!" Bremer drove his knee in again, and the Omas went limp.

Morgan stared at the heavy lock. "Bremer, can you pick this?"

"No time! Use your sword!" Bremer shouted.

Morgan hacked at the lock. Sparks flew as a series of high-pitched rings sounded throughout the antechamber.

Clank, clank, clank.

A third Omas appeared and slowly moved toward Morgan. She prepared for a fight, but suddenly Will charged forward, handgun raised. Morgan focused on the lock.

Clank, clank, clank.

The short Omas brought its staff around in a fluid motion. It struck the back of Rowe's ankles with enough force to break his footing. Rowe's arms swung upward as his legs were knocked out from beneath him, but his sword blocked the staff inches from his face. He slashed, forcing the Omas back a step.

Clank, clank, clank.

"Morgan, duck!" Will screamed as he came around the crate seconds before the third Omas attacked.

Morgan dropped to her knees.

Click! The gun misfired.

Morgan parried a split second before the staff struck her head, throwing the third Omas off-balance.

Will ejected a bullet and squeezed the trigger again. This time, everyone in the room cowered at the thundering sound.

Morgan let out an audible sigh as her attacker's dead body landed several feet away. She rose to her feet and redoubled her efforts on the lock.

Clank, clank, clank.

After Bremer had kneed the tall Omas in the head for the third time, he pulled a dagger from his brace and drove it into the Omas's neck, spilling blood that pooled around the dying warrior. As he removed the knife, Bremer was clipped in the head by the short Omas. The impact sent him into a somersault that he recovered into a kneeling position.

Four more Omasai appeared at the far end of the antechamber.

Clank, clank, PING!

As the broken lock fell, one side of the crate dropped to the marble floor. Morgan jumped backward.

The entire keep shook. Dust floated down from the beams above, and everyone in the room paused to face the crate. A crack slowly spread across the marble slab as another side of the crate fell, shaking the room again. The top section of the crate launched straight into the air. It crashed through a massive oak beam, bounced off the ceiling, then smashed down through another beam before hitting the floor near the red curtain. The crate's last two sections dropped in unison. Within seconds, spiderweb cracks covered the lustrous marble floor.

After dodging debris and covering their eyes, everyone gazed at the crate. As the dust settled, a stunning six-foot-tall woman stood to her full height. Her radiant sky-blue gown filled the room like the natural light of a clear spring afternoon. The brightness was dazzling, but her beauty was breathtaking. Gold-spun hair flowed in waves over her delicate pointed ears, framing elegant, high cheekbones. Her porcelain skin appeared youthful, but her piercing violet eyes settled upon each person in the room with the commanding authority of an ancient monarch.

Without a sound, she raised a hand and flicked her slender fingers, sending the Omasai warriors back through the air as if tossed by the might of a dragon. Their bodies crashed against the far wall, and the crushing sound left nothing to the imagination.

CHAPTER 34

IN THE PRESENCE
OF SIDARA

With the Omasai destroyed, the antechamber grew strangely silent for a brief moment. Morgan noticed Rowe had kneeled. She was about to do the same but realized she already had. Bremer and Will had also bowed as the stunning woman considered her new surroundings.

"Cinhalla, Queen of the Northern Elves," Rowe said, bowing his head.

"Rowe of the Nest," the elf queen said in a soft yet confident voice of recognition. Her voice was a soothing, captivating melody.

Her eyes, sharp yet serene, settled upon Morgan. The queen nodded as if pleased, then shifted her attention to Will.

"Most interesting," she said. "Rise, Callum Sage."

Will stood, keeping his gaze low to the ground.

"How are you called?"

"Will Owens."

"No fear resides in you. Tell me, Will Owens, what has happened to your fear?"

"It was taken." The words sounded strange in his ears.

"How?" she asked.

Will glanced at the others as if searching for the right answer. "I…uh, I'm not sure." He lifted a hand to his necklace. "Something powerful…like…love or…prayer?" He hung his head, and his cheeks turned red.

Cinhalla's eyes brightened further, clearly intrigued. "And yet, a sadness remains in you. Yes. It is a sadness for Sidara and what she endured as a child."

Will nodded. "I know what she has become, but…that could be me."

"Your bloodline draws deep from the pools of wisdom, Will Owens."

"Can you help me?"

A brilliant, knowing smile parted her beautiful lips. "You believe you require help?"

Will stared at her.

"I do not understand why you believe you require help," she said.

"Your Majesty—" Rowe's voice faltered.

"Surely you understand what is to happen here?" Cinhalla continued, ignoring Rowe.

Will looked at Rowe, hoping he would answer for him.

"A tempest approaches," the elf queen said.

"Forgive me, but—" Rowe stammered.

"The winds will be at his back," she said. "But even Will Owens does not understand why. Still, it approaches."

"Your Majesty, I…" Rowe's voice faded as a terrible heaviness drifted into the antechamber, choking the conversation. It wrapped around Morgan like sinister unseen arms, violating and probing her soul, exposing her secrets. Given the horrified expressions of the others, she assumed they were experiencing something similar. They each backed away in a desperate attempt to distance themselves from the intrusive force.

The large red curtain between the antechamber and the hallway blackened.

The elf queen reached out her hands, uttering something under her breath. A light sparked and slowly widened into a glowing sphere around her. It encompassed Rowe, who reached for Morgan's hand. She withdrew, shifting awkwardly as the probing presence intensified.

"Morgan!" Rowe called, snatching her wrist. He pulled her into the elf queen's light, and the moment she entered, the vile darkness withdrew.

A distant, bone-chilling cacophony of muffled screams drifted from the Unholy. As the terrifying sounds grew louder and more pronounced, a wall of churning shadows entered the room. The shadows morphed into ethereal creatures with tormented faces and mouths opened in distant, otherworldly screams. They swirled within the darkness, consuming what little light remained in the antechamber.

As the shadows filled the room, Morgan noticed that Will seemed to be fighting an inner battle that threatened to overpower him. She did not understand it but sensed death would follow should he succumb to the fear pressing in on him. She tried to reach out to him, but he was so far away, so lost.

Fleeting glimpses of ghost-like beings flew past as the wall of shadows floated ever closer. Faces flitted by, making it impossible to distinguish male from female or human from beast, each one gnashing their teeth as they materialized and disappeared into shadows.

Bremer stepped toward the dark wall with his sword extended before him. His legs were shaking. Morgan wanted to scream for him to turn and run, but she knew Bremer had come too far and was hell-bent on fighting Sidara.

The cloud of churning shadows now filled the antechamber floor to ceiling, hovering forward with deadly intent. Bremer stopped a few feet from the cloud and waved the tip of his sword through the shifting shadows. The blade passed through it without resistance. Several translucent, disproportionate humanoid forms drifted closer before disappearing.

With his empty hand, Bremer was about to touch the shadows when something reached out so fast that he was unable to pull away. An ethereal hand snatched his wrist in a viselike grip. He cried out and dropped to a knee. His eyes shot wide as his wrist twisted dangerously close to snapping.

Rowe's sword flashed. The dark hand disappeared, and Bremer shuffled back and tripped, landing on his backside before springing to his feet. He turned and ran past the elf queen, then slashed at the antechamber's large curtain that had turned from red to black. His sword rang off what sounded like a steel wall. He rushed to the edge of the curtain and tried to slip his sword past to push it sideways. Again, his sword struck loudly, to no avail.

"Rowe!" he called. "Your sword!"

Rowe left the magical sphere and ran to Bremer's side. He tried to push his sword through the solid curtain but failed to even scratch what had once been fabric.

"We're trapped," he said.

Cinhalla leaned forward, lowered her head, and began a slow chant. The light responded, and the sphere around her pressed outward until it contacted the shadows. Bremer and Rowe stepped into the sphere with Morgan as the shadowy figures darted around Cinhalla's impenetrable light. The darkness pressed into the light as if appraising strengths and weaknesses. Beads of sweat formed on the elf queen's weary brow as she struggled to maintain her protective spell.

Morgan spun around suddenly. "Where's Will?" she gasped. Sheathing her sword, she dropped to her knees, eyes closed as she whispered a prayer.

Sidara's presence beckoned from beyond the antechamber. Will knew he must answer the call but stood staring at the roiling shadows attacking his friends. A sense of helplessness overtook him. The physical darkness intensified, sending him into the gloomy caverns of his mind.

The deep loneliness he thought he had left back home resurfaced, clawing at his heart. He recalled the death and destruction that followed the odious creatures that had invaded Cochrane. Accusing voices attacked his thoughts. Why had he not stopped it? In all likelihood, Joe was dead, leaving the town without hope. How many more lives had been lost since he and Morgan left? And how many had died here since they arrived in the Fourwinds? How many lives had they taken without mercy?

His pulse and breathing quickened with the bleak realization that the dark forces of this world would probably win the war for the Fourwinds, spread back into Cochrane, and usher in unthinkable devastation around the globe. He was powerless against such evil.

He watched numbly as the shadowy hand reached out and gripped Bremer's wrist. Jolted into action, he pushed aside the despair and reached for hope like a drowning man's final desperate attempt to survive. The deep loneliness loosened its grip on him but lingered as if waiting for an opening.

Then Will heard something that reversed the course of his life. He listened for a moment, trying to place the sound. It reminded him of his mother's voice, comforting the most troubled corners of his soul and resonating with a power that defied all logic.

Let love be your guide.

Without a second thought, Will stepped into the swirling shadows of ethereal creatures drifting in and out of his vision. Darkness enveloped him. Although he could see nothing, he ventured across the antechamber and knew at once he had left the room.

The difference between the antechamber and the Unholy was like the difference between Cochrane and the Fourwinds. The moment he stepped from one room into the next, he lost his equilibrium and almost doubled over. Despite the acrid air and the foreboding evil in the room, he kept his feet beneath him.

Shrouded beings heightened their attack, tormenting Will to the core. In response, he pulled his Trannalun cloak tight against his chest and strained to see through the impenetrable shadows. All other sounds were suddenly drowned out by the unforgettable cries of countless tortured victims sacrificed upon the altar before him.

The shadows dispersed to reveal a massive stone slab less than twenty feet ahead. It was covered with blood—some old, some so fresh it ran freely—and a gruesome pile of body parts strewn about. Will's stomach lurched at the sickening sight and smell.

Hundreds of hateful yellow eyes stared down at him. He could not see the creatures but sensed these ranked much higher than the Lessers and harvesters. The room, vast and cold as a tomb, welcomed sorrow and pain like a war-torn town welcoming home wounded and broken soldiers.

Will managed a few clumsy steps forward through the gut-churning mess. He felt pushed and pulled at the same time. Basic natural laws were not applicable here, and the threat of losing his tenuous grip on sanity wore him down. He had no plan and no weapon remotely capable of defending himself. Through the noise, the voice echoed in his mind, carrying him forward.

Let love be your guide.

Below him lay bodies that had been tortured beyond recognition. Resisting despair, he jerked his head up and now floated toward the altar. The weight of Sidara's presence pressed upon him. It was impossible to tell exactly where she was, but he sensed her all around.

The faint light in the Unholy had no visible source. It barely illuminated the altar. The sound of claws scraping on stone was evidence of the multitude of hidden clerics, hellions, and minions of the darkest class positioning themselves along the great round rows of stone benches that formed the cruel cathedral. Somehow, Will understood their intentions as if something were impressing the thoughts upon his mind. They had all arrived to see the ultimate sacrifice, that of the elf queen, but they recognized this intruder was equally important to Sidara.

As the newcomer neared the altar, every creature in the Unholy leaned forward in anticipation. Again, Will understood their thoughts. None had ever seen a sacrifice approach the altar voluntarily. Usually, sacrifices were forced onto the altar by fiendish creatures or by dark magic. But not this one. Usually, sacrifices entered the Unholy screaming and fighting like cornered hellhounds. But, again, not in this case. This sacrifice was clearly unique. The room grew tranquil as the assembly waited with hushed anticipation.

Despite a strong aversion to the abhorrent altar, Will knew the battle would take place there. It was the most horrifying thing he had ever seen; nevertheless, his heart told him that his place was on the sullied slab. He gazed at the chest-high altar. It appeared to be lowering but, in fact, it was stationary; he was drifting upward. Without hesitation, he stepped onto the bloodstained altar and settled his footing. His knees trembled as the altar lurched. It now hung several feet off the floor.

An odious voice void of humanity broke the silence: "Welcome, Will Owens."

Even if Will had anything to say, his parched throat would not have cooperated. He forced a hard swallow.

"I can see your mother in your eyes, and you have your father's chin."

Will grimaced at the comment, prompting a gurgle of laughter from Sidara.

"I remember the day your mother stood there, much the same as you are. Only, she was not as calm as you are now. I can hear echoes of her screaming pleas for mercy." Sidara cackled.

A knot tightened in Will's stomach.

"What she lacked in courage, she made up for in constitution, I'm afraid. If memory serves, we had removed much…no, I believe we had removed *all* of her skin before her body yielded."

Will's mind railed against her words that struck like hammers in the back of his mind. No one had ever found his mother's body after the snowmobile had gone through the ice. Was it possible she had been here? But how?

"It was a shame we had finished with her before your father pulled the trigger. It is always best to have one watch the other, especially when we peel."

Will trembled as the crushing words settled around him. With tears forming from deep pools of sorrow, he sniffled and cleared his throat. About to scream against her words, he noticed movement around the altar. Six of the vilest inhuman creatures he had ever seen knelt around the floating slab, chanting.

"Would you like to see your mother?" Sidara asked.

Will said nothing.

"She will appear different to you, but she will always be… your mother."

A long silence lingered.

"Then perhaps…Ryowyn?"

Will tried to mask his confusion.

"You do not know, do you?"

Will stared at Sidara. The knot in his stomach rose to his throat.

"You mean, Rowe has not told you? I wonder why he told Morgan and not you?" Sidara paused, allowing her words to penetrate before continuing.

"When Aamon's warrior struck you with the bolt, you were killed, Will Owens. I was about to reach out to you, but Ryowyn bested me to your side. The love in her eyes was so strong, I was not surprised she gave her life so you could live."

"Liar!" Will shouted.

"It was the necklace that allowed her to do such a thing. The very thing she gave you in love now holds her imprisoned for the remainder of time. You see, Will Owens, that speck in the dewdrop is Ryowyn. Search your heart; you cannot deny this truth. What I find most intriguing is that you are the only one who can rescue her from her prison, and I am the only one who knows where that prison is."

A gentle crackling sound caught Will's attention. From below, flames with no fuel source crept up the sides of the altar. The six clerics kneeling around the altar continued their chant as the flames grew hotter and brighter.

"It seems our time is short, Will Owens. Ryowyn will be lost upon your death. Joe is already lost. Your mother begs for death every second of every day, and your friends here will soon taste the same fate. All for naught."

Will noticed a flicker of uncertainty in her voice. She was hiding something.

"Would you bow, not for your life but for the lives of your loved ones?" she asked.

Will worked his mouth, sensing the strength to speak rising from an unaccountable source. "For the life of everyone," he said in a voice foreign to him, "I forgive you, Sidara."

The Dark Queen recoiled. "You are about to burn, Will Owens, for eternity. And that pales in comparison to what your friends are already enduring in the next room. Have you nothing intelligent to say?"

The flames crept over the altar. Will shifted his feet. There was no place to go, but he realized there was nowhere else he needed to go. He knew he was in the right place, despite the intensity of the approaching flames. An undeniable strength rose within him, and he squared his shoulders.

"Not even your cloak will slow what is to come for you, Will Owens."

"I know about your time at the Academy," he said.

The creatures around the altar murmured and shuffled their feet. The atmosphere in the room changed as tangibly as if someone had just opened a large window. No one this side of the Stoneberg knew of Sidara's past, and if they did, no one would dare to speak of it. The chanting grew more intense. The flames responded by spreading faster, but calmness flooded Will's mind.

"I know what they did to you," he said. "And my heart aches for you."

Sidara rose and was about to lash out, but Will raised his hand.

"I'm so sorry for what they did, Sidara." He coughed and almost choked on the fumes. "It wasn't your fault."

The Dark Queen roared a curse as the flames licked Will's legs, but he remained undeterred.

"Even as we speak, I would give my life to have those scars healed," he said. "Let there be no illusion here: I am aware of what you have become, what you have done. But I have no judgment. I can only imagine what I would have become had I been treated the same. But the evil must stop. Forgiveness and hope will prevail. I know this to be true, and I want you to find both, Sidara."

The creatures' chanting grew so loud and the smoke so intense that Will was forced to stop talking. Closing his eyes, he held his breath as the flames erupted into a firestorm that enveloped the altar and what was on it.

Sidara leaned forward with tears burning in her eyes, possibly the first since her childhood days in Acttun. She gaped at Will's unmoving outline in the flames. One moment drifted into another, but still, he stood, unaffected. All at once, her hollow, tear-filled eyes narrowed at the sight of a second figure within the flames.

The Dark Queen's body shuddered as something deep within her soul jolted her back into the throne. The sound of snapping chains filled the Unholy. Clutching the chair to brace against another violent spasm, her eyes darted around the room, realizing the sound and powerful force had been meant for her alone. Grunting against the unseen force ravaging her spirit, she closed her eyes and squeezed the arms of the throne with a white-knuckled grip.

At the center of the altar, two silhouettes stood in the midst of a firestorm so hot that a cleric burst into flames while the others stumbled back with shouts of pain. A dull murmuring spread throughout the Unholy as the outlines in the firestorm remained unmoving. Sidara struggled to understand what she was witnessing and why she had responded so violently to Will's simple words.

The person next to Will was a woman. Her hair was radiant, her eyes sparkling with a life that made the surrounding firestorm dull and insignificant.

"*Who…are…you?*" Sidara shouted over the roaring flames.

"I told you once that my son would never succumb to hate." The words flowed like a massive waterfall, breaking the final chains that had enslaved Sidara since childhood.

"Forgiveness waits at the unchained door," the voice continued.

Sidara's heart was broken. For the first time since before her captivity in Acttun, light shone through the cracks. The light was invasive and pure yet dangerous. Feeling weak and vulnerable, she summoned the last of her energy to trigger a personal warding spell. A dark sphere surrounded the throne for a moment before exploding in a flash of light. When it faded, the Dark Queen's throne was empty.

Will raised his arms, and the fire swirled. The color and pattern of the flames had changed. What had once been born of darkness now danced and twirled as a free and holy fire burning with inescapable heat. Driven by something beyond him, Will turned in a circle and brought his arms up and around. A deafening rush of hot wind filled the room and sucked the air from the Unholy and the antechamber, consuming all darkness and every evil being in its path in a single great roaring flood of fire. What had once been flesh burned to ash, and then even the ash disappeared. What had once been ethereal burned into absolute nothingness. Even the bloodstains set deep in the altar were burned clean.

Will stood at the epicenter of the flaming torrents. He raised his arms again and sent the firestorm up in a great rush that burned through the roof of the Unholy before dissipating hundreds of feet above the castle.

Sunlight and solemn silence filled the Unholy.

CHAPTER 35

GENERAL RARIC

The firestorm destroyed the protective dark curtain between the hallway and the antechamber as well as the curtain separating the antechamber from the Unholy. As the dust and destruction settle, the three humans and the elf queen stirred.

Rowe was the first to race into the Unholy, but Morgan was right behind him. Seeing Will lying upon the altar, she groaned under her breath. "Oh no. Please…tell me the cloak saved him."

Will lay on his back next to his Trannalun cloak with one leg dangling over the altar and the other bent awkwardly at the knee. One arm was across his chest and the other straight up past his head. Desperate to see his eyes open and unsure of what to do, Morgan stepped around to see his face.

After a moment, Will's eyelids trembled. Hope flooded Morgan even though his eyes didn't open. She reached across the stone slab, brought her finger to his neck, and waited.

"He's alive," she exhaled sharply, like someone stepping back from the edge of a dangerous cliff.

"Help me get his cloak around him," Rowe said.

With some effort, Rowe and Morgan unraveled Will's cloak and laid it beside him. They straightened his legs and arms but failed to revive him. Rowe wrapped the garment around Will's body, and the fabric warmed as the cloak's healing power ignited.

Multiple footfalls and voices sounded from the stairway beyond the antechamber. Bremer ran in, wide-eyed.

"We need to leave, now," he said. "We've got company."

"The roof," Rowe said.

"Why?" Bremer snapped. "So they can corner us?"

"Trust me," Rowe said. "We cannot leave without General Raric."

"But how do we get out of here?" Morgan asked. She surveyed the Unholy, a semicircular cathedral of more than a hundred rows of stone benches divided equally by three sets of stairs at the opposite end of the room.

"That stairwell," Rowe said, pointing at the far-left staircase. "It leads to a hallway that connects us with the keep. There, we turn right, and another stairwell leads up into the eastern tower. I'm certain it is the tallest."

Bremer was nodding. "Fadua said the general is on the roof. I thought he was hallucinating, but maybe—"

More shouts sounded from the hallway outside the antechamber.

Rowe pulled Will up and over his shoulder and headed for the staircase. "We need to go," he said.

"Where's Cinhalla?" Morgan said. "We can't leave without her!"

Bremer was already running back to the antechamber.

Morgan followed and found Cinhalla there, down on one knee. Sustaining her protective sphere for so long had obviously drained most of her energy. "May I help you?" Morgan asked.

Cinhalla nodded. "Yes, but I need a moment to rest."

Bremer ran to the gaping entryway, now without its large curtain.

He almost collided with someone stepping inside from the hallway. The curious gnome had no chance to defend himself as Bremer thrust his sword through the gnome's chest. He pushed the body backward and removed his blade, then peered into the hallway.

Seven gnomes in similar old shirts and leather overalls stood near the top of the stairway, gaping as though they had never seen the antechamber without the red curtain draped across it. A few gnomes had sawdust in their hair, and one held an old hammer.

Bremer stepped toward them, and the gnomes floundered backward. "Sidara is dead," he informed them in a flat tone.

"Impossible," a worker breathed.

Behind the seven gnomes, several armed bush gnomes clad in crude banded armor charged up the stairs past the smoldering wooden beams.

"Who are you?" a bush gnome called as they slowed.

"The last person you will see in this life if you take another step," Bremer said.

All the gnomes stopped at once.

"What be the meaning of this?" the same gnome demanded.

"Gone the curtain is," another said. "How?"

Bremer remained motionless until one gnome pointed at the blood dripping from one of Bremer's blades. He shifted the blade slightly.

"Natas is feasting upon Sidara's carcass in the Unholy and does not wish to be disturbed at the moment."

"Only a tale told to frighten little ones that dragon is," one gnome said.

Bremer stepped to the side and motioned to the antechamber. "Maybe you would like to interrupt the dragon for yourself," he offered.

A heavy silence hung in the air. Morgan wasn't sure what Bremer was up to, but the gnomes did not seem convinced.

Bremer continued his ruse. "Natas has assembled an army that is marching down from the north. It will be arriving on the morrow, so you have time to collect your families and flee the ensuing destruction."

The gnomes murmured among themselves, visibly shaken.

Sheathing the sword at his left hip, Bremer wiped the other blade across his right hip to clean the blood before sheathing it. "I must return to the bidding of my master," Bremer continued, maintaining the lie.

He entered the antechamber, then turned back to face the stunned group as something heavy pounded up the stairs. Ash fell from the smoldering timbers stretching across the hallway ceiling.

A gnome soldier peered down the stairs, and a chill ran down Morgan's spine when the gnome screamed, "Moonwalker!"

The gnomes all dropped their swords and tools, bolting for the antechamber. Morgan had never heard of a moonwalker, but judging by the gnomes' response, she decided not to hang around and find out. She helped Cinhalla to her feet.

Bremer stepped between them and swept up the elf queen in his arms, racing to the Unholy where Rowe was already halfway up the stairs. Morgan kept pace with Bremer, amazed at his speed while carrying Cinhalla.

Frightened gnomes poured into the Unholy, scattering in every direction; some ran for the passages lining the outer walls, while others sprinted toward the three staircases.

The horrifying sound of a spiked iron ball meeting flesh and bone in the antechamber sent everyone into a frenzied state. The moonwalker's heavy footfalls rattled the walls as screams filled the air and fueled the panic.

Bremer sprinted, taking the first series of steps two at a time. Morgan was close behind but paused to venture a glance at the moonwalker.

Standing over eight feet tall, the creature was clad in massive iron plates that shifted across its large frame like a living game of Tetris. Some plates moved across its broad chest while others spun around its arms and legs. The plates changed position so quickly they distorted the light around the creature, revealing its molten lava body beneath. A giant dragon-like helm with flaming eyelets swayed from side to side, scanning the room.

In one gauntlet, the moonwalker held a length of blackened deadwood with a heavy chain dragging across the floor behind it. A spiked iron ball at the end of the chain glowed red hot, burning everything in its wake. The moonwalker hoisted the handle over its head and gave a sharp snap. The chain lurched, sending the iron ball in a low trajectory. The weapon caught one fleeing worker in the back, sending him flailing into a bush gnome with so much force, the spikes impaled them both before they burst into flames. With a powerful jerk, the moonwalker retrieved the spiked iron ball, and the chain retracted into the deadwood handle.

Morgan shrieked and dove to the side, narrowly avoiding a spiked iron ball that exploded into the steps. Stone shards flew in every direction. The moonwalker snapped the handle back, causing the chain to retract. The iron ball flew back, crashing several feet away.

Bremer shouted at Morgan as a second moonwalker entered the cathedral. Turning in the direction of Bremer's voice, it closed the gap between them. Morgan scrambled to her feet and ran up the stairs. She crested the final step and caught up with the others.

With muscles nearing the breaking point, she gasped for breath and nearly vomited.

Rowe buckled under the weight of Will's unconscious body. He had draped Will over his shoulders, clutching his legs with one arm. In his other hand, he held a long knife. Bremer cradled the elf queen in his arms, but he appeared to be strong and ready to continue.

The crashing and wailing continued from the Unholy.

"Keep going," Bremer said. "The gnomes will only distract the moonwalker for a while. We have to get to that tower!"

Rowe pressed on, struggling down the winding hallway. After several agonizing minutes, they entered a main hall and turned right. They passed several closed doors and eventually came to a gnome soldier standing guard by a spiral staircase.

"You there! Help me with this man!" Rowe shouted.

"What has happened?" the gnome called out in a heavy accent, raising his arms to prevent entry into the stairwell.

Rowe shuffled one last step and drove his long knife into the gnome's chest. The surprised guard tried to cry out, but his punc-tured lung caused a gurgling sound to escape his lips. He stumbled back against the wall and slumped to the floor.

Rowe stepped into the narrow opening of the tight spiral staircase and collapsed forward, catching Will's head before it slammed into the steps. He lowered Will to the floor and took a few heaving breaths before standing again.

"We cannot stop here!" Bremer hissed as the sounds of heavy footfalls and dragging chains reached their ears.

Rowe grabbed Will's wrist and, with a grunt, pulled him over his shoulder. "Bremer, go ahead of us and make sure the way is clear."

Bremer set Cinhalla down on the bottom step and climbed the spiral staircase.

Morgan reached out to help Cinhalla, who raised a hand to stop her. Turning, the elf queen brought both hands upward across the opening, then down the sides all the way to the floor.

"All right, now we can go." She wrapped her arm around Morgan's shoulder. "That protection magic should give us some extra time."

With great effort, Morgan helped Cinhalla climb the stairs as Rowe followed close behind carrying Will. Around and around, they ascended as fast as their burning lungs and stiffening leg muscles would allow.

Bremer was at the top, his ear pressed against a wooden door. He was on his knees, examining the locking mechanism.

"It's a security trap," he said.

Waving everyone back, he turned the large iron handle upward until it clicked. Three poison darts shot from the keyhole and bounced harmlessly off the stone wall. He pulled the handle down, and another set of darts shot out. He pulled it down farther, and the release clicked. The door swung inward.

Bremer drew a sword, kicked the door fully open, and stepped back in a low, expectant crouch. Inside, the room was still. A musty breeze and failing daylight streamed into the round tower through open embrasures in the stone walls. The room was furnished with a small table, a scattering of chairs, and several old books on a small shelf. Scraps of bones from abandoned meals littered the stone floor. At the top of a short wooden staircase by the far wall was a large opening in the ceiling.

Bremer crouched as he approached the steps. All was still, so he started up. When he reached the top, a gust of wind blew down some dirt from above. Sword in front, he peeked out.

Morgan breathed a sigh, realizing there was no one waiting to take his head off.

Bremer climbed onto the roof and froze.

"What's up there, Bremer?" Rowe asked.

A moment later, Bremer stumbled down the steps. His face was pale. "We've come to the right place," he said.

"Help me get Will up there," Rowe said.

The two men started to carry Will up the steps but stopped when something crashed in the stairwell.

"Bremer, get the door sealed," Rowe shouted.

"I'm afraid I have given us too little time," Cinhalla said.

Bremer closed the heavy door and threw the bolt sideways, shaking his head. "This will never stop a moonwalker."

He helped Rowe get Will up the steps to the roof. When Morgan and Cinhalla joined them, he lowered the heavy trapdoor across the opening. He found a long-handled crowbar and tried to use it to lock the door, but it was futile. Instead, he opted to use his own weight, and sat on it.

Morgan stood motionless, staring at the horrific scene on the roof. A solitary cross, made of enormous rough-hewn timbers, stood in the center of the small, flat roof.

"What is *that*?" she gasped.

With a heaving chest, Rowe approached the cross. Stretched wide and nailed into place was a naked man. The nail wounds in his hands and feet were scabbed over. A sickening umbilical cord stretched from his navel, down between his legs, and into the wood that pulsed with tiny veins. Rowe was speechless.

Two small cauldrons hung on either side of the crossbeam. Morgan grimaced. "Those pots…they're like the ones at the cabin in the Arden Forest. Joe said they were a power source and needed to be emptied." She shuddered.

A thin membrane stretched across the man's eyes like semitransparent patches. Several veins connected the membranes to his face as if crudely sewn in place. He appeared to be dead.

Rowe pointed at two long scars on the man's right leg. "I recognize those scars."

"Is it…?" Morgan asked.

"General Raric of the House of Aldor."

"What's that on his face?"

"It is an Illiack," Cinhalla answered. "It forces the wearer to see everything unfolding in the land."

Rowe's arms hung loosely at his sides. "I cannot imagine the agony of a general being forced to witness his armies scattered to the winds and his strongholds plundered…" He trailed off.

"Does that mean he's alive?" Morgan asked.

Bremer dropped the crowbar on the stone floor with a high-pitched *clank*. Morgan flinched—and so did Raric before lifting his head slightly.

"He's alive!" Rowe stepped toward the cross. "Bremer, help me with this."

Rowe reached down and pulled a large metal pin that fastened the vertical beam to an iron bracket bolted to the floor. The pin released after a second tug with both hands, and Rowe pulled it free as Bremer kept the cross from falling over. Rowe came around beside Bremer, and together they stepped back with arms outstretched, lowering the cross to the floor.

Morgan grabbed both cauldrons when they were low enough to reach and threw them off the tower.

"What do we do with *that*?" Rowe pointed to the umbilical cord.

"Let's cut it and tie it off the same way we would for a newborn baby," Morgan suggested.

Bremer raised an eyebrow but handed her a knife. She knelt beside Raric and drew a breath. After cutting a short length of shoelace from her boot, she grasped the cord and, with one quick motion, sliced it above her fingers. Dropping the knife, she picked up the shoelace and tied off the umbilical cord that was oozing black sludge.

"That should do for now." Morgan wiped her hands across the stone floor. Slipping off her cloak, she draped it over the general to cover his nakedness.

Rowe picked up the crowbar Bremer had dropped and found a small block of wood beside the cross. He placed the block next to the nail in Raric's right hand.

"Sure you want to do that?" Bremer asked.

"Why not?"

"The moonwalker will soon figure out where we are, and I can't speak for you…" Bremer glanced at Cinhalla. "But I have my doubts about a rescue. Shades! It would take a man a full day to scale this tower even with the proper ropes and harnesses. I don't see how we could all make it down. What I'm saying is, why bother putting the general through that agony only to get killed a few minutes later?"

"Is there no way to kill a moonwalker?" Morgan asked.

"Not that I'm aware of," Bremer said.

Rowe hung his head. "We have not come this far to die on this desolate rooftop."

"I suspect we'll find out soon enough," Bremer said.

Rowe positioned the crowbar hooks against Raric's palm. The general stiffened as his skin was pushed down around the spike.

Rowe winced as pus oozed from the wound, but he continued to press the bar around the spike head. Positioning the wooden block beneath the opposite end of the crowbar, Rowe placed his knee on Raric's wrist next to the nail and pushed the handle away from him. The spike sprang out in a single motion, and the momentum sent him tumbling over the general's arm and onto the floor.

Raric's back arched, and his mouth opened in a silent scream.

Rowe collected the block and moved to the other hand.

"Here, let me help you," Bremer said.

Together, they removed the spike in the other wrist and the much larger one through both feet. Rowe pulled Morgan's cloak up to the unconscious general's neck, covering his torso.

"What do you want to do about *that*?" Bremer asked, pointing to the Illiack on Raric's eyes.

"Can we cut it off?" Rowe asked.

"Use a pointed blade to puncture each vein attached to the membrane, and they will—" The elf queen closed her mouth and turned to face the trapdoor.

"What is it?" Rowe asked, although no one needed to hear the answer.

"It has entered the stairwell," she said.

Morgan stood over Will's motionless body. "Rowe, we have to revive Will!"

Rowe knelt beside Will and gently shook him.

Nothing.

He gave him another shake and a slap across the face.

Nothing.

"Come on, Will! Wake up!"

Nothing.

"What about my sword?" Morgan asked. "Will its magic work

against that creature?"

"There is always hope," Rowe answered.

BAM!

The tower shook from the impact.

Morgan pictured the moonwalker in the main stairwell outside the door positioning itself on the small landing.

BAM!

There was the distinct sound of wood splintering, followed by a roar of flames. Smoke leaked through the trapdoor.

"It's burned its way in," Bremer said.

"I would sooner face a thousand gnomes," Rowe said as he stepped away from the trapdoor.

He grabbed Will by the arms and dragged him as far from the trapdoor as possible before wrapping him in his cloak. He rejoined Morgan and Bremer. Three swords were drawn and ready. Cinhalla stood beside Morgan. If the elf queen had some magical way of protecting them as she had in the antechamber, she showed no sign of wielding it now.

"Any final words, old friend?" Bremer asked.

Rowe widened his stance. "Not yet."

As the moonwalker pounded across the room below toward the wooden steps, Morgan leaned close to Rowe and whispered in his ear. "I believe in you, Rowe. Have faith."

Splinters exploded from the trapdoor as a spiked iron ball smashed through and sent chunks of wood sailing off the roof.

"How about now?" Bremer asked.

Rowe said nothing but raised his sword.

"We go together," Bremer said.

A set of terrifying horns materialized as the dragon-like helm rose from the opening. With a monstrous dark-gray snout covered with small horns that stretched to each fiery eyelet, it turned and surveyed the rooftop. The creature stepped onto the roof and stood to its full height. The chain from its mace shortened as the spiked iron ball raked the wooden steps. With a billowing huff of steam, the moonwalker appraised the group but seemed unthreatened.

Morgan's mind reeled, unable to focus on a single thought. Fleeting images of battles recently fought flashed in her mind's eye. As a group, they had fought many dangerous creatures, but they had never faced a moonwalker.

Bremer stepped back, peering over the edge of the roof. Morgan wondered if he was actually considering jumping.

The moonwalker raised an arm over its head, sending the iron ball in a wide circle. As it gained momentum, the chain extended to reach the entire group. The ball whistled as it circled the entire roof with a single pass.

Fixated on destroying the intruders, the moonwalker failed to notice a flash of dazzling white descending from the evening sky.

Plunging from a dive that began high above the dark clouds shrouding the tower, the Ice Dragon flared her massive wings, stretching tendons from the pressure as she pulled from the dive. Her massive claws plunged into the moonwalker's chest, and the impact blew the creature off the tower in a thunderous explosion. Flaming body parts lit the sky above the farmlands of Gilesonia before slamming into the frigid waters of the Habina Ocean.

Alyssa roared past the tower and banked sharply to bleed off speed in a wide circle. After a final flare of wings, she settled on powerful hind legs, occupying the greater part of the roof.

Before a single word was spoken, pounding footfalls of the second moonwalker filled the tower stairway.

The dragon drew in a powerful breath with a loud swishing

sound as she reared the full length of her neck back to fill her lungs. She lowered her mouth into the narrow trapdoor opening and slowly exhaled. A great rushing sound shook the tower. Block and mortar groaned and cracked against the staggering pressure. The tower shuddered and swayed.

Morgan and the others tensed and struggled to maintain their balance as the tower shifted. Blocks crumbled and fell away as the foundation buckled.

"Come," Alyssa said. "It is time for us to leave this cursed place."

The Ice Dragon lifted her head and lowered her huge clawed hands before them. Rowe helped Morgan and Cinhalla into one of Alyssa's protective claws while Bremer carried Will and Raric into the other. Once they were all safe, the dragon flared her wings and stepped back. With breathtaking grace, she spun her body over the edge, dropping altitude to pick up speed as the tower collapsed in huge sections and thundered to the rocks below.

CHAPTER 36

A Tale of Two Worlds

Will opened his eyes and blinked several times. The sky transitioned from dreary darkness to breathtaking blue in a matter of moments, like a room slowly lit up with a dimmer switch. But this was no room. The vast expanse of an unclouded sky filled his entire field of vision. His senses awakened to the clear sky, a warm breeze, fresh outdoor scents, and soothing sounds.

A choir of songbirds greeted the sun's arrival with particular cheerfulness, unruffled by the paucity of listeners. Will enjoyed every note. He lay still with a soft pillow beneath his head, slipping in and out of meaningless dreams. In one, he was lying in a sweeping prairie with a gentle breeze rustling through endless wheat fields. A thin white bedsheet fluttered against his chin, making him think he was neither dreaming nor awake but somewhere in between.

He propped himself up on an elbow and looked down the length of the sheet at the short wooden bedposts. The mattress beneath him was as soft as the pillow, and for a moment, he considered lying down again. Instead, he sat up and realized he was naked…and clean. An unfamiliar freshness replaced the odors he had become accustomed to over the past few weeks.

Folded neatly on a small table beside his bed were the clothes he had worn the day he'd arrived in the Fourwinds. He shook his head and rubbed his eyes. The bloodwood bow was under the table beside the holster with his 1911. His Trannalun cloak was draped over the bedpost by his head, but there was no sign of his sword. That didn't bother him. He reached up for his necklace, rubbed the dewdrop pendant between his index finger and thumb, then raked his hand through his clean, soft hair. He was almost convinced now he was in a dream, but then a small rift opened in the sky beyond the foot of his bed. He tensed.

Rowe peeked his head through the rift, and Will laughed in bewilderment.

"I suppose you've never been in an elven healing tent before," Rowe said, unable to mask the grin that spread across his clean-shaven face.

"Wha-what?" Will managed, seeing light streaming in from around Rowe.

"Take your time; we're outside." Rowe nodded and disappeared.

Unable to contain his curiosity, Will slid his feet out from beneath the sheets and scrambled into his underwear and favorite cargo pants. He slipped on his black undershirt and poked his head through the flap. As he stepped through the rift, his breath caught in his throat.

Ten small green pup tents were evenly spaced around an enormous tree trunk. He had just emerged from one of them. Beneath the tents, smooth wooden planks spread out from the tree. Against the tree, each plank was barely a handbreadth wide but spread out from the tree to a dozen feet wide, like giant slices of a pie encircling the tree. A masterfully carved railing along the perimeter formed the walls, and a cedar shake roof provided a large overhang.

A gentle breeze rippled over the canvas tents. Even from where he stood away from the railing, Will knew they were high above the ground.

"Will! You're awake!" Morgan ran and embraced him as though she had not seen him for months.

"Good to see you too, Morgan." The way she hugged him so tightly reminded him of his near-death experience when Ryowyn gave his life to save him.

"Don't tell me I was dead again," he said as Morgan released him.

Morgan laughed heartily. "No, but I imagine you were close. We're in an elven outpost camp. The elves are amazing healers." She turned her head. "Rowe can tell you more."

About fifteen feet away, Rowe leaned against the railing and motioned for Will to join him. In a chair a few paces from Rowe sat the shimmering elf queen. Despite the distance, Will had to avert his eyes, which watered against the brightness of her presence.

"There is sweet water on the table there," Rowe said, pointing to a large serving table.

Will walked to the table and poured himself a large goblet of water. He took a deep drink and sampled a few bites from a wide selection of fruit in several large serving bowls. He walked over to the railing and gazed at the canopy of trees below. As if he were not relaxed already, the rustling leaves soothed his soul.

Morgan joined him. "We made it, Will. I honestly wondered if we would ever escape that horrible castle, but here we are. It's a miracle."

Will breathed deeply as he recalled recent events. "Did that all just happen?"

"It did."

Will turned to face Rowe. "How did we escape from the Waer-dreath?"

"You missed the spectacle," Rowe replied.

"I gotta stop getting knocked out," Will said.

Rowe smiled as Morgan stood next to him, slipping her arm around his waist. "The same dragon that saved Morgan and I down in the Tuxan Mines carried us all from the Waerdreath," he said.

"So…" Will paused, unable to recall anything beyond the fire in the Unholy. "So, how did the dragon know where to find us, not to mention the timing?"

Rowe hesitated a moment before answering. "Your mother… sent the dragon."

Will stared at him as if he had told a cruel joke.

"Quite the woman, your mother is—which explains much about you."

"She came to me in the flames," Will began. "The fire was burning my ankles, but she appeared, and immediately the pain was gone. She was something else—radiant…like ice with a powerful light behind it, and calm in the midst of terror. I've never felt so safe in my life."

"Her reach has become…remarkable."

Will was uncertain what he meant by that but continued his story. "She didn't die in the river, Rowe. She wanted to say so much more, but our time was short."

"Understandably."

"She said she will come to me when time allows. She said it with so much love that it was enough for me. I don't understand it… but I don't have to. Her love was enough, if that makes any sense."

"It does, my friend, it certainly does. And I take much delight in your good fortune."

Will nodded as a deep sense of contentment filled his heart. He smiled at Morgan, whose eyes were glistening.

"So, where's the dragon now?" Will asked, looking around.

"The Ice Dragon had other matters to attend to. Much is happening, and not all of it good, I'm afraid."

"That's okay by me, Rowe. Nothing we can't handle together, right?"

Rowe chuckled. "I share your sentiment. In the meantime, the queen would like to have a few words with you." He gestured to the vacant chair beside Cinhalla.

Will sat in the chair and fixed his eyes on the blue sky, self-consciously picking at a fingernail. He was uncertain how long he could remain so close to the elf queen. He closed his eyes and took a few breaths. When he opened his eyes, he was face-to-face with Cinhalla. This time, a sense of peace filled him.

She gazed into his eyes, allowing him to settle in her presence before speaking.

"Freely you have given, now freely I give to you." Her voice was melodious yet authoritative. "When the gnome bolt struck you down in the Hollowtangle, Ryowyn offered her life for yours. Despite the cost, she did so without hesitation or regret."

Will opened his mouth, but she raised a single slender finger to pause his questions.

"The magic embedded deep within the dewdrop that breathed life back into you has tried to take Ryowyn's life, as was its design. Your strength, however, has protected her. In response, the dewdrop has woven Ryowyn in a spell that has stopped her time, leaving her in a suspended state. Unfortunately, the spell placed her somewhere beyond my reach."

Again, she raised a finger to silence his questions as he wiped a tear from his eye.

"Her body was placed in the depths of a lake unknown to her people, but I believe you are familiar with this lake. The water is unclean and will destroy her if she remains there. I have gazed deep within the dewdrop around your neck and have been able to look out from where Ryowyn is held captive. I saw a lake surrounded by a stretch of bright, yellow bars. Beyond that, a smooth hard road with strange metal carriages that moved without horses. A steep treed embankment led to four large white dwellings. The scene was unfamiliar to me."

"That's Lake Commando!" Will gasped. "Down around Second Street!"

Cinhalla nodded slowly. "She was near the bottom of the lake, about sixty feet down."

"I scuba! I can get to her!"

"What will he find?" Rowe asked.

"She will appear as one sleeping," she answered.

"How do I wake her up?" Will asked.

Cinhalla leaned back. "I do not know. You must find a way."

Will jerked his head back as if she had struck him. He almost spoke but stopped as he struggled to collect his anxious thoughts. "What do I do, Rowe?"

"Do not concern yourself with the problems of tomorrow," he said. "What do you need to do *now* to free Ryowyn from the lake you spoke of?"

Will nodded and scratched his head. "We need to get back to the Gateway."

"Can we do that?" Morgan asked.

"The duke will have a sizable presence in the Upper West Hall to prevent our return to the library," Rowe said.

"I can have the eagles lower you atop the West Hall," Cinhalla said. "The moment your boots touch the roof, I can stop time throughout the entire castle for fifteen minutes."

"That would be enough," Rowe said.

Cinhalla folded her hands. "All is as it should be."

"When can we leave?" Will asked.

"The eagles have answered my summons. I believe a midday arrival would be accurate."

Morgan turned to Rowe. "You're coming with us to Cochrane, right?"

Rowe sighed deeply and nodded.

Will took an excited drink and set the goblet on the floor. "Where's Bremer?"

Rowe pointed at the tents. "The general is in one of them too."

"Can Bremer come with us?" Will asked.

Rowe shrugged. "You can ask him if he wakes in time."

"How long was I asleep?"

"Almost three days."

Will gaped at him. "Why did you let me sleep so long? We need to get moving."

"One wakes when the healing is complete," Rowe said.

"What?"

"These tents possess a powerful magic that heals whomever is placed within. It takes time, and it's impossible to wake someone before the magic is satisfied that the healing is complete."

"There are exceptions," Cinhalla said. "Given the condition of General Raric, for example, I cannot say whether he will be fully healed when he wakes. I might need to spend extra time with him, if he permits me."

"Why is Bremer still asleep?" Will asked. "He wasn't hurt, was he?"

"The journey has left him with a shattered spirit," Cinhalla explained. "His wounds are far deeper than physical injury. It is unlikely he will be able to join you."

"Over the past few years, and on our recent journey, Bremer has undertaken deeds no man should ever attempt," Rowe added in a quiet voice.

Will was silent for a moment, recalling their time at the Stoneberg and all that Bremer had endured. "And hopefully never again. What about the Iron Dragon, Natas?"

"He does not yet have a way to breach the warding magic protecting the Records of Time."

"That's good." Will was afraid to ask how long that would last.

"Make haste," Cinhalla said. "The creature known to us as Abaddon—the harvester responsible for the deaths in your hometown—knows of the heavy losses its master Natas has suffered here. I imagine Abaddon will destroy many lives in the wake of such knowledge."

"Is—is it alone?" Will asked.

"Abaddon has been joined by another called Eurynome."

Will met Morgan's gaze. "That must be the one Joe was locked in ice with when we came through the Gateway."

"I cannot say what has become of your friend Joe." Cinhalla seemed genuinely sympathetic.

Will leaned his head back and covered his face with his hands. After a moment, he cleared his throat and wiped his eyes. He grabbed the goblet, walked over to the table, and poured himself more sweet water.

"So, what happened to Sidara?" he asked.

"I cannot trace the darkness that once permeated her soul," the elf queen said.

"Is she…is she *dead?*" Will asked.

"I cannot say. She is beyond my reach."

Will studied Rowe and Cinhalla but realized they would say no more about the Dark Queen. "So, what happens to the Fourwinds now?" he asked.

"There are whispers of Natas in the ethereal," Cinhalla said. "Visions I see when I close my eyes of the Iron Dragon standing in the midst of a terrible destruction. A woman in ragged clothes stands against Natas. I cannot see clearly…" Cinhalla trailed off, closing her eyes.

"Well, why am I not surprised?" Will said. "One thing after another."

Cinhalla smiled, opened her eyes, and stood. "There is much good that you have done here, Will and Morgan. And now you must return to your people. It has been a pleasure to meet you both."

"What?" Morgan asked. "You almost sound like we're not coming back."

Rowe cocked his head and furrowed his brow. "I do not understand."

"Listen," Will said. "I'm going back to punch Abaddon and whatever the other one's called in the face so you and Morgan can kill them with your swords. After that, we'll finally find Morgan's mom. Then I'm gonna find Ryowyn, and we're all returning to the Fourwinds."

Will glanced at Morgan, who was beaming and nodding her head in agreement.

"I—I assumed you would remain with your people," Rowe said.

"I am."

GLOSSARY OF
TERMS AND NAMES

Abaddon: harvester who passed through the Gateway from the Fourwinds to the contemporary world

Acttun: \akt-un\ an eastern city in the Fourwinds, home of artists, fortunetellers, seers, wielders, warlocks, magicians, sorcerers, wizards, and more

Acttun Academy: school in Acttun for training wizards

Addolay and Marlay Bonicle: wizard brothers; taught at the Acttun Academy; their dispute over the young student Sidara led to a dual in which Marlay killed Addolay, putting an end to the Academy

Aerodice Mountains: western range in the Fourwinds that separates gnome and human realms

Akia Tibers: elder in Fairbay

Alarra: of the House of Aldor, High Queen of Dwenlin Thah; Raric's sister

Andy Barnet: OPP constable stationed in Cochrane; Tom Bondy's rookie partner

Arden Forest: fictional name of the large forest outside Will's home of Cochrane

Blackie: Lillie's horse
Bremer: Rowe's friend; former Callum Sage; rogue

Canadian Tire: national retail department store in Canada
CIB: Criminal Investigation Branch of the OPP
Coach: Morgan's fencing coach
Crow's Nest, the: castle in the Rainia Valley; home of the Records of Time and the Gateway

Dench: half-orc; half of Rowe's personal guard
Dwenlin Thah: capital city of the Fourwinds; throne of the High Queen Alarra

Ellywick: gnome healer
Epping Forest: wooded area east of the Misty Gorge, stretching from north of the Rainia Valley to the central valley; home of very tall, ancient trees and the tree-dwelling, apelike species known as holgs
Eurynome: \yoor-i-nome\ harvester who passed through the Gateway from the Fourwinds to the contemporary world

Fairbay: peaceful fishing village on the southern shore of the Niasa Sea

Gateway, the: magical passageway/portal from the Fourwinds (Records of Time) into the contemporary world (specifically, a cabin in the Arden Forest near Will's home)

Gauntlet, the: three-hundred-foot long entrance to the Crow's Nest castle

Gloriana: worker and friend of Rowe who lives at the Crow's Nest

Grant Finley: Morgan's father; pastor of Baptist church in Cochrane

Guilliad: \gil-ee-ad\ powerful elixir developed under Sidara's rule; when liquid form is released into the air, it turns into a vapor that disintegrates anything living it comes into contact with

Habina Ocean: \ha-bee-nah\ forms the western border of the Fourwinds

Half-orc: ostracized race born of union of orc and humans living east of the Hillron Mountains; tolerated in the Fourwinds but friends and allies of Callum Sages

Hammerclaw: stronghold city in the south-central region of the Fourwinds; commanded by the Iron Lord

Hansla: works at the Recovery Ale House and Inn

Harroc: Queen Alarra's and Raric's brother

Hillron Mountains: range south and east of the Rainia Valley; home of the half-orc community

Histories, the: books documenting the history of the Fourwinds; studied and preserved by the Callum Sages; kept in the Records of Time

Holgs: apelike creatures that live in the treetops of the Epping Forest

Hollowtangle: large forest west of the Niasa Sea; home of the Druid Forest and the Maidstone tower; former home to the People of the River Country

House of Aldor: royal family line in the Fourwinds

Homas: works at Recovery Ale House and Inn

Iron Dragon: also known as Natas, the so-called mythical creature of chaos

Jessman: bartender at the Recovery Ale House and Inn
Joe Cheechoo: Mushkegowuk; Special Investigator for OPP's Criminal Investigation Branch; Will's great-grandfather; *see*: Johanissan
Johanissan: Callum Sage from the River Country; *see*: Joe Cheechoo
Josh Morley: OPP CIB Special Investigator; Joe's partner
Julie Finley: Morgan's mother; nurse

Lessers: small, mischievous demon-like creatures from between worlds that infiltrate the contemporary world; visible only to Will
Lillie: orphan girl in the Crow's Nest; considers Morgan her mother

Meagan: server at the Cauldron's Stew in Acttun; friend of Rowe and Bremer
Misty Gorge: canyon west of the Rainia Valley; Serpentine River flows through it
Moonwalker: powerful armored creature over eight feet tall, sometimes used by gnome army; usually wields spiked iron ball as preferred weapon
Morgan Finley: Callum Sage; former fencing champion
Mushkegowuk: indigenous people of Canada, part of the Cree First Nation located in Ontario

Natas: mythical creature of chaos; also known as the Iron Dragon
Niasa Sea: saltwater home of the merpeople

old man Lafleur: resident of Cochrane; the harvesters' first victim
Onathe Wyeth: dark elf

OPP: Ontario Provincial Police

Phyriad: \fear-ee-ad\ a substance found in the Maidstone and used by Natas to create an infectious elixir that transforms living beings into dragon-like creatures
Plains of Ashron: large region west of the Niasa Sea, divided into Upper and Lower

Rainia Valley: community in the eastern Fourwinds; home of the city of Rainia, saltwater Rainia Lake, and the Crow's Nest castle.
Raric: commander general of the human army
Records of Time: library tower in the Crow's Nest, traditionally protected by the Callum Sages
Recovery Ale House and Inn: eatery and inn located in Fairbay
Renaldi: duke of the Crow's Nest
River Country: home of Johanissan
Rock Pincer: wild wolflike beast trained to kill
Rowe of the Nest: Callum Sage
Ruint: Dench's best friend; half of Rowe's personal guard
Ryodan Ayoust: \rye-o-dan\ mer king; Ryowyn's father
Ryowyn: \rye-o-win\ mer princess

Sidara: Dark Queen
Soveigh: boy who Rowe rescued from slave runners
Springfield 1911: a semiautomatic pistol; Will's preferred weapon
Stoneberg: wall between the eastern and western regions of the Fourwinds; commissioned by Queen Alarra's great-great-grandfather; key to its iron gate has often changed hands

Tevan root: found in Fourwinds forests, used for medicinal properties (pain relief) and also as a recreational narcotic
Thaudas: half winged horse, half unicorn
Tim Hortons: national coffee shop franchise in Canada
Tom Bondy: OPP constable stationed in Cochrane.
Tranas: councilman at the Crow's Nest
Trannalun cloak: worn only by Callum Sages; powerful magic woven into red fabric to protect and heal the owner

Uluk the Shadowfallen: \ew-look\ Dark Queen Sidara's minion; offspring of a fallen angel and a woman
Urk: \erk\ goblin; friend of Bremer

Will Owens: Callum Sage
Waerdreath: \ware-dreth\ castle in the western Fourwinds, on the coast of the Habina Ocean; ruled by the Dark Queen Sidara
Wrathan: \rayth-an\ mer prince; brother of Ryowyn

Did you enjoy *Across the Fourwinds?*

We're looking for a group of loyal readers who will help us continue writing stories like these.

Honest reviews help bring our books to the attention of other readers. If you enjoyed this book, we would be grateful if you could spend a few minutes leaving a review (as short as you like) at Amazon (or other online retailer) and on Goodreads.

What's Next?

Visit
www.MaidstoneChronicles.com

Featuring:
• Regular Giveaways for Fantasy Book Lovers
• Forthcoming Book Releases
• Author Details
• Details on our "Buy a Book / Give a Book" program
(for each book we sell, we're donating student workbooks
for classrooms in Haiti to help kids there learn to read and write)
• Social Media Links

**Everyone on our email list has a chance to win
in our regular giveaways of popular fantasy books.**

Read Book Two of The Maidstone Chronicles:
Beyond the Hollowtangle

Thanks for reading and engaging with us!
— *Shane and Darryl*